Worldwide Bestselling Author
LINDSAY ARMSTRONG

Return TO THE
OUTBACK

MILLS & BOON

RETURN TO THE OUTBACK © 2020 by Harlequin Books S.A.

WHEN ENEMIES MARRY
© 1995 by Lindsay Armstrong
Australian Copyright 1995
New Zealand Copyright 1995

First Published 1995
Third Australian Paperback Edition 2020
ISBN 978 1 867 20602 6

THE UNEXPECTED HUSBAND
© 2000 by Lindsay Armstrong
Australian Copyright 2000
New Zealand Copyright 2000

First Published 2000
Third Australian Paperback Edition 2020
ISBN 978 1 867 20602 6

THE CONSTANTIN MARRIAGE
© 2002 by Lindsay Armstrong
Australian Copyright 2002
New Zealand Copyright 2002

First Published 2002
Third Australian Paperback Edition 2020
ISBN 978 1 867 20602 6

Published by
Mills & Boon
An imprint of Harlequin Enterprises (Australia) Pty Limited
(ABN 47 001 180 918), a subsidiary of HarperCollins
Publishers Australia Pty Limited (ABN 36 009 913 517)
Level 13, 201 Elizabeth Street
SYDNEY NSW 2000
AUSTRALIA

MIX
Paper from
responsible sources
FSC
www.fsc.org FSC® C001695

Printed and bound in Australia by McPherson's Printing Group

CONTENTS

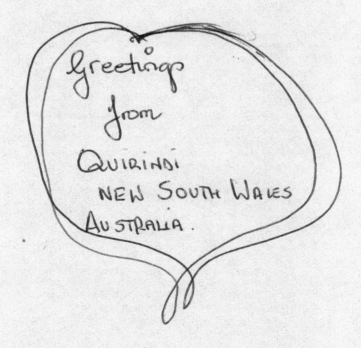

Greetings from
QUIRINDI
NEW SOUTH WALES
AUSTRALIA.

Lindsay Armstrong was born in South Africa but now lives in Australia with her New Zealand-born husband and their five children. They have lived in nearly every state of Australia and tried their hand at some unusual—for them—occupations, such as farming and horse training—all grist to the mill for a writer! Lindsay started writing romances when their youngest child began school and she was left feeling at a loose end. She is still doing it and loving it.

Recent titles by the same author:

MARRIAGE ULTIMATUM
THE BRIDEGROOM'S DILEMMA

When Enemies Marry

CHAPTER ONE

'JUSTIN, THIS IS unbelievable; there's a photographer—oh, sorry, I didn't realise you were with someone.'

Lucinda Waite paused on the threshold of her husband's study, then swept in, continuing, 'But it's only you, Sasha—well, you and someone else. How do you do?' she added politely to the third party in the study. 'I'm Justin's wife Lucinda, but most people call me Lucy. Who are you?' she enquired, extending her hand graciously.

'Robert Lang,' the third party murmured, rising hastily and taking the extended hand. 'How do you do, Mrs Waite?' He was about twenty-three and looked both embarrassed and slightly dazed.

'Not very well, thank you, Mr Lang,' Lucy Waite replied with a grimace. 'My privacy is being invaded—and I can't help feeling you might be responsible for it all.'

Robert Lang blinked beneath a clear blue gaze and made a mental note that registered some surprise. They *were* the colour of deep blue velvety pansies, her eyes, and her skin had the texture of cream rosebuds while her hair, caught back carelessly, was the colour of ripe wheat. Now, now, he cautioned himself, letting his gaze drift over the rest of Lucinda Waite, it can't be all perfection. Short legs possibly, out of proportion with the rest of her, or hippy and pear-shaped, *thick* legs—no, his eyes widened, talk about legs, they were sensational...

'You're staring, Mr Lang,' Sasha Pearson said all but inaudibly and not quite kindly. She was an elegant redhead in her early thirties but whether she was family hadn't been made clear.

But Robert Lang, despite his youth, was not without charm and ingenuity. 'I sure am,' he conceded boyishly. 'In point of fact, I'm quite bowled over. I don't think I've ever seen anyone as lovely as you, Mrs Waite—er—if you'll forgive me for saying so, sir!' He turned deferentially to Justin Waite still sitting behind his desk, not altogether in a further demonstration of his charm but because, to his mind, Justin Waite was not the kind of man one gave offence to and possibly least of all in the matter of his stunningly beautiful, flawless, twenty-year-old-if-she-were-a-day wife.

'You're forgiven, Mr Lang,' Justin Waite said. 'My wife has been having that effect on people since she was in her cradle.' He moved in his chair and stood up, revealing most of the over six foot, lean, muscled length of him that, coupled with rather hard grey eyes and a look of worldliness and experience, had kindled Robert Lang's wariness in the first place. 'My wife has also,' he went on coolly, 'been leading people up the garden path for almost as long.'

Lang's eyes widened and jerked to Lucinda. But, far from any expression of outrage, she merely smiled faintly, and murmured, 'What have I done now, Justin?'

'Invaded your own privacy, my dear, from what I can gather. Did you or did you not write to a certain publication and invite them up here to do a story on the place, and on you?'

'Yes, I did—so that's who you are!' Lucy said to Lang with a glorious smile. 'But you didn't let me know you were coming. I thought you must be one of those maverick journalists who turn up from time to time and make my life a misery.'

'Lucy, that happened once and has never been repeated,' Justin Waite said in the kind of voice that caused Robert Lang some trepidation, although it didn't seem to have any effect on his wife.

'And the reason you didn't know he was coming, Lucy,' Sasha Pearson—where *did* she fit in? Robert wondered—rose and picked up a letter from the desk, 'is because while Justin and I were away you didn't bother to open any mail although you assured me you would.'

'That's right,' Robert Lang said eagerly. 'I did write and suggest today if it would suit you.'

'Oh, dear,' Lucy Waite said regretfully. 'You really should have waited for a reply, Mr Lang, but now I know who you are, we might as well go ahead. I've got nothing else on. By the way, you are indispensable, Sasha, aren't you? Forgive me for ever doubting it! I'll just go and get changed.'

'You'll do no such thing, Lucy.'

'Justin,' Lucy protested. 'Why not?'

Blue eyes stared into hard grey ones and, despite only mild protest registering in Lucy Waite's expression, the atmosphere was suddenly electric and Robert Lang found himself, to his amazement, wondering what went on behind locked doors between Justin Waite and his wife. Did he beat her or did he throw her down on the bed and make punishing love to her...

'Because I say so, Lucy,' Justin Waite said with sudden detachment as he looked away from his wife thereby seeming to cut the electric current between them. 'Go back to your horses, my dear, and I will apologise for this misunderstanding.'

Lucy Waite shrugged. 'Whatever you say, Justin,' she murmured. 'Do forgive me, Mr Lang,' she added. 'I haven't been married very long, you see, so I'm not altogether familiar with the *rules*, I guess, but I—'

'Lucy—'

'Just going, Justin. Bye!' She strolled out with a wave.

* * *

'I gather,' Justin Waite said across the dinner table, to his wife, 'that today's events were more shots in the war you promised me the day you married me, Lucy.'

Lucy Waite smoothed down the skirt of the clinging, long-sleeved black dress with a heart-shaped neckline that she'd changed into for dinner and picked up her soup spoon. She'd also tucked a creamy gardenia into the hair that was lying loose and rippling on her shoulders. 'You gather right, Justin.'

'It wasn't much of a shot.'

Lucy sipped her soup then grinned. 'As a matter of fact I thought it quite got you off the bit for a moment, Justin.' She changed her expression to one of severity and mimicked, '"My wife has been leading people up the garden path from the cradle." But yes, it would have been better if it had come off,' she conceded. 'You do so hate publicity, don't you, Justin?'

'I can't believe you really enjoy it,' he commented drily.

Lucy wrinkled her nose. 'It was only a rural paper. I thought it was rather tasteful to choose a rural paper instead of a national daily. And all I'd planned to do was show them the house and some of...*our* treasures, and all your improvements to the property. It would have been quite a scoop for that young man, don't you think? Something about the Waites in a newspaper, even just a rural one. You've probably blighted his career, Justin, and he was rather sweet, really.'

'I haven't blighted his career at all, but he does understand now that my wife is off limits so you might as well forget him, Lucy. And any other young man who takes your fancy.'

Lucy laughed and pushed away her soup. 'You perceive me quaking in my shoes, Justin,' she murmured. 'Still, all may not be lost,' she mused. 'There's got to be at least one person out there now who's thinking that the Waites of Dalkeith and Riverbend have a very strange marriage.'

'On the contrary, there could be at least one person out there who is actually thinking that Lucinda Waite is a spoilt brat and deserves a good lesson.'

'From my experience of young men, Justin, they don't generally have those thoughts about me. It's only your generation—at least, you're the only one of your generation I have to go on, and I have to tell you that if you mean what I think you mean—'

'That you deserve to be put over someone's knee and ceremonially spanked?' he broke in lazily.

'How picturesque.' For the first time a little glint of anger lit Lucy's eyes. 'I have to tell you I should probably get so angry I'd even be capable of taking a pot-shot at *you*. Don't forget I'm an excellent shot and I would know exactly how to inconvenience you considerably without doing a lot of harm—and make it all look like an accident anyway.'

'That wasn't what I had in mind, Lucy,' he drawled, and reached for the decanter to pour himself some wine.

'How brave you are,' she retorted.

'What I had in mind—were I so minded,' he continued, holding his wine glass up to the light meditatively, 'was a lesson of another kind. Such as—' he put the glass down gently and their eyes locked '—removing your dress from your delectable body, uncovering your breasts and the rest of you and making love to you until you're—shall we say, in a much more amenable frame of mind? I have this theory on women,' he went on, idly inspecting the pulse that had started to beat rather erratically at the base of Lucy's throat. 'That without regular, satisfying sex they become fractious and troublesome, and in your case in particular, dear Lucy, that what you really need is a couple of kids to keep you out of mischief.'

It took Lucy several moments to gather enough composure to be able to speak, moments that were made worse for her because her tall, satanic husband did not relax his leisurely scrutiny of her in the slightest and then had the gall to pour her a glass of wine and push it towards her with a faintly amused twist of his lips.

In the end, as she sipped the golden liquid, it was he who spoke first. 'You don't agree?'

'I think,' Lucy said carefully, 'that it's a pity you didn't live in a different era, a bygone era for example, when women were treated like chattels and it was accepted practice to generalise about them as if they were so many...sheep. As if they had no minds, only instincts.'

'Then tell me this—you've ordered the course of this marriage so far; how happy has it made you?'

'You've gone along with it,' she said tautly.

'Were you secretly hoping I'd do something as uncouth and as—*exciting* as taking you against your will after you made your dramatic declaration on our wedding-night?'

Lucy gasped. 'Only minutes ago *you* were talking about... you *were* talking about...'

'Something quite different, Lucy,' he said.

'I can't see it, personally.' She looked at him defiantly.

'I was talking about finding out what your will really is in this matter,' he said and his teeth glinted in a sudden grin. 'Don't look so worried, I'm not going to do it. Not tonight, at least. But I do make the point that to a certain extent you've given me yourself as a hostage in this ridiculous war, Lucy, and perhaps you should bear it in mind the next time you decide to fire any shots. Would you care to dish up the casserole or shall I?'

Lucy put down her napkin and stood up. The silver casserole was on a hot plate on the sideboard. 'I will,' she said, but didn't move immediately. 'Justin, you gave me very little choice about marrying you. You made it very plain that I could lose everything I possessed, not the least my home, where I've lived all my *life*, if I didn't marry you. You put it to me that we could fight each other for years over Dalkeith and that you *would* fight for it although it was more or less all I had, while you'd inherited Riverbend and made yourself a huge fortune on top of it—'

'That's debatable—'

'Don't interrupt,' she commanded. 'But since you have, it

was never my fault that our fathers were foolish enough to own this place in partnership and then even more foolish to fall out with each other and leave us to inherit this mess—'

'Lucy, the cold, hard facts of the matter are a little different. Because Riverbend and Dalkeith are adjoining properties and because our fathers were friends, when your father got into financial difficulties, *my* father offered to inject some money into the place and accept a partnership in return—a *silent* partnership,' he said significantly. And waited while Lucy tried to look unaffected but failed. He went on, 'What broke up the friendship, despite this concession to your father's ego, despite trying to help save Dalkeith from going under the hammer, was that your father persisted in believing that Australia could ride on the back of its sheep forever and fought every suggestion my father ever made for diversification away from growing wool.'

Lucy bit her lip. 'I didn't know all that,' she said bravely, however.

'No, but that wasn't my fault,' he retorted impatiently. 'It was his fault that you didn't know, his fault that you were allowed to queen it over all and sundry as Lucinda Wainright of Dalkeith and never suspect you'd have to share this place with anyone, let alone with *me*, whom your father had given you the impression you shouldn't want to know any more anyway. Although—' his eyes glinted '—there were times when you didn't mind knowing me, Lucy.'

She coloured faintly but said with spirit, 'If you're referring to the days when I was barely out of rompers and didn't know better than to follow you around whenever you were here—'

'As a matter of fact I'm not referring to those days,' he said softly—and said no more.

She blushed properly this time, which made her angrier. 'If this is your revenge for—' She stopped abruptly.

'It isn't,' he answered equably. 'Not against you, anyway.'

'Then tell me this, Justin: what *was* your motivation for coming to see me only a fortnight after my father's funeral and telling me that the only sensible course for us to pursue was to get married?'

'Ah, well, my better nature did slip a bit then, I have to confess. You were so proud. I could also visualise the complications that might arise if someone else married you or got you pregnant before we'd sorted it all out. You have to agree, Lucy, that you left a trail of broken hearts around the district—it was really only a matter of time before you—er—fell. But of course, there was also the way you'd grown up, five foot six of sheer perfection, a bobby-dazzler in fact,' he said with a shrug. 'It occurred to me that not only would I not mind being married to you, but, since we had such a lot in common—' his eyes drifted around the beautiful room '—it would simplify matters considerably.'

'I'm only surprised you don't have another theory,' Lucy said through her teeth. 'That wives can be schooled and trained like horses. Or is that still to come?'

'Provided you get them young enough, it could be a possibility, even though you were so spoilt and indulged by your father,' he said indifferently and shrugged again. 'Lucy, how much longer do we have to wait to eat? We've had all this out before. And you were the one,' he said with sudden impatience, 'who accepted my proposal. Which to my mind, if we're really discussing moral superiority, puts us on a par. Although you mentioned earlier that I threatened you with something like poverty. In fact I offered to buy you out, and that would have been a long way from poverty, my dear.'

'But I didn't want to be bought out. I decided to fight in the only way I could think of for my birthright, Justin. My great-grandparents happen to be buried here, and my mother and now my father, I love every acre of Dalkeith and sometimes, when you love something enough, you're prepared to go to extraordinary lengths to preserve it. Besides which, it occurred to *me*,' she said softly, 'that you'd find it not considerably simpler but much more difficult to dispossess a wife, Justin.'

'A wife, yes, Lucy,' he said. 'But there are certain things you have to do to become a true wife.'

'It's only your word against mine—ah,' she said to herself. 'So that's why you haven't forced me to go to bed with you! You're keeping your options open, aren't you, Justin? But while an annulment on the grounds of non-consummation may entitle me to less of your property, it is only your word against mine.'

He lay back in his chair and watched her. 'Would you lie about something like that, Lucy?'

'Where you're concerned, I might. Don't forget, I have to put up with your mistress parading herself around my home—who knows what flights of fancy the mere fact of that might prompt in me—where is Sasha, by the way?'

'She's gone back to Riverbend and she's not my mistress.'

'Then she's dying to be your mistress.'

'She happens to be an employee, my private assistant in charge of the stud at Riverbend, as you very well know, and she's extremely good at her job, that's all; what makes you think she has...the ambition you're accusing her of?'

Lucy turned to the sideboard at last. 'You'd probably have to be a woman to understand that. But I would have thought even you could see the sort of censorious way she treats me.'

'There are times when you lay yourself open to that, Lucy.'

Lucy heaped a fragrant portion of lemon chicken on to a plate, and some steaming, fluffy rice, and laughed. 'Perhaps I do. But she does so obviously hold this conviction that you were mad to marry me whatever else she is or isn't, you see. On the subject of mistresses, by the way...' She turned and carried his plate over to him, not unaware that his gaze was following every move she made, then went back for her own. 'At thirty, you must have had some, probably dozens. You're successful, you're good-looking when you're not being critical and superior—did none of them prompt you to think of marriage for all the right reasons?' She sat down and helped herself to salad then courteously handed the crystal bowl to him. 'Take Joanna

Madden, for example,' she added pointedly. 'I'm sure a lot of people thought that was a *fait accompli.*'

'So did I—once upon a time,' she said musingly after a while when she thought he wasn't going to answer.

'What happened? Did she have nothing as enticing as the other half of Dalkeith to offer you?'

'She—had her reasons.'

'You don't seem particularly perturbed,' Lucy said witheringly.

He smiled fleetingly. 'One lives and learns, I guess. Lucy,' he said after a pause, 'considering our feelings on the subject of Dalkeith—and while I acknowledge mine aren't as unaltruistic and loving as yours, none the less it is very important to me—considering that we have its best interests at heart in other words, would it be so hard to see whether we couldn't make a go of this marriage?'

She considered for a long time then she said rather bleakly, 'That's like asking a nation to love their invaders. I don't think it's possible. I mean, for another thing, there's the problem that you don't respect me—you surely couldn't if you really believe that regular sex is all I need to keep me happy—'

'There's a difference between regular sex and satisfying sex.'

She shot him an oblique look. 'Your ego is really monumental, Justin, even for a man. All *right*, but I'm still just another giddy girl to you, aren't I?'

'I suppose it wasn't a help possessing such stunning looks on top of a father who spoilt you rotten, but you certainly don't go out of your way to dispel that image, Lucy.'

She looked across at him and there was something curiously haughty in her eyes. 'Perhaps not, but that might not be all there is to me. For example, I do know quite a lot about Dalkeith and how it runs—if young men can sow their wild oats, why can't girls have a few giddy salad days, anyway?'

He put his knife and fork together and stared at them for a long moment, before raising his eyes to hers. And then there was something curiously enigmatic in them as he said, 'I've told you, what's history can remain so. Your legion of lovers and my—multitude of mistresses. Unfortunately, you've got into the habit of sending out unmistakable signals—you're probably right about young Mr Lang and the kind of thoughts he's having about you now.'

Lucy grimaced.

'Not picking up the bait, Mrs Waite?' Justin said softly but with an undercurrent of mockery.

She tightened her mouth and subjected him to a deep blue look of considerable scorn.

He only laughed quietly. 'Just one more thing, Lucy. In case you haven't already got the message, if celibacy is becoming irksome then I am your only alternative. Remember that.'

She burst into speech. 'What about you? You don't really expect me to believe *I* am *your* only alternative.'

'Well, you are, so bear that in mind as well, my dear. But I'm afraid celibacy, inside marriage, certainly won't suit me forever.' He stood up. 'And you know, Lucy, while I give your devotion to Dalkeith full credit, there's no way a twenty-year-old girl could run it. There was no way you could have gone on without the kind of cash it needs again—and Dalkeith has become a rather expensive pastime for us Waites.' He stopped and watched her as she took the point and looked away uncertainly. Then he went on quite gently, 'But *this* way, here you are, mistress of it, and if you've got as much sense as I think you have in your more rational moments you must know it's in good hands. By the way, I'm taking a couple of weeks off and we're giving a house party this weekend. You might need to get in extra help. Goodnight.'

A couple of hours later, Lucy walked into her bedroom and closed the door.

As part of the austerity measures her father had been forced to introduce before his death, there was no live-in house help on Dalkeith. In fact Lucy had cut short her bachelor of arts degree to come home and look after her father six months ago and after her marriage, a curious marriage to say the least, she'd decided to keep it that way. It gave her something to do, and she'd discovered that, in lieu of her deep interest in Dalkeith being taken seriously, her interest despite herself in the crops Justin planned to grow and the sheep it still ran across its thousand acres of outback western New South Wales, that only left her horses for her to occupy herself with. And two mares in foal and two gelding hacks, devoted to them though she was, didn't take up a lot of time.

She did have a cleaning lady who came in daily and a farmhand to tend the fireplaces, but it had come as some surprise to her, in those last days of her father's decline, to find that she enjoyed cooking and gardening.

She sighed suddenly, pushed herself away from the door and picked up the silver-framed photo of her father from her dressing-table. No matter the things that she'd come to suspect even before his death, such as his being eminently suited to being a gentleman of leisure but *not* a gentleman farmer, and what she'd discovered about him after his death—that he'd tried to rescue Dalkeith from the brink again by gambling on horses, despite it all, she'd loved him and, only three months later, still missed him unbearably at times. If nothing else he'd certainly loved her unstintingly, and he'd taught her all the things he held dear to his heart, among them riding, shooting and fishing. He'd also taught her about art and music, he'd taken her to faraway exotic places, he'd helped her to fix her taste in clothes and all manner of things and yes, spoilt her wildly. But he'd never foisted a stepmother on her after her own mother, whom she couldn't remember, had died. In fact, she suspected he'd never got over her mother's death, and certain things in life hadn't had much meaning for him after it. Including Dalkeith.

He'd also sent her to a very expensive convent school where the Mother Superior had been strong-minded enough to persevere with the motherless, precocious, mischievous and often downright naughty Lucy Wainright despite the battles royal they'd had since Lucy had been placed in her care at nine and a half, and she'd continued there until she was seventeen and a half. They'd even parted on terms of mutual respect and by that time quite some mutual affection, although each was loath to admit it.

But had her father, Lucy wondered, as she stared down at his handsome likeness, never really realised how much Dalkeith, above all else, had meant to *her*? That even in her giddy salad days when she'd been queening it over all and sundry—her eyes flashed briefly—it, even more than her father, had been the rock to come back to. Did she have more of her Scottish great-grandparents in her than he'd ever had? A spiritual affinity with the land that was like a physical tie? Had he not known that, without him and without Dalkeith, brave, bright Lucinda Wainright, darling of society, was in fact lonely and more than a little frightened? But he had known how much she loved Dalkeith; wasn't that why he'd never told her he'd lost half of it to Justin's father?

She pushed off her shoes and curled up in the pink velvet armchair beside the fireplace, and stared into the flickering flames with a faraway look in her eyes.

It was ironic but true that she had hero-worshipped Justin Waite as a child. It was also true that Justin had, without her quite understanding it, achieved the status of a hallmark in her mind during her adolescent years. A hallmark that she had involuntarily found herself measuring other boys, then men up against, and finding most of them wanting. This had also led her, once she'd left school and on the few social occasions that they had met, to treat him with cool hauteur, yet to experience an undoubted desire to be *noticed*.

'And he noticed,' she murmured a little bitterly, her cheeks feeling warm again. 'Although the only sign he ever gave of it was that hateful little glint of amusement in his eyes—I really do hate him now!'

She sat up breathing quickly but also feeling a curious mixture of confusion and guilt. Why hadn't she pressed her father for details about his rift with the Waites, despite his extreme reluctance to say more on the subject? Well, I did try, she admitted. And of course I know now that he couldn't bring himself to tell me what was going on—the fact that Riverbend did diversify and go into breeding racehorses with spectacular success must have been an awful blow to his pride, but why couldn't I have realised it at the time? And then what he did say, about us no longer being good enough for the Waites, set my back right up. With the result, she conceded gloomily, sinking back in the chair, that I made myself ridiculous by treating Justin the way I did. But did I really offend him enough for him to take this kind of revenge? To make me marry him although he didn't love me and so he can get all of Dalkeith? she asked herself miserably.

And answered herself a little tartly—apart from amusing him, I doubt it. I mean, I never *saw* him without some beautiful woman on his arm or doing something spectacular like playing polo or crewing on some twelve-metre yacht, and of course he then proceeded to make his own fortune.

She brooded darkly for a moment on how Justin had taken a run-down saddlery business and built it into a nationwide success story—another one—and so not only did Riverbend Stud produce top-flight progeny, but Riverbend Saddlery produced saddles of the finest quality, with an international reputation and all sorts of horse products, as well as clothing—riding boots et cetera. Yes, Justin was clever and not only with horses—and there was a ten-year age gap between them, damn it!

She got up and paced about angrily. 'So what?' she murmured to herself, and picked up her silver-backed hairbrush and turned it over and over in her hands. Then she stopped and looked down at it and fingered the ornate 'W' engraved into the handle, and drew herself upright and stared at her reflection with cold eyes.

'Just remember what he said when he proposed. He said, "We won't even have to change the monograms, will we? Surely that demonstrates what a *practical* arrangement it would be."'

But she shivered suddenly because, in a moment of rage and panic, she *had* accepted. And then, in a moment of further panic on her wedding-night had made her 'dramatic declaration'. That she'd never willingly sleep with him. Had she in fact been seriously unbalanced by grief and everything else?

CHAPTER TWO

'I NEED YOU. Justin—'

'Well, well—' Justin Waite put out a lazy hand and grasped his wife's wrist '—did my little lecture set you thinking, dear Lucy?'

Lucy closed her eyes, attempted to free herself to no avail and ground her teeth. 'I need to *talk* to you. About this party.'

It was a bright, chilly morning but Justin had apparently been up well ahead of her, which was how she'd encountered him coming in through the kitchen door as she was on the way out. Normally she'd have kept on going.

'Ah.' He released her wrist. 'Then talk away while I start my breakfast.'

'What have you been doing?' she said involuntarily as she followed him reluctantly back into the kitchen where his breakfast was keeping warm on the range. He had on jeans, boots and a yellow sweater, his thick dark hair was ruffled and the cold morning air seemed to have agreed with him. In other words he looked fit, tough and capable, alert and slightly mocking, and more than a match for her. But when did he look any different these days? she wondered bitterly.

'I've been out and about,' he said idly, and carried the plate of sausages, scrambled eggs and toast to the kitchen table. There was a pot of coffee bubbling gently on the stove.

Lucy went over to it and poured two mugs which she carried to the kitchen table and sat down opposite him. 'You can tell me, you know. Not only is the place still half mine but I'm *interested*,' she said with extreme frustration before she could stop herself. 'Wouldn't I under normal circumstances have some sort of voting power or some *say* in what you do?'

'I've only been inspecting fences in the twelve-mile paddock, Lucy,' he said mildly. 'I made no momentous decisions other than that they need repairing.'

Lucy drew a breath and thought how much she'd have enjoyed a gallop down to the twelve-mile before breakfast instead of the lonely, aimless ride she'd been about to take. 'What about the boundary rider's hut?' she asked tonelessly. 'The last time I saw it it was a bit ramshackle. Grandad always liked to keep it provisioned and weatherproof because the twelve-mile can flood, but it's on the only high ground, so if you did get marooned out there—'

'That too. They're starting on it today.'

She lowered her lashes instead of glaring at him. 'Well,' she said even more tonelessly, 'tell me about the house party. You haven't given me much notice.'

Justin spread marmalade on his toast. 'I can get someone in to do it all if you like. I have mentioned that there's no need for you to do so much of your own work, Lucy.' He put the lid on the marmalade with some impatience.

'And I've told you, I'd go round the bend that way, Justin, not to mention feeling as if I was on the receiving end of your patronage.'

He smiled. 'I can assure you it's not patronage to provide one's wife with household help.'

'But then we've agreed I'm not much of a wife. Look, I can do it. I can get Mrs Milton and her sister to come up—as I've done before on Dalkeith.'

'Then do it,' he said curtly. 'What do you want to know?'

'When they're arriving, when they're leaving, who they are and just what kind of a weekend you have in mind!'

'Why, the kind of weekend Dalkeith is famous for, Lucy,' he said blandly. 'I'm sure I don't have to tell you. There'll be four guests and Sasha.'

She stared at him then forced herself to relax. 'Well, if they come on Friday afternoon, we'll have an informal dinner, a buffet and a simple evening—music, cards and so on. Saturday, a picnic at the creek, some sightseeing around the place, some target shooting or archery, a little gentle croquet for the ladies, then a formal dinner to which I could invite some locals.' She considered. 'Yes, I could invite the Simpsons, and Miles Graham for Sasha! That should even things up.' Her eyes glinted. 'Then on Sunday morning a late breakfast, and they can do what they like until they leave after lunch.'

'And you and Mrs Milton and her sister can cope with all that?' he queried.

Lucy shrugged. 'They've got it down to a fine art. Mrs Milton does the cooking, although a lot of it is prepared beforehand, and her sister makes the beds, tidies up, waits on table et cetera. It's all in the preparation, Justin. So long as you feed people really well, the rest seems to take care of itself.'

'It's Tuesday today, Lucy,' he warned.

'That gives me three full days, Justin,' she said wearily. 'Besides, I think I need a challenge,' she murmured, and propped her chin on her hands.

He regarded her steadily then said quietly, 'You're making things awfully hard for yourself, Lucy.'

'No, you're making them hard for me, Justin.'

'I hesitate to labour this point, but if it weren't for me you wouldn't be here.'

'Perhaps. But I might have felt I'd gone down in a fair fight—who knows?'

'How are you going to handle us in front of these people?'

She blinked, then grinned. 'I hadn't thought of that—yet.' She sat up suddenly and tossed the thick plait she'd braided her hair into over her shoulder. 'Do you mean we'll have to put on a loving show?'

'It's not unexpected in newly-weds,' he observed.

'Oh.'

'And I don't expect I'd take kindly to being made a fool of,' he added without the least emphasis, yet a curious underlay to his words that made her nerves prickle oddly. Perhaps it was something in his eyes as well, as they rested on her.

She opened her mouth, closed it then said with dignity, 'It's not a pre-requisite to... I mean, some of the people I've known who really were in love didn't...sort of flaunt it.'

'Perhaps not,' he agreed. 'What I'm trying to get at is, are you prepared to be sensible or are you going to cook up something like yesterday to advertise to the world that we're not in love?'

Lucy pursed her lips. 'I might just be normal and let them work it out for themselves,' she said thoughtfully. 'I don't think you can expect much more from me, Justin.'

'When you say normal, do you mean you'll include me in your *come hither*—?'

'I *don't* do that,' she cut in sharply.

'Perhaps you don't realise you're doing it. Perhaps it's second nature now. Didn't you notice Robert Lang going weak at the knees when you smiled at him yesterday?' He lifted a dark eyebrow at her.

Lucy set her teeth.

He waited then gathered his plate and took it over to the sink.

'I can't help how I smile!' she said in a goaded sort of voice at last.

'No, but with a bit of age and maturity you should be able to use it with discretion. Otherwise you could find yourself in a situation you might find hard to handle one day.'

Lucy tossed her head and stood up, with not the slightest idea, as he came back to the table, what he had in mind. 'Like this,' he said softly, standing right in front of her so she had to tilt her head back, and taking her in his arms as her eyes widened. 'In the position of being kissed by your sworn enemy.'

Her lips parted. 'Justin...'

But he ignored both the look in her eyes and the incredulity in her voice, and held her closer so she couldn't help being aware not only of the feel of his hard, muscled body against her own but of the faint tang of aftershave and sheer maleness about him—and finding it curiously heady, like some primitive assault on her senses. This both stunned her slightly and made her less able to cope with what followed. A searching, not particularly deep kiss to which she didn't respond particularly yet which didn't exactly repel. It was really strange, she reflected afterwards. It was as if her body had gone languid and her mind was suspended above her, recording and storing the event, monitoring her own reactions but, above all, searching for his.

And when he lifted his head at last she blinked once then stared into his eyes, with her heart in her mouth suddenly at what she might see.

What she did see was the way he narrowed his eyes immediately, and then the little laughter-lines beside them creased. 'Well, Lucy,' he said wryly, 'you have got that down to a fine art, haven't you?'

She licked her lips and said huskily, 'What do you mean?'

His hands slid down her back to her waist and he lifted her off her feet and moved her away, and steadied her but didn't take his hands away. 'The art of kissing and giving nothing away at the same time.'

A tinge of pink came to her cheeks and a pulse beat at the base of her throat, a pulse of anger as it happened. 'If that's not exactly what you did, I'll eat my hat,' she retorted, and removed herself from his grasp but sat down almost immediately.

'Then why are you so cross?' He leant against the corner of the table and folded his arms.

'Perhaps I'm tired of having it continually pointed out to me what a *femme fatale* I am.' She picked up the lid of the sugar bowl and replaced it not gently. 'And if that was a warning of the deluded sort you were issuing yesterday—'

'It was a warning to behave yourself this weekend, Lucy.'

'*Listen*, Justin!' Her eyes were a deeper, decidedly stormy blue now.

'No, you listen to me, Lucy.' He unfolded his arms and pinned one of her wrists to the table as her hand wandered towards the sugar bowl again, and he lifted her chin in his other one, also not gently as she resisted stubbornly. And his eyes were a cold, hard grey as he said, 'You can fight me all you like in private, but not in public, because if you do, I'll retaliate, believe me, in a way you wouldn't like at all, and in a way that will make your little war look like child's play. Do we understand each other?'

It was Mrs Milton who broke into Lucy's reverie. Mrs Milton came in daily and Lucy was still sitting at the kitchen table where Justin had left her, staring into space, as she arrived.

'Morning, Miss Lucy,' she said brightly and placed a parcel on the table. 'There's those sheets that needed mending.'

'Oh!' Lucy jumped. 'Oh, thank you, Mrs Milton—sorry, I was miles away. How are you?'

'Fine, love. Miles away where?' Mrs Milton poured herself a cup of coffee.

Lucy grimaced. 'Are you doing anything this weekend? You and your sister?'

'No. Got a party on?'

'Yes, and I want it to be—something special, Mrs Milton. Hang on, I'll get a pen and paper.'

Whether by design or not, Justin stayed out of her way over those next three busy days, although they did meet for breakfast on the Wednesday morning.

'You have a dirty mark on your chin, Lucy,' her husband

said after a more formal greeting had got him a cool look and a barely audible murmur in reply.

This time she responded with a raised eyebrow and a shrug, causing him to narrow his eyes and appear to drop the subject. But as they passed each other later, he stopped her with a hand on her shoulder and put his forefinger on the 'mark' on her chin.

'Did I do that?'

She merely nodded.

He took his finger away and inspected the faint blue bruise. He also let his gaze wander over her mouth, innocent of any lipstick yet rose-pink and finely chiselled, the smooth lucent skin of her cheeks, the deep pansy blue of her eyes with their sweeping lashes, darker than her hair, and the escaping tendrils of wheat gold curling on her forehead. 'My apologies,' he said. 'I didn't know you bruised so easily.'

'I don't bruise so easily. Perhaps you don't know your own strength. Or perhaps you do.'

'What I haven't known,' he said with a twist of his lips, 'is anyone quite as stubborn as you. I suppose you've now added the fact that I'm a callous brute to your list of my sins.'

'Some of your threats left me in no doubt of it at all even before this,' she murmured coldly. 'May I go now? I have a lot to do.'

'How's it going?'

'It's all under control.'

'Do you need any assistance? From me,' he said gravely.

Her look spoke volumes. 'All you have to do is be here, Justin.'

'I still haven't told you who's coming—apart from Sasha.'

Lucy shrugged. 'I rang Sasha myself and got it all from her. She was a mine of information, in fact. Two couples, although one unmarried couple who will nevertheless share a bedroom—'

'Unlike some *married* couples I know. I wonder if it's a new trend? Go on,' he said politely.

'Yes, well,' Lucy said evenly, 'Sasha also told me that although it's not strictly a business weekend, they will be inspecting some yearlings at Riverbend on their way here and might be interested in buying them at the upcoming yearling sales in Sydney—she said that very significantly, Justin. In other words—don't rock the boat, Lucy, *if* you can help it! And, she also gave me some helpful suggestions which—'

'You will go out of your way to ignore,' Justin said amusedly.

'Indeed I will.' Lucy's eyes flashed briefly, recalling Sasha's helpful advice which had included the maxim that keeping things simple might be a good idea. 'How you put up with her I've no idea!'

'I've told you, she's very good at her job.'

'She's certainly got a superiority complex. Is that why you two get along so well?' she asked innocently, and went on impatiently, 'Besides, being good at your job doesn't mean you have to be treated as a friend, necessarily.'

'Well Sasha is both actually, Lucy. And since I moved to Dalkeith, so that you might remain in your ancestral home,' he said and held her eyes in a suddenly cool look, 'she is more up to date on matters relating to the stud and this crop of yearlings than I am. So she will be here in what you might call an unofficial business capacity.' He paused then added with that same cool look. 'Don't upset Sasha, Lucy. She may rub you up the wrong way but she has a brain like a computer when it comes to horses, and extremely good judgement.'

'As a matter of fact I believe you, Justin. I've even thought she has a certain horsey look about her—nothing less than a chestnut thoroughbred with wonderful lines, of course!' she finished with a grin. 'As for upsetting her,' she added, 'I wish you would tell me how to, because it doesn't seem possible.'

They stared at each other—rather, Lucy found it suddenly impossible to evade his gaze or to understand why it made her suddenly feel a bit small, but it did and she said at last, 'Oh, all right! I *won't* upset Sasha—so far as it's humanly possible for me not to!'

'Good.' He said nothing more but moved out of her way.

'Am I being dismissed now?' she demanded.

'Why not?'

'There are times, Justin Waite, when you irritate the life out of me,' she said precisely. 'And what with you and Sasha telling me what I should do and what I shouldn't do, it will be a miracle if this weekend doesn't turn out to be a disaster—' She broke off and made a disgusted sound.

'And there are times, Lucy, when it's impossible to tell you anything—I wouldn't be too happy about this weekend turning into a disaster, so if you have any doubts tell me now.'

'*I* don't—'

'I suppose the proof of that will be in the pudding,' he said drily, and studied her. 'By the way,' he said, flicking his gaze over her denim overalls, and the two pigtails she wore her hair in, 'Would you mind not wearing your hair like that over the weekend?'

She blinked. 'Why not—as if I would, anyway.'

'I could be accused of cradle-snatching, that's all. Off you go.'

'Perhaps you are!'

'Now, Lucy, we both know I'm not. Don't we?' His grey gaze bored into hers until she reddened and turned away abruptly and angrily but without words.

Fortunately for her seething state of mind, there was enough to be done to calm her and force her to concentrate—and not only that. There was the knowledge that both Justin and Sasha had doubts about her capabilities as a hostess. In her less angry moments she recognised that it was a useful spur, in her more angry moments she told herself she would certainly show them a thing or two. And by Friday midday the fruits of her labour and Mrs Milton's were very evident. The house was polished and shining and filled with flowers. The guest bedrooms were impeccable, with not a wrinkle in their bedspreads, and the cold room was filled with a selection of pies and pastries, cold meats, quiches, fruits and vegetables and three splendid, plump ducks hung there, ready to be roasted for Saturday night's dinner.

It was also not long past midday when disaster struck, in the form of a distraught phone call from Mrs Milton who'd gone to pick up her sister to take up residence in the staff quarters for the weekend.

'...Your mother? Oh, I'm so sorry, Mrs Milton,' Lucy said into the phone and a moment later, 'Yes, of course if it's that serious, I do understand. Um...you and your sister must be worried sick and will want to be with her... Look, if there's anything I can do, please—'

'You've got enough on your plate as it is, pet,' Mrs Milton said down the line in tones quite unlike her normal cheerful ones. 'I've been racking my *brains* and all I can come up with is my niece, Shirley. How would it be if I send her up, Miss Lucy? She's a good cook, that I can guarantee, and doesn't mind what she turns her hand to. There's only one problem and that's—'

'Oh, Mrs Milton, please do,' Lucy said into the phone. 'I'd be so grateful, and between us we've done most of it, haven't we? What's the problem?'

'Well she'd have to bring her son, Adrian—'

'That's no problem!'

'Mmm, I haven't told you about Adrian, have I? Look, just... if you're *firm* with him he's fine, but his father ran off when he was two, so... And Shirley worships the ground he walks on.'

'Don't worry, I'll tie him up if...no, of course not, Mrs Milton, I wouldn't dream of it, but I'm sure we'll be able to cope with him between us. Now you just worry about your mother and give her my love—I'll be thinking of you all.'

She put the phone down and took several deep breaths, then remembered she'd forgotten to ask how old Shirley's Adrian was.

He was ten, with red hair, prominent blue eyes and buck teeth. He walked with a swagger and didn't reply when spoken to.

His mother had faded blonde agitated-looking hair but otherwise was clean, neat and presentable and obviously anxious to do her very best.

'Well, Shirley,' Lucy said with a dazzling smile, half an hour before the guests were due to fly in, 'I guess the important thing is not to panic. Everything in the buffet is either cold or only needs heating up so tonight will be quite simple, and I'll nip in later to give you a hand.' And she took Shirley step by step through the evening's requirements. Then she showed them to their room and showed Adrian the television and even fetched some of her old books and games for him.

'He's not much of a reader,' his mother said with an apologetic smile, 'but it's lovely of you to bother, Miss Lucy. Now, Adrian, you will be a good boy, won't you?'

At five-thirty, the long, lovely veranda room played host to the glow of lamplight, the chink of glasses and some exuberant conversation. And despite the fact that part of her mind was elsewhere, Lucy was in the thick of it.

She wore slim scarlet trousers, matching flat shoes and a cream pullover with a wonderful red, green and cream scarf worn shawlwise. Her hair was loose and she was faintly pink from some of the extravagant compliments she'd received—most on the subject of new brides and early wedded bliss. Their guests were of course all older than she was, the two women in the same mould as Sasha, elegant late twenties or early thirties, experienced and articulate and both with careers of their own. But apart from that aspect of it, it was a milieu she was very familiar with and one her father had taught her to hold her own in some years ago. She'd been hostessing his parties since she was about eighteen, after all. And if she had fewer resources to hand than she'd ever had before, plus one Dennis the Menace on hand, she was damned if anyone was going to know it. Least of all Justin, although she'd caught him looking at her once or twice with something oddly alert in his eyes. But he's not a mind-reader, she reassured herself, and there's no earthly reason for him to go into the kitchen tonight, anyway. The longer I can keep him in the dark and still cope, the better, she reasoned—somewhat obscurely, she realised briefly, but didn't have the time to elaborate.

All the same, at six-thirty, when she suggested to everyone that they might like to freshen up although not to worry about changing, she breathed a sigh of relief when they all took themselves to their bedrooms and she repaired to the kitchen as unobtrusively as she could. To find Shirley standing in the middle of the room looking wild-eyed and tearful.

'What's wrong?' she demanded.

'He's gone!'

'Who?'

'Adrian! He could be anywhere out there! He's not a country boy, Miss Lucy; we're just spending a holiday with Auntie Vera!'

'The little...um, calm down, Shirley. I'll find him. You just keep on with the buffet. We've got an hour.'

It took her half an hour to locate Adrian in the loft above the garage. And the mild lecture she gave him brought no visible reaction from him even when she told him he'd frightened the life out of his mother. 'Now just stay put,' she admonished as she marched him back to his room. 'Tomorrow you can go out and see the horses, I'll organise a ride on a tractor for you, whatever you like—and your dinner's coming in a moment.'

'Are you all right, Lucy?'

'Fine, Justin,' she said brightly, finding him alone in the lounge. He'd added a sage-green sweater to his informal gear and his hair was brushed and tidy, his grey eyes watchful. 'No one down yet?'

'No. Have you been running somewhere?'

She laughed. 'No. Why?'

'You look a little—harassed. Are Mrs Milton and her sister coping all right?'

'Everything's fine. If you could just have some confidence in me, it would be a big help.'

'Very well, Lucy. Ah, here are the first of our guests.'

The buffet went off smoothly and with plenty of compliments and afterwards for a while they played music and all chatted together, and then the men tended to group together at one end of the room, leaving the women at the other and Sasha looking for once in her life as if she didn't quite know which group to join.

Lucy seized the opportunity and murmured in her ear that she'd be grateful if she could deputise for her for a moment, while she checked that all was well behind the scenes. Sasha looked gratified, as much, probably, Lucy reflected, that 'behind the scenes' should need checking. But she did as she was asked.

Behind the scenes, there was another story. The dining-room was cleared, the kitchen was tidy and a tea tray was set out but there was no sign of Shirley. What she was doing in fact, was swabbing out the staff bathroom and passage leading to it because Adrian had allowed the bath to overflow. He'd got so wrapped up in the television programme he'd been watching, his mother explained, he'd forgotten.

Lucy closed her eyes and counted to ten. And, on opening them, noticed Adrian watching her interestedly. Why, he's testing me out, she thought, the little wretch.

'Isn't it time he was in bed?' she said as mildly as she could.

By the time she got back she was feeling decidedly limp—it had taken the two of them a good twenty minutes of vigorous mopping to dam the flood, her feet were damp inside her shoes and she had trickles of sweat running down her back, but no one appeared to notice and the party had come together again and was dancing to the CD player.

'Oh damn,' she muttered to herself.

But two hours later her ordeal was ended, or so she thought.

The party broke up at last and everyone went up to bed appearing happy and contented with their stay on Dalkeith so far.

'Let's hope I can keep it that way,' she murmured to herself as she tidied up. She'd sent Shirley to bed, reasoning that it might keep Adrian out of more mischief as well as having her bright and fresh for the next day. But when it was all done she stood in the middle of the dining-room, thinking about the three other women in the house, excluding poor Shirley.

Thinking about them in a context that surprised her a little. In other words, how much more appropriate any one of them would be as a consort for Justin than she was. How, for example, *they* would react to being told that without regular, satisfying sex they could become—what had he said—fractious and troublesome?

Well, she mused, she couldn't imagine him saying something like that in the first place. To them. So how would communication on the subject take place with someone older and wiser? A more sophisticated play on words? A simple expression of need—with Sasha he'd probably only have to crook his finger, she thought somewhat maliciously, then sighed.

But a moment later she discovered herself feeling a sense of righteous indignation—talk about her *come hither* smiles! Had he not noticed that despite two of their female guests being partnered there had been throughout the evening a discreet summing up of Justin taking place, an awareness—yes, very subtle, but *there*. Of course it was always there with Sasha and he must be blind not to notice it. Why didn't he? But not only that, her thoughts ranged on, a subtle summing up of herself had been taking place all evening, in the direct context of her suitability for Justin.

She stood in the middle of the dining-room deep in thought, wondering if it was all part of the games people with a bit of age and maturity played, wondering if he played it himself, or wondering finally if he just had this devastating effect on women and had got so used to it that he didn't notice it any more!

'*Lucy.*'

'Oh!' She turned with a start to find the object of her deep, dark musings regarding her with some amusement. 'You—I didn't hear you,' she said lamely.

'I gathered that. You seemed to be a hundred miles away.'

'Not really,' she replied ruefully. 'Well, that's all done. I think I'll go to bed now—goodnight.'

'I'm coming up myself.' He strolled beside her to the foot of the staircase. 'It was a very successful evening, by the way.'

Lucy paused with her hand on the banister and tried to think of something to say but ended up unsuccessfully trying to smother a huge yawn. 'Sorry, I—'

'You're exhausted. Come,' he said, and without further ado he picked her up and started up the stairs.

After a moment of supreme surprise, she lay quiet and composed in his arms, her lashes fanning her cheeks, her only thought to wonder what was coming.

But all he did was to put her down on her bed and turn away to stoke up her fire. She lay quite still, watching him and feeling an odd little sense of loss, which translated upon a moment's thought to the realisation that she hadn't felt quite so lonely or strung up in his arms as she did lying alone on her bed the way she was... She bit back a husky exclamation and sat up, feeling unreasonably annoyed and stung to retaliation.

'It's a pity we couldn't have done that for the benefit of the gallery,' she said ironically. 'Justin, is it important to you the kind of impression I make on these people? I mean, are they going to judge you on me, sort of thing?'

He straightened and came over to the bed. 'Why?'

'Why what?'

'Why are you asking me that, Lucy?'

She stared up at him. 'Why shouldn't I? I'm curious, that's all.'

He looked faintly sceptical but said, 'I guess it's human nature to wonder what people see in each other and make some sort of judgement.'

'So,' she said slowly, 'were I to be judged—if they were to think for example, well, she's pretty enough and all that but mightn't she bore Justin to tears after a while?—how will that affect how they think about you?'

He frowned. 'Lucy, if I knew what was behind this I might—'

'You're the one who wanted me to make a good impression and not look as if I'd been snatched from my cradle,' she broke in tartly.

He smiled. 'Is that how you've been feeling tonight? A little out of your depth? I thought you were a bit wrought up about something.'

The accuracy and the inaccuracy of his words brought a faint blush to her cheeks and a further sense of maltreatment to her heart. 'You can't have it both ways, Justin. You did marry me, even if it was for all the wrong reasons, but they don't know that, so—'

'Lucy,' he interrupted gravely, 'let me set your mind at rest. I don't give a damn what people think about my private life; I never have. My concern about how you might behave this weekend was motivated by this—when you invite people to spend time with you, especially way out in the backblocks like this where they can't get up and go that easily if they want to, I think you're fairly obliged not to make them feel uncomfortable and as if they're in the midst of a domestic brawl. Don't you agree?'

She opened her mouth, closed it then said scathingly, 'Of course! That doesn't explain the cradle bit, though.'

'Well, as to that,' he said musingly, and picked up a strand of her hair, 'I wondered if it mightn't be part of your strategy, that's all.'

Lucy blinked at him. 'I don't understand.'

'Don't you? I thought since I'd made it plain that your *femme fatale* act—your words, not mine, but not inappropriate—was something I wouldn't approve of you might—change tack.'

Lucy closed her eyes. 'Funnily enough, it didn't occur to me at all,' she said bleakly.

'You wouldn't be losing your grip on this—war, would you, Lucy?' he queried, slipping her hair through his fingers then smoothing it back into place and standing back a step.

For the briefest moment Lucy wondered if she was. But she said, 'I'm rather tired, Justin, that's all.'

'Is it, Lucy?'

The way he said it, on a different note entirely made her open her eyes. 'What more could there be?'

'Unless you tell me, I don't know.' His eyes searched hers.

She looked away and found herself considering telling him that she didn't have Mrs Milton and her sister, only one flustered and anxious substitute—and Adrian, and that if the rest of the weekend went well it would be something of a miracle—he'd probably find out soon enough, anyway. But almost immediately she decided she couldn't stand his scorn, not tonight, so she said wearily, 'There's nothing,' and lay back exhaustedly.

'Perhaps you're trying too hard, Lucy.'

She stretched her throat and rubbed it. 'I really don't know what I have to do to *make* you approve of me, Justin.'

He moved so his face was in the shadows and she couldn't read his expression. 'Just the one thing you won't do.'

For the life of her she couldn't help it, couldn't stem the images that flooded her mind, of lying in his arms and being made love to, of not being lonely, at least. Images of surrender in the most complete way a woman could to a man, but... 'But then I might not approve of myself. It's a real dilemma, isn't it?' she whispered, and sat up suddenly with her hands to her face as hot tears sprang to her eyes. 'Please, just go away, Justin. I can't cope with you and all this at the same time.'

He stared down at her shaking shoulders for a long moment, then he said evenly, 'All right, I'm going. But if there is a problem you don't have to—'

'There's nothing!' She raised her tear-streaked face abruptly.

'Other than that you've now managed to undermine my self-confidence.'

'Why, Lucy, I never thought to hear you say that. Goodnight, my dear. Don't do anything stupid, will you?'

She didn't, not then, but before the weekend was over she seriously interfered with Adrian's freedom and committed a social solecism of considerable proportions.

CHAPTER THREE

IT WAS SASHA, who else, who broke the news on Sunday morning.

She came into the veranda room where everyone was lounging around comfortably just prior to getting ready to leave, still commenting on the great dinner party last night and lovely day they'd had yesterday, and she said into a lull in the conversation, 'Justin, there's a child handcuffed to a fence outside. He says Lucy did it and that she threatened to shoot him.'

Everyone sat up with wide eyes and turned to Lucy.

'Oh,' she swallowed, 'that's Adrian. He's only been there for about ten minutes. I…' She stopped and blushed bright red.

Incredibly, it was Justin who came to her rescue. 'What's he done now?' he said resignedly, and added for everyone's benefit, 'Adrian is the son of our cook, Shirley—a great cook, I'm sure you'll all agree.'

Lucy stared at him open-mouthed but he murmured gently, 'Tell us, Lucy, otherwise people will think you're some sort of a monster.'

'He…' Lucy licked her lips. 'Yesterday *he* handcuffed *me* to the towel rail in the kitchen. Um—one of his uncles is a policeman and he gave him this set. Fortunately his mother came to the rescue—eventually… And today,' she said hastily, 'he actually picked the lock of the gun cupboard—I caught him at it but of course luckily we keep the ammunition in a safe and I *didn't* threaten to shoot him…but in light of the fact that he laid waste every tomato plant in the vegetable garden yesterday, lit a fire in the chicken shed and downed all the washing on the line in the duck pond, I thought some of his own medicine might be good for him… You *knew*!' she said to Justin. 'All the time you knew.'

'Not all the time. Where are the keys? I'll…let him out on parole.'

But a combination of all sorts of factors worked powerfully in Lucy and she was deaf to discretion. 'How could you?' she accused. 'Of all the low-down things! To let me go *on* pretending…oh!' She ground her teeth. 'I hate you, Justin Waite, you're the most arrogant, self-opinionated man I've ever met and that's only some of the things I hate about you.'

The silence was electric but Justin laughed, as if he was really amused. 'Well, we nearly made it,' he said obliquely. 'Sorry, friends, but Lucy has had a traumatic weekend, haven't you, my love? I'm sure you only need to apologise, though. To them, not necessarily to me,' he added, and his eyes mocked her.

Lucy glanced round, flinched visibly as no one's eyes quite met hers, then became aware of an agitated murmuring she was coming to know well behind her. She dug into the pocket of her jeans and removed a set of keys. 'Here you are, Shirley,' she said swinging round. 'He hasn't been there long and if I were you I'd confiscate those handcuffs—they're more of a temptation than some people can bear. I am sorry,' she said contritely, swinging back. 'I've been short-staffed this weekend and I have an unfortunate temper, apparently. I do hope you'll all forgive me.'

She lay on her bed with her eyes closed but knew it was Justin when she heard the door open and close. She'd heard the plane take off about half an hour earlier but she'd made her farewells—she winced as she thought of it—from the house.

What caused her to open her eyes was the sagging of the

other side of her double bed, and she saw before she closed them again that, not content with sitting, he'd stretched out with his hands behind his head. He also said, 'You're not sulking, are you, Lucy?'

She sat up abruptly and crossed her legs. 'No. I'm still angry as a matter of fact, so if you've come to *lecture* me you're wasting your time.'

'The thought never crossed my mind,' he murmured.

She frowned then turned to him. 'Aren't you—angry?'

'Do I look it?'

She hesitated because in fact he looked perfectly relaxed and at home and there was only a sort of bland query in his eyes. 'I—there are times when I don't understand you, Justin,' she said at last.

'That's rather obvious.'

'I mean, I've just done the one thing you didn't want me to do: discomfited our guests in other words—yet you—'

'They *were* on their way out, but go on.'

She breathed deeply. 'All right. I displayed sentiments not exactly common to new brides, I'm sure; I probably gave them cause to wonder whether I wasn't round the bend, handcuffing children to fences! Isn't that enough?'

'And all without even trying.' He smiled unexpectedly. 'Are you so annoyed because you feel its sheer spontaneity robbed it of malice aforethought and robbed you therefore of some satisfaction?'

Lucy bit her lip.

'As for my—low actions, what actually happened was that I knew something was up so I bearded a lady I *thought* must be Mrs Milton's sister in the kitchen yesterday morning, only to have the whole sad story explained to me—although she didn't tell me what a monster young Adrian is. I then acted as if I'd in fact known and decided to resume my mantle of ignorance with you mainly because you did seem to be coping admirably and I thought it would help restore your confidence. That same confidence you accused me of undermining. I now realise I should have bucked in and helped or something like that but then that would have meant explaining to people like Sasha—'

'That I'd got myself in a bind,' Lucy said gloomily.

'I thought you might not appreciate that.'

'I wouldn't have.' She pulled a fold of the bedspread through her fingers. 'Well,' she said grudgingly after some thought, 'I suppose I'm now in the wrong on all counts.'

'Is that an olive branch?' he queried.

She shrugged. 'Of a kind. Which means we're only back to square one, so—'

'Don't get any ideas, Justin. In other words.' He said it with utter gravity but when she looked at him there was a wicked little glint in his eyes.

She turned away hastily with her heartbeat doing an odd tattoo. 'I still have to live with the thought of at least five people seriously wondering about me,' she said with a toss of her head.

'I wouldn't worry about that; one of them even suggested you could be pregnant,' he said placidly.

'Well, I'm not!' Lucy sprang off the bed agitatedly.

'You know that and I know that, but they don't.' He stretched his arms lazily.

'In a few months' time they're all going to know it. What will they think then?' she demanded.

He regarded her in silence for a moment. 'Things could change in a few months' time.'

She made an exasperated sound and stalked over to the window. 'I still can't understand why you're quite happy for everyone either to know I do hate you or to think I have such a volatile disposition you must have been mad to marry me!'

'I told you, I don't give a damn what people think. I also happen to prefer you when you're being spontaneous, even if a shade volatile, Lucy.'

She stared out of the window. It had started out as another

bright, cold day but it was pouring now. She shivered. 'Remind me to be spontaneous the next time...it happens.'

There was silence, then she tensed as she heard the bed springs creak, but she refused to turn even when she heard his soft footfall across the carpet stop right behind her. She said, with her tension reflected in her voice, 'Where do we go from here?'

'I don't know. Any ideas?'

She couldn't contain herself any longer. She swung round. '*No.* I'm the hostage, don't forget.'

'You're also seriously overtired and overwrought,' he said impatiently. 'Why don't you have a bath and go to bed?'

'At three in the afternoon!' she said jerkily. 'Apart from anything else, Adrian is still on the loose—'

'He's not. I've had a chat with Adrian and I doubt if we'll have any more trouble with him. I've also told Shirley to relax for a couple of hours and thanked her for her considerable efforts.'

'And she's no doubt got stars in her eyes now and thinks you're just marvellous,' Lucy said bitterly.

He raised a mocking eyebrow. 'Being bitchy doesn't become you, Lucy.'

'I wish I knew what did—other than gracing your bed! As a matter of fact I also thanked Shirley and apologised for what I did to Adrian,' she said with irony.

'Then you won't mind if they stay on for a few days. Shirley to help you and Adrian to perhaps benefit from some male supervision.'

Lucy's eyes widened causing him to say with genuine irritation, 'He's only a kid suffering from the lack of a father. As a kid yourself who suffered from the lack of a mother, surely—'

'Oh, shut up, Justin,' she broke in. 'Don't you think I feel guilty enough as it is? In any other circumstances I'd never have...' She grimaced. 'I was just surprised you would want to take the time, that's all. Is that really—' she hesitated '—what you feel is the root cause of all my so-called problems, as a matter of interest? The lack of a mother?'

He shrugged. 'It mightn't have helped.'

'Thank you,' she said very formally, and added, 'Do you know what? I think I will do as you suggested after all. There just doesn't seem to be any alternative.'

'There is,' he said drily. 'And one day you'll take it, Lucy. Because I'll tell you what it is. Assuming you and I were in any kind of mental unity—let's leave the physical aspect out of it for the time being.' He smiled but it didn't reach his eyes. 'Assuming we were mentally attuned, we could go downstairs and have tea in front of the fire in the library, we could discuss the plans I have for the next week, all to do with Dalkeith and the kind of things that have been begging to be done for years, you could play the piano for a while—it's that kind of afternoon and I would enjoy listening while I read the papers the plane brought in this morning—then we could have dinner, watch a video and go to bed early. You would sleep like a top and be all bright-eyed and bushy-tailed in the morning.'

Her lips had parted as he spoke and she stared into his eyes with a kind of longing dawning in her own, which he saw, but he made no movement, no gesture.

She turned away.

She took a long bath and in a sudden spirit of urgency tried to sort out her thoughts in the process and to reduce her dilemma to stark facts rather than overheated, panicky emotion.

But the results *were* stark, she decided as she added more hot water and stared dismally through the steam. She was married to a man who didn't love her, who'd stood to gain by marrying her and had virtually forced her into it. A man, she mused, who must have taken a conscious decision that a marriage of convenience suited him best and had possibly decided he could mould her into the the kind of wife he wanted. What kind of man would do that? A man with a grudge, perhaps, yet it wasn't really *his* affair, more his father's, and it seemed an extreme length to go to surely, especially when he could have had virtually any wife he chose. No, there had to be more to it, she reflected, and wondered if there'd been anything in the Justin she'd known as a child to indicate this...hardness, sort of.

'He was always—I don't know,' she murmured to herself, 'you just knew he would always get what he wanted somehow, that's true. He was self-contained and...and of course, talking about mothers, he didn't have one either after she ran off with someone. Perhaps he suffered from a lack of it more than I did.' She sat up with a frown in her eyes. 'Perhaps that's why he thinks he can treat women like this: because he never had a woman he could respect or appreciate in his formative years. I bet that's got something to do with it!'

But a moment later she sank back ruefully, as it crossed her mind that coming from *her* this character-analysis of her worldly, sophisticated husband would probably be treated as laughable. Her thoughts ranged on. Assuming she did give in, she moved uncomfortably in the water then forced herself to consider the possibility. Assuming she did, what kind of a husband would he be for the rest of her life? Always a little distant, always the boss, so to speak—what kind of a marriage would that be? Or would she really, once she was *bedded*, be so besotted it wouldn't matter, or it would all come right in some mysterious manner she just couldn't foresee.

'And I *can't*,' she said with some force, 'because if he's an enigma now, he always will be, and even if he isn't a terrible husband it will only be half a life. Of course, there's always Dalkeith...is it such a price to pay?'

She shivered suddenly, and not because the water was cold but because it was occurring to her more and more that she was going to have to pay a price for her beloved home.

She also slept for a couple of hours, something that was unheard of for her during the day but although she woke feeling less tired she also felt cold and lonely as the rain-laden dusk blotted out the landscape. She pulled on a navy-blue tracksuit and sat brushing her hair for a long time, staring at her image in the mirror because it was in her mind to take a step she hadn't believed she ever would...

Justin was reading the papers in the library as she entered and closed the door behind her. He raised his dark head and watched her thoughtfully as she stood just inside the door, her hand still on the handle as if she might change her mind and leave again.

Then he said, 'Feeling better? Dinner's nearly ready, I believe.'

'Oh. Yes. I am. Justin—' She stopped as he stood up and was nearly overcome by nerves and by something else. A sudden sense of frustration, because knowing Justin Waite was like knowing the cover of a book you'd never read and because there were some ways she knew him that were infinitely disturbing, and not things she'd taken into account during her bath-time analysis of her situation. Things, for example, that only struck her when she was in his presence—or in his arms. Things like the feel of him and the feel of his mouth on hers, the easy strength of his arms and shoulders. And the knowledge that he was a dangerously attractive man, and suddenly being in the position of having to admit to herself that she'd always known it and that no amount of taboos on him could make her completely immune to it. It had been there, of course, when she'd been measuring other men up to him, there when she'd resolutely ignored him but noted every little detail of the women he was with. There now, as he stood watching her looking big and casual in his jeans and green sweater—and the treacherous thought came to her that if she just walked across the room into his arms, if he would just hold her and perhaps smooth her hair and touch her face gently, before he did anything else, it *might* all come right...

'Justin.' She released the door-handle and took a couple more steps. 'What you said earlier,' she went on hurriedly, 'about being *mentally* attuned. Could we—talk about that a bit more?'

His lips twisted but he said after a moment, 'Sure. Would you like a pre-dinner drink to—help it along?'

'Thanks,' she murmured and sat down opposite his chair.

He poured her a brandy and soda and one for himself and came back but didn't sit. Instead he propped an elbow on the mantelpiece and sipped his drink, not looking at her. 'Go ahead.'

Lucy took a large swallow of hers. 'Would it compromise me if I said,' she paused and licked her lips, 'if I said I could give it a try?'

'Compromise you how?' he enquired.

'I mean, would it lead you to think that it's a preliminary to going to bed with you?' she said tartly.

He considered gravely. 'Probably.' He lifted his head at last and there was amusement in his grey eyes.

She tried consciously to stem the tide of pink that came to her cheeks but of course that wasn't something one could consciously control so she said evenly, 'Well, you'd be wrong.'

He moved his shoulders briefly and murmured, 'My mistake. What would it mean, Lucy?'

She hesitated then said honestly and bleakly, 'I can't think what else to do, that's all.'

'Are you proposing, in other words, that we spend the rest of our lives in only mental affinity?'

Her nostrils flared and she took a huge swallow of her brandy this time which caused her to cough and splutter a bit before she got out, 'I can't *think* that far ahead! All I'm suggesting is that—all I'm saying is that I can't go on like this. I'm... I just don't know what else to do. For the moment. And while I'm in this awful situation, which is all your fault, don't forget, life is sort of slipping away from me and I feel useless and...' She gestured helplessly.

He studied her in silence for quite some time and until her

nerves started to prickle. Then he said, 'You're very young, aren't you, Lucy.'

'Are you asking me or telling me?'

He smiled faintly. 'Telling you, I guess. All right, we can give it a try. So long as you understand I won't be content with it forever.'

She raised her eyebrows ironically, 'Who knows, things might change in a few months.'

'Yes, well, you're also very articulate, my dear,' he said drily, 'for someone so curiously...naïve, sometimes.'

'That's a change—again. Has it occurred to you, Justin, that you haven't really worked out what I am?'

'On the contrary, I know exactly what you are, Lucy. I wouldn't be married to you if I didn't.'

Her eyes narrowed and another faint flush stained her cheeks and her heart started to pound uncomfortably. But he can't know, she thought. Everything he's ever said has gone along with... 'And what would that be?' she asked with a quiver in her voice.

'Oh—' he shrugged and stared into the fire for a moment '—a bit confused, a bit volatile at times—' he lifted his head and that wicked glint was back in his eyes '—stubborn but not without courage, bright as a tack, possessing a sense of style— quite a lot of admirable virtues, in fact.'

'Is that a fact?' Lucy tossed her head and grimaced. 'Then I was right—I think I mentioned it to you before. I'm trainable in your eyes, aren't I? You really feel you can mould me into a suitable wife, don't you? You must also feel I'm not too far gone down the path of *femme fatality* to be redeemed, and of course I'm also a Wainright of Dalkeith, let's not forget that. I'm just wondering what I'd get in return—assuming I ever allowed you to mould me into anything. In other words, Justin, say I had ideas about the kind of husband I'd like you to be— am I allowed to do that?'

'Why not?'

She blinked.

'What did you have in mind, Lucy?' he asked casually.

'I...' It was one thing to tell yourself in a bathtub exactly the kind of husband you'd want him to be, another to tell him to his face, she decided darkly, as the words were curiously difficult to formulate.

'I've always held the theory that honesty and openness between men and women is the best way, if that's what you mean,' he said seriously after waiting politely for a moment. 'But women, some women,' he amended, 'find it rather difficult—uh—they have a natural reticence on the subject. Are you naturally reticent about those things, Lucy?'

'What...what things?'

'How you like to be made love to, for example, how you like to be touched and what turns you on—all things that are really at the core of a marriage wouldn't you agree?' he said softly, and added, 'I certainly think it can make or break a relationship so, yes, if you have any preferences I'd be quite happy to go along with them.'

It was a moment or so before Lucy realised that her facial muscles actually felt stiff with effort. The effort not to contort with anger. Her voice, she realised, sounded even stiffer, but there was nothing she could do about it. 'I didn't mean that. Do you ever think of anything else?'

'Frequently.' His eyes were amused again. 'In the context of a marriage it just seems to spring to mind, however.'

'But there must be more to it!' she burst out. 'There should be *love*, otherwise you grow tired of each other. There should be—there shouldn't be the kind of unequal feeling our marriage would have to have, and the gaping chasm of me knowing I'm being altered and made suitable for you—of just not understanding you, Justin, and why you've done this!'

'Or why you agreed to it,' he said significantly.

'Or why I...' She stopped and sighed.

'What if I told you I had no desire to make you feel unequal, Lucy?' he said into the silence.

'But you do.' She grimaced at the slightly forlorn note in her voice. 'And just the fact that this is a marriage of convenience for you will always make me feel unequal and I'll always feel I don't understand you.'

'Is there anything, apart from the way I married you, that you particularly dislike or distrust about me, Lucy?'

She'd turned her head to stare into the fire dispiritedly but she looked up with a frown because there was no amusement in his voice now. And she saw that his eyes were rather intent as they rested on her.

'I...well...' She stared at him helplessly. He waited as her lips worked again but all she could say finally and foolishly was, 'Why?'

'I mean, does the thought of going to bed with me fill you with disgust and make your skin crawl, and do you seriously believe that I don't have the best interests of your beloved Dalkeith at heart?'

She stared at him fixedly and discovered she was breathing rapidly as she wondered frantically how to answer him. She licked her lips. 'I haven't *really* thought of going to bed with you; I—'

'Haven't you, Lucy?' His impenetrable grey gaze was nevertheless mercilessly compelling and her cheeks flamed right on cue.

She took a deep breath. 'Not...seriously, then.'

'What was the verdict—unseriously?' His lips twisted.

'I thought I mightn't feel so lo...' She stopped abruptly.

'So lonely?' he said very quietly.

'Yes,' she whispered.

'You wouldn't.'

'Justin,' she got up agitatedly, 'this—'

'What else did you think?' he overode her. 'Any revulsion, Lucy?'

She closed her eyes. 'No. But that's not the same thing as *wanting* to, with every fibre of your being!'

'I agree, but it's a start. How many times have you really wanted to with every fibre of your being, Lucy?'

She tightened her lips. 'That's for me to know and you to worry about, if it worries you at all.'

'All right—what about Dalkeith?'

What about Dalkeith—the words seemed to reverberate through her brain. 'Yes,' she said and the word was torn from her, 'I think you do have its best interests at heart, but—'

'Then, Lucy, I think it's time you grew up and accepted that life isn't all roses and sweet dreams, and that, when reality comes, most of us pick ourselves up and make the best of it. And the reality is, I am—and I apologise for it, but I am—to some extent a disillusioned cynic, I do want Dalkeith, for a variety of reasons, and if you want it too, and as badly as you say, then this is the price tag for it. On the other hand, I wouldn't have married you if I hadn't believed that, while it might not have been made in heaven, it could be made to work. Many, many marriages have worked on less. Nor do I expect you to be grateful or feel patronised; in fact if you made it a *commitment* I wouldn't expect a passive, unequal-feeling wife at all. I'd expect and be happy to accommodate your feelings for this place as well as your spirit and your courage—and even those times you feel justified in losing your temper with me.' He stopped and lifted his head. 'Dinner's ready, by the way. I hear the bell. Bring your drink, it's quite informal tonight.'

It was, in fact, macaroni cheese served at the kitchen table in company with Shirley and Adrian.

Lucy managed to contain her surprise—she was still a bit dazed by what Justin had said anyway—and then there was this facet to him that she'd not suspected. That he'd take seriously the plight of one fatherless boy and his mother.

It was obvious he'd already worked a small miracle with Adrian. Not that Adrian was suddenly a model of virtue but his surliness had disappeared and he caused Lucy to all but choke when he handed her his handcuffs and said, 'Mum reckons you better keep these until I'm reformed.' And she recognised that, coming from Adrian, this was equivalent to an apology.

But there were more surprises in store. Justin remarked, 'It's school holidays, Lucy. Adrian has three weeks so he's going to stay with us—'

'And Mum too,' Adrian said through a mouthful of macaroni.

'Of course, darling,' Shirley said. 'Mr Waite's asked me to help you out for the three weeks, Miss Lucy, and he's going to set Adrian some chores every morning to make up for the... damage he did.' She blushed, then brightened. 'And if he's good, he's going to take him up in the plane and teach him to ride a horse and drive a tractor. Is that all right with you?' she added anxiously.

'Fine!' Lucy said heartily. 'Yes, that'll be great, Shirley.' But she avoided Justin's eyes because of two simultaneous thoughts she had—a sudden ridiculous affinity she felt with Adrian, and the rather indignant thought that, given the right time and circumstances, she could have managed him just as well. Why the affinity? she pondered. Oh, I get it. There are times when Justin makes me feel just like a recalcitrant child and times when he uses the reward system, the old donkey-and-carrot trick, she thought bitterly, just as he's doing to Adrian. And, just like Adrian, I've got the feeling I've met my match, she reflected.

She couldn't help brooding on this, but no one seemed to notice her reticence—she winced at the thought—as Shirley responded to Justin's conversation yet didn't for a moment lose her deferential air, as if to assure him she would never take advantage of this lapse in normal household relations, and Adrian ate his way solidly through three helpings.

But as Shirley was bustling about, making coffee and clearing away, Lucy looked directly at her husband at last and said suddenly, 'Do I have to make a decision right now?'

'You could think it over for a few days.'

'I will.'

He smiled faintly and changed the subject—or did he? 'I thought of doing an aerial inspection tomorrow if it's stopped raining. Care to come?'

CHAPTER FOUR

THE NEXT WEEK proved to be a comfortable, peaceful one—for the most part.

They did all the things Shirley had enumerated and Adrian trod the road of being "reformed" quite successfully while Lucy discovered herself delighted to be included in the goings on of the property for a change—for the most part. It did sometimes sadden her to realise how neglected it had been, and occasionally it irked her to watch Justin in the role of owner, a role he played not flamboyantly at all but with a cool, businesslike practicality, a deep knowledge of the needs of Dalkeith and the unmistakable aura of a man who was not to be trifled with.

Like the great white hunter, she thought irreverantly once, but was conscious that she couldn't help secretly admiring his stewardship of her home at the same time. Which places me in an awkward position and no doubt induces this ambivalence in me, she thought with some bitterness.

It was that same afternoon that she was in her bedroom trying to decide what to wear to a dinner party being given by their nearest neighbours, twenty-five miles away, that Justin walked in on her as she was conducting a conversation with herself.

'Why, Lucy,' he murmured, stopping on the threshold and

raising an eyebrow at the colourful array of clothing that littered the bed, 'are you moving out? And I thought I heard voices.'

Lucy put her hand on her hip and surveyed him imperiously. 'I was talking to myself, something I do frequently and always have—perhaps you should take that into account if you intend to persist in being married to me. And I'm trying to decide what to wear tonight—perhaps you should *also* take into account that it can sometimes take me *days*, let alone hours, to decide what to wear.'

'Dear me,' he said gravely. 'Mind you, that's not uncommon in women.'

'It may not be,' she replied with a toss of her head, 'but I don't intend to change.'

'I'm not asking you to. On the other hand—' he strolled over to the bed and picked up a dress '—husbands can be quite useful at times likes these.' He picked up a dress. 'I don't believe I've seen you in this one.'

It was a grey flannel straight dress with long sleeves and a white, lace-trimmed collar and cuffs. 'Funnily enough,' Lucy said. 'I'd almost—' She stopped abruptly.

'Almost decided on it?' he said with a lazy lift of an eyebrow. 'I'm quite sure you're about to change your mind, then.'

Lucy bit her lip and said stiffly, 'I'm not that stupid.'

'Why don't you give me a preview, then?'

'Why should I?'

'We could both reassure ourselves it's the right dress for the occasion. This is the first time we've been invited out as a couple,' he added.

'I know that only too well,' Lucy said with irony.

'Is that why you're a bit worked up?' he queried. 'You shouldn't be. We've both known the Gardiners for as long as we can remember.'

'Who said I was worked up?' Lucy countered coolly, because she would rather die than admit she *was*, on top of everything else, at the prospect of having to parade with Justin before a set of people she had known all her life, but as Lucy Waite now. 'Anyway, if I am it's not without cause,' she added shortly. 'I feel—' she paused '—I feel like a yearling about to go on display.'

Justin moved away from the bed and sat down in her pink velvet armchair. 'Sometimes you remind me of a long-legged yearling,' he commented. 'Why don't you try this dress on so I can give you the benefit of my wisdom on the subject?'

'Not with you sitting there—I mean...'

He scanned her jeans and jumper. 'I presume you have underwear on?'

'Of course I do, but I'm not about to even give you a glimpse of my underwear,' she said virtuously.

'Is it—particularly saucy?' he suggested with a perfectly straight face.

'It's not saucy at all; well—' Lucy hesitated '—all underwear is—'

'Suggestive?' He laid his head back and his eyes were wickedly amused although his face was still straight.

Lucy frowned. 'Justin—this conversation doesn't become you, you know,' she said scathingly then. 'In fact I find it particularly gratuitous, if you must know!'

'I don't think it is, not between a husband and wife, Lucy,' he replied politely, and stayed where he was, apparently perfectly relaxed in her favourite chair. 'But if you'd care to change in your bathroom, I wouldn't mind.'

Lucy muttered something beneath her breath then scooped up the dress and went to do just that. But once out of her jeans and jumper she looked at herself in her pretty white underwear with little red bows and felt a *frisson* run down her spine as she wondered several things. How would she look to a worldly, experienced Justin Waite in said underwear, and why was he doing this? But the most concerning of her mental processes was the undeniable little mesh she suddenly found herself caught in of being so aware of him sitting only feet away and then, like a tide growing in her and causing her to tremble foolishly, the thought that she could go out to him as she was, the thought *again* that she could stop fighting and put it all into his hands; this was a perfect opportunity to do just that...

Is that what he's trying to create? she asked herself, and observed that her eyes were wide and stunned in the mirror. The next instant she was climbing into the grey flannel dress hastily.

'There!' She glided out of the bathroom, did a couple of pirouettes and came to rest in front of the pink chair. 'I do think we're right about this dress, Justin. I'm quite sure the Gardiners would approve, anyway; they're extremely strait-laced and absolute sticklers for modesty and propriety, aren't they, fond as I am of them? And I wouldn't be at all surprised if Colonel Howard is there, and he's a real old fuddy-duddy, fond as I am of *him*, so—I will wear it.'

For a couple of moments Justin simply stared at her and Lucy was quite sure, with a piercing sense of embarrassment, that he knew exactly why she was talking nineteen to the dozen, and knew the rest of her tangled emotions all too well also. And she held her breath as their gazes locked.

But at last he stood up, although he still said nothing as he smoothed the lace-trimmed collar about her throat and let his gaze linger down the lines of her figure beneath the grey flannel that ended just above her knees. Then he said gently, 'Yes, dear Lucy, it is a model of modesty and propriety. You look almost Quakerish in it. However, you also look young and lovely and infinitely desirable, as I'm sure even Colonel Howard and the Gardiners will recognise.'

Her eyes widened and she could feel his hand that still rested on her shoulder as if it was burning through the cloth, as well as being devastatingly aware of everything else about him that attracted her so much, she thought with a jolt. The tall, lean lines of his body, the clever eyes... So much...she thought with another jolt, and said because she couldn't help herself, 'Do you

mean that in a general way? Of course you do, how silly of me.'
She swallowed and went on hurriedly, 'Well, I can't think of
what else to wear, I mean that would be less—'

'Lucy.' He put a finger to her lips. 'The dress is fine, in fact
it's perfect for you, but then so would sackcloth be, probably.'
He smiled slightly, but not with his eyes. 'And yes, I did mean
in a general way—but also in a very private way, and by that
I mean just between the two of us. When you're ready to acknowledge and accept that, my dear, I promise you life will be
a lot easier.' He stepped away and said then, perfectly normally
and with a slight grimace, 'I guess it's time I got changed.'

'Well, it wasn't such an ordeal after all, was it?'

'No,' Lucy said quietly as they drove through the dark, chilly
night back to Dalkeith.

'You're very quiet,' Justin said a couple of miles further on.
'Sorry.'

'Lucy, you've got me seriously worried,' he said wryly.

She moved restlessly and wondered how he would react if
she told him he'd got *her* seriously worried. 'It's nothing, I'm
just tired,' she said, and managed to yawn right on cue because
she was a bit tired as well as everything else. 'It's quite a tiring
business playing at being a wife, you know, Justin,' she added,
and could immediately have kicked herself.

But he didn't make the rejoinder she expected. He drove on
in silence, although he did speed up rather abruptly while she
held her breath then cast a curious glance at him from beneath
her lashes. But all she could see was the familiar angle of his
jaw, the way his hair lay, thick and dark, and not much else as
the powerful Land Rover chewed up the miles of the uneven,
unmade road.

And some little devil of perversity was just about to prompt
her into further, no doubt foolish observations, when there was
a sudden dark shadow on the road in front of them, the Land
Rover swerved wildly then skidded off the track, hit a large

boulder with a sickening thump, came to rest at an angle with the engine cutting out—and Justin slumped forward over the steering-wheel.

'Oh, no! Justin! Are you all right. Oh, no!' Lucy scrambled on to her knees awkwardly on the seat and felt for a pulse in his neck. It was an all too familiar scenario on outback roads, either a kangaroo or some form of stray livestock bounding in front of a vehicle at the last moment, and then an unhandily placed boulder causing Justin to crack his forehead on the steering-wheel and knock himself out.

'That's all it is, please God,' she said to herself as she found a pulse, 'something temporary—oh, don't let him have fractured his skull or anything like that. And what do I do in the meantime?'

But after a few panicky moments she calmed down and decided all she could do was make him as comfortable as possible so, with quite some effort, she eased him back so his head was resting on the back rest. There was already a livid bruise on his temple, she saw by the interior light, and decided to apply a cold compress from the water bottle that no self-respecting vehicle travelled without, attached to its front bumper, in the bush.

So she climbed out, retrieved the thankfully undamaged water bottle, tried quickly to estimate whether the Land Rover would go again, and climbed back in because it was very cold.

It took him half an hour to come round.

Thirty minutes while the chill inside the vehicle grew, and it resisted all attempts to start the motor so she could have the heater on, and she stopped putting the compress on and concentrated simply on keeping them warm. Thirty minutes that felt like hours and acted in a strange and powerful way upon her for two reasons—the lurking, terrible fear in her heart that he might be more seriously injured but at the same time, the unaccustomed freedom of being able to look her fill upon him and not to have to hide anything from him...

Oh, dear, she thought, as she realised all this, it's no good trying to pretend I haven't fallen deeply in love with him, is it? It doesn't even help in the slightest to remind myself of all the injustices of the situation, not now when I'm alone with him like this, holding him and wanting to be nowhere on earth but here because he intrigues me and fascinates me and attracts me and I fear for him—and I can't imagine life without him.

Indeed, she was still looking her fill with her head on his shoulder, her arms around him, when his eyes fluttered open, and although they were dazed with pain, his lips twisted into a semblance of a smile as he said, 'Lucy? Is it you?'

Her heart lurched and her breasts felt curiously heavy and her stomach tightened beneath a sudden onslaught of sheer longing for him that told its own tale. 'Yes, it's me,' she said softly, sitting up. 'I'm trying to keep you warm—you hit your head. How do you feel?'

He groaned and gathered her back against him. 'Like hell.'

'Justin,' she said urgently.

But he chuckled huskily and stilled her movement. 'No, I'll survive. I just didn't feel like letting you go.'

Lucy subsided but only briefly. 'Are you sure you haven't fractured your skull or something,' she said anxiously, but didn't move as he started to stroke her hair.

'Quite sure—well, reasonably sure. It's all coming back now. Did I do much damage to the Land Rover?'

'It won't start. We hit a big rock—'

'Are you all right, Lucy?' He pushed her away a little at last and looked into her eyes.

'I'm fine,' she reassured him.

'You look quite pale,' he said slowly, his eyes roaming over her face.

'I was... I was worried about you.'

'How long have I been out?'

'Half an hour. I was putting a cold compress on your head but then I thought I might give you hypothermia because it's so cold anyway!'

He raised a hand and touched the bruise on his temple, wincing as he did so. But he smiled ruefully at her, touched her cheek gently and said ruefully, 'Thanks. I feel like a bloody idiot,' he added drily, pushing himself up. 'I was driving far too fast—well, let's see if we can get this show on the road.'

Somehow he did get the Land Rover going again and they limped home at a very sedate pace.

'Look, are you sure you're all right?' she said anxiously again as they came into the warmth of the kitchen and he flung the keys on the table. 'You look terrible now.'

'Nothing a couple of aspirin, a cup of tea and a good night's sleep won't help. What's this?' He took a piece of fine Swiss cotton, white with little blue flowers on it, out of her hands and held it up.

'Oh. It's my half-petticoat. It was the only thing I could think of to use as a compress.'

His lips quirked. 'Very... Lucy,' he said. 'Is it part of a matching set by any chance?'

'As a matter of fact, it is,' she said slowly.

'I thought it might be—don't look like that.'

'How am I looking?' she asked uncertainly.

'As if you're not sure whether to subject me to another lecture on the impropriety of discussing your underwear or—something else.' And for once his eyes held a sober, direct enquiry.

Lucy blushed, to her chagrin, then heard herself say gruffly, 'If you're sure there's nothing more I can do to help, I think I'll go to bed.'

'Nothing—I think that would be a good idea,' he said with a certain irony but, curiously, she couldn't tell if it was directed at her or him, and her confusion caused her to murmur goodnight and leave rather precipitately.

But as she lay in bed listening to him moving around the adjoining room—and then deep silence—the turmoil in her heart and the bereft feeling she experienced didn't make for a peaceful night.

* * *

And for the next few days the fact that he was not in a good mood at all didn't help.

'It's his head,' Adrian said philosophically when he'd received a cool, sharp set-down over something very minor.

'Yes, it's his head,' Shirley agreed with adoring overtones that caused Lucy to grimace.

'Well, I don't know why he doesn't take his head to the doctor,' she said, forgetting for the moment how concerned she'd been over Justin Waite's head.

'I'm sure it's nothing serious, Miss Lucy,' Shirley said very seriously. 'But a bump like that can give you a headache for a couple of days. I'll think up something extra nice for him for dinner!'

'Well, I think I'll keep out of his way for a while,' Adrian remarked, causing Lucy to grin this time and utter a similar sentiment, but this was something she didn't prove successful in.

Nor was the confrontation she finally had with him helped by her feelings of uncertainty and restlessness, the new awareness that she'd fallen in love with him up against the old awareness that he didn't love her...

It started when Sasha came to lunch two days after the accident. Justin was looking much better but he still had the bruise on his temple, which prompted Sasha to make enquiries, not unnaturally, Lucy supposed.

Justin explained briefly and then was called away to the phone as they sat down to a meal of soup and quiche.

'I hope you're looking after your man, Lucy,' Sasha said archly with her soup spoon poised but a highly unfriendly little glint in her green eyes at the same time.

Lucy raised an eyebrow. 'What makes you think I wouldn't?' she countered coolly.

'Why, nothing,' Sasha murmured. 'It was just one of those things one says. But, come to think of it, the last time I saw you two together you were, well, not in the greatest harmony, shall we say?'

Lucy gritted her teeth. 'That has nothing to do with you, Sasha.'

'Oops! Sorry,' the other girl murmured. 'Now I've upset you,' she added blandly.

'I'll tell you what should upset *you*,' Lucy retorted, 'is the fact that you wouldn't have the courage to say things like that if Justin were here.'

'Courage to say what?' Justin enquired coldly as he re-entered the room.

There was a short silence then Lucy said, 'Nothing.'

'If you two are squabbling,' he said sardonically, 'would you mind cutting it out? Sasha, we have quite a lot to discuss, so I'd appreciate it if you turned your mind to the business of the upcoming yearling sales.'

Sasha actually blushed, but Lucy smiled sweetly at her, turned an equally sweet smile upon her husband although she was thinking that she must be mad to feel herself in love with him, and said in a grave, hushed voice, 'We're suitably squashed, Justin. You don't feel we ought to write out a hundred lines after lunch? Do not squabble, do not squabble—that kind of thing?'

His mouth tightened and his eyes were very grey and hard as they rested on her. He also said with the kind of precision that would have cut through a steel plate, 'You're not very long out of school, are you, Lucy?'

If Sasha hadn't been there she might have poured her soup all over him, although what she did do was nearly as bad. She clanked her spoon down but said meditatively, 'I don't know why, but I seem to have lost my appetite, so why don't I leave you two to have a very adult discussion—yes, because to be honest, both of you *grown-ups* bore me to tears. Have fun!' And she got up and walked as lightly as she was capable of out of the room.

But when Justin found her in the stables ten minutes later,

there were real tears streaked down her face, tears of anger and anguish as she employed a pitchfork with considerable energy to lay down new hay in an empty stall.

It was his tall shadow that fell across the floor of the stall that first alerted her to his presence and she stopped what she was doing, turned to him and said brightly but witheringly, 'Finished already? That *was* quick.'

'Lucy—' he reached over to take the pitchfork from her '—no.' And as she resisted, added curtly, 'Don't be an idiot, you'll only get hurt waving that thing about.'

Whereupon she resisted even harder, but after an undignified, quite unequal little struggle he wrested it from her and leant it against the wall. So she glared at him, stalked past him and plonked herself down on a bale of hay. 'All right, go ahead! I'm sure you've come to tell me how childish I am again.'

'I haven't, as a matter of fact, but I did warn you once, Lucy, that you could fight me all you liked in private, but in public— it would be a different matter.'

'Fight you!' she marvelled with magnificent scorn. 'You started it! And I'll tell you something, Justin Waite—I don't enjoy fighting in public either but I will *not* put up with being insulted *in* public. You're only lucky you didn't cop a bowl of soup.'

'For someone who doesn't enjoy it you seem to indulge in it fairly frequently,' he said drily.

'Only when I'm provoked,' Lucy said proudly. '"If you two are squabbling…"' she repeated. 'Who do you think you are?' she added intensely. 'If you really want a wife then you better start treating me like one.'

'And if, Lucy,' he drawled, 'I were treating you like a *wife*, this wouldn't keep happening.' Then he added with a relaxed little smile suddenly playing around his mouth, 'But I have to give you full marks for sheer spirit and courage. I'm also beginning to wonder how your father ever coped with you, not to mention your school.'

Lucy stared at him then whispered suddenly, 'I hate you, Justin. I was mad to think anything...anything—' She stopped abruptly.

'Anything...?' He raised an eyebrow.

'*Nothing.*' She got up, but found he was barring her way. She looked up at him for a long, tense moment, then her shoulders slumped suddenly and she said wearily, 'What now?'

'What *did* she say to you?'

Lucy's lips parted. 'Do you mean...?'

'I mean Sasha.' He lifted a hand and traced a tear streak down her face then kept his fingers on her chin.

Several emotions chased through Lucy's eyes but finally she said with simple dignity, 'I'm not going to tell you, Justin. I was quite capable of dealing with it on my own.'

'Until I stuck my oar in?' he suggested, looking wry.

'Yes,' she said pointedly.

'Something to do with the fact that we—don't always get on?' he hazarded.

But Lucy refused to speak, although her pansy-blue gaze did not attempt to evade his and after a long moment he laughed softly, kissed her lightly on the lips and released her chin. 'Such a proud, stubborn little wife. For what it's worth, I've sent Sasha back to Riverbend with a lecture.'

Lucy's eyes widened. 'Why?'

'Why?' He grimaced. 'You are my wife, while she is only my assistant.'

'If that's the case, why did you—?' She stopped and frowned bewilderedly up at him.

'Why did I say those fatal words in the first place? About squabbling?' He paused and shrugged. 'Well, Lucy, I have to be honest and confess to you that there are times when it's not easy—*playing* at being a husband,' he said with a significant little look up and down her figure.

A slow tide of colour started to travel up the line of her

throat. 'Is that…is that why you've been in such a bad mood?' she whispered, her eyes wide. 'Not your head?'

'Well my head hasn't helped,' he said amusedly.

'I didn't… I didn't realise,' she said confusedly. 'But now I do, I don't quite know what to do about it. I can't…just suddenly…come to bed with you,' she said agitatedly. 'Only a moment ago I was quite sure I hated you!'

'And now, a moment later?' he queried with a wicked little glint in his eyes.

'I haven't entirely forgiven you yet; I may still feel quite annoyed even to think about it for a time!'

He looked down at her with something in his eyes she couldn't read, something that made her feel very young, though, and realise the total irrationality of what she'd said, and she closed her eyes suddenly in a fever of embarrassment.

'Then why don't we approach things from a different angle for a while?'

Her lashes lifted and she frowned up at him. 'What do you mean?'

'We began this week in a kind of harmony; let's just try to get back to that,' he said seriously but his grey eyes were amused again.

'All right,' Lucy replied slowly.

'Good.' He took her hand. 'Shall we finish our lunch now? I don't know about you, but I'm starving.'

CHAPTER FIVE

SO THAT WAS what they did, and once again their household started to shape up in a rather jolly way.

Adrian spent a few hours each day in the vegetable garden and the chicken house, repairing the damage he'd wreaked, and was rewarded for his efforts each day with a flight over the property or a tractor ride or just being allowed to accompany Justin. Lucy again took part in these expeditions and Shirley, seeing more contentment in her son than she'd ever seen, probably, cleaned and polished, washed and ironed and cooked up delicious meals. She even began to lose her agitated look.

But Lucy was hauntingly conscious that it couldn't go on like this forever, that she would have to make some decision soon, and confess to herself that, her own feelings aside, these glimpses of what harmony with Justin and Dalkeith could be like were nearly irresistible. Where did all my hostility go? she wondered once, and felt her cheeks burn as she remembered the rash thought that she could somehow make him regret marrying her, and another even rasher thought—the crazy idea that she might enslave Justin Waite—only to end up the one who was ensalved herself... What she would have done once that was accomplished was not quite clear, but that she should even have entertained it proved to her, now that she could think more clearly, that being really married to him had never been so un-thinkable. Indeed, perhaps at the back of her mind there had always been a fatal fascination about it.

I think I must have always been a little in love with him, she mused painfully, and all that anger was caused more by hurt pride than by anything else, because he doesn't love me the same way. What would be worse, she wondered: to be married to a man you hated or married to a man you loved who didn't love you? And even if you did decide to live with it, how did you take that final step...?

It was ironic thus that what in the end did help her should also be the cause of Justin Waite's not loving her as she believed she loved him... She had thrown Joanna Madden's name at him once—their relationship had after all been long-lasting and well-documented. Come to think of it, Joanna's was the only name Justin had been linked with like that... Then, out of the blue, Joanna had married an older man who was very wealthy and twice divorced. But what Lucy had not expected was to meet Joanna Madden in the flesh and at Riverbend.

They'd taken Adrian and Shirley to see the yearlings that so soon would be going to the sales—Shirley in quite a flutter of excitement because this was her first flight. They'd not alerted Sasha other than buzzing the stud office, which was Justin's way of saying he was arriving, and they'd arrived. There was another light plane on the runway which Justin had stared at with a frown—the Maddens'. And they'd all met up in the stud office with Sasha looking pink and confused and as if she couldn't believe this was happening to her.

'Oh, Justin,' she said as he walked over the doorstep, 'I... um...the Cawnpore filly...that is Mr Madden here...is very interested in her breeding and he called me up on the HF and said they were flying over Riverbend and asked if he could take a look...'

'That's no problem, Sasha,' Justin said smoothly as his grey gaze swept the room and took in the couple standing across it. 'Joanna, Tim, how are you? I don't know if you've met Lucy?'

Joanna Madden, Lucy decided a bit dazedly as there was a slight pause, was still lovely. About thirty, she was dark, tall and graceful and she had an air that marked her as a person of inner grace—she had had it when Lucy had met her briefly years before but now it had another quality that was hard to define except to say that it was slightly haunting...

'Yes.' Joanna came forward, breaking the pause that had begun to stretch. 'We did meet once, Lucy; I don't know if you remember? Tim,' she turned to her husband, who looked to be in his early fifties but was tall and spare, 'this is Lucy Wainright from Dalkeith, Justin's next-door neighbour.'

This time the pause was crashing. Sasha actually closed her eyes before Justin said quietly, 'In fact Lucy and I got married a couple of months ago, Joanna.'

Joanna's eyes jerked to his, but that was the only sign she gave that this news might be momentous, because the next moment she murmured, 'We've been overseas for so long! Oh, I do wish you both every happiness. *We* do, don't we, Tim?' And she turned to him and slipped her hand into his.

'Justin?'

'Mmm...?'

It was that same evening and, as they'd got into the habit of, they were sitting in the library after dinner. It was raining again.

'I think you should tell me about Joanna Madden, Justin,' Lucy said.

He stretched his legs and looked into the fire for a while. 'What do you want to know?'

'Why she didn't marry you. Why she looks...sort of sad. Why she couldn't hide for a moment what a surprise it was that we'd got married. And why, considering past history, her husband should even consider taking her to Riverbend, let alone buying the Cawnpore filly.'

He turned his gaze to her at last. 'Taking things unchronologically, Lucy, that Cawnpore filly is the best of the bunch. She shows signs of wonderful conformation, she has marvellous bloodlines on the distaff side—so much so that I've put a reserve price on her even Tim Madden might find hard to fork out.' He looked towards the fire again and his gaze was extremely meditative.

Lucy was briefly diverted. 'If that's the case, why are you even contemplating selling her?' she queried.

After a long moment he shrugged. 'I own her dam and her grandam and—' he gestured '—Cawnpore. He was a gamble but he's proving himself as a sire now, so you could say I'm on a bet to nothing. It's all still there at Riverbend, the genes. Not that everything is ever a certainty, but then again, I could keep the filly and race her and have her break down on me or a hundred other things go wrong with her—it happens. It happens all the time with horses. I've hung on to what I've thought were the best before, only to find it wasn't so.'

'But mares—well, fillies,' Lucy protested, 'even if they don't race well—'

'They can be barren, they can run into fences, they can get colic. I think too,' he frowned, 'that while I would have liked to retain an interest in her if I didn't have her dam and grandam, I see myself essentially as a breeder. Racing horses is another game in a sense.'

Lucy stared at him. 'All right. I guess I can see the logic in that,' she said slowly. 'But why would Tim Madden want her? From you, I mean.'

Justin smiled faintly. 'Tim is a racing man above all else. Horses are a subject that transcend everything with him.'

'Even to putting his wife through—an experience like that?'

Justin didn't move but he transferred a slightly wry grey gaze to her. 'What makes you think it was such an experience? Joanna and I broke up two years ago.'

Lucy hesitated then she said simply, 'Why?'

She thought he wasn't going to answer so she then said, 'I'm not asking this because I want to poke or pry—'

'Don't you?' He raised an eyebrow at her.

'No,' she insisted a little heatedly. 'But my intuition tells me it could have something to do with why you married *me*. So why should I be kept in the dark?' She lifted her chin defiantly at him.

He smiled again, idly and as if at some inner thought. 'Very well. Joanna discovered she was unable to have children.'

Lucy felt her eyes widening and had to stop herself from staring at him open-mouthed as well. 'So she wouldn't marry you and—and married a man who already had a family. Justin! Oh—how terribly sad!'

'Now don't get all carried away, Lucy. It's not nearly as dramatic as you make it sound.'

'But it must have been! When two people really love each other—'

'That's fairy-tale stuff you're talking, Lucy,' he said drily.

'But she looked so—haunted for a moment or two!'

He said nothing, and his expression was indecipherable as he looked into the fire until Lucy said, 'And you've never forgiven her, Justin, have you?'

He looked up then and said impatiently, 'Of course I have. The sadness you see in her is probably to do with not being able to have anyone's children.'

'I—well—Justin—' Lucy looked at him confusedly '—I don't know about that but are you sure you didn't marry me because it didn't matter much to you who you married after—her?'

'Lucy,' his lips twisted and his eyes were suddenly amused, 'if that were the case, that I married simply for the sake of it, don't you think I would have found myself a much more *compliant* candidate for a wife?'

Lucy's brow creased. 'I suppose so, but don't forget they didn't have the other half of Dalkeith.'

'That's true,' he said wryly. 'So you're unique in several senses.'

She tightened her mouth. 'I also very much resent being married because it's so *practical*,' she said bitterly. 'That's what you said to me!'

'My apologies,' he replied gravely. 'If I'd put it to you that we'd once been good friends, how would that have affected you?'

'I'd have probably liked it better,' she said but grudgingly.

'Would you have admitted it, though?'

She opened her mouth, closed it and reddened. Then she said haughtily, 'I don't know what point you're trying to make, Justin, it's quite lost on me. But the point I'm trying to make is that we're locked in a loveless marriage—and I'm beginning to see why!'

'Lucy,' he said evenly, 'I've never denied the practicalities of our marriage. But its lovelessness hasn't been put to the test yet. I've told you that from my point of view it's a commitment, not some nine-day wonder, and I mean that. When you try it, you'll see what I mean.' He stood up and stretched. 'And here endeth that lesson, but perhaps I could say one thing more. Romance and moonlight and declarations of never-ending love are all very well—indeed, I wouldn't expect you to live without them entirely.' He smiled down at her unexpectedly and added wryly, 'Not you. But there's a whole lot more to it, as many a romantically inclined girl has discovered to her cost. So don't be too scathing about practicalities; they often build into something strong and enduring *because* they have a basis to build up.'

Lucy's lips parted and she frowned. 'Why not me?'

He lifted a lazy eyebrow. 'Why not you what?'

'Why wouldn't you expect me of *all* people—you didn't say that but you might as well have—to live without—well, all those things *you* were being scathing about?'

His lips twisted. 'Are you not the Lucy Wainright about whom some bloke flew a plane over Sydney Harbour trailing a banner asking you to marry him?'

Lucy's eyes sparkled with indignation. 'I don't think it's fair to blame me for that! I'd given him absolutely no cause to imagine I would!'

He grimaced. 'Perhaps not. I do remember the papers writing you up as rather heartless because you declined.' He grinned. 'Still, some very romantic gestures have come your way, you must admit.'

'They did,' she said with youthful dignity and a very steady gaze from her pansy-blue eyes. 'It may have escaped you that I didn't take any of them up, Justin. No one rushed me into marriage because of moonlight and roses. You were the one who did the rushing.'

'You're only twenty,' he said mildly, ignoring the rest of her speech.

'I may be, but I'm not entirely a fool.' She stood up herself. 'I'll have to think about *this* revelation now! I hope you have no objection to that?'

He took his time replying. He studied her brave stance and her outfit of grey cords and a lovely chunky grey and white sweater. His gaze lingered on her loose hair and finally her face and there was something in it that caused her to catch her breath slightly and be suddenly aware of him differently, something undoubtedly admiring in his eyes; it was as if they were a man and a woman caught in a moment of intimate curiosity. *No*, she thought, as a sensation that was becoming familiar coursed through her body, a sensation of leaping pulses and trembling anticipation. He can't do this to me. Not when he's just told me about Joanna! And she switched her gaze away confusedly.

'By all means, Lucy,' he merely said after a moment.

She turned away and walked towards the door, praying he wouldn't guess what an effort it was to appear completely normal.

Yet despite that puzzling look, over the next few days Lucy couldn't help feeling that Justin was withdrawn and preoccupied, in fact he spent a lot of time at Riverbend, much to Adrian's disgust.

And she couldn't help wondering how much that unexpected encounter with Joanna had affected him. It also occurred to her that he had never denied being in love with Joanna. And she thought to herself often, it's all falling into place, isn't it? It has to be. You don't marry someone the way he married me unless there's a reason like that behind it. So what do I do now?

It also struck her as unfair that during those few days she could settle to nothing because of a curiously bereft feeling…

What she did do was quite unexpected, as it happened, and it all boiled up one evening out of the blue…

She was sitting at the piano playing Chopin when Justin came in—she hadn't seen him for two days and he'd arrived after dinner, which Shirley had kept warm for him, and elected to eat in the kitchen where Adrian had regaled him with *his* doings of the past few days.

Lucy had stayed for a while then wandered into the library and started to play softly. She looked up now as he closed the door, and felt her heart contract. He was wearing jeans and a black sweater and there were marks of weariness on his face beneath his ruffled dark hair and something drained and moody in his eyes. He also said briefly, 'What's wrong?'

'Nothing. I… I was going to ask you the same.'

'Why?'

She played a chord quietly. 'I thought you looked—tired and disenchanted, that's all.'

He shrugged. 'I am tired. A consignment of twenty-five yearlings to break in and get ready for a sale is a tiring business.' He sat down in an armchair and lay back. 'Play some more,' he suggested after a minute or so. 'How come you play so well?'

'Mother Angelica, at school,' Lucy said with a grimace. 'She used to tie me to the piano stool—no, not really, but she was a very determined person, and eventually I grew to love it.'

'She was your music teacher?'

'She was much more than that,' Lucy said wryly. 'My head-mistress, the bane of my life often, yet, looking back, rather wise and someone I'll always admire.'

He said no more, so she played, and noticed out of the corner of her eye that his hand on the arm of the chair clenched and stretched a few times, then relaxed. What she didn't notice was the way he watched her straight back, the sweep of her eyelashes as she concentrated, how she sometimes, as a lovely melody evolved beneath her fingers, bit her bottom lip.

She also found herself thinking about Mother Angelica as she played, that hard-headed but wise nun who had had very clear ideas on a whole host of subjects including the role of wifedom that would come to most of her charges...

And she must have played for nearly an hour with those thoughts on her mind, until she began to wonder if he'd fallen asleep, but, as she closed the piano softly and stood up, she saw that he had not.

'Sorry,' he said, and grimaced. 'I'm not great company to-night, am I? That was very...relaxing.'

Lucy hesitated then sat down opposite him. 'Strange to say,' she said very slowly, 'I'm sorry I can't offer you the more conventional form of relaxation wives are supposed to provide—but I don't think it would help to try to be a substitute tonight—do you?'

She saw his mouth harden briefly then thought he might have forced himself to relax as he drawled, 'So that's what's bothering you—Joanna again.'

'Yes,' she admitted composedly, 'but it may surprise you to know all my thoughts on the subject.'

He lifted one black brow wryly. 'Well, go on, surprise me.'

She looked down and smoothed the fabric of the long tartan skirt she wore with a dark green angora cardigan that had little pearl buttons. Her hair was tied back simply with a matching green ribbon. And she answered obliquely, 'Do you…could you believe that I think domesticity is overtaking me, Justin?'

He narrowed his eyes. 'I think you'll have to explain a bit better than that, Lucy.'

'I… I just have it in me at the moment to believe I could be quite a good wife, to be modest and industrious—you're probably going to laugh—'

'No,' he said slowly with a frown in his eyes. 'But when did all this hit you?'

When you walked in tonight, she answered in her heart, and when I thought of Mother Angelica, that's when it all crystallised, but she said, 'Over the last few days, I suppose.'

'Well—' He paused and watched her searchingly. 'What are you suggesting?'

'That's up to you, really. I mean—' she hesitated '—if you still feel we could make a go of it.'

'I've never changed my mind about that. Lucy—' he paused '—you're not about to sacrifice yourself on the altar of your no doubt highly dramatised version of what happened with Joanna, are you?'

'Not while she's still so close to you,' she said, and thought he swore under his breath but made herself go on bravely, 'and not that, no. Just—well, you yourself told me it comes to most people, a time when they have to make the best of things, so…that.' And she lifted her chin and stared into his eyes with dignity.

He swore properly this time and said roughly, 'Do you know how old you look, Lucy? About sixteen.'

She flinched. And said honestly, 'I feel a lot older than sixteen, Justin. I know how young I must appear to you but right now I feel like a woman for the first time in my life probably.' She stopped awkwardly and licked her lips nervously as she sought to explain what was in her heart. 'And I'm beginning to understand what my options are, I guess. Go away from here, or try to build something worthwhile with you. And I suppose it came to me that if I'd had the courage to go away, I would have done it at the beginning. It's also come to me that even if you couldn't love me as you did Joanna, if you did care all the same, then you're right, there is something to work on.'

'What if,' he said very quietly, and she thought she saw a tinge of pain in his eyes, 'my...the way I love you doesn't come up to expectations?'

'You mean if I really fall in love with you but it doesn't happen the same way for you?' She stopped, but he didn't answer or make any gesture so she said, 'Then I'll have to pour it all into Dalkeith, and you'll have to give me some children, Justin. But there's one thing I've got to tell you before you make up your mind.' She hesitated, then took a deep breath. 'It's one of the reasons why making this decision has been so difficult for me—I don't know if you'll believe this but I'm not very experienced about lovemaking. In point of fact... I've never actually done it.'

'I know—'

'Now if that alters *your* decision I'd quite understand. I mean it's a bit different for two reasons at least—you *what*?' She stared at him with her lips parted and her eyes huge.

'I know that you're a virgin, Lucy.'

'But how can you possibly—know?' she whispered.

'Because your innocence in these matters—shines like a lamp,' he said with irony, self-directed irony she thought, but such was her confusion that she didn't give it more than a passing thought.

'But everything you've *said*,' she protested, and bit her lip.

His lips twisted. 'It suited me to—go along with everything *you* said with such bravado, my dear. I also—' he paused and regarded her crestfallen countenance with something unusually gentle in his eyes '—have known you for a long time and always had quite a bit of respect for you, Lucy.'

'Respect,' she murmured dazedly. 'But what about—' she licked her lips '—what about getting a proposal of marriage from a plane over Sydney Harbour? And, I did have—well, quite a few boyfriends, although—' her eyes flashed suddenly '—I certainly deny "queening" it over all and sundry!'

'My apologies. In fact you were a sight for sore eyes when you were—in full flight. Is that a better way of putting it? But still quite obviously a lovely, laughing girl who had given herself to no one.'

'Oh.' Lucy groaned and put her hands to her hot cheeks. 'This is so humiliating!'

'On the contrary, it's something to be proud of.'

'So you married me—you don't mind, in other words?'

'Why should I mind?' He smiled faintly.

'Well, I could turn out to be frigid for one thing,' she said starkly. 'And isn't it a little bit different—taking someone untouched into a marriage like this, other than someone who might have a better idea of…all sorts of things!' She eyed him indignantly.

He sat up abruptly. 'You're not frigid, Lucy.'

'That sounds so essentially male!'

'It may be,' he said with a tinge of impatience, 'but believe me, it's true.'

'Do all men know so much about women?' she asked then with turmoil and confusion showing in her eyes.

He shrugged. 'I don't know. And you're only one young woman we're talking about. I don't claim ultimate wisdom on the subject. All it means is that I'm quite a few years older and have a lot more experience.'

She stared at him for a long moment, then said, barely audibly, 'Do you know what I wish? I can't help wishing at this moment,' she whispered desolately, 'that I were planning to be a modest, industrious wife to someone who didn't necessarily have any experience but who loved me so much that it wouldn't matter.'

'Strangely enough,' he answered very quietly, 'at this moment, so do I.'

'Justin—'

But he stood up and walked over to her and held out his hand. 'Lucy—you could still take my other offer. You talked of an annulment once...' He paused as she put her hand into his uncertainly, and pulled her gently to her feet. 'If that's really what you want to do,' he finished.

She didn't realise the leap of fright that showed in her eyes, but she did make herself say, 'Because you saw Joanna again, is...is that—'

'Lucy, that's over and done with,' he said grimly. 'I—'

But she wouldn't let him go on. Speaking from a deep well of fear in her heart, she said haltingly, 'Well, perhaps if you can't have her and I can't have—an imaginary person who might never exist anyway, could we console each other, do you think?'

It was his turn to stare down into her eyes with something like real regret in his, until he said, 'We could try.'

'Well—'

She got no further, because he put a finger to her lips and murmured, 'I think we've probably said as much as one can say on the subject. I think the time has come now to—let things take their course. Like this.' And he took her into his arms and started to kiss her.

It was quite some time later when his mouth left hers and she discovered that just about everything else had left her mind, Joanna Madden included, because it seemed she was wholly focused on Justin Waite and the rapture his lips and his hands had inflicted on her body and imprinted on her soul. It was also a revelation because she hadn't expected it, yet this kiss couldn't have been more different from the only other time he'd kissed her, and that was what she'd expected—another give-nothing-away experience. And it was what she'd expected to bestow, she realised shakily. But she'd received and bestowed far more, and her breathing was undoubtedly erratic as she stared up at him, not wanting to be released. Heady again with the feel and the taste of him but completely abandoned to it this time, her skin trembling finely in anticipation as his hands wandered down her back and found the gap between her cardigan and skirt and lingered on her waist, then slipped beneath the elastic waistband of the skirt and slid down to her hips, scantily clad in a tiny pair of fine silk bikini briefs.

Her breath jolted in a little flare of shock and his eyes narrowed as he saw it, but the shock waned almost as quickly as it had flared, and she came unresistingly as he pulled her even closer because there seemed to be a current flowing between them, or from him to her, she thought, a sort of sensual pull that both amazed her and filled her with an inner quivering that was a mixture of longing and excitement—and the knowledge that she wanted to be nowhere else on earth but in Justin Waite's arms.

It was like a compulsion such as she'd never known, and an awareness that made her drink in everything about him, the way his dark hair fell and those little lines beside his eyes— they weren't creased in amusement, she noted, in fact his eyelids were half lowered in a rather intent way and he seemed to be watching her mouth with interest, just her lips, which sent another tremor through her as she remembered how his own had explored the soft skin of her neck and a little further down when he'd flicked open a couple of little pearl buttons...

And she made a helpless little sound because it was also terribly unfair that he could make her feel like this, though of course, to be perfectly honest, it had been growing in her for a long time, hadn't it? It had probably been there when she was fourteen and measuring up her very first date at the school dance...

'And what is going through your mind at the moment, Lucy,' he said very softly and kissed the corner of her mouth chastely.

'I still think we should wait until...'

'No, now,' he said and took her back into his arms. 'This has gone on long enough, and it will be all right, I promise you.'

'Justin,' she whispered, her colour fluctuating, her breathing erratic, 'do you mean...?'

'Yes, now, tonight.' And stopped anything further she might have said by kissing her.

'I feel—I feel so different,' she said later.

'Do you?' Justin drew his hand down her pale, slender body and rested his dark head on his hand so he could look into her eyes. There was one lamp on in her bedroom and the bed was rumpled, the fire now low. 'Tell me.'

'I feel translated somehow.' Her voice was low and husky. 'Does that sound odd to you?'

'Not at all.' He stroked her cheek. 'I feel a bit that way myself. You're incredibly lovely, you know.'

'But was I any good?' she said very quietly. There were faint blue shadows beneath her eyes, her hair was damp and disordered and there was something young and bewildered in her eyes, as if she couldn't quite believe what had happened, couldn't quite make the transition to having him lean and strong, dark and naked in bed beside her.

He smiled and pushed some golden strands of hair off her face. 'You were tender and—delicious. Didn't you notice my reaction, incidentally?'

She thought for a moment and closed her eyes at the memory of the feel of his hard body on hers and how he'd made her want everything he'd done to her, how he'd made her feel soft and smooth and told her she was like a work of art—how there'd been no pain at all, how her eyes had opened and her hands on his back had fallen slack and she'd gasped as sheer pleasure had risen in waves through her body and she'd felt the convulsion of his with a sweet sense of triumph.

'And you came yourself, didn't you?' he said as all this passed through her mind.

'I...yes, something happened to me that was quite wonderful,' she confessed.

'Then—' he pulled up the sheet and held her close '—all is well.'

But she said seriously, 'Justin, I just have this feeling I may have given myself away and I'm a little worried about it, you see.'

He moved his chin on her hair and she thought he laughed softly. 'Given yourself away how, Lucy?'

'Let you know that I do love you—'

'You don't have to worry about that.'

She grimaced. 'I suppose you knew that too all the time I was—pretending to myself. But what I'm worried about is that it might be a burden to you so—'

'No, Lucy—' he put his fingers to her lips '—it's not, it never can be, so don't say any more. Let's just relax and be happy. Go to sleep, in other words, my sweet, talkative wife,' he said wryly, and kissed her brow.

Lucy subsided, although part of her wanted to have it out with him, but the rest of her couldn't help but feel warm and safe, and it was so lovely lying against him and feeling his hand stroking her back that she ended up falling asleep before she knew it.

And morning brought her some reassurance.

She woke to find him watching her with something unmistakably tender in his eyes. He also said, 'How do you feel, Mrs Waite?'

Her lips curved. 'Fine, thank you, Mr Waite.'

'Then would you mind—if I did this?' And he drew the covers aside and touched her nipples until they started to unfurl and a sense of longing travelled down her body, and her eyes widened in such surprise that he laughed and kissed her. 'Don't look like that, it's quite normal to wake up feeling sexy. I've been doing battle with it for about half an hour.' And he eased his weight on to her gently.

They showered together afterwards and she ate a huge breakfast then went for a ride, during which, for the first time since their marriage, she told him about some of her ideas for Dalkeith and he listened attentively and with approval. But after lunch he said he had some work to do so she, somewhat to her surprise, found a book and curled up with it for the whole afternoon.

'Lucy?'

She looked up to see Justin standing over her with something wry in his eyes.

'Hi!'

'I wondered where you were—the place was so quiet.'

She stretched and yawned and closed the book then glanced at her watch and blinked in surprise. 'It's nearly dinnertime! Is this what being married does to one?' she asked with a glint of humour.

'There's no sin in it,' he replied, helping her up and kissing the top of her head.

'It seems very slothful, however,' she commented, and leant against him.

'Perhaps that's what honeymoons were designed for.'

'Oh! Perhaps you're right!' She glinted a smile up at him. 'To help new brides get over the shock of it all.'

'Shock?' he queried tilting her chin up and with something quizzical in his expression.

'What I mean is—'

'Did it come as such a shock, Lucy?'

'No, not really.' She lowered her lashes. 'But something has to account for the fact that I seem to be—' she paused '—in a state of suspended animation at the moment,' she said thoughtfully. 'I mean, after all the weeks of trauma, it's finally happened—you'd think I'd at least be analysing it, turning it over and over, trying to poke holes in it—that sort of thing, instead of peacefully reading a book all afternoon. Oh, no!' And she looked up at him with a curiously comical, wide-eyed look of horror.

'Lucy, you've got me seriously worried,' he said wryly. 'Oh, no what?'

'I've just remembered something you said to me!'

'Well, tell me.' He fingered the collar of her blouse and his lips twisted. 'Before I die of curiosity.'

'I don't think I should—you'll be able to say I told you so! And I don't think I'd appreciate that one bit...'

He grimaced. 'I can see I'm going to have to use strong-arm tactics, Mrs Waite. Shall we go up to our bedroom?'

'What do you mean?' She was genuinely wide-eyed now.

'Just that I could kiss you there until you were happy to confide in me without the possibility of Adrian or Shirley stumbling upon us, and just in case it went—further than that.' His grey eyes were entirely grave.

'That's...incredible blackmail, Justin!'

'I know but one of much the nicest forms of it you'd probably find.'

'Then I'll spike your guns here and now, sir,' she said and started to laugh. 'It's just that you did say to me once that without regular, satisfying sex I could get troublesome and fractious—'

'Actually I said *women*—'

'It was still an amazingly superior kind of thing to say, whether you were generalising or being particular, or so I thought. Now I have to wonder if you were right, which is rather demoralising actually—'

'Then perhaps this will help,' he interrupted. 'From now on, without regular, satisfying sex with you, Lucy, I'm the one who could become fractious and troublesome.'

She stared up into his eyes and was so totally intrigued and fascinated by this possibility, she forgot to say anything at all.

Until he said softly, 'What deep, dark plans are you concocting for me now, Lucy Waite?'

'Nothing!' But she blushed and got hotter as he laughed quietly and kissed her on the lips, and said, 'If it weren't for the fact that dinner *is* only ten minutes away...' But he didn't go on as they heard Shirley come into the dining-room next door; instead he raised a rueful eyebrow—and Lucy breathed a tiny sigh of relief.

It was after dinner that he brought up the subject of honeymoons again.

'You know,' he said as they sat down before the library fire, as it was raining again, 'once the yearling sales are over we should take our delayed honeymoon. Where would you like to go?'

They were sitting side by side on the settee and Lucy raised her hands above her head and said, 'Oh—the Seychelles, where I could get around in a bikini all the time and if it rains it's warm. Or—Tahiti sounds nice, Justin,' she said, parodying a television advertisement with a pert look.

'It does indeed, but seriously—'

Her expression grew serious. 'Closer to home? I don't mind—that didn't sound very modest or industrious, did it?'

He laughed quietly and pulled her onto his lap. 'The thought of you in a bikini all the time in the Seychelles is seriously electrifying, all the same. What I was going to say was, do you have a *serious* desire to see them or were you teasing me?'

She considered for a moment then all of a sudden found herself with tears in her eyes.

'What's the matter?' He frowned down at her.

'I don't know—how very embarrassing! I think being in a position *to* tease you, Justin, is something of a revelation and... and...' She couldn't go on.

'Lucy,' he said quietly and stroked her hair, 'this is only reaction—it has all been pretty traumatic but it's *over* now.'

Lucy laughed shakily, and Adrian stuck his head around the door. 'Mum's looking for you two.'

Justin stilled Lucy's sudden movement. 'Ask your mum if we can have our coffee in here, Adrian. Is something wrong?'

Adrian advanced into the room and continued his critical study of them from close quarters. 'She sick?' he asked at last.

'No. Just tired,' Justin said gravely.

'Didn't know you two felt like that about each other,' he said with the extreme unselfconsciousness of youth and because he was Adrian anyway, and extremely perceptive with it.

'As you see, we do. I hope you approve?' Justin enquired.

Adrian shrugged. 'Don't know much about it. I haven't got a father so my Mum doesn't go in for it.'

'Yes, well, that could change one day, Adrian, and if it does I'll tell you how to handle it. The best way is to ignore it and leave them in peace.'

Adrian considered. 'OK,' he said at length. 'I reckon I get the message. I'll tell Mum to knock like the clappers when she brings the coffee and not to rush it.'

'You're a bright boy, Adrian,' Justin said with not a breath of laughter. 'In fact I'll add to that, I reckon you'll go a long way.'

'Thanks,' Adrian replied off-handedly. 'By the way, I've changed my mind. Not sure about being a farmer any more. I think I'll be a pilot. See you later.' He withdrew and closed the door behind him.

But Lucy could contain herself no longer. She began to laugh uncontrollably and felt Justin's iron control give way too. 'Oh, God, he's a character, isn't he?' she gasped.

'One of the best.'

It was minutes before they were quiet again, although Lucy was still subject to the odd breathless little chuckle.

'Feeling better?' he asked.

'Mmm.' She moved her cheek against his chest and thought how warm and safe she felt and how she'd like to stay like this all night. And as the thought took possession of her mind, she raised her lashes and whispered, 'I can, can't I?'

'Can what?'

'I'm just thinking aloud; it doesn't matter.'

'Yes, it does.' He put his fingers under her chin and made her look up at him.

'I can spend the night with you—that's what I was thinking, that's all,' she said, and shrugged and coloured all at the same time. 'You're probably wondering if I've gone feeble-minded,' she added ruefully.

He laughed quietly—and then swore as the phone rang.

It was Sasha with the news that the Cawnpore filly had severe colic.

'I'll have to go—Lucy, I'm sorry,' Justin said intensely.

'But it's dark and it's raining, Justin, and you—'

He sat down and took her hands. 'It's stopped raining and it's clear over Riverbend, and I have an instrument rating for night flying—Lucy, that filly could bring a hell of a lot of money at the sales if we can save her and I don't have to tell you that colic can be fatal in a horse. I have to go, much as I hate to.'

Her hands quivered in his but she said, 'Of course. Good luck with her. Will you ring me when you arrive?'

'Yes.' He leant forward and kissed her. 'Sleep well, Mrs Waite.'

'I'll try...'

She was actually in bed although not asleep when the phone rang, but it was Sasha to say that Justin had arrived safely, and that they looked as if they had a difficult night ahead of them and not to expect him home until tomorrow.

Lucy replaced the receiver and regarded it balefully for a moment. 'I don't know why I put up with that woman,' she also murmured. 'Only she could, in the space of a few short sentences, contrive to make me feel quite useless while she's being so strong and competent,' she marvelled.

She put the lamp out with a snap and slid down to curl up beneath the covers in her pink and white polka-dot silk pyjamas. Then it occurred to her to wonder what Sasha and the rest of the world would make of the latest development in the Waite marriage, assuming they'd been privy to what had gone before—which they hadn't, she reminded herself, but might have sensed or guessed it.

But her overriding emotion, she discovered, was a hauntingly new feeling of vulnerability. Because I'm alone? she asked herself. I didn't feel like this earlier today, I felt serene and—well, *happy*. She grimaced suddenly and tried to think back over what had happened and how it had happened but, as she'd found all day, it all seemed dreamlike and not susceptible to analysis...

It was as if all she could think of now was how much she loved Justin Waite, and how, oddly, that had opened up a whole new field of vulnerability for her.

She fell asleep with it on her mind.

CHAPTER SIX

LUCY WOKE UP to a warm, clear morning the next day and a call from Justin this time, to say that the filly was responding to treatment but still not out of danger, and he'd have to stay with her until she was.

'Of course,' Lucy said down the line. 'I quite understand.'

'What will you do?'

'As a very new wife who's lost her husband on the second day of her—well, what should be her honeymoon?' she said with a chuckle. 'I'm not altogether sure, Justin.'

'Lucy—'

'No—I'm only teasing, I really am fine,' she said wryly, and they chatted for a few minutes more. And when she put the phone down she discovered she did feel a lot better, with none of the shadows of the night before lurking in her mind, and after helping Shirley during the morning she had lunch then saddled her horse and went for a ride.

It was such a pleasure, after all the rain they'd had, to be out in warmth and sunshine, that she actually found herself singing as she rode along. She also thought wryly that she was exhibiting classic symptoms of being in love—and that just a few words from Justin this morning had achieved a minor miracle.

It was quite unwittingly that she rode towards the twelve-mile paddock, which true to form could be more accurately described as a bog in parts. Any more rain and it would flood as it often did, she thought and paused to breathe in the air and the sky and take off a jumper as she let her horse pick its way. And since she'd got this far, she decided to check the repairs to the old boundary riders' hut.

The hut could not even by a long stretch of imagination be described as anything but rough and ready but the roof and door had been repaired, a supply of firewood laid in for the stove as well as some basic provisions and there were new mattresses on the two bunks and some heavy duty blankets that resembled horse blankets in texture. She grimaced as she felt them then raised her head suddenly as she realised that in the half-hour or so she'd been poking around the afternoon had gone curiously still. And the fine hairs on her body stood up in the eerie silence which was broken, as she swung open the door, by a sheet of lightning that filled the sky and an enormous clap of thunder that caused her to jump about a foot in the air. What was worse was the fright her horse got, which caused it to rear and whinny and break its lead, and, on discovering itself free, show her a clean pair of heels as it headed for home.

'Oh, no!' The words were torn from her as the sun went out in a manner of speaking and the first raindrops fell like bullets from an enormous thunderhead and more thunder and lightning split the sky.

But it was 'oh, yes'; she was marooned, the twelve-mile was bound to flood with this storm; she should have realised the unusual warmth in the air could lead to storms and she'd told nobody where she was going...

'Well, I'm quite safe,' she told herself as she closed the hut door against the uproar outside, 'it's just that nobody knows it. And it did come up so fast; anyone could have been caught napping—well, anyone with other things to think of. Could I be blamed for this? Not really,' she reassured herself, resolutely stilling the slight niggle of her conscience by adding, 'All's well that ends well, don't they say?'

It was nine o'clock before it finally stopped raining, but there was still thunder in the air, and, when she peered out, an obliging flash of lightning illuminated an eerie scene—water lying everywhere below the high ground the hut was built on, more water than she'd ever seen in the twelve-mile, probably waist-deep in some parts, she guessed, and she shivered as she remembered her grandfather telling her about a flash-flood that had swept through the paddock once and lapped the door of the hut. So she closed the door and concentrated on the fact that she was dry and safe. In fact it was quite cheerful inside the little hut. She had a roaring fire going in the stove, she'd eaten a dinner of baked beans and biscuits and there was a pot of coffee bubbling away. She'd also pulled the two mattresses off the bunks and put them on the floor in front of the stove—it was now very cold, and a wind was getting up which would probably blow the storms away—good news really, although the danger of flash-flooding still depended on how much water was draining into the paddock.

It was probably due to the rising wind and the crackle of the fire that she heard nothing as she sat huddled on a mattress under one of those hairy blankets and sipped her coffee. In fact her first intimation that she was not alone came when the hut door opened precipitately, nearly blew off its hinges and a tall, dripping figure stood there.

She nearly died at the unexpectedness of it, spilt her coffee and yelped with pain then gasped as she put her cup down. 'Justin! You frightened the life out of me! Couldn't you have knocked—?'

But with a swift lunging movement her muddy, torn and tattered husband hauled her to her feet and grated through his teeth, 'What the *hell* are you doing here, Lucy? Have you no sense at all? Just how long are you going to be a giddy, thoughtless, brainless eternal schoolgirl?'

If he'd just not said those last words, the short fuse to her own temper might not have lit, but it did in a blinding flash because she knew she was no longer a schoolgirl or giddy or thoughtless and brainless, in fact she knew she was a woman in just about every sense of the word with a lot of the heartache that seemed to go with the condition—and all at his hands. So she wrestled an arm free, spat at him, 'I *hate* you, Justin Waite! I wouldn't *be* here if it weren't for you.' And she hit him hard and accurately on his cheekbone.

His grey eyes blazed beneath his dark, dripping hair, and his mouth twisted in a frighteningly savage way, then he jerked her into his arms, stared briefly into her widening eyes, darkening with fright as her face paled, and started to kiss her ruthlessly.

She sagged to her knees when he let her go at last, her heart pounding, her mouth bruised and her whole body shaking.

He stared down at her for a moment, their eyes locking, then he said grimly, 'Don't you realise that every able man on the place is out searching for you, that we've even called in the State Emergency Services helicopter?'

She gasped. 'I…but there was no way I could let you know I was all right. My horse b-bolted, you see—' her teeth chattered '—it was the thunder, then it started to pour—it was really all just…one of those things,' she finished helplessly in a bare little whisper, and dropped her head into her hands.

'No, it wasn't,' he said precisely. 'It was a case of plain thoughtlessness, Lucy, and in future don't you ever go galloping off into the blue without telling someone *where* you're going. Do you understand?'

'Yes. Look, I'm sorry—'

But he cut her off. 'And for someone who knows as much as you do, or claims you do, to come *here* when you know the history of this bloody paddock was sheer lunacy. Look at me, Lucy,' he commanded.

She did, and could have cried because of course he was right. If only she hadn't been so happily preoccupied! But she refused to allow herself the luxury of tears. 'You're right,' she said in a stiff little voice. 'I was extremely stupid. I won't do it again. How did you get here?'

His mouth set in a hard line then he pulled off his oilskin. 'I drove as far as I could then I walked and finally I swam.' His eyes glinted with mockery and she winced. 'I just hope,' he continued, pulling a two-way radio wrapped in more oilskin out from under his shirt, 'this survived the experience.'

It had, and she breathed a sigh of relief as he called off the search, thanked everybody, and it was decided they'd be safe for the rest of the night and a rescue attempt would be made in the morning.

'We'll bring a boat this time,' the voice on the other end promised with more good-naturedness than one would have expected.

But it didn't appear to improve Justin's humour. He put the radio down, glanced at her coldly then started to remove the rest of his wrecked, sodden clothes.

Lucy took a breath, wondered incredulously if she was being sent to Coventry, but some impulse made her guard against putting it to the test immediately. And she turned away and busied herself.

'Here,' she said after a while, and handed him a cup of steaming packet soup. There was a pot of canned braised beef simmering on the stove and she'd hung his clothes over the bunks. He'd stripped to his underpants and was wrapped in a blanket. She'd earlier found a coarse old towel and he'd rubbed himself down with it and the muscles of his shoulders and thighs had rippled under his fire-bronzed skin.

He took the soup and drank it in silence then started on the beef, and all he said was, 'Aren't you having any?'

'I'm not hungry—I had something earlier.'

He didn't reply and she busied herself at the rudimentary sink which was a bucket on a table, and wondered how long it would be before she was considered suitably chastened and worthy of talking to.

He finished the coffee she poured for him and lay back with his hands behind his head. She hesitated, then sat down cross-legged on the other mattress half turned away from him and sipped her own.

And she nearly spilt another lot of coffee as he said suddenly, 'Would you care to explain, Lucy, why you wouldn't be here if it weren't for me?'

'I—what I meant was,' she said carefully, 'that I had some things on my mind. And so I wasn't quite as—um—'

'On the ball as you should have been,' he completed for her drily. 'That's no excuse.'

'Well—'

'Lucy,' he said dangerously.

She grimaced and sipped some coffee. 'Perhaps you're right.'

'Perhaps?'

'All right,' she said quietly. 'I've admitted it was stupid, *I* am stupid—'

'All the more so if those things you had on your mind,' he said sardonically, 'are to do with us.'

She took a breath. 'I can't quite agree with you there, Justin.'

He swore beneath his breath and turned to look at her, resting his head on one hand and then for reasons she couldn't fathom, he swore again but added in less abrasive tones, 'For what it's worth, I don't usually go around kissing little girls quite as brutally as that.'

Involuntarily, Lucy raised a hand to her mouth, and she said a little foolishly because she couldn't think of anything else to say, 'I'm glad. It's a bit—well—' She paused, then hastened to say, 'I don't usually go around slapping people's faces either, but I did think you'd done me an injustice, you see. I still do.' She paused and looked at him resolutely, then she said, 'What I didn't take into account at the time was all you'd been through. Could we both have been just a bit at fault?'

Justin Waite stared at her expressionlessly and she was entirely unaware that the firelight enhanced the gold of her hair, deepened the blue of her eyes, had brought a delicate flush to her cheeks so that she looked troubled but almost ethereally lovely. Nor did she understand why he closed his eyes briefly and sighed as he said, 'What injustice, Lucy?'

'Well I'm not just a little girl, I'm your wife for one thing and what I meant about—not being here if it wasn't for you—was the simple but awkward fact that...that I was in a bit of a love-struck daze and *that's* why I wasn't completely on the ball,' she said in a rush. 'But now I can't help wondering when you're really going to start treating me like a wife, Justin. Maybe one who makes mistakes occasionally but who doesn't deserve to be treated like a child.'

His expression hadn't altered during her speech and all he said at the end of it was, 'Come here, Lucy.'

Her eyes widened. 'Why?'

He raised a wry eyebrow. 'So I can start treating you like a wife—why else?'

But a defiant little spark lit her eyes. 'If you think that's all it's going to take—'

'Yes, I do,' he interupted. 'It's a time-honoured custom between men and women—'

'But I think it should be *said*,' she objected.

'As a matter of fact, this will probably say a lot more than either of us could say in words—let me show you.' And he knelt up and reached for her and when she made a convulsive movement he sighed quietly but didn't release her and said abruptly, 'Trust me for once, Lucy.'

She looked up into his eyes and blinked away the tears she was still determined not to shed. And the faintest smile touched his mouth as he observed the tilt of her chin and he said, 'All right, I apologise. But when you've been wondering whether the body of your wife is going to float past you, it tends to—well, as you saw. Do you think you could see your way clear to allowing yourself to be undressed now?'

She licked her lips and her pulses started to beat erratically.

'Well—only if you'll allow me to say that I seriously regret hitting you.'

'Thank you,' he said gravely and pulled her sweater over her head then removed her blouse, and with her help, her jeans so that all she wore in the glow of the fire was a navy blue bra with little white flowers on it and matching briefs.

'Very—fetching,' he murmured.

'They're French,' she confided, sitting on her heels, her hands on her thighs.

'There's one thing I can think of that would be prettier than you in them—and that's you out of them.'

She laughed then sobered as she gazed at him. 'You're—I have to tell you I think you're quite magnificent, you know,' she said huskily. 'Just in case you thought I wasn't affected or something like that. Indeed, the truth is, I'm quite seriously affected.'

'Lucy—' he reached behind her and released her bra '—any more words along those lines and I'm liable to become uncontrollable.'

'Well, that I can't imagine,' she said, and caught her breath as he touched her naked breasts, and she lifted her hand, not sure what she wanted to do, but he caught it and raised it to his lips and kissed the palm.

'Firelight becomes you,' he murmured, turning his attention back to her nipples until they unfurled. And he stroked all the soft, silky places of her body—her armpits, the back of her neck, the curve of her waist, but each time returning to weigh her full, high breasts that quivered on the slender stem of her body like luscious fruit. Until she could stand it no more and she leant forward and slipped her arms around his neck and laid her brow on his shoulder and said his name pleadingly.

She woke slowly to a dim grey light filtering into the hut. And she made a contented little sound and closed her eyes again, but then her lashes flew up and she was staring at close range into Justin's eyes. She blinked and other things intruded upon her consciousness, that she was nestled in his arms, that they were covered by two scratchy horse blankets—and it all came back to her and her eyes widened.

'It's all right,' he said softly, and raised a hand to brush her hair off her cheek.

Lucy relaxed and said with a little sigh, 'This is terribly nice, you know. Even here.'

'I'm glad,' he replied, his lips twisting slightly. 'It is for me too. I take it I'm quite forgiven?'

'Of course,' she said. 'I thought I'd made that obvious last night.'

'Well, you did let me make love to you last night,' he said thoughtfully.

Lucy's eyes widened. 'Wasn't that enough? I also apologised for hitting you...'

'So you did. I was only wondering whether I had sufficiently apologised for kissing you the way I did.'

Lucy took a breath and looked at him earnestly but with a trace of shyness. 'To be honest I'd forgotten all about it, and if that didn't show—well, don't forget I haven't done this often.'

He smiled rather quizzically down at her. 'All the same you do it with a lot of style.'

She forgot to feel shy. 'Do I really? In what way?'

He moved the blankets aside leisurely and his grey gaze skimmed her body. 'Well, there's the way you move, the things you say—and sometimes the things you don't say, but I can read them in your eyes all the same.'

She grimaced. 'I had the feeling I was a dead giveaway.'

'There's nothing to regret in that. It's very appealing. And there's the way you're lying here discussing this so gravely with me, with not a stitch of clothing on—believe me, that's intensely appealing, speaking as a man,' he said seriously but with laughter lurking in his eyes.

Lucy blushed but laughed a little herself. 'Speaking as a

woman, you're tremendously appealing, I have to say, Justin.' And she put her hands on his shoulders tentatively.

'Go on.'

Her lips quivered and she moved her hands across his shoulders. 'Well, you're tall, dark and handsome for one thing—I did tell you that last night. You can be very nice at times, for another. I must say it's also very reassuring to have you around, yes, even when you're cross with me,' she said airily. 'Let me see,' she continued, 'you—'

'Lucy,' he interupted, 'you're teasing me.'

She opened her eyes very wide. 'I wouldn't dare!'

'Oh, yes, you would. But I have to tell you I have the perfect solution for pert girls.'

'You do?' She frowned. 'Let me guess.' And she leant forward so her breasts brushed against his chest and kissed him lightly on the lips. 'Something along these lines?' she asked with her eyes dancing wickedly.

'Precisely. You're learning very fast, my dear.'

She laughed and rested against him. 'I think I couldn't have a better teacher. Justin—are you asking me to make love to you again? Because, if so, it would be a pleasure...what's the matter? Is something wrong?' she queried anxiously as he moved suddenly then swore.

'Depends on which way you look at it.' He grimaced. 'But I think I can hear our rescuers approaching. Does that sound like an outboard motor to you?'

She listened then sat up abruptly. 'Yes!'

His lips twisted. 'Well, it's not cause for alarm but they're bloody early.'

Lucy scrambled up. 'You better put some clothes on.' And she gathered an armful of his clothes, felt them anxiously then handed them to him. 'They're pretty dry.'

He sat up more leisurely. 'So they are. There is no stigma attached to being caught in bed with your husband, Lucy.'

She cast him a rueful look as she started to dress hurriedly herself. 'I know, but...'

'You think there is?' He drew on his shirt and pushed the other blanket aside. Then he stood up with his shirt still unbuttoned and the hut seemed to shrink.

'No stigma, no,' she said, 'of course not—'

'The lady doth protest too much, methinks,' he said wryly, and caught her hand. 'Tell me, Lucy.'

She stared up at him and for a moment forgot entirely what she was going to say as she studied the blue shadows on his jaw, his dishevelled hair and decided he looked younger this way, and that she rather liked it...

'Lucy?'

'Oh.' She bit her lip and coloured. 'Sorry—what was I saying?'

'Nothing,' he replied amusedly, 'but you were looking—perturbed about being caught in bed with me.'

'Ah, that—um...' she said, dragging her mind away from her thoughts with difficulty. 'Even married couples probably don't relish being caught in bed.'

'True,' he agreed gravely, buttoning his shirt and reaching for his mud-stiffened trousers. 'But there are probably a lot of people out there who were wondering when we were going to take up our marital bed.'

Several expressions chased through her eyes before a look of indignation took hold. 'I know, but it has nothing whatsoever to do with them!'

'True again,' he murmured, and looked with disfavour at the thick jumper he'd worn under his oilskin. 'That doesn't usually stop people wondering.'

'I'm quite sure Sasha for one,' Lucy said with considerable hauteur. 'If you must know, Justin, it will give me a lot of pleasure to...demonstrate otherwise to her.'

He grinned and pulled the jumper over his head. 'That

doesn't seem terribly consistent with your desire to get up out of our bed a few minutes ago, Lucy.'

She thought for a moment then tossed her head and smiled mischievously up at him, 'Well, you see, Justin, there's a difference. Being caught in bed, even with my legally wedded spouse, by a boatload of grinning, knowing men would quite possibly have rendered me all blushing and coy. Whereas dropping the odd subtle hint to Sasha would not.'

'Lucy.' He laughed and caught her again as she went to go past him and took her chin in his hand,

'Yes, Justin?' she said demurely.

'Don't change, will you?' he said after a moment but she got the oddest feeling he'd been about to say something else. He also added wryly, 'They're here.'

They were, and the news they brought with them was not good. Not only was the twelve-mile flooded, but the whole property was in danger of inundation.

'Please, Justin, let me help!'

'Lucy—'

'You can keep an eye on me. You can give me orders as you do to the others. I promise you I'll obey them to the letter!'

He raised a wry eyebrow. 'That would be a new experience but all the same, Lucy—'

'Justin.' She put a tentative hand on his sleeve and tried to mask the hurt in her eyes. 'Don't leave me out. I love Dalkeith, and to sit by and watch this happening, to know that stock are drowning and so on, is more than I can bear. You said yourself you need all the help you can get—and I can ride as well as any of them!'

'Lucy.' He paused and stared down into her eyes. 'I know that. But there are some things you won't want to see, some things you won't be able to do.'

'Perhaps,' she conceded, 'but there must be some things I *can* do. Please.'

He hesitated. 'All right—but I have to say this: if you become a liability at all, if we have to divert someone to look after *you*—well we just can't afford the manpower.'

'You won't,' she said quietly.

She was as good as her word and for the next week, as the floodwaters peaked then started to recede, she spent every daylight hour in the saddle, herding wet, bedraggled sheep from one soggy paddock to another. And she fell into bed every night exhausted. She noted though that she was never allowed to work on her own and, as Justin had predicted, there were sights she wished she hadn't to see. But she never flinched other than inwardly or turned away.

Once, during the week, Justin who had not only Dalkeith but Riverbend to worry about and divided his time between the two, although by a freak of nature Riverbend wasn't as badly affected, stopped her as she was about to set out at the crack of dawn, and inspected her face intently. 'How are you?' he queried.

'Fine!'

'Don't overdo it, Lucy,' he warned.

'I'm not. You must be worried sick about the yearlings and the foals.'

'I've got all the yearlings out. And so far we haven't lost a mare or a foal but it's touch and go. Look, are you sure—'

'Quite sure,' she said quietly but firmly.

He narrowed his eyes then smiled unexpectedly. 'They tell me you've been as good as any bloke on the job.'

It was what kept her going, those words of praise. But finally the day came when the crisis was past and she walked into the kitchen late in the afternoon, knowing she wouldn't be needed the next day.

Shirley fluttered about her anxiously as she sat down at the kitchen table. 'Oh, look at you, Miss Lucy, you've been doing too much! You're only a slip of a girl—'

'No, I haven't,' Lucy protested, and stood up again, but her knees buckled unexpectedly and if Justin hadn't come through the door, she'd have fallen.

'Lucy,' he said grimly through his teeth as he picked her up. 'I warned you!'

'But I helped, didn't I?' she whispered, and closed her eyes.

His expression softened slightly. 'You were a bloody marvel,' he said. 'But one day you're going to learn to really do as you're told.'

'You were the marvel,' she said huskily. 'If you hadn't been here to co-ordinate it all...' She shivered and didn't seem able to stop, and buried her face in his sweater.

'Shirley,' he said over his shoulder, 'in about an hour, could you bring our dinner upstairs?' And he shouldered his way out of the kitchen with Lucy in his arms.

'I'm fine really,' Lucy said as he set her on her feet.

'So I see,' he commented as he started stripping her clothes off. 'Lift up your arms.'

Lucy obeyed, and he removed her pink vest, which left her standing in her bra and jeans, the fact of which she seemed unaware as her brow creased. 'It hasn't been a total disaster, has it? I know we lost some but we saved plenty too... Justin,' she said on a sudden jolt of breath, as she realised he was releasing her bra, 'no...'

Their eyes locked for an instant and her cheeks started to burn but he continued what he was doing saying quietly, 'This is a bit strange, Lucy. Not that I can blame you for wondering when we're ever going to be at leisure to consummate our marriage properly but—I have done it before. And all I intend to do at the moment is inspect you from top to toe. Seven days in the saddle is tough on most people.'

'You're right, I don't know what got into me,' she said breathlessly. 'Is there any chance of the Seychelles?'

He laughed and kissed the top of her head. 'Unfortunately the blasted Yearling Sales are almost upon us.'

An hour later she was ensconced in bed in her pink and white polka-dot pyjamas, and Shirley had brought up dinner for them both, and was unfurling napkins and fussing around them.

'We'll be fine, thanks, Shirley,' Justin said eventually.

'Well, if you need anything just give me a call!'

Justin looked expressively at Lucy as she left but he said, 'I've had a thought. How would you feel about taking Shirley on permanently?'

Lucy blinked. 'I think it would be great, but would she want to stay?'

He laughed. 'Would she ever? Not only does she worship the ground you walk on, but the son of her heart is a reformed person. I'm sure she would. She'd be close to her aunts as well and Adrian could enrol in the School of the Air with the rest of the property kids. I get the feeling it might be hard to tear Adrian away, anyway.'

'I think he worships the ground you walk on,' Lucy commented.

He shrugged and said. 'Eat up, Lucy. We don't want you wasting away.'

She picked up her knife and fork. 'I don't think there's the least danger of that—'

'You certainly felt a few pounds lighter.'

Lucy ate some roast beef in silence.

'What's wrong?' he said after a minute or so.

'I don't know,' she replied, her brow creasing as she put her knife and fork together. 'Well, yes, I do, although it's a little hard to put into words.'

'I think you'd better try,' he said with a smile in his eyes.

'Would you...would you come to bed with me? Now? Not to...well, whatever you like, but I'm just feeling a little shell-shocked, sort of, and I think I need some help.'

Ten minutes later, when he'd got rid of their dinner plates and she was lying in his arms, he said, 'Feeling better?'

'Oh...yes,' she whispered with a relieved sigh. 'Sorry.'

'Don't be. You did far too much but, be that as it may, will you come to Sydney with me for the sales?'

'I'd love to,' she said huskily. 'Would I be in the way, though?'

'Of course not. You might even be a considerable asset. There's an enormous amount of socialising that goes on. You could also, much enamoured as I am of your French underwear, collect yourself a trousseau, meet old friends—have a break, in other words.'

But Lucy, much to her embarrassment when he reminded her of it the next morning, was fast asleep.

'Right. I have a few things to do—why don't you hit the shops, Lucy?'

'I will, in a while,' she replied over her shoulder as she completed a tour of the downstairs area of Justin's townhouse in a fashionable inner suburb of Sydney. 'I love it!' she added enthusiastically, looking out over the tiny courtyard. The living area was furnished mainly in subtle beiges and sandy pinks with sandstone walls, wooden-framed windows and multi-paned French doors with brass knobs. There were big comfortable chairs covered in ivory fabric and the dining table was clear glass and forged iron tinted a soft, old green.

'I'm glad,' he said gravely. 'It's yours to command.'

'Oh, I won't change a thing!'

His lips twisted. But he said, 'By the way, we've been invited to a cocktail party this evening. It's a pre-sales do. Would you care to accompany me, Mrs Waite?'

'I'd be delighted to, Mr Waite,' she said grandly.

He smiled but his eyes were faintly probing as they rested on her face. 'You're very chipper, Lucy.'

'Why shouldn't I be?' She eyed him innocently.

'You've just been through a rather harrowing experience, my dear,' he said after a moment.

'I recover quickly,' she said ruefully. 'You really don't have to worry about me.'

'Sometimes the effect of these things can be—more insidious than one realises. And I can't help thinking you have a look about you of the kind of high spirits that give way to tears before bedtime.'

She swallowed suddenly and hoped he didn't notice. Because of course he was right in a way. Her high spirits were a front for a little spring of tension that had hit her rather suddenly because on the flight from Dalkeith, it had begun to dawn on her that she and her marriage to Justin Waite were going to be very much on show over the next few days. But she was curiously loath to let him divine this. So she said with a laughing look, 'I got over that kind of thing when I was about ten, Justin,' she said with a laughing look. 'I'm just a naturally ebullient kind of person.'

'I see. All right.' He looked her over narrowly once more then shrugged. 'I'll be back at five, we're due at the party at six. In the meantime, these are for you.' He drew his hand out of his pocket and held it out to her. In it was a key-ring, a wad of money and a bank card.

Her eyes widened and she licked her lips. 'I... Justin, you don't have to—'

He picked up her hand and closed it over the contents of his. 'Of course I do,' he said lightly. 'You can't shop without money, you need transport and you need the keys of the house. Go ahead and enjoy it.' And he kissed her briefly on the top of her head and walked out.

She got back to the townhouse at three o'clock, parked the racy little sports car that was apparently hers in the double garage, and carried quite a few packages into the house. But only one of them contained clothes, the rest holding food. A quick tour of the pantry before she'd left had shown her that it was bare. She'd also bought a percolator, the one bit of equipment the kitchen didn't seem to have, and before long the aroma of coffee was drifting through the house. And she took her mug with her as she made a more detailed inspection. There were three bedrooms upstairs, the main one done out in white and yellow and overlooking the courtyard. She opened the linen closet and discovered it packed with thick, thirsty towels and matching linen sheets and pillow cases, some of them not even out of their wrappers.

And the impression that this house wasn't used a lot was reinforced when she checked the china cupboards and discovered glasses and cutlery still in their boxes. She grimaced and wondered who had bought it all. Perhaps he'd got an interior decorating firm in, she surmised, and they'd supplied it. Or perhaps... But she closed the door of her mind on that thought at the same time as she closed cupboard doors, and thought instead, resolutely, well, whoever did it, it's *nice*.

She was dressed and almost ready when she heard the front door open and close, and she looked over the banister and called out that she'd be down in a tick.

'No hurry,' he called back. 'I've got to get changed yet—is that coffee I smell?'

'Yes, it's on the stove.'

They met as she was halfway down the stairs and he was starting to come up.

'Hi!' she said gaily as he stopped with his foot on the bottom step. 'How was your day?'

'Lucy...'

'Are you lost for words? I do hope not in a *disapproving* way.'

He moved away and said wryly, 'Come right down and I'll be able to give you a proper evaluation.'

She hesitated briefly, although she wasn't sure why, then continued down and went to stand in the middle of the room.

'Turn round,' he said.

She did so obediently, then looked up at him gravely. 'Short skirts are in, Justin.'

He said nothing as his gaze flickered over her again. She wore a midnight-blue Thai silk suit. The jacket was short and fitted into her waist with a wide collar that exposed her throat and the tops of her shoulders and the sleeves were elbow-length. The straight little skirt came to six inches above the knee and she wore very pale frosted stockings and high-heeled blue shoes that matched the outfit. Her hair was piled on top of her head with some curly strands framing her face.

'What do you think?' she asked at last, unable to stand the suspense and quite unable to read his expression.

'I think,' he said expressionlessly then smiled faintly as her eyes grew anxious, 'that you look simply stunning, my dear. And that I shall have to watch out in case any susceptible blokes out there take to flying banners over the harbour again.'

Lucy relaxed and had to laugh. 'I quite thought you didn't like it!'

'Why wouldn't I?'

She gestured. 'I wasn't sure it was a terribly—modest, wifely outfit, somehow.'

'But you chose to wear it all the same?'

'Don't you think it is?' She looked at him seriously.

'Not at all. I didn't say that. And wives are allowed to look stunning. Husbands are usually quite keen on that, in fact.'

'Then why do I get the feeling you don't entirely approve?' she said slowly.

'I don't know—why do you?' he countered.

'Well,' she frowned up at him, 'you did—sort of stop when you first saw me.'

'Ah. So I did. But that's easy to explain. I was simply bowled over, particularly by your legs.'

Lucy's eyes widened and then her lips curved into a smile. 'Thanks,' she said huskily. 'I needed that.'

'Lucy,' his lips twisted, 'it's true—you would be able to bowl a block of wood over. Hell—' he looked at his watch '—I'd better get moving. By the way, I see you did the grocery shopping. Thanks. I always forget.'

'You don't have to thank me; that's what wives are for, especially industrious ones,' she said, but distractedly. 'Aren't they?'

A wicked little smile lit his grey eyes. 'Among other things. I'll be about ten minutes.'

Lucy drew a deep breath and Justin looked down at her with a faint frown. 'Something wrong?'

They were just about to enter the cocktail party venue, she could hear the buzz of voices and clink of glasses, but she paused and realised she had a vaguely uneasy feeling at the pit of her stomach.

'Lucy?'

'Um—I'm fine, Justin,' she said with a glance at him. But that made things worse, she discovered. He wore a grey suit with a pale blue shirt and navy blue tie and he looked both worldly and enigmatic, tall, broad-shouldered and incredibly attractive—and way out of my league? she enquired of herself with a little sigh.

'Are you feeling sick or something?' he asked with a frown in his eyes.

'No,' she said uncertainly. 'Well, not really. But it's just occurred to me that there could be four people here who know about me handcuffing kids to fences, let alone telling you I hate you. And that the whole of Sydney might now know of it! And, much as I hate to admit it, my stomach is doing strange things right now and I'm not terribly sure that I can…do this.'

'Lucy—'

'*Justin*—'

'No, Lucy, listen to me.' He took her hand and turned her away from the double doors, at the same time as he gestured to a passing waiter carrying a tray of glasses, and after a short enquiry relieved him of one that contained neat brandy. 'Here, have a sip of this.' He handed her the glass but didn't release her other hand.

'It might make me sick…'

'No, it won't,' he said positively. 'It'll settle your nerves.'

She looked up at him out of huge eyes and with her lips trembling, but he pressed her fingers gently, and she raised the glass to her lips and took a sip, and then several more. Then she shuddered, but as the fiery warmth made its way down to her stomach she felt herself steadying. 'You're right,' she said blinking several times.

'I'm quite often right,' he replied wryly.

'All the same—' a frown creased her brow and she looked anxiously past him '—it—'

'Lucy—I've told you this before but it's true—I don't give a damn about what other people think and neither should you. This is between us and it's all over anyway. But in point of fact, you do know what most people will be thinking? That if I couldn't make you happy, I must be out of my mind. In other words—' his lips twisted '—it's me they'll be wondering about, not you.'

Her lips parted. 'If they do,' she whispered, 'they also must be wondering if you're still in love with Joanna Madden— don't you see?'

'No, that's over and done with,' he said firmly, his grey gaze as steady as a rock. 'Now, we can do one of two things. We can go home if you still don't feel up to this and it won't worry me in the slightest. Or we can go in there—and give them something else to talk about.' He smiled unexpectedly.

'Wh-what?' she stammered.

'Well, should you choose never to leave my side—that kind of thing—they might very well say to themselves that Justin Waite is doing it right at last.' He stared down into her bemused eyes and grimaced slightly, but he added, 'Why don't we try it?'

CHAPTER SEVEN

WHICH WAS HOW it came about that for the first time in her life Lucy Waite née Wainright had an attentive escort who was also her husband. And it was a revelation. She wasn't quite sure how he did it but he somehow contrived to make her feel special, as if he were as interested in her as if not more so than anyone else they met. Nor did he give her the opportunity to stray from his side even if she'd wanted to. And she couldn't help noticing that they were the centre of quite some attention.

It's incredibly heady, she thought a little dizzily at one stage, as she stood beside him and glanced up to see him watching her with a faint smile on his lips and a look in his eyes that was exclusively for her, a look that contrived to make her feel ravishing and *interesting* and of singular importance to him. Also to see the envy in other women's eyes as they looked at him, particularly Sasha, who had come forward to meet them as soon as they'd entered, and stayed glued to their side ever since.

Yes, well, Lucy thought privately, as Sasha, who was dressed in mint-green that went well with her red hair, moved restlessly, perhaps you won't be quite so superior with me now?

And she had almost decided to let herself just be happy— she'd certainly got over her bout of nerves and was laughing at something someone was saying to her—when she looked across the room and straight into Joanna Madden's lovely, haunting eyes. And that was when it all collapsed like a pricked balloon. It was no coincidence that their eyes had caught, she knew that in her bones. Joanna had been looking at her for some moments, she was sure, and didn't seem to be able to look away either, so that it was Lucy who did. And, as she did, it crossed her mind to wonder whether what Justin had said about "giving them something else to talk about" might have been directed more at one particular person?

'Lucy?'

'Oh, sorry, Justin,' she said a few minutes later. 'Did I miss something?'

He looked her over thoughtfully. 'No. But enough is enough, I think. Shall we go home?'

She could only nod gratefully.

'Why don't you change into something more comfortable while I make us a snack?'

'I'm not hungry, Justin, but thanks all the same.'

'Lucy—' he caught her hand as she went to walk past him '—do it.'

A spark of rebellion lit her eyes. 'Why should I?'

'Because you'll make yourself sick if you don't eat,' he murmured with nothing other than a slight tinge of amusement in his eyes. 'I only had a sandwich in mind, and coffee.'

Her shoulders slumped. 'OK.'

He let her hand go but his gaze held hers. Then he smiled absently and turned away.

She changed into a creamy satin nightgown and a white towelling robe and sighed as she let her hair down, brushed it then tied it back in a simple pony-tail. For reasons she didn't think had much to do with her exertions at Dalkeith, she felt really tired and dispirited—in fact she knew the reason all too well, she chided herself, Joanna Madden—is she going to haunt me forever? she wondered. Why can't I just take what I've got and make the best of it? I shouldn't have come, she thought finally, I'm OK at Dalkeith but this is like being on a rollercoaster ride… How am I going to be now, for instance?

When she got downstairs, Justin had laid out his supper on an occasional table and drawn it up to a settee. There were open toasted cheese sandwiches, a bowl of fruit and a fresh pot of coffee.

'Mmm. Smells nice,' she said very mundanely. 'I didn't know you were a cook.'

He grimaced. He'd taken off his jacket and loosened his tie. 'A very ordinary cook. Sit down.' He indicated the settee. 'Would you like to listen to some music?'

'Yes, please.' Lucy sat down and watched him glance through a pile of compact discs. Then moments later some lovely guitar music flooded the room. He turned it down and came to sit next to her.

'Help yourself,' he murmured. 'It's cheese or cheese.'

'I like toasted cheese,' Lucy heard herself say, and wondered why she should be feeling unwittingly soothed. The music? The fact that Justin had gone to the trouble of making this snack? She grimaced.

'Something wrong?'

'No!' she denied hastily, and concentrated on eating her sandwich. When she'd finished he peeled and quartered an apple for her and poured the coffee.

'Tell me what else you bought today?'

She cradled her mug in her hands and tucked her feet under her. 'I bought an outfit to wear tomorrow to the sales, a dress for the ball you mentioned tomorrow night, and that's all.'

He raised an eyebrow. 'Is that all you intend to buy?'

'I don't know. One has to be in the mood.'

'How does one get into the mood?'

'I don't think one can consciously do that—you either are or you aren't.'

'So events outside you are the telling factor,' he commented.

She wrinkled her nose. 'Probably.'

'Is that to say if you were feeling happy and confident you would go out and splurge?'

Lucy considered with a faint smile. 'It could be the other way around; sometimes people do things like that when they're down in the dumps and need cheering up.'

He drank some coffee then sat back with his arm along the back of the settee. 'What I'm trying to get at,' he said after a while, 'is which of those states you might be in.'

She turned her head to look at him and whispered one word. 'Why?'

'Why do I want to know? Why shouldn't I?'

'Sometimes I'm happy and confident, sometimes I'm not—' She stopped abruptly and put a hand to her mouth.

'For a little while this evening you were both.'

'Justin,' she said huskily, and to her consternation she felt tears in her eyes, 'I...it's not easy to...' She broke off frustratedly.

'There's one thing that makes it all much easier. Don't cry,' he said with a faint smile quirking his lips and he took her coffee cup from her. 'This.' And he took her into his arms.

'Justin!' she protested on a suddenly panicky note.

'There's nothing to be afraid of.'

'It's not that I'm *afraid* of anything.'

'Good,' he said wryly, and lifted her onto his lap. 'Then you should be able to relax.' And he did nothing more than hold her lightly and after a while it seemed only natural to rest her head against his shoulder rather than sit tensely upright against his arm.

Although she did say, challengingly, 'I am rather tired.'

'So am I. Cocktail parties can be an exhausting form of socialising and I'm not at all sure why people inflict them upon themselves.'

She smiled against his shirt. 'That's what my father used to say. Why stand around doing a juggling act with drinks and bits of food stuck on toothpicks when you have to shake hands with people all the time? He used to say it was a cheap form of entertaining.'

Justin laughed.

'How are the yearlings? Is that what you did today?'

'Yes. They all seemed to have settled in well.'

'Will they go under the hammer tomorrow?'

'Six tomorrow, the rest the next day.'

'I suppose Sasha has everything in hand?'

'Sasha has,' he agreed. 'With her usual superb efficiency. She is in fact being quite painful at the moment.'

'Justin!' Lucy beamed a marvelling blue gaze up at him. 'I never thought to hear you say that.'

He grimaced. 'I don't know why, but lately it's occurred to me that Sasha doesn't have a sense of humour.'

Lucy giggled. 'Poor Sasha.'

He looked down at her ruefully. 'You don't say that with a lot of feeling.'

'No, I don't,' Lucy replied unrepentantly. 'She makes me want to bite sometimes.'

He grinned. 'She probably envies you terribly.'

'I'm sure she does, but only over you... I mean...' She stopped and moved restlessly.

He stilled her movement and put his fingers under her chin so that she had to look into his eyes. '*I* meant,' he said quietly, 'that she envies how young and fresh you are, how lovely, how natural, how vibrant your personality is—those things.'

'Little to know if so,' Lucy whispered, 'what a trial some of those things are to me.'

Something flickered in his eyes. 'They shouldn't be. They aren't to me.'

Her lips parted and her eyes widened.

'In fact they're often the opposite,' he went on, releasing her chin and pushing some strands of hair off her face. And he bent his head and started to kiss her.

'Oh,' Lucy said breathlessly some minutes later. 'Oh.'

'May I take that as approval?' he murmured.

She swallowed and moved her cheek on his shirt and was unable to reply because the fact of the matter was, she was still unbearably affected by his kisses and she couldn't help thinking how ridiculous it had been to try to pretend to him that she was too tired for his lovemaking when she seriously doubted that would ever be the case...

'Lucy Waite?' he said gravely.

'Justin—' it came out rather cracked '—I can't talk. I know that sounds ridiculous and I'm sure you're aware that I'm talking right at this moment, but—'

'I am. Aware of it.'

'Well, it's not the same thing.'

His lips twisted. 'It's not?'

'No.'

'All right. Then let's devise a system of non-talking for those things that can't be talked about. If you would like me to kiss you again, you have only to nod your head.'

'I...'

But he waited no longer and it was the same wonderful experience, although this time he slipped his hand beneath her robe and slipped down the narrow strap of her nightgown. And, far from resisting, Lucy sighed with delight as she felt his fingers resting very gently on her breast.

'Nice?' he queried against the corner of her mouth.

'Lovely,' she breathed. 'I didn't know it could be so...'

'Didn't you?'

'Not until you did it to me—I feel a bit of a fool,' she said ruefully, but he took no notice and continued to touch her.

'Justin?' she said, because in spite of her delight she felt slightly chagrined, she found, and *young* as well as foolish. 'Is this doing anything for you, Justin?'

He'd been looking down at her in a curiously heavy-lidded way, but all of a sudden he stopped what he was doing and that heavy-lidded look changed to one of open amusement. 'Of course it is. I wouldn't be doing it otherwise,' he said wryly, and added, 'What is going through your mind at the moment, Lucy?' as he kissed the corner of her mouth chastely.

But she didn't want to be kissed chastely, she thought rebelliously; it was too late for that now, when her breasts were feeling tight and tingly and she was dying to slide her hands over his skin—all of which added to her inner turmoil and sense of injustice. 'I was wondering if you can turn this on and off like a tap—men can, can't they?' she said tartly.

He raised an eyebrow. 'That's a rather cynical remark. As a matter of fact there is a point of no return to which men are very vulnerable.'

Lucy said scathingly, 'I know that! It wasn't what I meant.'

'What did you mean?'

'I wondered why you—stopped. I mean to say,' she said, 'one minute you were kissing me, then you were laughing at me. It's not a very elevating experience, to be perfectly honest—'

'And probably entirely new to you? I'm so sorry,' he said seriously, 'but I wasn't actually laughing at *you*. Because as anyone with you in their arms would know—'

Lucy sat up abruptly. 'I hate the thought of that, Justin, so don't say another word!' she commanded.

He grimaced. 'It was meant as a compliment.'

'No, it was not! It was just like saying, give a man a girl who is reasonably attractive and—bingo. Which is something I resent very much.' Her eyes smouldered.

'Lucy,' he said thoughtfully, watching as she pulled her nightgown up, 'if you think it only takes a pretty girl who is eager—' their eyes clashed '—I grew out of that quite a few years back. Moreover, I was actually laughing at myself.'

She blinked. 'Why?'

'Because I was approaching that point of no return rather quickly,' he said with a faint, dry smile, twisting his lips.

'In spite of me trying to pretend I was too tired?'

'Are you?'

Lucy paused then said hollowly, 'I get the feeling I might never be.'

'Well, now,' he said gravely but with his grey eyes perfectly wicked, 'that's entirely appropriate for a wife.'

'But not essentially modest,' she whispered with a reluctant smile tugging at her lips.

'Wives are allowed to be sexy with their husbands. So long as it stops there.'

'But—'

'In fact so far as being a wife goes,' he overrode her, 'there's only one serious flaw I've found in you, Lucy.'

'I...' her lips dimpled at the corner '...talk too much?' she hazarded.

'Much too much. Will you come willingly and happily to bed with me now?'

She opened her mouth to say something along the lines of, Did he know why she'd been unwilling and unhappy earlier? But in the end she said simply, 'Yes, please.'

'Lucy—can't you drive any faster? The first yearling is due to go under the hammer in half an hour.'

'We won't be late, Sasha, trust me, but I don't want to get caught speeding,' Lucy said reasonably.

'I know, but all the same—I should have been there hours ago,' Sasha said fretfully. 'Not only for the horses but there's the hospitality tent to be set up and the Riverbend Saddlery display—why, oh, why did I have to break down in the middle of the most terrible peak-hour traffic?'

'These things can't be helped,' Lucy said soothingly but with an unholy inner wriggle of amusement. For once in her life Sasha was looking less than her usual soignée self. Her hair was ruffled, her face was hot, there was a streak of grease down her beautiful tight-fitting designer jeans, her handmade leather boots were scuffed and her expression was strained. What had happened was, when her car had broken down on the way to the sales complex, she'd rung them from a phone booth and Justin had said he'd go to the complex immediately and that Lucy should bring Sasha once she'd extricated herself from her difficulties. 'I'm sure Justin can cope,' she added, and couldn't help the faintest tinge of irony that accompanied her words.

'You don't like me, do you, Lucy?' Sasha replied as she scrubbed the grease mark then cast an almost vengeful look at Lucy's attire, which consisted of a simple but striking coffee linen, A-line button-through dress with a longish skirt, flat bronze suede shoes and a marvellous straw hat with the brim upturned. Her hair was loose beneath it and gleamed like silk, her skin was clear, flawless and glowing, her lips were painted a frosted bronzy pink and the lightest touch of Miss Dior lay on the air as she moved.

Lucy couldn't help but be conscious of this scrutiny, and she drew a deep breath and said as mildly as she was able, 'You make it rather hard for me sometimes, Sasha.'

'*You*...' But Sasha stopped, perhaps fortunately, and went on in an entirely different strain as Lucy swore beneath her breath and slowed down and stopped as she was flagged so to do by a policeman, 'You must have been speeding after all!'

'I was about two kilometres over the speed limit,' Lucy said tartly, 'And only because *you* were so—oh, well, if this isn't a sucker spot, I've never seen one, anyway. Which I will tell him!'

Sasha groaned. 'We'll be later than ever! He's liable to throw you into gaol if you argue with him!'

'Argue with him?' Lucy smiled sweetly. 'I wouldn't dream of it—Officer,' she said to the large young policeman at her window, 'before you write a thing down on that ticket, may I say a few words in my defence? In fact, if you let me get out, I could say them even better!'

'Of all the...' Sasha appeared lost for words as they drove off, unticketed, several minutes later.

'What was wrong with it?' Lucy queried, grinning. 'I merely

explained why we were in a bit of a rush, pointed out to him, quite deferentially I thought, that he really should be policing *dangerous* traffic situations and not sitting behind a bush picking off lone cars only exceeding the limit by a couple of kilometres, and I offered to donate the fine to his favourite charity if he would reconsider his position. Which he did.'

'Because he was drooling at the mouth,' Sasha said bitterly. 'But don't think Justin will be taken in by these schoolgirlish ways forever, Lucy. Oh, you may think you have him enslaved at the moment but it won't last. You're too young for him. And there's always Joanna... She did up the Sydney house, by the way; did you know it was all her doing? And I can't help wondering if Justin's flaunting you at her because he's still punishing her for marrying Tim Madden.'

Lucy clenched the steering-wheel until her knuckles went white but surprised herself as she said quite steadily, even gently, 'Sasha, I'll try to forget you ever said that to me. We're here,' she added flatly.

Try to forget, Lucy marvelled, as she sat in the stand reserved for vendors later and watched Sasha, none other, lead the Cawnpore filly into the ring to an excited buzz of the crowd.

Somehow or other Sasha had got rid of the grease stain, she saw, and was wearing a navy blazer with 'RIVERBEND' on the back, and she handled the filly lightly but expertly. And she was a magnificent filly, you couldn't deny it, with powerful quarters, a splendid deep chestnut coat with a small white blaze and one white foot, and an alert, intelligent eye as she surveyed the crowd with her ears pricked. And for a moment Lucy forgot all else as she watched.

Then Justin slid into the seat beside her and said wryly, 'She's handling it all like an old stager.'

'She's magnificent,' Lucy said with an odd lump in her throat.

'We could be in for a magnificent bidding duel too,' he said significantly as the auctioneer read through the filly's bloodlines. 'Apparently there's a South African syndicate here rather interested, as well as a sheikh from Saudi Arabia.'

'Oh! Where is he?'

'I doubt if he's here in person but that's his trainer over there.' He pointed.

'And the Maddens,' Lucy murmured. She'd spotted Joanna and Tim almost immediately—Joanna was dressed in eye-catching yellow that went superbly with her dark hair.

'Uh-huh. Here goes.'

But the bidding opened quietly and after a few minutes Lucy turned a concerned face to Justin—to see that he was quite relaxed. 'They're playing cat and mouse,' he said.

And indeed they were, because, as the tension mounted, the bids crept up then started to leap up and the buzz from the floor grew and flashbulbs popped while television crews crept among the crowd as they passed the quarter of a million mark, then you could have heard a pin drop as Tim Madden appeared to drop out and the South Africans competed with the Saudi sheikh's trainer until they too dropped off. And Lucy clutched Justin's hand, thinking it was over as the auctioneer called...*for the final and last time*! But before he could drop his hammer, Tim Madden's hand went up. There was pandemonium briefly then silence again, and finally a huge roar that sent the Cawnpore filly dancing across the ring with Sasha clinging grimly to her rearing bit, as she was knocked down to Tim Madden for a sales record.

And it was all recorded for posterity in the next day's newspapers as well as being on television that night—Lucy holding Justin's hand tightly and concentrating fiercely during the bidding, Justin hugging Lucy as the final hammer went down. Tim Madden, smiling quietly into his wife's eyes—both the Maddens and the Waites posing with the filly, Sasha posing with the filly—it went on for the rest of the day and half the night. People congratulating them, people interviewing them and in between the other five of the Riverbend consignment allotted to that day being sold most successfully to buyers who also wanted to be photographed with the breeders.

So that by the time they got home Lucy was genuinely exhausted. 'What a day!' she said as Justin closed the door behind them.

'I know—want anything?'

'Only bed.'

He picked her up, carried her upstairs and laid her down on the bed. 'You were wonderful.'

Lucy grimaced. 'I didn't do much! Cawnpore's daughter did it all.'

'I mean—' he started to unbutton her dress '—you were wonderful with the Press, with the proud new owners of six Riverbend progeny, everything a wife should be in those circumstances,' he said with a smile at the back of his eyes. 'A considerable asset.'

'I'm glad,' she said huskily. 'But you bred her, you saved her life when she got colic.'

'All in a day's work,' he said lightly. 'Sit up.'

Lucy did so obediently and he continued to undress her like a child, then slid her cream nightgown down her body. She suffered these ministrations gratefully then said thoughtfully, 'Justin?'

'Uh-huh?' He'd got up to change himself and looked over his shoulder at her.

'Tim Madden must have an *awful* lot of money.'

'He does.'

'More than the sheikh, do you think?'

'I doubt it—but enough. Why?'

'I just wondered.'

'Go to sleep, Lucy,' he said but gently, and sat down beside her again. 'No,' he put his fingers to her lips, 'not one more word—well, unless you'd like to explain to me why Sasha arrived today muttering about you corrupting the due processes of the law?'

Lucy sat up indignantly. 'Is that what she *said*? Why, if it hadn't been for her, I wouldn't have had to talk myself out of a speeding ticket in the first place. She really—'

'Talk yourself out of a speeding ticket, Lucy? I didn't think that was possible.'

'Well, it is. Provided you get them before they've written anything.'

He looked quizzically into her eyes. 'You've had a bit of experience in these things?'

'No, that's the first time—all it takes is a bit of eyelash-batting—oh, no,' she said on a descending scale. 'Justin, I wasn't being a *femme fatale* if that's what you're thinking, I never was, not really and anyway, there isn't a part of me now that's not wholly taken up with you and—' But she stopped abruptly and bit her lip.

'Then that's fine,' he said gravely. 'I approve wholeheartedly of what you just said. So don't look,' he said softly, 'as if you feel you ought to retract it. And now, my dear, it's definitely lights out and silence. But only if you'll let me get in with you and only if you'll allow me to hold you, because, as you once told me, that's very relaxing.'

Which was how Lucy came to fall asleep in his arms, still unable to deal with all the impressions of an exciting yet turbulent day—what Sasha had said, how Joanna had looked, how Tim and Justin had, for one brief but piercing moment before shaking hands, registered a cool yet battle-laden tension between them.

CHAPTER EIGHT

'LUCY, WHY DON'T you go home?' Justin said at about three o'clock the next afternoon. 'There's the Breeder's Ball tonight, don't forget, and you've been yawning for the past hour.'

'Sorry,' Lucy said, and promptly yawned again. 'OK.' She smiled up at him and he bent his head and kissed her lightly.

And once home, she changed, lay down on the settee to relax and bring her mind to bear on everything that had happened over the past few days, but fell asleep for a couple of hours. What is wrong with me—why am I so sleepy, why can't I come to grips with anything? she wondered as she woke up feeling terrible.

It proved nothing that a soak in the bath didn't cure, and she started to do her hair and her make-up but she was still conscious of a failing to come to grips with things. Perhaps, she lowered her brush, and stared at herself in the mirror, I shouldn't even try. What can I do to change things, anyway? How can I alter that deep hostility between Justin and Tim Madden? How can I help Joanna, and so far as Sasha's concerned, I can only hope to God she's wrong and perhaps it's about time I was a bit more charitable...

'Lucy?'

Her eyes widened as she registered Justin's image in the mirror. 'I didn't hear you come home!'

'I know, you were miles away,' he said wryly. 'What I'm wondering is, where?'

'So *much* has happened lately,' she said hastily. 'It must be that. I slept for a couple of hours and woke up feeling like a log of wood!'

'You don't look anything like a log of wood at the moment.' His grey gaze drifted down her.

She smoothed her towelling robe, took an inward breath and turned to him with a mischievous little glint in her eye as she said softly, 'You ain't seen nothin' yet, brother!'

He laughed and looked rueful at the same time. 'I only hope I can bear it.'

Her ballgown was rather modest in design, a long flowing skirt with a matching sleeveless gilet that buttoned to the throat and came to her knees. What made it quite stunning, however, was that the lined silk chiffon it was created from matched the deep pansy-blue of her eyes and the buttons down the front of the gilet were beautiful little prancing pearl, amethyst and diamante horses...

'There,' she said, standing before Justin at last. She'd put her hair up again, and dotted in it were tiny flowers fashioned from the same silk chiffon as the outfit. Her purse and shoes were silver.

He started to smile as he surveyed her. 'Where did you find it?'

Her mouth dimpled at the corners. 'I've got the feeling it found me. As soon as I saw it, I thought, now how could I wear anything else to a Breeder's Ball!'

'How indeed.'

'It's also very comfortable.' She twirled before him to demonstrate. 'Very suitable for dancing, and I know there'll be nobody in another one because it's unique and—cost an awful lot of your money, Justin.' She came to rest in front of him again and put a hand to her mouth just a little awkwardly. 'Not that these are real—' she touched a button '—but I hope you don't mind.'

'Why should I mind?' he queried.

'Well, even my father,' she said soberly, 'used to get a bit shocked about the price of these kinds of clothes. Oh, dear, I'm beginning to wish I'd never said those words about being a careful, prudent wife. I've got the feeling they're going to haunt me.'

'Lucy—' he touched the point of her chin '—I, on the other hand, am quite happy to fork out a small fortune to see you looking so happy and stunning. Just remember that.'

'That's...lovely,' she said with an odd attack of shyness, 'but it won't take that, I promise. You know,' she went on before he could reply, 'you look rather devastating yourself.' And indeed he did in a black dinner suit, pleated white shirt and hand-tied bow-tie. 'I might have to keep a sharp eye out for any ladies on the loose!'

In the car, she said suddenly, 'I suppose they'll all be there.'

'I guess so.'

They were.

The Maddens, Sasha although with an escort, a tall, good-looking man, the South Africans, the sheikh's trainer—and courtesy of the Breeder's Association they were all at the same table...

I can handle this, Lucy told herself after taking a deep breath, and went forward with her head tilted regally.

It was Sasha she had to handle first, Sasha who came to sit next to her after dinner had been cleared and a general loosening up of the company occurred as the band struck up.

Sasha said stiffly as she slipped into a vacant chair next to Lucy, 'I would like to apologise.'

Surprise made Lucy's eyes widen as she surveyed the other girl, who was wearing a black strapless gown and a troubled expression in her green eyes. 'Well, thank you,' she said slowly. 'Perhaps I've been—a bit at fault too.'

But Sasha brushed that aside. 'I should never have said what I did. It was only…sheer jealousy that made me do it. You see, after he broke up with Joanna, who incidentally is a friend of mine, I,' Sasha stopped and looked unbelievably uncomfortable. 'Well, I thought there might be some hope for me—only to have that idea crushed by a slip of a girl—by you, I mean, and it…rather brought out the worst in me, I'm afraid.'

Lucy blinked and sought a little frantically for the means to cope with this. 'Uh… I, well I wondered about that; I mean to say—'

'You don't have to say anything, Lucy,' Sasha said drily. 'I was never a contender; I just couldn't bring myself to believe it.'

'What did… I mean, why now?' Lucy asked involuntarily.

Sasha looked away, looked oddly flustered then her eyes came to rest on her escort and she said perfunctorily, 'I've met someone else.'

Lucy stared at her averted profile and wondered why this didn't ring true.

Then Sasha spoke again, 'I'm leaving Justin, by the way.'

Lucy sat up. 'Oh, dear! Do you have to? I mean, I—'

'Yes, I have to, Lucy—I should have done it years ago. I'll tell him tonight.' She looked up as a shadow fell across them but it was Joanna Madden and she said gaily. 'May I join you? All the men of the party are talking bloodlines!' She grimaced expressively. 'So I swapped my seat with one of them.'

'Of course,' both Lucy and Sasha said, but perhaps for the only time in their acquaintance they were united in the oddly very brief but wary glance they exchanged as Joanna sat down. And Lucy, looking across the table, discovered Justin watching them before he switched his grey eyes away as someone spoke to him. How strange, she thought. Three women either in love with him or having loved him. What is he thinking? What is everyone else thinking? Probably, she thought with an inner tremor, they're wondering how Lucy Waite will cope with an old mistress and a would-be mistress, so I'll just have to show them...

'Have you thought of a name for the Cawnpore filly yet, Joanna?' she said brightly.

'I've thought of sixty,' Joanna replied whimsically, 'but none of them is quite right. Did you have any thoughts on the subject, Lucy? Or Sasha?'

'Well, I always give them pet names,' Sasha said wryly. 'I used to call her Flopsy because as a baby she used to flop all over the place, but I did think of—well, he *did* save her life and I wondered about—Justine.'

Sasha, Lucy thought. How could you put your foot in it like that? As if Tim Madden is going to have any horse named after someone who lived with and loved his wife...

But Joanna handled it superbly. She said, 'Tell me how he saved her life!'

And Sasha launched into graphic account of the colic and how Justin had kept the filly on her feet and walked and walked her, how he was the only one she trusted enough to help her through her pain and misery.

'Were you there too, Lucy?' Joanna said in a bid, probably, to stem the tide.

'Well, no; Lucy,' Sasha said, 'chose to get herself lost that day—'

'It was the next day, actually,' Lucy inserted gently, 'and I didn't choose to do it, it happened quite out of the blue—oh!' She looked up as she felt a hand on her shoulder and was intensely grateful to see it was Justin.

'May I have this dance, Lucy?'

'I'd be *delighted*,' she said and stood up with a flourish, adding under her breath, 'I really need to get away!'

But it wasn't until they'd joined the growing throng on the floor and he took her in his arms that he said with a smile lurking in his eyes but also something rather querying, 'Care to tell me why you needed rescuing so urgently?'

'Well, to be quite candid,' she replied, 'I was about to... It was Sasha,' she said ruefully. 'She has about as much tact as a tank!'

'What's she said now?'

Did that odd question mark in his eyes subside, she wondered then suddenly remembered Sasha's apology and the fact that she was leaving Justin. 'Oh, it was nothing,' she said.

'Lucy—'

'No, Justin, I'd rather not be trite and petty,' she said determinedly, then grinned up at him. 'Have you any idea how good a dancer I am?'

'You could always show me.'

She did, and she really let her hair down and soon the whole party caught her enthusiasm.

But what came as stunning little surprise to someone who could and had quite frequently danced the night away was how, just before midnight, she suddenly discovered she didn't want to be doing it any more and there was only one thing she did want to be doing but Justin was dancing with someone else, and she could only sit and stare helplessly at him as she thought of the way he made love to her or just held her in his arms when they went to bed.

And when he came back she responded mechanically to the conversation for a little while until he frowned slightly and stood up and made their farewells.

Of course there were the usual friendly remarks passed about 'the night being young but then so was their marriage', and more friendly raillery, when Lucy suddenly blushed brightly.

They didn't speak until they were home.

Then he led her into the bedroom and turned her to face him in the middle of the floor.

'Lucy?'

She winced.

He put a finger beneath her chin and made her look up. 'What's wrong?'

'Nothing...'

He raised his other hand and started to undo the little prancing horses. 'You could have fooled me.' He slid the gilet off.

'I just—didn't want to be there any more.'

'That was increasingly obvious.'

She grimaced, wondering if she'd caused another set of people to wonder seriously about her.

'On the other hand, if you wanted to be here, like this—' he reached for the zip of her skirt and it slipped to the floor '—there's nothing wrong in that.'

'You knew,' she accused, blushing again, and her body trembled.

His gaze was slightly amused as it roamed over her, wearing nothing now but a bra, a lacy suspender belt and equally lacy undies and sheer nylons, all blue, as she stepped over her skirt.

'I suspected,' he murmured.

'So did everyone else,' she said rather wretchedly and put her hands to her cheeks. 'How embarrassing.'

'There still nothing wrong in it. In fact, I'll go further.' He released her bra and drew it off her breasts. 'Don't change.'

'But I'll have to—I can't go around being so transparent!'

He laughed softly and put his hands round her waist. 'So long as I don't mind, that's all there is to worry about, my beautiful ch...' He stopped.

'Child?' she whispered. 'You must really think I am one now.'

He stared down at her naked breasts and the lovely curve of her hips, the delicate satiny softness of her skin. 'No, you're not, Lucy,' he said at last, 'and don't let me ever make you feel like one; you're just...you. Rather perfect, in fact.'

She wanted to ask him if he just meant her body or if it was the kind of perfection he could love, really love, as he'd loved Joanna. She desperately, she suddenly realised, wanted to ask him to be honest about Joanna Madden and ask him why he was subjecting her to this close contact, although, she supposed, the alternative would have been to leave her at Dalkeith and realistically she couldn't expect to avoid them forever. But something held her back, she couldn't really say what, other than the feeling that the ball was in her court now—she loved him, she was married to him and it was up to her to make the best of it, in other words. And at least one problem had resolved itself— Sasha. And yet, had it? Why was there this question mark in her mind about Sasha?

She sighed inwardly but said in a deep, husky little voice, 'Well, so are you.'

He smiled absently. 'No. Far from it, unfortunately, but—'

'Justin—' she reached out and placed her fingertips to his lips '—do you know why else I wanted to get away?'

'No.'

'I—seriously want to be alone with you for a while. Just us. We only seem to be together in a passing sort of way, don't we?'

'We don't exactly do this in passing, though. But I know what you mean—Lucy, I'm sorry about all this,' he said abruptly. 'And that includes Sasha, Joanna—'

'Did Sasha tell you?' Lucy asked, her eyes widening.

'Yes—'

'*I'm* sorry about that. I didn't—it really wasn't anything I did.' She hesitated, then added honestly, 'Other than being married to you.'

'I know.' He smiled, but it didn't reach his eyes and he moved his hands on her waist then pulled her into his arms. '*I* really didn't mean for it to be such a traumatic experience, marriage to me. And unfortunately, with Sasha leaving like this, I won't be able to do anything about the Seychelles for a little while, but as *soon* as possible, we will. In the meantime, though, at least we'll be at home alone together. How about that?'

She didn't have to tell him what she thought. It must have shown in her eyes.

But first thing in the morning came the news via the newspaper that Tim Madden had suffered a massive heart attack at the Breeder's Ball and was critically ill.

'Justin!' Lucy whispered, her face paling. They were in bed together and he'd made some tea and brought the paper up without unrolling it. And for a long moment they simply stared at the newsprint picture—the one of themselves and the Maddens with the Cawnpore filly. 'It must have happened after we left.'

Justin lifted his face and in spite of herself Lucy was shocked at the deep lines of tension scored into it. But before she could say any more the phone rang—it was Sasha, but it was difficult from his monosyllable replies to make much sense of it. And when he put the phone down he got out of bed immediately and started to pull some clothes on almost at random—jeans and a black T-shirt.

'What did she say?' Lucy asked.

He came to sit beside her and took her hands in his. 'She was there when it happened, Lucy. Apparently he's had a history of heart disease although very few people knew about it. Joanna is devastated and has no one to turn to. His family always resented him marrying someone so much younger, and she has no family of her own. Sasha has been with her all night but there's quite a bit of unpleasantness floating around. One of his sons actually accused Joanna of driving him to an early grave and tried to keep her from his bedside. He also made the accusation that spending so much money on the Cawnpore filly as a thrust in his private duel with me over her, was the *coup de grâce*. Lucy...'

'You have to go to her,' she whispered.

'Will you come with me?'

'I...no, Justin. Not this time.'

'Lucy—' He broke off and looked tortured for a moment. Then he said very quietly, 'It's *over* between us, just remember that.'

'I will, I promise,' she whispered. And he kissed her and held her hard. He also said, 'I love you, Lucy Waite.' And was gone.

She lay back and thought that it was probably true, in a way. She also lay and wondered what good his presence in the midst of the Madden family crisis would do. And she couldn't stop herself from wondering what would happen if Tim Madden died...

That day was the longest of Lucy's life as Tim Madden's life hung in the balance. Justin rang a couple of times but in between those times all she could do was think. And find herself going over everything in her mind, round and round in circles, and coming up with some surprises... Sasha, for example, who she had not known was an old friend of Joanna's and who had proved to be a good enough friend to support her during the awful night that had just passed. Sasha, who had admitted it was only after Joanna and Justin had broken up that she'd allowed herself to hope there could be a place for *her* in Justin's life. Sasha, Lucy thought, who so suddenly and surprisingly ended her little war with me but couldn't truthfully tell me why. Because she knows now, if she ever doubted it, that it's *still* Joanna she would have to fight for Justin in his heart if nothing else, not me?

She was sitting in the lounge staring into space when Justin came home. It was a dark overcast afternoon and she wore jeans and a long-sleeved cream silk blouse with her hair tied back in a blue ribbon. And her eyes were shadowed and wary as she stood up slowly when the door opened.

He came wearily into the lounge and she was shocked again to see the lines of tension in his face. Nor could she find any way to frame the query that was uppermost in her mind.

And his grey eyes ranged over, standing so still before he said quietly, 'He's going to be all right. The crisis is past but it will be a long, slow recovery.'

'Oh, thank God,' Lucy whispered, and sank down as her legs seemed to fold up beneath her.

He came to sit beside her on the settee, took her hand laid his head back wearily. And they simply sat like that for some minutes in silence. Until Lucy made herself say, 'How is Joanna?'

'All right now.'

'And the...his family?'

He sat up and pressed her hand before releasing it. 'They've come back to earth a bit; a lot of what was said was said under awful pressure.' He rubbed the blue shadows on his jaw wearily. 'Lucy—'

'Justin,' she said before he could go on and because she couldn't help herself, 'didn't they think it strange you should be there?'

He grimaced. 'It didn't exactly help at first, but I think I made them realise I was only there as an—intermediary. Joanna, you see—'

But Lucy stood up suddenly. 'You must be—would you like something to eat? You probably haven't had anything all day. I'll make us something now. How about a drink in the meantime? Stay there, I'll get it,' she said brightly, but to herself she was saying, I'm sorry, I know I brought it up but I can't talk about Joanna Madden any more, Justin, I just can't!

'Lucy—' He stood up, caught her wrist and for a moment towered over her, dark and powerful, and she trembled inwardly but didn't know that she looked both frightened and rebellious.

'Don't,' she stammered, not quite sure what she meant but suddenly sure it was all too much for her.

He paused, his eyes narrowed. 'Don't what, Lucy?' he said evenly after a long moment.

'I... I—let's just leave it, please, Justin.' Her voice shook but there was the sudden light of determination in her eyes. 'Let's just...pretend it's all over.'

'Lucy, it *is*, and—'

'Well, good! Now if you'll let me go I'll get us something to eat—really, Justin,' she tried to laugh, 'you're hurting me.'

He released her wrist abruptly then picked it up again and inspected the white marks of his fingers on it. Then he looked into her eyes and said drily, 'I'm only trying to reassure you, Lucy—'

'Oh, I'm reassured,' she broke in again. 'Is there any hope that we could go home now, by the way, Justin?'

He said after a tense moment, 'Tomorrow morning if you like—Lucy, will you come to Riverbend with me for a while?'

Her eyes widened. 'Why?'

'Because that's where I'll have to be for most of the time until I find a replacement for Sasha.'

'Well...' She hesitated, because in her heart she was dying to get back to Dalkeith.

'We could bring Shirley and Adrian from Dalkeith.'

'All right,' she said slowly.

'After all, it is your second home now and,' he grimaced, 'it certainly needs someone to take an interest in it.'

But although that was what they did, things were different.

CHAPTER NINE

I KNEW THIS wasn't a good idea, coming to Riverbend, Lucy thought a week later. Which was not to say there was anything lacking at Riverbend other than a little tender loving care, which Shirley was more than happy to provide. It was a more modern house than Dalkeith but still a pleasant, gracious home. But its relative unfamiliarity was unsettling in her mood of the moment, which alternated between a kind of numbness and a kind of grief that contrived to make her stiff and awkward with Justin, withdrawn and then trying too hard and altogether right off balance.

She would also look around the rooms at times, and wonder if Joanna had designed them… There are no ghosts at Dalkeith, she thought more than once, that's why I'd be better off there. But, there was no doubt Justin couldn't have been at Dalkeith at this time; it was the peak of the foaling season and without Sasha there was undoubtedly a mountain of work entailed in running the stud, not to mention the personal interest Justin took in the horses.

For not only did Riverbend run its own mares but it stood four stallions, each of which had a list of outside mares booked to it, and nearly all of these mares arrived to be served with a foal at foot and they had to be accommodated in pastures, they had to be served and kept on the property until they tested positive to the service and their foals had to be looked after as well.

She said once to Justin, 'It's like a production line! No sooner have they dropped their foals than they're put *in* foal again; it doesn't seem terribly fair to me.'

'But it can't be news to you either, Lucy,' he replied with a faint look of amusement.

'Well, no, it's not,' she confessed, 'but on *this* scale... I mean, we're all but swamped with mares and foals and...' She gestured helplessly. 'It's a logistical nightmare if nothing else.'

'I can only agree, at times,' he commented wryly. 'That's why Sasha was so good; she had the kind of brain and horse-sense that excelled in these circumstances.'

'Have you...have you heard what she's doing now?'

'Yes I have. She's got a job with the Magic Millions organisation.'

'Oh! You mean the Queensland sales where all the yearlings sold are eligible for the Magic Millions race?'

'None other. It should suit her eminently.'

'How are you going finding a replacement for her?' Lucy asked after a moment.

'I've had a flood of applicants. It will take a bit of whittling down.'

'Could I help in the meantime?' Lucy said suddenly. 'I... I need something to do.'

They were breakfasting together but Justin had been up all night with a foal that had got entangled in a fence. The fact of this, that they had so little time to spend together, was something Lucy didn't know whether she was glad about or not. Because, in truth, whatever had snapped within her that last afternoon in Sydney had stayed snapped, and she knew she was subtly holding Justin at arm's length, knew he knew, but perhaps the most heartbreaking aspect of it all was that he'd made no real effort to break down her defences.

Well, look, he's been incredibly busy and I can understand

why, she told herself a little drearily several times. All the same...

Which was not to say she hadn't shared his bed since that day, nor that he hadn't made love to her. But what she couldn't say in all honesty was that the thought that they might be interrupted by an emergency call from the stables, as did happen once when a very valuable mare got into difficulties foaling late one evening, was the real reason for her subdued, slightly tense response, although she'd offered it when she'd sensed he was about to say something. Offered it with a strained little smile then tried, too hard, to be bright and perky while she was feeling like dying within, and more so when he'd let it go...

'If you want to, Lucy,' he said at last, his grey eyes lingering on her.

'Yes, I do.' She realised immediately that she sounded defiant and stubborn, for no good reason probably, was cross with herself then tossed her head in a further gesture of defiance.

He said nothing as their gazes caught and clashed. Then, with an oddly dry inflection, he said abruptly, 'What's wrong, Lucy?'

'Nothing. Nothing in the world!' she answered brightly, and forced the tears that were so close to stay away. 'Where shall I start and what shall I do?'

She held her breath as she thought he was going to contest her statement, but although his mouth set in a rather hard line, he said unemotionally, 'There is something you could do. When the outside mares are delivered or picked up by their owners, it would be handy to have someone in the stud office who could give them a bit of a tour of the place, spend a bit of time with them—that kind of thing. It makes them feel wanted.'

Lucy's eyes widened with genuine interest. 'I think I'd like that,' she said slowly.

'I think you'd probably be good at it,' he commented.

'That would be a change,' she murmured, and bit her lip.

'Lucy—'

'No, Justin,' she sprang up and managed to grin at him, 'don't take any notice of me. I *do* know I'm very good at talking the hind leg off a donkey! Can I start today?'

'By all means,' he said, but after another lingering, narrowed look. Then he shrugged and stood up himself. 'I'm going to grab a few hours' sleep. I don't suppose you'd care to—join me?'

Her lips parted, her eyes widened and her heart started to beat erratically. But she said, 'I've not been…up that long, Justin. I mean…' She trailed off awkwardly.

He looked down at her enigmatically for an age then he touched the point of her chin gently and said, 'I know what you mean, Lucy. Never mind. Why don't you wander off to the stud office and—get started?' But there was a look of irony in his grey eyes that pierced her heart.

She hesitated then turned and walked away, her emotions in turmoil. What does he expect? she asked herself miserably. Surely he must *know* I can't help wondering what would have happened if Tim Madden had died, that I just can't stop thinking about it as well as everything else…

And for the next few weeks she threw herself into her newly created job as the flow of mares went both ways, incoming and outgoing. She also unexpectedly met an old friend, a young man who'd just qualified as a vet and was assisting their regular vet. He was a couple of years older but he'd been born in the district and they'd moved in the same crowd after she'd left school but only as friends. He was apparently delighted to meet her again and they had a few chats, recalling old times and laughing a lot. He was a tall, well-built, open-faced young man with a shock of blond curly hair and with one serious passion in his life, horses—Lucy gathered he had no romantic attachment at the moment. But in the uncomplicated pleasure she found in his company, she failed to notice that he looked at her occasionally with new eyes. It didn't occur to her for two reasons: because she wasn't looking for it and because she didn't imagine, now she was a married woman, that men would seriously think of her in those terms.

Nor would she ever have been aware of it if she hadn't one day been laughing over her shoulder at something he said as she walked past then looked ahead to see Justin watching them, standing curiously still.

She took an unexpected breath as she walked towards him, her eyes widening as he still made no move, but his grey gaze seemed to pierce hers for a blinding moment. Then at last he moved and said with a wry twist of his lips, 'Hi, Lucy. Having fun?'

'Yes—no, I mean... Justin?' She frowned at him. 'Is something wrong?'

'No, of course not, Lucy,' he said easily. But it was that evening he told her that he had to go to Sydney for several days...

'Lucy?'

'Oh! Justin.' She looked up with a smile from the brown study she'd been in since returning from the stables. 'I didn't hear you come in. Finished for the day?'

'Yes.' He threw down his hat and stretched. 'You're looking very pensive,' he remarked.

'I was feeling a bit pensive,' she confessed but added as she stood up, 'Dinner is actually ready but I'll tell Shirley to hold it for half an hour so you can have a shower. Would you like a drink?'

For a moment, his grey gaze roamed over her narrowly and she thought he was going to ask her what she'd been pensive about, but then a faint smile touched his lips and he turned away saying, 'I'd love one. I'll be back in ten minutes.'

And they had their dinner then took their coffee on to the terrace where a crescent moon laid a silvery glow over the landscape.

'Summer's really here,' Lucy murmured, and once again he

let his gaze drift over her, taking in her sleeveless white blouse and white cotton skirt splashed with yellow daisies.

'Mmm. It will be Christmas before we know where we are. Lucy, now that things have calmed down a bit, I have to go away for a few days—a week at the most. Sydney mainly, and all business. I've narrowed the applicants for Sasha's job down to two and I'll be seeing them but if you'd like to come—'

'No, thank you,' she said hastily, then forced herself to relax. 'There are still a few mares coming and going. I can keep on with my job here if you like.'

'It's what *you* would like,' he said, and there was something curiously watchful and narrowed in his eyes.

She frowned faintly. 'I know you keep asking me this but it seems to be my turn now—is something wrong? I've—' she paused '—known Rob Redding for years and years, if that...' She stopped and stared at him.

But he only, once again, said wryly, 'So have I. It makes me feel quite old. Good to see him qualified. I think he'll make a top vet from what I've seen so far. No, nothing's wrong, Lucy—as you keep telling me.'

She sat back and grimaced. 'I wondered if you thought I was being a *femme fatale* again.'

'No.' He was silent for a long while then he stretched and yawned. 'I don't know about you but I'm knackered, and I've got a crack-of-dawn start tomorrow.'

'Oh,' Lucy said with some concern. 'I promised Adrian I'd help him with a composition he's got to have in for the School of the Air tomorrow. He has to read it out over the radio.'

'Never mind,' Justin said, curiously gently, as he stood up. Then he bent over and kissed her briefly on the forehead. 'Goodnight, my dear. I'll try not to wake you in the morning and I'll ring you from Sydney.'

'Goodnight,' Lucy said in a strange little voice, and watched him walk away unhurriedly with a stabbing sense of grief in her heart.

* * *

It didn't go away over the next couple of days, that sense of grief, nor did her job, or Rob Redding, or even Adrian's getting an A for his composition mitigate it. All she could think of was lying stiff and silent beside Justin that night when she did go to bed, longing for him to wake up and take her in his arms, willing herself to reach out and touch him but not being able to do it as she wondered whether he would be seeing Joanna in Sydney…

Then came the proof that he had in the form of a picture in a two-day-old newspaper she normally wouldn't have bothered reading if Shirley, who was still avid for her hometown news however late it might be, hadn't left it on the kitchen table.

She stared down at it and drew in a long, shaky breath. Ever since they'd left Sydney, she realised, she'd longed to ask Justin for news of the Maddens, but it had seemed like tempting fate as well as establishing whether he'd been in touch—if he had, would she mind? And yet it was not unreasonable for him to do so, but… Well, he has now, she thought unhappily, and wiped away a foolish tear. For the picture that had captured her attention was one of Justin and Joanna, with his hand on her elbow, leaving the Sydney hospital where Tim Madden was still recovering, and it was dated the day after he had arrived back in Sydney two days ago. It also bore a simple but cryptic caption to the effect that the Waite-Madden feud appeared to have been halted in its tracks.

Why didn't he tell me? she wondered miserably. That it wasn't *all* business.

To make matters worse, she was out riding when he rang that day—he'd rung daily—so what she got was a message that he'd call early the next morning, and would she please make sure she was in the house? To explain? she wondered dully. He's left it a bit late, or perhaps he thinks the odds against my seeing it are pretty long. And why doesn't he ring back this evening when I'm *sure* to be here? Is he with…her? I don't know how much longer I can stand this uncertainty and torment.

And the next morning Justin explained nothing, nor did he mention the Maddens, but he did say he would be home the following day late in the afternoon, that he'd appointed Sasha's replacement, and asked her how she was.

'Fine. Fine!' she reassured him.

'Good. No other problems?'

'Not that I know of!'

'OK—see you tomorrow, Lucy.' And he rang off.

It was a moment before she put the phone down, and she said to it before she did so, I'm not terribly sure about that, Justin. Because, you see, I just don't think I can go on living with the thought of you and Joanna…any longer.

And two days later she sat in Mother Angelica's study at her old school, a room she was very familiar with and which was quite unchanged since she'd first come to know it at nine, and said jerkily, 'I need some advice—thank you for seeing me at such short notice, by the way, but I'm afraid I've got myself into a bit of a bind.'

Mother Angelica's hair was grey now beneath the short veil and there were new lines and wrinkles in her skin, but her tall, spare figure was the same and her keen blue eyes especially were as uncomfortably all-seeing as they'd ever been. 'So it would appear, Lucy,' she said thoughtfully. 'And talking of by-the-ways, I would have liked to know about your marriage at least; it would have been a courtesy if nothing else.'

Lucy sighed. 'No, it wouldn't. Because, you see, I married my worst enemy—or so I thought at the time. I married for all the wrong reasons, not to say *crazy* reasons only—then I fell in love with him and realised I'd probably *always* been a little in love with him but he loves someone else, someone he can't have, except that her husband nearly died a few weeks ago and if he had…well, I just can't stop thinking about it. You see, *if* he had, they could have been together again—if it weren't for me.'

'My dear child—' Mother Angelica began, but Lucy interrupted her.

'I'm *not* a child any more,' she said intensely, her eyes suddenly flashing blue fire in her white, weary face. 'That's how *he* thinks of me but I'm a living, breathing woman now. In all respects save one: I haven't had a child myself yet.'

'And you think that's what it takes?' Mother Angelica said quietly.

Lucy stared at her. 'What do you mean?' she said hollowly after a moment.

'Well, neither have I. But it's to me you've brought your problems, Lucy.'

Lucy grimaced. 'That's because you more or less brought me up, thankless task though it may have been, but—'

'On the contrary, Lucy. I always felt I was working with the finest material.'

'*What*?' Lucy whispered, her eyes now astounded.

'But what was more,' the nun went on in that same thoughtful, quiet way, 'despite our frequent conflicts, I always hoped that you acquired enough respect for me to benefit from my upbringing—however old-fashioned it may have seemed at the time.'

Lucy blinked several times then said hoarsely, 'Yes, I did. And yes, that's why I'm here, but—'

'Very well. Let's take this step by step, my dear—and I apologise for calling you a child.'

So that was what they did. And at the end Mother Angelica sat silent for a time then she said, 'I'm surprised at you, Lucy. I thought you had more spirit.'

Which was not what Lucy was expecting, and her eyes widened. 'Do you mean...?'

'I mean, if you really love this man, why aren't you fighting for him?'

Lucy actually laughed, although it was a pale imitation. 'You know,' she said, 'I came here all prepared for you to talk about the sanctity of marriage, but not this.'

'It's not a lot different,' Mother Angelica commented.

Lucy was silent for a moment, then she said painfully, 'But he does make me feel like a child sometimes and there are...' She stopped, then said awkwardly, 'And there are things between men and, well, women that are hard to explain—'

'Especially to a woman who has no experience of men in that way? I believe you,' Mother Angelica said, 'but I don't believe it should change one's morals or the things *you* believe in or be a cause to run away—does he know where you are?'

'No,' Lucy said distractedly. 'What did you mean about the things *I* believe in?'

'That you're a woman not a child, that you love him, have given yourself to him and are entitled to do all those things. But I wouldn't be saying this, Lucy,' Mother Angelica narrowed her eyes, 'if it didn't seem to me that you also respect him. Or if I felt he was some sort of bounder who had taken terrible advantage of a rather innocent young woman—which is how it would appear to a lot of people on the face of things.'

'I know, but that's not quite... It wasn't quite like that. As a matter of fact, I respect him as much as I do you,' Lucy said shakenly.

'Then you've forgiven him for marrying you the way he did?' There was an even more acute than normal little glint in those blue eyes now.

Lucy paused. 'I did have another option; I couldn't bring myself to take it, as I told you,' she said at last. 'What I didn't realise at the time was how difficult it would be to live with the thought of him loving someone else.'

'You haven't done it for very long.'

'No.'

'And apart from this feeling that he doesn't love you the way you love him, how has he treated you?'

'Very well—look, I'm not denying that he might love me in a

way,' Lucy said desperately. 'Or that he would ever stop taking care of me and all that. I don't even think he would dishonour me intentionally, although...' She stopped. 'It's just this awful feeling that I'm not his...soulmate, and she is.'

'Why don't you give him the benefit of the doubt? Men,' Mother Angelica said, 'can change their minds. We all can.'

Lucy sat in confused silence for about two minutes, then she said, 'Could I stay here just for a while?'

'Of course, but I do think you should get in touch with him in a day or two if you've run away and he doesn't know where you are.'

'You do?'

'Wouldn't it feel cowardly to hide away from him for any longer?'

'Well I suppose so...'

In the event she wasn't given the opportunity to do so for any longer by Justin either, but it was quite by accident that she over-heard what he and Mother Angelica had to say to each other when Justin arrived at the convent to look for her quite early the next morning. She *had* been with the junior boarders play-ing an early game of rounders; that was where Mother had left her when she was called away, following her obvious intention of not allowing Lucy to mope or brood in the plain, rather cell-like guest-room. The previous afternoon Lucy had been called upon to umpire a couple of tennis matches and in the evening she'd been roped in to play the piano at an end-of-year concert rehearsal, then have a late supper with that year's senior girls.

But in the middle of the rounders she'd been struck by a mix-ture of regret that things were no longer so simple for her and the urgent thought that she had to sit down somewhere peace-ful and private and *think*. She chose the little walled garden that was off limits to the girls and thus was new to her, without stopping to think that it was also directly below Mother An-gelica's first floor study.

There was a bench, a patch of lawn, a bird bath, creepers along the grey stone walls and a riot of roses. There was also, as she sat down and leant back in the early sunlight and closed her eyes, the sound of voices suddenly from above, quite distinct and very familiar...

'How do you do, Mother Angelica? I'm Justin Waite and I've come to enquire whether you've seen or heard anything about my wife who would have been known to you as Lucy Wainright of Dalkeith.'

Lucy swallowed and sat upright abruptly.

'Ah, Mr Waite! I have as a matter of fact been looking forward to having a few words with you. Please sit down.' There was a slight pause and the sound of a chair on wood. 'Now,' Mother Angelica continued in a voice Lucy recognised only too well, and her eyes widened, 'would you please be so good as to tell me *why* you took a girl as naïve and vulnerable as Lucy and forced her into a marriage of convenience? I can think of a very unpleasant name for the likes of you, you know.'

Lucy gasped.

'Is that what she told you, Mother Angelica?' There was the faintest suggestion of a drawl in Justin's voice, but it was mainly as hard and cold as the nun's.

'No, it is not what she told me. She apparently admires and respects you and indeed, thinks she *loves* you. So much so that she is prepared to leave you so that you and some other woman can be together again and be—soulmates,' Mother Angelica said with utter, icy contempt, then, 'I'm waiting, Mr Waite.'

'Madam,' Justin said softly but equally as icily, 'I have no intention of being soulmates with anyone other than Lucy, so—'

'Then how come she's not aware of this?' Mother Angelica broke in imperiously. 'How come this lovely child who was so radiant, so spirited even when she was so lonely at times, who made it a better day in most people's life even when she was being wayward, a child who is nevertheless completely *wholesome*—is like a broken flower now? Tell me that, Mr Waite?'

Lucy dropped her head into her hands and could have died.

'Look, Mother Angelica, just tell me where she is,' Justin said harshly. 'It may come as some surprise to you but I care as much about Lucy and her welfare as you do.'

'Then you have a strange way of showing it, Mr Waite.'

'Would you rather I'd abandoned her after her father died, ma'am?'

There was a little pause and the tension of it seemed to float down to where Lucy sat so that she raised her head—and waited.

'Why did you marry her, then—will you tell me that?' Mother Angelica said in a very slightly, less hostile voice.

'I'll tell you this—I have no thought of *corrupting* her if that's what you fear; I have only her best interests at heart. I too, you see,' he said with considerable irony, 'was aware from the start of not only her innocence but her vulnerability when her father died, her loneliness, the terrible burden of debt and so on she'd been left with. And if I may bring this to your notice, Mother Angelica, I've known her for even longer than you have, so I too know all about the quite—special person Lucy Wainright is.'

'Will you at least admit you haven't been able to make her happy, Mr Waite?'

Lucy twisted her hands until her fingers went white.

'So it would seem so far,' Justin said drily. 'That doesn't mean to say I'll stop trying. Is she still here?'

A pause then Mother Angelica said, 'Yes,' and went on in a different, thoughtful voice, 'If I've misjudged you in some ways, Mr Waite, I apologise. But I still must admonish you to banish all thoughts of this other woman from your mind, because I hold you entirely responsible for Lucy—do I make myself clear?'

'Eminently, Mother Angelica. It so happens I hold *myself* entirely responsible for her, so we are—in some agreement...'

Lucy heard no more, because she sprang up suddenly and ran to her room, where she started to pack hastily. But she wasn't quick enough, because there was a brief knock on the door— and Mother Angelica opened it with Justin just behind her.

'Lucy...what are you doing?'

Lucy cast one look at Justin from beneath her lashes and was shocked to see how pale and tired he looked before she rushed into speech. 'Packing. Hello, Justin. I... I didn't expect to see you. Oh what's the use?' she said under her breath and sank down on to the bed, 'Look, quite by accident I happened to overhear your conversation so I have to say some things— thank you for defending me the way you did, Mother, but I'm not quite such a broken flower as you imagine and—'

'*Lucy*!'

'It wasn't my fault, I just happened to be sitting in the garden below your window; I wanted to be somewhere quiet where I could think,' Lucy said tiredly, and turned to look at Justin properly for the first time. 'And thank you for feeling so responsible for me, but I probably know better than most how... impossible it is to banish someone from your thoughts unless there's no hope, and even then perhaps, so—'

'Mother Angelica,' Justin said quietly but quite compellingly, 'would you allow me to handle this on my own?'

The nun hesitated, then she went out and closed the door behind her.

'Justin,' Lucy said, 'don't think—'

'I'm not.'

'You don't know what I was going to say!' she objected after a moment.

'Was it along the lines of—don't think I'm coming back to you after what I overheard this morning?'

Lucy took a breath then sat down on the bed. 'Well, yes,' she said baldly, and added, 'If you must know, I was highly embarrassed this morning. How did you find me so quickly anyway?' she said exasperatedly.

'I remembered what you said about Mother Angelica once. I thought you might have—turned to her. But why embarrassed?' he queried.

'Because...because I felt as if I'd never left school, for one thing!' She subjected him to an indignant pansy-blue gaze.

'Some of the things you heard this morning are true, though, Lucy.'

She turned away, picked up a blouse and started to fold it on her lap. 'I know, I do know,' she said suddenly. 'I...it was one of the reasons I married you. I didn't know where else to turn, I didn't have the maturity to stand on my own, and now look at me: back here,' she said, barely audibly and with a rueful look around.

He smiled drily. 'With two people who love you nearly coming to blows over you this morning.'

Her eyes widened. 'She *wouldn't*!'

'She certainly looked as if she would have dearly loved to flatten me when I introduced myself.'

'Well—but that doesn't change things.'

'It does for me,' he said. 'That—and finding that you'd left me.'

'What do you mean?' Lucy whispered, and her heart started to beat erratically. 'Look, I have to tell you, I saw you and Joanna in the paper, holding hands! But in any case, since he nearly died—Tim—things have been different, and they were never quite right in the *first* place so—I couldn't help knowing you were thinking of what might have been. After all, you were the one she turned to. Then—' her voice cracked '—then this morning I had to listen to all those things you said about responsibility and vulnerability and innocence as if I were your *ward*, not your wife. How can you expect me to believe I'm really anything else to you, Justin?'

'I don't,' he said, 'not yet. But I'd like the opportunity to explain. Will you let me try to do that, Lucy?'

'H-how?' she stammered.

He grimaced. 'For one thing, not here. Will you come away with me now?'

'What if it doesn't—' she stopped to brush away a tear '—make sense to me?'

'Then I'll do whatever you want me to do—bring you back here, if you like.'

She hesitated. 'Well I have to warn you I'm no longer a pushover, Justin. Nor am I a broken flower.'

He was silent, just watching her as she sat straight-backed on the bed, her chin tilted although her eyes were still wet, and there were tired faint blue shadows beneath them. Then he moved as if to ease some mental burden and said, 'You never were, Lucy. Should we perhaps—get some breakfast? It's about that time.'

'Not if you live here; I've had breakfast *and* a round of rounders,' she said with a sudden faint smile, though sobering almost immediately.

'Coffee, then?' he suggested.

'All...all right, but...' She gestured almost futilely.

'I'd better make it good,' he said with a sudden touch of humour.

Lucy caught her breath, but said bravely, 'Yes.'

CHAPTER TEN

JUSTIN DROVE HER to the Rocks and chose a restaurant over-looking Circular Quay with an open veranda where they had the Sydney Harbour Bridge almost overhead, the sails of the Opera House rising across the Quay and the waters of the harbour dancing before them in the morning sunlight. And he went inside to place their order, taking quite a few minutes.

Not that Lucy minded; she was trying desperately to get herself together and even wished he'd been away longer when he and the waiter arrived together with orange juice, a pot of coffee and two waffles spread with syrup and heaped with ice-cream.

And she said quite spontaneously, 'Oh, dear! I don't know if I can fit it in.'

'Try,' Justin murmured, sitting down opposite her. 'Look upon it as brunch; that's what I'm doing.'

And they ate in silence for a while until he pushed his plate away and poured the coffee. 'Lucy—'

'Justin…'

They spoke together, and he smiled slightly and said, 'Go ahead.'

'No.' She pushed her plate away and wiped her mouth. 'I'm not sure what I was going to say anyway.' She shrugged desolately.

'All right. Lucy, you were right about Joanna—once. When she left me and married Tim, a kind of blackness came over me and I swore I would never forgive her, or him.' He paused and watched her searchingly, 'And, while it *wouldn't* have been true to say it didn't matter whom I married after that, it was not a true marriage that I offered you.'

Lucy closed her eyes then made herself take a sip of coffee. 'Go on,' she said in a gruff little voice.

'But it *was* nevertheless a gesture prompted by all those things that Mother Angelica and I catalogued so embarrassingly for you this morning. In other words, I did care very much about what became of you, not only Dalkeith, and I did know how much Dalkeith meant to you and I did mean to... always have your best interests at heart. Unfortunately—' he paused and stared into the middle distance for a moment then returned his grey gaze to her with something bleak and sombre in it '—certain things happened unexpectedly, as you know, and while I would never have gone out of my way to flourish you at Joanna, when it happened I couldn't help feeling—a certain sense of revenge.'

'Go on,' she whispered.

'But—' He stopped and looked at her white face. 'When I realised that, it very quickly changed to a feeling of remorse and I came very close, when you offered to make our marriage a real one, to letting you go.'

'I wish you had,' she whispered, then her eyes widened. 'Well, you did try, didn't you? That night. I wouldn't take you up, though...oh...'

'Lucy, don't blame yourself for that, blame me,' he said harshly. 'I could have done it if I'd set my mind to it.'

'Why...why didn't you?' she stammered.

His grey eyes held hers. 'Because I found I didn't really want to.'

'So you could go on avenging yourself?'

'No. So I could really have you.'

'But...but why?' She stared at him bewilderedly.

'It had become a matter of growing urgency for me, that's why, Lucy.'

She sat in stunned silence for a moment then said, 'Because you're a man and not a monk sort of thing?'

His lips twisted into a dry little smile. 'You've accused me of that once before. No. Because of *you*. An enchanting, sometimes wayward source of increasing fascination for me in every way, including the most intimate way—that's why I did it.'

'Are you trying to tell me you started to fall in love with me, Justin?' she said with difficulty.

'You've hit the nail on the head, Lucy,' he agreed.

'I don't know if I can believe you...'

'I think you should try.'

'But look here—' she sat up agitatedly '—it didn't stop you treating me like a child sometimes—don't you remember what happened that night in the twelve-mile?'

'Very well, as a matter of fact. May I point out that it didn't stop me from treating you like a woman either?'

Lucy sat back and felt the colour rising from the base of her throat but with an effort, tried to compose her thoughts. 'Well, it didn't blot Joanna out entirely, though, did it?' she said huskily. 'I know because,' she paused, 'for one thing I saw how you and Tim looked at each other after the sale of the Cawnpore filly, and there could be only one reason for you two to feel so hostile towards each other, couldn't there? Joanna,' she said miserably.

'No, it didn't blot out Joanna *immediately*, Lucy,' he said and unexpectedly reached across the table and put his hand over hers. 'But that was partly habit, I suspect, and mostly a sense of remorse towards *her* by then. You see, seeing us together, sensing my frame of mind that day they flew into Riverbend to look at the filly, opened it all up for Joanna again. And I began to wonder if I was some sort of monster, letting her see that flash of revenge so that it all came back to her at the same time as I was falling in love with you.'

'Did she tell you this?' Lucy queried very quietly. 'That it had all opened up for her again?'

'Yes, but not until the day after Tim nearly died.'

'But you knew it was happening to her all the same?'

'Yes, I guessed,' he said and both his voice and eyes were completely sombre. 'The kind of thing that in my black days I'd dreamt of planning, only to find a growing horror when it happened quite unplanned. And I guess most of the hostility I felt towards Tim Madden then was motivated by something you put into words once. How could he put Joanna through it, all over a horse? Which was why I was glad he had to pay so much for it in the end.'

'Oh,' Lucy said on a breath. 'But that still leaves—I mean, you still *cared* about her otherwise…not that I mind, I mean… I don't know what I really mean except that Joanna Madden is very hard to hate,' she said frustratedly. 'And she did turn to you—'

'She didn't,' he said drily. 'Sasha did that without Joanna even knowing, which was just the kind of thoughtless thing Sasha was so prone to doing. Joanna was actually horrified when I turned up at the hospital, horrified and terribly guilty. Because she blamed herself for Tim's heart attack, you see.'

'Why? And if so, why did you stay with her nearly all day?' Lucy whispered.

He moved his fingers on hers. 'I stayed because she *didn't* have anyone else to turn to and once the damage was done, I couldn't stand by and not try to bring some sanity to the situation.' He paused. 'Why did she feel guilty? Because Tim knew what she was going through too, perhaps he'd even deliberately brought her to Riverbend to find out if she'd got over me—I don't know, but I'm quite sure it was his perhaps subconscious shot in *our* war, buying the Cawnpore filly for such a high price. I think he was trying to prove something to Joanna.'

'I see…oh, yes, I see,' Lucy said, her eyes widening. 'So

they were right, his children, after all?' She stared at him with her lips parted.

'Partly right,' Justin agreed grimly. 'What they didn't know was that by then what I felt for Joanna was an affection I probably will always hold but that I was no longer in love with her, and never had been in love with her the way I love you. The other thing they didn't know was that the shock of seeing Tim at death's door had opened Joanna's eyes to her love for him.'

Lucy sat staring at him, absolutely arrested. Then she said shakily, 'Do you really believe that?'

'Yes, I do. In fact, that picture you saw, which I wasn't even aware had been taken until Shirley showed it to me because she'd seen you looking at it with tears in your eyes—that picture was the final chapter. I went to see Tim with Joanna and together we told him all this, but I *only* did it because he'd had a relapse just after I arrived back in Sydney and she was desperate enough to contact me and beg me to do it. I think we got through to him. And I wasn't holding her hand as such; she'd tripped on an uneven tile and I stopped her falling, that's all. We parted outside the hospital.'

'But why—Justin, did you know how Joanna felt the day after Tim's heart attack?'

'Yes.'

'Why didn't you tell me?' Lucy whispered. 'How could you tell Tim and not me?'

'Lucy, when I came back from the hospital the day after Tim's heart attack I wanted nothing more than to do so. But—' he paused and looked deep into her stricken eyes '—you went away from me. You made it quite clear you didn't want to hear any more on the subject. You even looked...repelled by it all. And I thought it was too late, that I'd lost you and I didn't deserve any better because I'd been such a bloody fool for so long. I thought, why would you want to go on being involved with me after all I'd done? I felt, to put it mildly, as guilty as hell as I watched you withdraw further and further from me. Then I saw you and Rob

Redding, I saw you laughing again, becoming in his company your old, natural, lovely—it's hard to put it into words—self. And I saw the way he looked at you and I thought…how much better it would be for you to be loved by someone with no dark past, someone young and uncomplicated—'

'Justin,' Lucy broke in urgently, 'yes, I did go away from you, although not because I was repelled but because I couldn't stop thinking about what might have happened if Tim had died, and wanting to die myself out of sheer misery. You see,' she dashed at the tears brimming in her eyes, 'you don't know this but Sasha… Sasha seemed to confirm my worst fears just the night before at the dance.' She told him what Sasha had said and how it had all seemed to add up to the fact that Sasha genuinely believed it wasn't over between him and Joanna. 'Then, when it was Sasha who rang up…' She stopped and the tears fell unchecked now.

'I might have known,' he said grimly, and closed his eyes briefly. 'You were right, why I put up with her I'll never know. But she was wrong.'

'She did apologise for all the things she'd said before,' Lucy said involuntarily.

He looked at her piercingly, 'Such as?'

'Oh, Justin,' Lucy looked away, 'I don't think there's much point—Sasha…was Sasha, I guess.'

'Do you—believe what I've told you this morning, Lucy?'

'I…' She bit her lip and swallowed, wondering if she dared to believe it.

'But there's more,' he said very quietly. 'When I got back to Riverbend and you were gone, when I confronted Mother Angelica and came close to hating a nun of all people because she thought she loved you and understood you more than I did, I knew then I could never let you go, Lucy, even if I believed you'd be better off with someone like Rob Redding. I just—in the end, couldn't do it.'

Lucy stirred. 'This morning you said you'd take me back to the convent if I wanted it.'

'Do you?' he queried quietly. 'I was hoping to persuade you to give me a second chance. I was hoping if I told you all this and told you how you've grown into my heart and life so that I'll be lost and lonely for the rest of it without you, you wouldn't want to. I was hoping to be able to prove to you that we are soulmates.'

But although he looked deep into her eyes, Lucy twisted her hands and said disjointedly, 'I want... Justin, I want to believe you with all my heart but...'

She stopped and became aware of a droning noise overhead, then aware of some of the waiters and some passers-by stopping and looking upwards and starting to smile and gesticulate, so she looked up herself and saw a light plane flying over the harbour bridge flying a banner. A banner that said in high, rather hastily painted letters by the look of it but quite clearly all the same, 'I LOVE YOU, LUCY. JUSTIN'.

She choked, looked upwards incredulously again then turned to him and whispered urgently, 'Justin, is it really true?'

'If you let me, I'll spend the rest of my life proving it to you, my darling Lucy,' he answered, and then she was in his arms and everyone's attention turned to them as it became clear to all and sundry who Justin and Lucy were, and people started to cheer and applaud.

'I think we ought to get out of here,' he said into her hair.

'Oh, yes, please,' she said. 'Oh, no! Do you think it will get into the papers again?'

'I hope it does,' he replied, and added with a grin. 'It would also make my day if Mother Angelica were to see it. Let's go.'

'How did you arrange it?' she asked laughingly as they were ushered into a suite at the Regent very close by.

'When I went to order the waffles. I rang a friend of mine who owns the plane. He gives flying lessons and trails banners and was just about to take-off, fortunately—although I'm afraid he thought I'd gone mad.'

'I should get in touch with Mother Angelica,' Lucy said sobering. 'Actually, I got the surprise of my life when she verbally attacked you this morning, because her advice to me had been to fight for you if I really loved you, you know, Justin.'

'Was it?'

'Yes—that's strange, isn't it?'

'Not so strange if she'd perceived that you do really love me.'

Lucy grimaced. 'I don't think anyone ever doubted that— Justin,' she breathed as he suddenly held her very hard.

'Sorry. I don't know how I could have been such a bloody fool, that's all.'

'Should we...should we go to bed, then?' she suggested. 'It might stop you feeling like that.'

He lifted his head and she caught her breath at the blaze of love she saw in his grey eyes as well as the laughter.

'Did I say something wrong?'

'No. Oh, no. Lucy, another thing you said once was that you'd rather you were married to someone with no experience but who loved you so much it didn't matter—that's how I feel right at the moment. Delighted, devoted, renewed—and dying to go to bed with you.'

'That's lovely,' she said softly, and moved in his arms.

They made love twice before lunch and spent the afternoon in bed recuperating, as Justin put it. They watched a movie on television holding hands but at about four o'clock he went into the adjoining sitting-room and made a couple of phone calls, telling her just to be patient when she asked about it. Half an hour later there was a knock at the door and he brought into the bedroom a large box and a slim envelope.

'What's this?' Lucy asked.

'Open it, the box first.'

So she did and discovered two dozen bikinis inside. 'But—'

she stared at the colourful throng dazedly then lifted her eyes to his '—if this is what I think it is, I only need a couple.'

'What do you think it is?'

'The Seychelles?' she hazarded.

'More or less. Open the envelope.'

So she did and this time her eyes nearly fell out of her head. '*Justin...*'

'What do you think? We've missed the QEII here but we pick her up in Singapore then cruise to the Seychelles, Mombasa, Durban, Capetown, so you could well need more than two bikinis—hey,' he said softly, 'don't cry.' And drew her into his arms.

'I'm not. I mean, I am, but only from happiness. Do you remember saying something to *me* about romantic gestures—well, yours are the very best!'

'Well, my first one wasn't the most original, but perhaps I'm learning,' he commented, and kissed her leisurely. Whereupon they made love once more and then he had dinner and a bottle of champagne sent up.

'I still don't need two dozen,' Lucy remarked with an impish little smile, later.

'I know. I had an ulterior motive there, I'm afraid,' he drawled. 'I ordered them on approval so you could try them all on and select the ones you liked. With my help,' he added gravely.

'Ah,' Lucy murmured then laughed.

He raised a wry eyebrow at her. 'That amuses you?'

'No, it delights me actually, and very shortly I shall do just that, try them all on, but first of all I think I'll do this.' And she leant over and kissed him fleetingly on the mouth. 'Thank you. For everything,' she said a little shyly.

'Lucy—' he caught her wrist then pulled her on to his lap '—God knows I feel guilty enough about you as it is—'

'Justin, don't say that,' she whispered. 'It will make me start to wonder again if—'

'Then let me tell you this,' he said quietly, holding her against him gently. 'I have a vision of my life now that's inextricably linked with yours. I'll always have the memories of the beautiful girl who became a woman in my bed and told me she felt… translated, and I know I'll want to keep on translating her for the rest of my life. As well as living in love and laughter with her, as well as fathering her children, as well caring for her—and receiving the special sort of sunlight you bring to me, Lucy.' He tilted her chin and stared deep into her eyes. 'There is only one way to say it. I love you, I love your body and your soul and I can't live without you; it's as simple as that…'

If she had any last doubts they were dispelled the next morning when they went to see Mother Angelica together.

'Ah,' that wise nun said as they stood before her together in the study that hadn't changed for so many years, 'you've resolved it. Mr Waite, I *was* rather hard on you yesterday but one thing in the end convinced me that you loved Lucy and that was the look of inexpressible relief that came into your eyes when I told you she was still here safe with me. God bless you, my dears, and don't you dare have any christenings without me!'

And to Lucy's joy things like that kept happening, little touches of proof. Such as the occasion on their delayed honeymoon aboard the pride of the Cunard Line somewhere in the Indian Ocean between the Seychelles and Mombasa. It was a formal evening and she'd dressed in a strapless midnight-blue evening gown that moulded her figure and had a slit up the front, and put her hair up.

But she had to return to their state room when her tights laddered and it took about twenty minutes to change them and assure herself she was perfectly presented again. When she returned, Justin, looking magnificent in a black dinner suit, was standing with a group of people all superbly groomed, indeed he was flanked by two stunning women who seemed to be vying for his attention. And Lucy's heart missed a beat as she saw, as she approached, the distant, shuttered look on his face, something that had been missing these past few weeks. And when he looked up into her eyes, for a moment his own were moody and disenchanted.

Then they changed and he excused himself briefly and came towards her almost as if he was heading her off.

'Is something wrong?' she whispered.

'Yes. Come outside.' He put a hand on her elbow and steered her out onto the deck, and kept steering her until they reached a secluded area with no one around. 'This.' And he took her in his arms.

'But...but why?' she asked minutes later when she'd been thoroughly and urgently kissed. 'Not that I'm complaining...'

'I missed you,' he said simply. 'I couldn't work out why you were taking so long, particularly as everyone was asking me where my gorgeous, sensational wife was. I wondered if you'd fallen overboard—or found another man.'

'Justin!' she breathed her eyes wide and stunned.

'Moreover, Lucy,' he continued and while his eyes were amused there was something else lurking in their grey depths. 'I need to be reassured.'

Her lips parted. 'How...do you mean right now?'

'Indeed I do, Mrs Waite.'

'Like this?' she said not much later but in the seclusion of their state room, and reached for the zip of her dress.

But he stilled her hand as he stood before her, his dark head inclined, and murmured, 'Just so. May I?'

And he released her hair first and ran his fingers through its golden length and then undressed her item by item until there were only her new tights over brief silk panties. He laid her on the bed and drew them off slowly letting his fingers lie cool and firm on the inside of her thighs until she moved with desire and said his name in a grave, husky little voice.

Then he ripped his own clothes off and lay down beside her and took her with a lack of finesse that he apologised unevenly for, but an unmistakable hunger that told its own tale and took her to heights she'd never reached before.

And in the sweet, drowsy aftermath of their love, she cradled his head to her breasts, and felt herself to be Justin Waite's true partner in all things.

'I don't know what got into me,' he said after a while with her now lying in his arms, as he stroked her hair. 'But when I looked up and saw you coming back at last, so...utterly lovely, I just knew I had to do this very shortly.'

'I'm glad you did,' she said and drew her fingertips down his face. 'If I thought I'd been—translated before, it was nothing to this.'

He laughed quietly and hugged her gently. 'We've missed dinner.'

'It's well lost. I love you.'

'Even after—wrecking you like that?' he said wryly.

'More so, and—' Lucy paused, then sat up and looked down at him wickedly, '—you're also the man who flew a banner over Sydney harbour telling me you loved me, don't forget.'

'The second man—is it any wonder I could get a bit paranoid at times?' he replied lazily, his eyes on her pink-tipped breasts.

'The only man. For me,' she said firmly, and lay down again.

'So you do...believe me now, Lucy?' he said in a different voice as he took her into his arms again.

She turned her face to his and laid her cheek on his chest. 'Yes, Justin. Is it...is it so important to you?'

'The most important thing in the world,' he said very quietly.

'Well, you're the most important thing in the world to me, so it's worked out astonishingly well, in fact.'

'Yes, it has. Thank God, it has.'

* * * * *

The Unexpected Husband

CHAPTER ONE

'OF COURSE I don't want to go to bed with you!' Lydia Kelso said.

Joe Jordan stared at the woman who had just rejected his offer with such stinging contempt, and he registered mental surprise tinged with amusement. Surprise because Lydia Kelso was as different from her sister as chalk from cheese...

She had an unruly mane of sun-streaked dark fair hair that looked as if she didn't bother to torture it into any kind of style. Her skin was smooth and her eyes a deep velvety blue. Whilst she didn't have immediately turn-your-head kind of looks, that lovely skin, the delicately cut yet severe pair of lips, as well as her stunning eyes, redeemed her to a rather unusual attractiveness. She wore no make-up at all.

Her neck was long and elegant—so was the rest of her: tall and almost boyishly rangy beneath a pinstriped navy trouser suit she wore with black leather loafers. Her shoulders were straight and her hands were narrow yet capable-looking, with short, unpainted nails, and she wore a man's signet ring on the little finger of her left hand and a man's watch.

Whereas her sister Daisy was drop-dead gorgeous, with dark hair, true violet eyes and a sensational figure...

He shrugged, raised an ironic eyebrow at Lydia Kelso, and murmured, 'I asked because that was the proposition your sister put to *me* when we first met. I thought it might run in the family.'

'You should never generalise about people, even when they come from the same family, Mr Jordan,' she said coldly.

'Does that mean you don't approve of your own sister?' he asked wryly.

Lydia took a breath and subsided somewhat. Then she moved her hands and decided to be honest. 'I don't approve of you,' she said flatly.

'We've only just met,' he pointed out, with open amusement in his eyes now.

'Your reputation precedes you, however, so—'

'All right.' He sat up straighter and reached for his pen. 'Tell me exactly what you know about me, Lydia Kelso. We may then be able to sort the wheat from the chaff.'

Lydia looked around Joe Jordan's colourful studio and reflected that she could have been outmanoeuvred. At the same time she took in the posters on the wall, the books and magazines overflowing from a whole wall of honey pine bookshelves, the polished timber floor with a slightly ruckled rug in jewel-bright ruby swirls on a yellow background. There were two computers on the table behind him, an easel, a skylight above, and a particularly healthy Kentia palm flourishing in a wicker basket in one corner.

Then she looked back at him across the wide expanse of his untidy desktop, saw the challenge in his eyes and stiffened her spine.

All the same, it took her a few moments to compose her mental processes. Because it had been one thing to think dark thoughts about this man in his absence, but being confronted by him, and suddenly able to see what Daisy had obviously seen in him, made it a slightly different matter.

He wasn't, as she'd expected, to-die-for handsome. On first impressions, that was. She found herself amending the thought. He had thick, straight sandy-brown hair, hazel eyes, a smattering of freckles, and golden hairs glinted on his arms beneath the rolled up sleeves of his khaki bush shirt as a mote of sunlight came in through the skylight. He wore his bush shirt with blue jeans and brown desert boots.

So what was it? Well, he was tall enough—tall enough even for her. Lean, yes, but with wide shoulders, well-knit...

A smile touched her mouth as she wondered exactly what that meant. If it meant all in proportion, with a well-balanced look and the hint of smooth, easy strength beneath his outline, that was exactly the impression Joe Jordan gave. But he was also—interesting, she decided. In a way that was hard to define. You couldn't help gaining the impression that here was a man it could be exciting to know, especially if you were a woman...

She shook her head, reminded herself of his offer to take her to bed although they'd only just met—her blue eyes blazed at the memory—and said, 'We all know how clever you are, Mr. Jordan. One of the better known cartoonists in the country, but—'

'Why would you hold that against me, assuming it's true?'

'Because you have the ability to make people look stupid?' she countered sweetly.

'Only when they deserve it,' he responded mildly.

'Ah, but who's to say your judgement of whether they deserve it or not is always accurate?'

Joe Jordan frowned and sat forward. 'Have I offended someone you know?'

'No. But you can't deny it would be possible.' Lydia gazed at him seriously.

He shoved a hand through his brown hair, leaving it standing up in spikes. 'And that's cause to disapprove of me in regard to your sister?' he queried sardonically.

'That's cause for *me* to have reservations about you, Mr Jordan,' Lydia said precisely. 'It's your playboy reputation I fear in regard to my sister. Can you deny that you're often seen escorting beautiful women around?'

'Lydia, you wouldn't be a tad jealous of your very lovely and

feminine sister, by any chance?' he asked smoothly. 'This—'
he gestured towards her, managing to convey that she wasn't
particularly feminine '—has the taint of sour grapes about it,
if you'll forgive me for saying so.'

Lydia smiled with genuine amusement. 'Not in the slightest,
Joe! I hope that doesn't disappoint you. But the fact of the matter is, my sister has plans that you may be unaware of, plans
that might not feature on your agenda at all.'

'Such as marriage plans,' he said wearily. 'Look, I can—'
But he stopped at the sudden look of searing contempt in Lydia's eyes.

'You can—take care of yourself?' she suggested gently. 'I'm
sure you can.'

'Bloody hell,' he muttered, and rubbed his jaw. 'Daisy and I
have made no commitments whatsoever, Miss Kelso,' he added.
'So if you're imagining I've led her up the garden path, you're
wrong,' he finished flatly, then frowned. 'Isn't she your *older*
sister?'

'Daisy is twenty-nine going on nineteen. I'm twenty-six.
What you may not understand, Mr Jordan, and I can't blame you
for this, is…' Lydia paused and wondered how best to explain.

'Do go on, I'm agog,' he murmured with considerable irony.

'OK. Our father is a poet. Our mother, a pianist, died when
we were little and we were raised by an aunt. She's my father's
sister and she's a sculptress—'

'An artistic family,' Joe Jordan commented, looking only
one step away from utter boredom as he doodled desultorily.
'Daisy plays the violin—I can't wait to find out what you do,
Miss Lydia Kelso! Wrestle the double bass?'

'Oh, I'm quite different,' Lydia said flippantly. 'I'm a vet.'

She had the satisfaction of seeing sheer surprise in his hazel
eyes. He said slowly, now looking at her rather intently, 'So?
Where does all this lead?'

'I'm the only one of the family who is not in the least artistic
and happens to have her feet planted squarely on the ground.'

'Are you saying your whole family is mad?' He blinked at her.

'Not at all. But I can't deny they can be quite—eccentric and naive at times, then madly passionate at others, and, well, given in those moments to doing some rash things. Otherwise they're warm and wonderful and I would kill rather than see them get hurt.' Lydia folded her hands in her lap and looked at him serenely.

'What...' Joe Jordan could have killed himself for the slightly nervous way he said the word '...um—rashness has Daisy concocted towards me? I gather that *is* the problem?'

Lydia smiled at him. 'At least you're quick on the uptake, Mr Jordan. I'll tell you. She's decided to have your baby, with or without the benefit of wedlock.'

Joe Jordan's jaw dropped involuntarily, although he snapped it shut immediately. But before he could utter the cynicism he was prompted towards—*I've heard that one before!*—Lydia went on.

'At the moment she's rather in favour of *out of wedlock*, I have to tell you. I think she looks at herself and sees Jodie Foster, Madonna—there are quite a few famous single mums around—and when you're as devoted to your career as Daisy is, it's certainly easier if you only have a child to worry about. She also adores kids, and although twenty-nine is not old, she's not getting any younger.'

'Why me?' Joe Jordan asked faintly, after a long pause.

Lydia smiled quite warmly at him this time. 'You should feel complimented. She's gone into it very seriously, so she tells me, and she feels that you may contribute the brains she—not exactly lacks, but you're obviously *very* clever.'

Joe Jordan stood up and planted his fists on the desk. 'I said this before but—bloody hell! So that's why she suggested going to bed when...' He let the sentence hang unfinished in the air, and had to suffer Lydia Kelso looking at him with obvious sympathy—something that annoyed him all the more. 'Are you sure you're not making all this up?' he said then, through his teeth.

'Quite sure.'

'What if I did decide to marry her?'

'I'd be only too relieved, Mr Jordan,' Lydia said sincerely. 'Provided you love her, of course. She really needs someone to look after her, especially if she has a child, and I can't always be there. You know, she'd make a wonderful wife.'

'How can you say that?' he demanded bitterly. 'You've just led me to believe she's as mad as a March Hare! Something the whole Kelso clan could suffer from, if I'm not mistaken, despite your assertion to the contrary,' he added pointedly.

'Look,' Lydia responded coolly, 'it's not that I approve, necessarily, but it's a choice a lot of women are making—and not because they're mad but because they deem it a viable option in today's society, where women can aspire to having careers and continuing to have them instead of retreating to the kitchen sink once they start a family.'

'Go on,' he ordered tersely.

She shrugged. 'Some can cope with it, but I don't think Daisy would be one of them. And, whilst a lot of mistakes you make in the heat of the moment can be corrected, a fatherless child is not one of them.'

Joe Jordan sat down, propped his chin in his hands and considered that this rangy twenty-six-year-old girl knew how to pack her punches. She shot from the hip and was unusually mature, perhaps. 'You said you didn't necessarily approve—apart from Daisy. Why not?'

'I happen to believe a child needs both its parents. Of course it can't always be helped, as in my own case. And it's not that being a natural parent makes one automatically a *perfect* parent. But at least if you have kinship with a child it has to help.'

Joe raised his eyebrows thoughtfully. 'It so happens I agree with you. Nor would I countenance being used as a stud. Do you happen to know whether Daisy intended to put me in the picture? Or did she plan to disappear out of my life with a little bundle of joy I was never to know about?'

'It's the one thing that's causing her a bit of a problem,' Lydia said gravely. 'Well, there are two. While she feels she may be in love with you, she can't be sure that you are with her. If you were, then I'm sure she'd abandon all this nonsense.'

'I'm speechless,' Joe Jordan remarked with considerable feeling.

'Would you like to tell me exactly what you do feel for Daisy?' Lydia suggested.

'No! That is,' he corrected himself irritably and ironically, 'I have no intention of marrying her. I have to be honest. Or *anyone* at the moment,' he said moodily. 'But—look, this has been a light-hearted—I couldn't even call it an affair. She was the one who...dammit!' He glared at Lydia.

'Well, now you know why. But you must have liked her? Or do you pop into bed with every woman who indicates they're willing?' She eyed him innocently.

He swore, seriously this time.

Lydia waited, looking absolutely unruffled.

He gritted his teeth. 'I like her. She's fun to be with, she's extremely decorative, but...' He groped for the right words, then sighed savagely.

'You don't miss her when she's not there?'

He narrowed his eyes. 'Is that a true test? You sound as if you...know what you're talking about.'

'I got married when I was twenty,' Lydia said quietly. 'We had a year together before he was drowned in a boating accident. That's how it happened for me. He was always on my mind. Tucked into the background at times, yes, but always there.'

Joe Jordan swallowed visibly and looked discomforted.

Lydia went on before he could formulate any words. 'Please don't feel you need to apologise for anything you may have implied. Nor did I tell you to make you uncomfortable—'

'Then why?' he interrupted. 'And how come you use your maiden name?'

Lydia stood up. 'My husband's name was also Kelso, although we were not related at all. It was one of those strange coincidences because it's not very common. As to why I told you—it was to establish my credibility, I guess. This is not sour grapes, and I do have some experience in these matters.'

'So what do you suggest I do?' He lay back and eyed her narrowly.

'I'll leave that up to you, Mr Jordan. But if you do what I think you intend to—let her down lightly, please.'

'I gather you'll be there to pick up any pieces?'

Lydia hesitated briefly. 'I'm just about to start a position on a cattle station. It's only temporary—I'm filling in for a friend while he takes leave—so, no. However, my father and my aunt are in residence at present. Now, my father,' she said, with a faint smile touching her mouth, 'may not be quite as civilised as I've been should Daisy be inconsolable.'

Joe Jordan stood up with disbelief written in every line of his face. 'Is that a threat?'

'Oh, I don't think he'd do you any bodily harm. But he might come and harangue you, that kind of thing.'

'I don't believe this!' He thumped his fist on the desk, then doubled up in pain clutching his shoulder.

Lydia blinked, then moved around the desk with her boyish stride. 'Can I help?'

'No, you can't! I'm a human being. Why would I need a bloody vet?'

Of course it was surprise, he figured out, that had allowed him to be overpowered by a woman. Mind you, he told himself, she was quite strong, even unusually strong, because he'd ended up back in his chair with her long, capable hands massaging and gently manipulating his neck and shoulder in a way that brought him almost instant relief.

'How did it happen?' she asked conversationally.

He sighed. 'I was playing tennis and pulled a muscle. Just takes time, so they say. How...you did tell me you were a vet, didn't you?' he enquired bitterly.

Lydia laughed down into his upturned face. 'Animals also have muscles, tendons and nerves. I specialise in horses and I've done quite a lot of work with racehorses and polo ponies; they often pull muscles. There. What you need is regular physiotherapy, probably.'

She moved round to stand in front of him and held out her hand.

Joe Jordan didn't take it immediately for the very good reason that he was suddenly struck by the insane desire to see this girl without her clothes. To unbutton her mannish jacket and watch the pinstriped trousers sink to the floor, to find out how her figure was curved and how she could be strong yet so slim, to watch that fascinating stride...

'Goodbye, Mr Jordan,' she said gravely. 'I feel we understand each other quite well, don't you?'

If you can understand going from one sister to the other. If you have any idea how enigmatic you appear, Lydia Kelso. If you can understand that you've successfully made me feel like a piece of horseflesh... He bit his lip on all that was hovering on the tip of his tongue and said instead, 'I guess so. Goodbye, Miss Kelso. You have magic hands, by the way.'

'So I'm told. Oh!'

He followed her dark blue gaze to see it resting on his sketchpad. 'Ah, I apologise,' he murmured. 'I do these things without thinking sometimes.'

But Lydia was laughing down at the cartoon of herself, immensely tall and obviously haranguing a diminutive, seated Joe Jordan in short pants, whose feet didn't even touch the ground. 'It's so good,' she said, still chuckling appreciatively.

'It's not meant to make *you* laugh,' he replied with dignity.

'Then I must have an odd sense of humour! May I have it?' She paused, then added blithely, 'I can use it to warn myself against being too dictatorial and overpowering, even bossy.'

'You don't believe that for one moment, do you?' he countered.

She laughed again. 'How could you tell?'

He paused. 'I just have the feeling you...' He hesitated, and wondered what use it was to ponder any further about Daisy Kelso's surprising sister. 'Oh, well, it doesn't matter, I guess.' But as he stood up he was curiously relieved to discover he was an inch taller than she was.

'No. It doesn't,' she agreed, with an oddly significant little glance.

He shook her hand, then tore the drawing off the pad and gave it to her.

'I'll get it framed—don't bother to come down; I'll let myself out,' she murmured, with a look of delicious mischief in her eyes now. And she went round the desk, slung her navy bag on her shoulder and strode out.

She was still chuckling as she walked along the street in Balmain where Joe Jordan had his townhouse. It was a lovely afternoon and, since its revival in the 1960s, Balmain was a pleasant spot.

One of Sydney's oldest suburbs, on a peninsula into the harbour with a few miles of coastline, its fortunes had been varied. But although there were plenty of interesting and historic buildings from its early times of affluence, it now had a trendy population, and she wouldn't mind a townhouse there herself, she thought, as she waited for the ferry to take her across the harbour. Especially one as nicely restored as Joe Jordan's.

But then, he could be described as trendy himself, she mused, which she was not, particularly, yet he wasn't *quite* what she'd expected...

The ferry came and she stepped aboard and turned to have a last look not only at Balmain but at the home suburb of, yes, she had to admit it, a slightly intriguing man.

That evening, as she was putting the finishing touches to her packing, Daisy wandered into her room and sat down at the dressing table.

'I'm going to miss you, Lyd,' she said as she unpinned the glorious fall of her dark hair and started to brush it.

'Me too.' Lydia sat down on the bed and eyed her sister's back. 'But you'll have plenty to occupy yourself, what with the Musica Viva tour and the start of the symphony season.'

Daisy sighed and lowered her hand. 'Can't seem to get excited about it, somehow.' She swung round on the stool. 'It's my biological clock,' she added. 'I can feel it ticking away madly.'

'It actually ticks?'

Daisy pulled a face. 'You know what I mean. I just wish,' she said intensely, 'you could meet Joe and give me your opinion. Then I'd know whether to go ahead or not.'

Lydia experienced an inner tremor of guilt, but she said easily, 'There's an old saying—when in doubt, do nowt. To be honest, Daisy, I think you should put up with your biological clock a bit longer and wait for the right man to come along.'

'So you've said. But you're not twenty-nine—I'll be thirty in two months!'

'Maybe you're confusing the dreaded thirty—remember when we used to think anyone over thirty was ancient?—with the biological clock?'

Daisy smiled briefly. 'I just keep thinking my life is slipping away from me, and that there may not be a Mr Right out there for me.'

'So Joe,' Lydia said carefully, 'is not necessarily Mr Right?'

'Joe's lovely, most of the time. He can also be moody and sarcastic, and there are times when I don't think he knows I exist.'

Lydia smoothed a pair of khaki shorts across her lap as she wondered how to ask her sister whether she'd actually slept with Joe Jordan. This was one point Daisy had been reticent about, but then she was always reticent, if not to say capable of closing up like a clam, with her family on this touchy subject, because they, above all, knew how frequently she fell in and out of love. But would Joe Jordan squire around a beautiful woman he was

not sleeping with? A woman who had indicated her willing-
ness on their first date? She doubted it deeply, Lydia decided.

She asked cautiously instead, 'Would you say you're having
an affair with him, Daisy?'

'Not *exactly*. I mean, when I decided I wanted him for the
father of my child, I made most of the running, you could say.
Then I thought—Hey, this guy is also something else; he can
give you goosebumps just by looking at you, let alone the rest
of it, so...' She paused with an uplifted expression on her face
that Lydia felt answered her question better than words might.
'So,' Daisy went on, 'then I thought, Perhaps I should hang on
to him but, put simply, Lyd, he's not that easy to hang on to.'

Daisy's eyes were a true violet. She wasn't tall, she had a
perfect oval face, a lovely figure, she was exquisitely groomed,
even for a dinner at home, and she looked every inch a sophisticated twenty-nine-year-old. Nor did her just uttered sentiments
belie this—unless you knew her well enough to know that of
the two of them she was the much more naive.

'Does he have other women?' Lydia asked, packing her shorts
and reaching for a blouse.

'I don't think so. But the fact of the matter is he hasn't had
much of me lately. He's losing interest, I would say.'

Thank heavens, Lydia thought. She said bracingly, 'Then he's
not worth it, Daisy. Besides, you could end up with a moody
kid!'

'All the same, there's something about him—'

'Listen, Daisy.' Lydia was suddenly serious. 'I went along
with this when I thought you were theorizing as opposed to
actually doing it, because you're a lot like Dad. Once he gets
an idea into his mind nothing can change it until he gets it out
of his system.'

'Thank you,' Daisy said gravely.

'But now it's time for straight talking,' Lydia went on pointedly. 'If you love Joe Jordan and he loves you and wants to
marry you, you have my blessing. Otherwise it's a dangerous

game you're playing—don't do this to yourself. You're worth much more than a life of seducing men so you can have a baby.'

Daisy turned the brush over in her hands. 'You don't know what it's like, Lyd,' she said slowly. 'You fell in love once and it worked out perfectly—well, until Brad died, of course. But it never works perfectly for me.' She brushed away a tear.

'Could you be…could you be a shade too generous, Daisy?' Lydia suggested, picking her words with care. 'Why don't you play hard to get for a change?'

Daisy lifted her head as if struck by inspiration. 'Oh. Maybe Joe would respond to that!'

'Forget Joe Jordan—' Lydia broke off and bit her lip.

'Why?'

'Uh—you told me yourself that he's very clever and that he can be moody and sarcastic. That's always hard to live with unless you're clever in the same way. What you need is someone musical, someone who could share the area where you're really sensitive and creative.'

Daisy stared reflectively into the distance. 'There is a new oboe player who's just joined the orchestra. He's rather sweet, and I can tell he's interested, but, no, it wouldn't work.'

'It's probably far too early to tell whether it would work,' Lydia commented practically, 'but how can you be so sure it wouldn't?'

'He's younger.'

'Younger… How much?'

'He's about your age, I guess.'

Lydia was struck silent for a long moment, struck by the irony of her sister plotting to have some man's child to bring up on her own yet unable to contemplate a normal relationship with a man because he was a little younger…

She said, at length, 'Three years—that's nothing, really.'

'Oh, yes, it is. When I'm thirty he'll still be in his twenties. More importantly, when I'm fifty, he'll still be in his forties.

I'm sure it should be the other way around because men tend to age better than women, don't you think?'

But Lydia was suddenly gripped by the feeling that a younger man could be just what Daisy needed. Might it not bring out a so far latent streak of maturity in her? As well as getting her over Joe Jordan, of course. Then she sighed and decided she'd done enough interfering in her sister's life for one day.

'Why don't you just wait and see what happens?' she murmured, and reached for the silver-framed photo of Brad on the dressing table. She stared down at it, blinked a couple of times, then laid it gently face down on top of her clothes in the suitcase.

Daisy was on her feet in a flash, and she knelt in front of Lydia and took her hands. 'Do you still miss him so much, darling? I had hoped it was getting easier.'

'It is, mostly,' Lydia said tremulously. 'Just sometimes it's actually harder. I don't know why. Unless it's because I'm afraid I'll forget.'

'You know,' her sister said, 'you worry an awful lot about me, but I can tell you that Brad loved you so much he would not want you to be unhappy for ever. And it's been five years now. Time to stop living a half-life. Time to have no guilt about finding someone else.'

Lydia smiled painfully. 'The problem is, I couldn't care less if I never did find anyone else. Men don't seem to interest me much, apart from—' She stopped abruptly as it surfaced in her mind that Joe Jordan was the first interesting man she'd met for a long time. To make matters worse, she'd been just about to say it.

'So there is someone?' Daisy said eagerly.

'No!' Lydia denied hastily.

'But you said—"apart from…"?'

'Um—the ones you can't have,' Lydia improvised madly, then thought, Well, that wasn't so far from the truth either.

'Still, that could be a start!' Daisy frowned. 'Anyone I know?'

'No. No—'

'Is he married?' Daisy asked, with both understanding and sympathy. 'A lot of the best ones are.'

'You're right—was that Chattie calling?' Their aunt Charlotte was universally known as Chattie Kelso, and she still lived with them in the big old house at Bronte, a beachside suburb of Sydney where both Daisy and Lydia had grown up.

Daisy rose. 'She's cooked roast pork,' she said conspiratorially. 'You know how paranoid she is about getting the crackling crisp. We'd better not keep her waiting.'

James Kelso, who was renowned for his bush ballads and poetry written under the name of Kelso James, as well as renowned for always wearing a bush shirt and jeans, raised his glass and cleared his throat. 'I'd like to propose several toasts. First to you, my dear Chattie, for the crispest crackling you've ever produced.'

Chattie, a spinster in her fifties, with Lydia's colouring and build although her hair was sprinkled with grey now, looked gratified. She raised her glass in return and her fine eyes glinted with mischief. 'Thought so myself, although I didn't like to say it.'

'And to you, my dear Daisy—' James inclined his head towards his elder daughter '—for looking sensational, as usual. No one would think you were a day over nineteen.'

Daisy smiled fondly at him. 'Dad, you're sweet, but you tell awful lies!'

'May one enquire how your love life is going at present?'

'One may—it's going, but it's at a critical stage, you could say.'

'Hmm. Dangerous age, twenty-nine. Would you agree, Chattie?'

'No. They can all be dangerous. I consider myself at my most dangerous when I was seventeen, closely followed by thirty-nine. At seventeen I would have done anything to have a boyfriend and be like the rest of the girls, and at thirty-nine I would have done anything to have a husband.'

'What about children?' Daisy asked.

'That too. I gave serious thought to having one without a husband—'

'Chattie!' James reproved. 'Don't put silly ideas into their young heads.'

Lydia ate her roast pork and thought that if Joe Jordan were a fly on the wall he might be able to judge for himself how eccentric her family could be.

'If you'd let me finish,' Chattie said, 'I decided against it because I realised it was extremely unfair to a child to deprive it of a father.'

Lydia put her knife and fork down and glanced at her aunt through her lashes. Had a whiff of Daisy's state of mind got through to her?

'I have to agree,' James said. 'For example, do you or do you not think I've enriched your lives, girls?'

Daisy masked her expression almost immediately, but Lydia saw her sheer horror at the thought of never having known their father, and she felt like cheering at the same time as she wondered whether her father had also divined Daisy's dilemma…

She said, 'Dad, you've not only enriched our lives but your wisdom never ceases to amaze me—when you're not driving me mad with your forgetfulness, your inability to find your glasses, even when they're on top of your head, and the way you persistently wear odd socks—when you remember to wear them at all.'

'Well, that brings me to you, Lydia, my younger and most practical daughter,' James said humorously. 'We're going to miss you, my dear. Who else will we have to fix fuses and start our cars when they break down? You know how hopeless I am at that kind of thing.'

'I do.' Lydia grinned. 'Heaven alone knows where that expertise came down to me from, but if you just look in the *Yellow*

Pages you'll find there are electricians, mechanics, plumbers and so on galore—on second thoughts, I'd better write you out a list.'

'Now that makes us feel really small,' James Kelso admonished, 'but I'd be much easier if you did! And I know I speak for the rest of us when I say we're all happy to think of you enjoying a new challenge, a new experience—may it be a wonderful one!' He raised his glass again.

'Hear, hear!' Chattie and Daisy echoed.

'So let's think up a suitable limerick,' James went on.

It was a game they'd played ever since Lydia could remember...

'Lydia Kelso is going to Queensland,' Daisy started.

'To...look after cows...with a magic hand,' Chattie supplied.

'Not for too long,' James said.

'You won't know I'm gone!' Lydia laughed.

There was silence until Daisy said frustratedly, 'The last line is always the hardest! What rhymes with Queensland? We've got hand...'

'Wedding band?' Chattie suggested.

'Oh, no!' Lydia protested. 'There's not the least likelihood of that happening, and anyway, I didn't like to interrupt the creative flow, but I'm actually going to the Northern Territory.'

Everyone groaned. 'Oh, well,' James murmured, 'that's right next door, so we won't start again—and you never know! So... *And she'll come home complete with a wedding band.'*

'Very amateurish,' Lydia said. 'But thank you all for your good wishes!' And she looked round the dining room, with its heavy old oak table, dark green walls, examples of her aunt's sculpting and some lovely gold-framed paintings on the wall. 'I'll miss you,' she added. 'Just promise me you'll all be good!'

It struck her as she got ready for bed that she could go away with a much easier mind, now. A quiet word with Chattie had revealed that she was aware of Daisy's dilemma and would keep a weather eye out for her.

'We won't tell your father,' she'd said. 'He's liable to go and want to have things out with this Joe Jordan.'

Lydia had confessed that she'd already done that, but that Daisy was unaware of her actions.

'What's he like?' Chattie had asked curiously.

'Interesting, but not serious about her—nor, I suspect, did he stand much chance. She made the running, so to speak.'

'So she is sleeping with him?'

'She hasn't actually admitted to that, but she looks, well, you know...'

'I do. But he could have knocked her back. How like a man!'

They'd looked at each other, then grinned simultaneously.

'Daisy, in full flight, is a sight to behold,' Chattie had acknowledged. 'Perhaps I was being a bit hard on him. What about you?'

Lydia had blinked. 'What about me?'

'When are you going to lay Brad to rest and start living again?'

'Not you too!'

'Your father been giving you a hard time?'

Lydia had shaken her head. 'Daisy. But I am living, and enjoying myself and really looking forward to this job!'

'All right.' Chattie had looked as if she'd been about to say more, but had desisted and hugged her niece instead. 'Leave them to me; I'll look after them!'

Lydia took off her pinstriped trouser suit, donned a velvet housecoat and sat down at her dressing table to brush her hair, after removing a few very dark strands from the brush.

She'd returned to this room and this single bed after a year of marriage, and some days it was hard to believe she'd ever left it.

She and Brad had met at university, he'd been studying economics, and the first thing to draw them together had been their common although unusual surname. But the attraction had been almost instantaneous, and mutual. It had also been a revelation to Lydia, because he'd been her first serious boyfriend, and to find someone she clicked with so completely had been totally unexpected.

To fall so much in love when she'd expected to spend her university years working hard to achieve her career goals had also been disconcerting, but that had been another wonderful part of their relationship. They'd been quite happy to allow each other the space to study.

So, after two years, and before she had graduated—although he had, and had joined an eminent firm of stockbrokers—they'd got married, got themselves a small flat and had a year of idyllic happiness.

It had been a matter of surprise to many, her family included, that she should have been the first sister to marry, and so young.

He'd been such fun, she thought sadly, the night before she went—not to Queensland, although via it to the Northern Territory. Not that you'd necessarily have known that behind his glasses and his computer-like brain there had lurked a delicious sense of humour. And he'd handled her growing ardour with surprising passion for a man who had always been able to tell you how many points the All Ordinaries or the Dow Jones had gained or dropped overnight.

It wasn't fair. She'd thought it so many times, when her body had ached physically for him, and her mind had yearned for the warmth, tenderness and laughter they'd generated together.

She'd also suffered the growing conviction it would never happen for her that way again. So that, despite their good intentions, she hated it when people told her it was time to think of falling in love again—even her own sister.

She brushed steadily for a few minutes, trying to compose herself, and finally found some relief from her sad thoughts coming from an unusual direction... Joe Jordan and his hints that she was not as feminine as her gorgeous sister.

She put the brush down and studied herself in the mirror. What would he have thought, she mused, if he'd known that under her suit she'd been wearing—these?

'These', beneath her velvet robe, were a midnight-blue silk camisole deeply edged with lace and a matching pair of panties.

She stood up, opened her robe and, putting her hands on her hips, twirled slowly in front of the mirror. True, she conceded to her image, she was not like Daisy, who had an hourglass figure, but—how had Brad put it? Beneath her clothes she was slim, sleek and surprisingly sensuous, and her legs were to die for.

Of course, she told herself as she sat down again and grinned at herself, what appeals to one man may not appeal to another! And although her clothes were sometimes mannish it was only for comfort, and they were beautifully made. She also had a passion for shoes and bags and the finest lingerie.

So there, Mr Jordan, she thought, and was tempted to stick out her tongue at a mental image of him.

Then she sobered and wondered what on earth she was thinking. Only minutes ago she'd been consumed by sadness and the unfairness of fate—how could she be thinking of another man? A man her sister might be in love with—might even have slept with, moreover.

She closed her eyes and clenched her hands until Brad came back to her in her mind, and she remembered how he'd loved to cook, but had been quite hopeless at clearing up after himself...

CHAPTER TWO

SEVERAL DAYS LATER she was winging her way to Katerina Station in the Victoria River District of the Northern Territory, five hundred kilometres south of Darwin. She'd flown first to Townsville, to spend two days with Brad's parents in North Queensland, then on to Darwin to spend a day in the veterinary science department of the Northern Territory University.

The vet she was filling in for, although not precisely as a vet, was a friend from university, Tim Patterson. They'd kept in touch over the years, and several months ago he'd written to tell her that he was taking a break from his practice and doing something he'd always wanted to do—joining a mustering team on a cattle station where not only his horsemanship but his veterinary expertise would be useful.

Then, a few weeks ago, he'd written again to say that he was having the time of his life mustering cattle, that it was also wonderful experience for a vet interested in large animals, but for business and personal reasons he needed to take six weeks off and would she be interested in filling in for him? He'd assured her that the Simpson family, who ran Katerina Station, would welcome her enthusiastically and provide accommodation for her in the main homestead—when she wasn't sleeping under the stars with the rest of the mustering team.

That had done it. She'd gone, cap in hand, to the senior partner of the practice she was working for in Sydney and showed him the letter. He'd given her six weeks' leave and added enviously, 'Half your luck, Lydia!'

She was now staring down at the grassy plains, rolling savanna and rocky outcrops of the Victoria River District, known locally as the VRD, as it glided past below. It was a fine, clear day and the sky was huge, so was the panorama beneath it, giving Lydia a sense of the vastness and the emptiness of the ancient continent she called home.

The VRD supported one of the most successful grazing enterprises in northern Australia, but to look down upon it you wouldn't think a soul lived in it.

The station pilot was young and friendly, and he smiled at her wonderment and took an extra ten minutes to show her the various sets of cattle yards and bores as proof that cattle did exist in large numbers, then he buzzed the Katerina homestead to alert the occupants of his imminent arrival.

He also filled her in about the Simpson family. 'Sarah is a daughter of the pioneering family that started Katerina,' he explained. 'She and her brother inherited it, but when she married she divided her share with her husband, Rolf, and he actually manages the place.'

'What about the brother?' Lydia asked.

'He spends time here, he's still the major shareholder, but he doesn't live here—look, there's a mob on the way to the main yards.'

Lydia stared down at the dust being raised by a mob of cattle as they were moved along by horsemen.

'Do you only muster by horseback?' she asked. 'I thought most of it was done by chopper these days.'

'Used to be, for a time, but the ringer's coming back into fashion nowadays. You can't educate a bunch of cows from a chopper.'

'Does that mean you'll be out of a job?' He'd already told her he piloted a Bell 45 helicopter too.

'Nope! We work in conjunction. Choppers still have their uses in really difficult terrain and for moving large mobs. OK, here we go.'

He set the light plane down on a grass airstrip in what looked like the middle of nowhere until a large shed came into view.

Lydia emerged as the dust settled. She breathed deeply and looked around. Tim had confided that being a vet did not necessarily confer any special status on a member of this mustering team. They did most of their vet work themselves, and how you rode and handled cattle was the prime consideration—although some of the bigger stations did employ vets as vets.

She'd found this amusing, because he'd also told her that Katerina Station covered a million acres. What was big if not that? she'd pondered. But he'd gone on to say that once they'd realised you knew what you were talking about and doing, you'd find them deferring to you. So, she would have to prove herself first, she reflected. It would be a nice kind of challenge.

She turned as she heard a vehicle approaching, expecting either Sarah or Rolf Simpson. But as another cloud of dust started to subside as it skidded to a stop beside her, a pale gold Labrador dog leapt off the back of the battered utility and raced towards her, only to sit down in front of her and extend a paw.

'Hello!' Lydia squatted down in front of the dog and shook the paw gravely. 'And who might you be? I have to tell you I think you're gorgeous, and so well-mannered.'

The dog grinned widely and a voice above Lydia said, 'Glad you approve of my dog. OK, Meg, back in the ute.'

Meg obeyed, but not before giving the owner of the voice a loving lick as he put his hand down to her.

Lydia straightened dazedly. Because there was no mistaking that voice, nor any chance of mistaking the tall man standing in front of her, although he looked so different from the last time she'd seen him.

'What the hell are you doing here?' It came out before she could help herself as she took in the stained, dusty clothes he wore and the battered felt cowboy hat he dangled—none of which diminished the impact of that 'well-knit' tall body and 'interesting' face beneath his brown hair...

'Good morning to you, Miss Lydia Kelso—or rather Mrs,' Joe Jordan drawled, and leant casually against the bonnet of the vehicle as he allowed his hazel gaze to run over the olive-green stretch moleskins and cream shirt she wore with a sleeveless quilted olive vest and brown boots. Her hair was tousled, but he couldn't imagine it any other way, he found himself thinking, and it was a gloriously free head of hair, that framed those delicate features admirably.

Lydia, on the other hand, shook her tousled head and looked around, blinking experimentally. 'Am I on Katerina Station in the Northern Territory run by the Simpson family, or have I been kidnapped?' she queried.

'Not at all—'

'So how did you get here from Balmain?'

'As I was about to explain, Sarah Simpson is my sister,' he said mildly.

'You're the brother who owns half of the place?' Lydia stared at him incredulously.

'None other. I don't usually trade on it,' he added modestly, 'but after you left me the other day, I suddenly thought to myself—Didn't Rolf let me know that Tim had to go away for six weeks but he'd found someone to take his place who also happened to be a vet? My next thought was that it would be an interesting coincidence should you be the person replacing him.'

'I'm speechless,' Lydia said, in a parody of what he'd said to her three days ago.

Joe Jordan straightened. 'You weren't exactly speechless the other day.'

Lydia gestured futilely. 'So what are you doing here now?'

'Decided to come up for a bit of R&R at the same time as

I check out how the new vet handles herself, amongst other things.'

Lydia muttered something beneath her breath.

'That doesn't recommend itself to you?' he asked, with the most wicked spark of mischief in his eyes.

'No, it does not. You're the last person I want peering over my shoulder all the time!'

'Now why would that be?' he asked ingenuously. 'I thought anything taking me out of reach of your sister would meet with your approval.'

Lydia stared at him. 'Because the circumstances in which we met were not exactly auspicious,' she said deliberately. 'And did you just walk out on my sister?'

His eyes glinted with irony now. 'As a matter of fact, no. I told her that I had to be out of town for a while.'

'Was she devastated?' Lydia demanded.

'If so she gave no hint of it. I had actually prepared a sort of—not exactly farewell address, but a letting-down-lightly kind of thing, as you so thoughtfully recommended—only it never got said because she took the words right out of my mouth. She said that she thought it would be an excellent idea if we had a bit of a break from each other.'

Lydia digested this, then swore beneath *her* breath this time.

'Which indicated to me,' Joe Jordan said, with a wryly raised eyebrow, 'that she's losing interest in me and the idea of me fathering her child.'

No, she's not, she's playing hard to get!

Lydia didn't say it, she bit the words off on the tip of her tongue, but she experienced a sinking feeling in the pit of her stomach that generally indicated she was right about her lovely sister Daisy's state of mind.

'I can't believe this,' she said instead. 'I was really looking forward to this experience.'

He frowned. 'Surely my simple presence couldn't provide that much of a blight?'

'Your presence is not simple at all,' she retorted.

He stared at her thoughtfully. 'Does that mean you were rather intrigued about me, as I discovered I was about you, dear Lydia?' he queried.

She'd never been a blusher, but she undoubtedly coloured. She could feel the heat of it beneath the smooth skin of her cheeks and down her neck, all of which he noted with a flicker of amusement twisting his lips.

It was his amusement that got her going again, when she really would have loved to crawl into a handy hole to hide. 'How *could* you—apart from anything else—transfer from one sister to another just like...clicking your fingers?' She demonstrated, and he laughed openly this time.

'Funnily enough, I asked myself that,' he murmured. 'The only conclusion I could come up with was that your sister had singled me out from the herd, slightly against my better judgement, whereas *you* and I...came together differently.'

'We didn't,' she protested. 'We came together—we *met*—because of my sister!'

'Whatever.' He waved a negligent hand. 'This interest we share, however, sprang up of its own accord. Daisy had nothing to do with it.'

'I'm not admitting to...' She bit her lip and suffered a moment of dread that she would blush again, but she didn't. 'I am not interested in you, Mr Jordan. Let's put it like that.' She stared at him defiantly.

'I would have said your first assertion was more truthful, Lydia. The one about not admitting things. But let's not get ourselves all tied up here and now. Pete's got your gear off the plane. Would you allow me to drive you up to the homestead? Sarah has lunch waiting.'

Lydia was sorely tempted to press her point, if not to find some way of driving it home with a sledgehammer, but she contained herself and only looked supremely frustrated.

Joe Jordan watched her for a moment, then said, 'Good. I

wouldn't have believed you anyway, and it's hot enough without getting oneself unnecessarily hot and bothered. After you, ma'am!' He walked round the ute and opened the passenger door for her.

She did say stiffly as they drove away, 'It is hot, for the middle of winter.'

'Ah, but the nights are deliciously cool at this time of year, in comparison. Ever been up this way before, Lydia?'

'No.'

'Then you're in for a delightful surprise. The country is superb at the moment. We had a good wet season, everything's still flourishing, you can get about easily—do you ride?'

'Of course!' She looked at him scathingly, then looked out of the window.

'Excellent. Unless, that is, you intend to converse with me only in monosyllables for the next six weeks?'

She turned back to him wide-eyed. 'You're not going to be here for six whole weeks, are you?'

He shrugged. 'More or less.'

'But why? Surely you don't usually spend so much time up here!'

'How would you know?' he countered.

'I...well, I assumed you lived most of your life in Sydney,' she offered—a shade feebly, she couldn't help thinking.

'As in making generalisations about people from the same family, one shouldn't make assumptions based on very little knowledge of the facts, Lydia,' he reproved gravely.

They were driving along a rocky dirt road towards a stand of tall trees and between them she could see a large tin roof with 'Katerina' painted in big black letters on the silver surface: the roof they'd flown over.

Lydia blinked several times and said tersely, 'I was told you didn't live here.'

'Who told you that?'

'Pete, the pilot. I had no idea, of course, that he was talking about you!'

'Sprung,' Joe Jordan remarked with a charming smile as he wrestled the gear lever and they bounced over a large rock. 'Must get this road fixed, by the way. Uh—no, I don't actually live here, although I spend quite a bit of time up here.'

Lydia waited, then said pointedly, 'So?'

'Several things have happened, that's all. Rolf and Sarah need a bit of a break. Modern technology means that I can still pursue my chosen career from up here, and—well, the other thing that happened may not recommend itself to you, so I might wait.'

'Tell me!' Lydia ordered through her teeth.

He brought the utility to a halt outside a low white pole fence surrounding a lush acre of garden that in turn surrounded the homestead. There were colourful parrots swooping amongst the trees, there was a carpet of thick green grass, the house was old and sprawling, but well maintained, there was a riot of purple, pink and white bougainvillea smothering the tank stands, and a woman standing on the front steps was waving to them.

'All right.' Joe Jordan cut the motor and turned to look at her fully.

He didn't start to speak immediately, however, and, much as she would have wished otherwise, Lydia felt an erratic little frisson run through her at the proximity of this man. Nor was it so hard to define his attractiveness suddenly. It was all there in the lines and angles of his face, the well-cut mouth, those broad shoulders and lean hips, the pair of strong hands, those intelligent hazel eyes, and in the distinct feeling that not only might he be exciting to know, he was also a connoisseur of women.

And he waited until their gazes clashed before he said, 'I've been plagued by the curious yet nevertheless powerful desire to see you without your clothes, Ms Kelso. And the way you walk has taken to invading my thoughts. I do apologise for putting it so plainly, but it is the truth and you did command me to tell you.'

* * *

Lydia washed her hands in the bathroom attached to her bed-room and brushed her hair vigorously.

She'd been welcomed warmly by Sarah Simpson, shown her room and asked if she'd like to brush up before lunch. She hadn't responded to Joe Jordan's statement, beyond bestowing upon him the fieriest of blue glances before she'd jumped out of the utility. It hadn't abashed him in the slightest as he'd introduced her to his sister and brother-in-law.

How on earth she was going to face him over a lunch table and for the next six weeks she had no idea, she mused savagely as she flung her brush down and stood with her hands on her hips. And there was Daisy to think about. Daisy, putting her own advice into practice, unless she was much mistaken.

'Rolf and I have to take a little while off, although it's such a busy time of the year,' Sarah said over lunch.

She was in her early thirties, Lydia judged, with the same colouring as her brother. She was also what one would call 'horsey' but in a not unattractive way. Horses were never far from her conversation, and the verandah room, closed in with glass louvres, where lunch was set out, was decked with rib-bons and trophies she'd won for dressage and show jumping, and she wore jodhpurs with a pink blouse.

Another clue to Sarah's preoccupation with horses was that, from what Lydia had seen of the house, and while it was com-fortable enough, the furnishings were old-fashioned, and it didn't give off the glow of a dedicated homemaker being in residence.

Sarah had also been boarding-school-educated, and there were photos on the wall depicting a young Sarah Jordan as school captain. She had a rather bracing, authoritative air, as if she were a school captain born and bred. One thing she wasn't, by her own admission, was much of a cook.

Lunch, while plentiful, was plain. Cold meat and salad, a fruit bowl and cheese.

'Do, *do* make free use of the kitchen, Lydia,' she invited. 'I only do the basics, I'm afraid.'

'Watch it,' Joe advised Lydia. 'You could find yourself not only the resident vet but head chef.'

'Just because you got my share of the cooking genes, Joe, there is no need to be smug. We're twins,' Sarah confided to Lydia. 'I sometimes think things got a bit muddled up. I should have got the artistic bent, one feels, but...' She shrugged.

'Hang on, beloved,' Joe advised his sister this time, 'you could be giving the wrong impression here.'

Sarah blinked her hazel eyes at her brother. 'Darling,' she murmured, 'one only has to count the trail of broken hearts you've left amongst the female population of the Territory alone to know otherwise.'

Joe Jordan looked hurt and outraged at the same time. 'Now you've really done it, Sarah!'

'Done what?' She eyed him innocently.

'Lydia already classes me with Casanova!'

Sarah transferred her gaze to Lydia with some interest. 'Joe mentioned that you two know each other. I didn't realise it was in *that* way.'

'It's not,' Lydia replied coolly. 'It's my sister he knows in "that way".'

Rolf Simpson, a man of few words so far—in fact to Lydia he epitomised the fair dinkum cattleman: tall, lean, sparse of speech and with far-seeing blue eyes—said, 'It's never a good idea to come between sisters, mate.'

Lydia flashed a triumphant look at the main shareholder of Katerina Station, then turned her attention to her lunch and the dodging of some uncooked pieces of potato in the salad of the same name.

'I'm suitably chastened; however—' Joe took a draught of his beer '—*I* didn't seek out either of the Kelso sisters.'

'Gosh!' Sarah enthused. 'We could be in for some interesting times, by the sound of it. I'm almost tempted to put our little holiday off, Rolf. She turned to Lydia. 'I must tell you, if what I think is going on between you two, *is* going on between you two, I should be delighted to have a vet for a sister-in-law. Just think how handy it would be for my horses, let alone Katerina.'

This time it was Joe Jordan who flashed Lydia a look that, while not exactly triumphant, spoke volumes.

'When, exactly, do you plan to take your holiday?' Lydia enquired of Sarah.

'In a fortnight,' Sarah replied. 'We'll be taking three weeks. But Joe'll be here, so it's not as if we're abandoning you!'

'I imagine,' Joe Jordan commented, 'that Lydia doesn't quite see it that way.'

'Why ever not?' Sarah looked perplexed.

'She'll probably tell you herself; she's a plain speaker, our Lydia.'

'Joe, I wish you'd stop talking in riddles,' Sarah protested, then turned her attention to Lydia with a smile. 'You do look awfully young to be a fully qualified vet.'

'Twenty-six, although I agree she looks younger,' her brother commented. 'But I can assure you she's very strong.'

'Ignore him,' Sarah said to Lydia. 'He can be impossible.'

But it was Rolf who changed the subject. 'We are Brucellosis and TB free in the Territory now, Lydia—did you know?'

'I...yes!' Lydia murmured, wresting her mind from his brother-in-law, who was sitting back in his chair with the most devilish little glint in his hazel eyes.

'What do you want now?' Lydia asked arctically, much later in the day.

It was after dinner, and she'd spent the rest of the day with Rolf and Joe, doing a tour of the main yards and the vet station, and she'd even been able to practise her science on a lame stock horse. She'd found a nail in its hoof and been able to extract it.

Neither man had said much during the operation, but she'd known they were watching keenly. After the nail had come out, and she'd injected the horse with an antibiotic and a tetanus needle, Rolf had remarked that no one else had been able to come up with the cause of the horse's lameness. It had been a way of saying well done, she gathered.

But instead of going to bed after dinner, despite yawning several times, she'd pulled on a dark green pullover, moved a comfortable cane lounger from the verandah onto the lawn and sunk down in it to watch the millions of stars overhead. That was how Joe Jordan had found her.

'Nothing. I thought you'd retired.' He went away and came back in moments with another chair. 'Mind if I join you?'

She glanced at him sardonically and shrugged.

'Thank you,' he returned politely. 'Hang on again; I'll be right back.'

This time he was away for five minutes, and he came back with a pottery wine cooler supporting a frosted bottle and two glasses. 'Thought you might appreciate some kind of a nightcap. Because Sarah doesn't drink, she forgets others do. And most people drink wine.'

Meg had followed him, and she put her muzzle in Lydia's lap for a pat before lying down at her master's feet.

'I have no intention of drinking half a bottle of wine.'

He pulled the cork from the pocket of his jeans and showed it to her. 'We can drink as much or as little as we like. It's quite a sight, isn't it?' He gestured skywards.

Lydia hesitated, then accepted the glass he'd poured for her and laid her head back. 'You're not wrong.'

'There's only one better way, and that's to be camped out. No tent, just a swag beside a small fire, the horses hobbled not far away.'

'That's the kind of stuff my father writes about,' she said dreamily. 'He was a jackeroo as a young man. He always says it got into his blood.'

'I've read some of his work. It's good. I'm surprised he didn't take you outback.'

'Oh, he did. Just not to the Northern Territory. Cooper Creek, the Barcoo, Lake Eyre—I've seen those.'

There was a long silence; Lydia sipped her wine and made no attempt to break it.

It was Joe who finally said, 'Why are you so mad at me?'

Surprise held her further silent for a moment, then she said wearily, 'I'm not.'

'You could have fooled me, but if we discount Daisy as a possible reason—what's left?'

It was no good trying to study his expression, it was too dark, despite the Milky Way seeming to hang just above their heads, but she had the feeling he was serious.

'You don't really hold being a cartoonist against me?' he queried. 'As you see, it's not the only thing I can do.'

'No...' She sighed.

'And you shouldn't believe Sarah's stories about a trail of broken hearts—'

'Why not?'

He paused. 'Because it's not true. I... Lydia, are you laughing at me, by any chance?' he asked ominously.

She sat up chuckling. 'Yes. Heaven alone knows why, Mr Jordan, but I'm quite sure it *is* true, or was when you were a young man in these parts.'

'What tells you this?'

'You'd probably have to be a woman to understand.'

'It's funny you should say that—I read a quote the other day that intrigued me. On the subject of women.'

'Do tell me,' she invited.

'"Any man smart enough to understand women is also smart enough to keep quiet about it."'

Lydia smiled. 'Do you?'

'Understand women? I would have thought so,' he murmured thoughtfully. 'Until I met you.'

'Oh, come now. This is only the second time we've met, and I've got an early start tomorrow, so...' She drained her glass and handed it to him.

But he merely reached for the bottle on the grass beside him and refilled it. 'One more won't hurt, surely? Besides, I got the feeling it was loosening you up, Ms Kelso.' He put the glass back into her hands.

'Is that how you do it? Ply them with alcohol?'

'Not at all,' he denied. 'But I thought you were uptight, feeling less than restful, and it might help.'

Lydia hesitated, then settled back. 'If you hadn't been the first person I bumped into on Katerina I might be feeling a lot more restful. If I didn't think my sister Daisy was—' She broke off.

'I told you what happened.'

'I know. You also told me you had this *curious* desire to see me without my clothes. As if I might be some sort of circus freak.' As soon as she'd said it Lydia regretted the words, and was amazed to discover that she had subconsciously taken umbrage at that particular word.

'Ah.' Joe Jordan drained his glass and refilled it. 'That wasn't what I meant at all, but I apologise for phrasing things awkwardly. What I meant was, if I'd thought you were some sort of circus freak, the last thing I'd want is to see you undressed. Do you perceive the difference, Lydia?'

'I perceive that you're getting yourself tangled up in technicalities, Joe! But, no, you don't have to explain further. I know exactly what you meant.'

'You do? Would you be so kind as to tell me what I meant?' he asked, with some chagrin.

Lydia grinned fleetingly. 'That at first you didn't find me feminine and to your taste, especially compared to my sister Daisy. You know, I would have had to be particularly dense not to have got that message loud and clear, Joe.'

She could see enough to see him flinch, and had to laugh softly. 'Look, don't let it come between you and your sleep,' she advised. 'I grew up in Daisy's shadow; I'm quite used to it.'

'And once again I'm speechless.'

'Good,' she said unfeelingly. 'Because I'm getting tired of this conversation and I am going to bed.'

'Mind you, I'm relieved it's not because of some of the things Sarah said—the other things about mixed up genes and being able to cook,' he said humorously.

'I wouldn't hold that against a man,' Lydia replied. 'My husband was a fantastic cook, although disastrously messy.'

Joe Jordan stared down at the wine glass cradled in his hands, and said at last, 'Is that it, Lydia?'

She stood up in one lithe movement. 'Yes, Joe, that's it. You see, it was so wonderful I...can't forget him or believe it could ever happen that way for me again.'

He stood up, and Meg rose like a wraith in the dark to stand patiently beside him. 'Then Daisy is not part of it?'

'Daisy *is* part of it,' she contradicted. 'If...' She paused and chose her words with care. 'You are at all serious about an interest in me, then you've run into a double whammy, so to speak. My memories of Brad and the impossibility of having anything to do with a man my sister may love. Goodnight.'

This time she took her glass with her as she walked inside.

Joe Jordan sat down again after a moment and took his dog's face into his hands. 'My dear Meg,' he murmured, 'who would have believed I could have been such a fool? Not that I was to know—all sorts of things—but I've been about as heavy-handed as a bull in a china shop—if you'll forgive my mixed metaphors. However, it would be fair to say I'm all the more intrigued. You do like her, don't you?'

Meg gazed lovingly up at him and wagged her tail.

'Good. As they say, tomorrow is another day. And another strategy is obviously called for. We shall see!'

* * *

About a week later, Lydia got up at the crack of dawn, then remembered it was a Sunday, so she got back into bed and fell asleep until ten o'clock.

There seemed to be no one about as she padded into the kitchen then and made herself some tea and toast. She took it back to her bedroom and spent the next hour leisurely engaged in doing the things she'd hadn't had much time for over the previous week.

She washed her hair, left the conditioner on and wrapped her head in a towel. She attended to her nails and smoothed moisturiser all over herself at the same time as she checked herself for bruises and saddle sores; there were no sores but a few colourful bruises. She paused to wonder whether her skin and hair would ever be the same again, despite this treatment, and sat down to write a long letter home.

Finally, she unwound the towel, rinsed her hair and dressed in a pair of cool pink linen shorts with a pink and white floral cotton blouse, luxuriating as she did so in clothes that were not khaki or definitely working clothes, and slid a pair of light sandals on.

She wondered again why the homestead was so silent, then shrugged. A week at Katerina had been long enough to discover that one day was very much like another, although she'd been told firmly to take Sundays off. Sarah would most likely be with her horses, and Rolf and Joe, if they weren't working on the road or the cattle yards or the airstrip or the maintenance of some vehicle or another, could still find a hundred other tasks.

She went out onto the verandah and pulled a chair into the sunlight so she could dry her hair, and ran a mental review of the week as she closed her eyes and lifted her face to the sun.

A faint smile curved her lips at the memory of how stiff she'd been for the first few days, and was still stiff at times. This was despite begging a friend in Sydney, as soon as she'd decided to come to Katerina, to let her exercise his polo ponies every day to get herself fit for what was to come. Although she'd ridden since she was six, and although horses were by no means the only way to get around Katerina, she'd done more riding in a week than she'd done in the past year. But it had been exhilarating and more.

She'd read respect in the eyes of the Simpsons when she'd refused to complain about her aching muscles or to take to the 'bull buggy', an open four-wheel drive vehicle suitable for getting around rough terrain with fearsome bars on the front capable of repelling charging bulls.

But Joe Jordan had surprised her. There had been no more overtures of a personal nature. In fact he'd treated her exactly as he treated his sister.

Even when, without quite knowing how, they'd taken to preparing the evening meal together. He had explained solemnly to her that Sarah was not only unhandy in the kitchen but notoriously difficult when it came to getting along with household help.

'Can't tell you how many cooks she's gone through!' he'd said.

'You'd think she'd be only too happy to have someone do it for her,' Lydia had responded.

'She is, at first. But it's not easy to get good cooks prepared to bury themselves beyond the black stump, and being an extremely fastidious person, as well as a "do-gooder", it's not long before she's interfering and, worse, trying to make them over into what she believes they should be. In other words nondrinkers, non-smokers, no bad language, extremely moral, even regular churchgoers, and all the things *she* is.'

Lydia had grinned. 'I see. She's quite a character, your twin sister.'

He'd looked at her curiously. 'But you two seem to get along pretty well.'

They did, Lydia had mused. Sarah could do most things the men did, and apart from her lack of domesticity she was a born country woman—and it was obvious she loved every inch of Katerina. She was also the perfect foil for her tall, unemotional husband. 'We do. I like her very much, actually. And she hasn't, so far, tried to change me in any respect.'

'Well, you don't have any of the above vices, apart from an occasional glass of wine. That could be why.'

'It could indeed. So that's why you and I are cooking dinner together?'

'I did warn you about this.' Joe had been basting a roast chicken and Lydia preparing an apple crumble for dessert. 'And I can take her cooking for so long, but not much longer. There.' He'd closed the oven door.

'Rolf doesn't seem to mind.'

'Rolf's a man who likes peace above all else. But, contrary to Sarah's belief that she has him well and truly housetrained, et cetera, he's one of those strong, silent types, and you don't really know what is going on beneath the surface.'

'Unlike you,' Lydia had said flippantly.

'Well, I don't know about that,' he'd replied, but had made no attempt to enlarge on the issue.

Lydia thought, coming back to the present on this Sunday morning when the house was as quiet as a church, that she must have got through to him with what she'd said about Brad and Daisy. They'd certainly spent quite a bit of time together, enough for him to have made all manner of passes.

She'd spent her first couple of days learning the ropes, with either Joe or Rolf at her side.

It was hard work, mustering and drafting cattle. First of all a mob of cattle was mustered by helicopter into a yard. Then they were sorted into various categories and other yards: weaners and calves to be branded, calves to be returned to their mothers as soon as possible, or weaners old enough to be separated and educated, breeding cows and bulls that went straight back whence they came, provided they were in good condition, sale cattle—steers and bullocks—and cattle to be culled from the herd for various reasons.

At one stage each beast was put into a yard by itself for evaluation, and this was when Lydia was able to make a fast assessment on whether they needed any medical treatment. But you had to be quick, and she soon realised that most of the members of the muster team knew as much about cattle as she did.

It had been a bit sobering, but she'd pushed herself to work as hard as any other member of the team, and had thanked heaven for the polo ponies—otherwise she'd have needed a wheelchair!

But Joe and Rolf had made a point of including her in their discussions on all sorts of things including their breeding programme. Most of the stock on Katerina was now Brahman, or crossed with Brahman, but there were still some wild scrubber bulls and inbred shorthorn cows to be dealt with, and their influence eradicated from the herd.

She hadn't slept out under the stars yet—the paddocks being mustered were close to the homestead at this stage—but she'd gone to bed in her bed each night to dream of dust and grit in your teeth, hair and every fold of skin, and endless hooves, and the hot sun beating down on you until you were dizzy...

But she'd enjoyed it, she couldn't deny. And she'd enjoyed becoming known to the men who worked the mobs and being treated with growing respect.

Yet, she mused, whilst others had treated her with growing respect, including his sister, Joe Jordan had given no indication as to whether he was impressed or not.

'How like a woman!' She had to laugh as she said it out aloud, and was referring to herself. She stood up and went inside to brush her hair now it was dry, then decided to plait it in one thick plait, because it was looking quite wild with energy despite the conditioner.

And her laughter faded as she did so, because it was sobering to contemplate that she could now be slightly peeved because a man she had given the flick to, in a manner of speaking, had taken the hint.

Nor was she really peeved, she assured herself. Just a little puzzled.

Her thoughts turned to Daisy. She had spoken to Chattie the day after she'd arrived at Katerina, but her aunt had only been able to tell her that Daisy had embarked on the Musica Viva tour, which would take her away for a few weeks, and had appeared to be in good spirits. Lydia had not, for reasons she wasn't too sure of, enlightened her aunt about the principal shareholder in Katerina.

She shrugged and walked through to the kitchen, and decided to make a cake.

It was when the cake was ready to go into the oven that Joe came in and slung his hat accurately on to a hook in the hall.

'Morning, Ms Kelso. What a picture of domesticity you present!'

'Thank you! Where is everyone?'

He didn't reply.

Lydia closed the oven door, hung the oven mitt on the handle and turned to him, to find him leaning back against a counter with his arms folded and his eyes on her legs.

She went still, and he took his time about raising his gaze to hers. Then they simply stared into each other's eyes for a long moment. But Lydia discovered her mouth had gone dry and her heart was beating strangely. It was the first time Joe Jordan had seen her legs out of trousers...

He broke the moment. She'd found herself curiously mesmerised. He turned, discovered the mixing bowl on the counter, and picked up a wooden spoon to scrape some mixture out of it. 'Mmm,' he pronounced, 'ginger and good. Where is everyone? Gone to church.'

'Church...how?'

'By plane. Sarah asked me to tell you that she hadn't liked to disturb you on your first day off, and she forgot to mention last night that there was a service being held this morning on an adjoining property. They have a circuit,' he added conversationally. 'She and Rolf will also being staying on Dunoon Station for the night. They're having a bit of a get-together.'

'Oh. I see. Didn't you want to go?'

'Well, we couldn't leave you here on your own, now, could we?'

'I'd have been quite safe here on my own, I'm sure,' Lydia murmured, and moved at last. She went over to the sink and began to gather the utensils she'd been using.

He handed her the mixing bowl. 'Besides, I thought you might enjoy a swim this afternoon.'

'Where?'

'There are some water holes a few miles away. We could take a couple of horses—'

'Not horses,' she said involuntarily. 'I mean,' she added, 'I—'

'I quite understand,' he said wryly. 'I'm often as stiff as a plank after I've been away from here for a while. We could take the bull buggy.'

'Well...' Lydia hesitated.

He raised an eyebrow at her. 'That's not what you were going to say?'

'I...um... I was stiff, but it's getting better. What I was going to say—'

'I promise not to cast lecherous looks at your legs,' he murmured. 'They caught me off guard, that's all. Being a mere male and...that kind of thing.'

Lydia turned the tap on so forcefully they were both hit by a spray of droplets.

He reached over and moderated the flow. 'We could take a picnic meal and your cake. It's deliciously cool there, under the trees. There are birds to watch, brolgas and storks, and water lilies, and there's not a cow for miles, because we've fenced it off from them—we like to think it's our own little equivalent of Kakadu.'

'Kakadu? Are you joking?'

'Come and see for yourself. Meg adores the place. So you'd be responsible for denying her a favourite outing if you said no.'

'That is sheer bribery and corruption!'

'Perhaps,' he said gravely. 'But I know you and Meg like each other.'

'Oh, all right!'

'I can't believe this,' Lydia said on a breath.

Kakadu National Park, world-heritage-listed and famous for its wetlands and rainforest, its Aboriginal rock art and sheer beauty, was in fact a long way from the Victoria River, Lydia knew, although still in the Northern Territory. But the idyllic spot Joe had brought her and Meg to in the bull buggy looked for all the world as if it *should* be in Kakadu.

From the vast savanna, a small creek originating from a spring had carved its way through a rocky outcrop, creating a waterfall, then a series of pools surrounded by lush vegetation. The banks were sandy, the water lilies were open in splashes of pink, white and lilac, and as they pulled up white egrets rose in slow flight to perch in the tall trees.

'Wait until you try the water,' Joe recommended. 'For anyone feeling at all stiff or sporting saddle bruising it's pure magic.'

'I don't think I can wait.' Lydia jumped out of the buggy, pulling her shorts and blouse off. She had a one-piece yellow costume on beneath, and she and Meg hit the main pool at the same time.

'Just don't tell me there are any crocodiles!' she called as she surfaced, gasping at the same time. 'I'd fight them bare-handed for this pool.'

He laughed.

'Oh, isn't this wonderful!' She dived under the water and surfaced again. 'It's so clean and cold and different from the tank water. Do you know?' She wiped her hair out of her eyes. 'I never thought I'd get rid of the dust and grit. I mean, I showered twice a day, but...' She raised her arms above her head and slid under the water again.

Joe was in when she surfaced this time. 'Sit under the water-fall,' he suggested. 'There's a ledge there.'

They swam together for the ledge and pulled themselves up as Meg barked delightedly and tried to scrabble up.

'Here you go!' Joe put his arms around the dog and lifted her bodily on to the ledge, only to almost immediately grasp his shoulder and grimace in pain.

'I thought you must be over that,' Lydia said breathlessly, as she moved her face behind the stream of water gushing down over them. 'I haven't seen any sign of it all week!'

'I'm gratified to think you were watching,' he murmured, 'but I've been very careful all week.'

'No, you haven't,' Lydia contradicted. 'Everything I've done you've done.'

'There are a lot of things I can do! It's just—it must be a certain angle, or something like that—what are you doing?'

Lydia was climbing carefully to her feet on the slippery rock. 'What I did last time. Any objections?' She knelt behind him and put her hands on his shoulder.

'I wouldn't dream of it,' he murmured.

Ten minutes later, she said, 'Well?'

'I beg your pardon?'

'Is it any better? It should have worked on a horse by now.'

He considered. 'I could be different. I could need it for longer and on an hourly basis, for example. Or do you treat all men as if they were horses so as—?'

He didn't finish for the simple reason that Lydia removed her hands from his shoulder to the middle of his back and pushed him into the pool. Unfortunately the exertion caused her to slip, and the only way she could save herself was to twist sideways and dive into the water. Meg, thinking it was all wonderful fun, jumped in almost on top of her.

But when she surfaced Joe Jordan was right beside her, and he took her into his arms.

'What do you think you're doing?' she spluttered.

'This,' he responded, and started to kiss her.

They went under, and when they came up she choked, 'More like drowning me, you idiot!'

'OK.' And he flipped her on her back and started to tow her towards the bank in a lifesaver's grip.

'I...you...' Lydia twisted and fought, then felt her feet touch the sandy bottom, and with a few more strokes they could both stand in water up to their waists.

'You're right,' he conceded, 'much easier to do it on one's feet—well, in certain circumstances.' And he started to kiss her again.

Despite his sore shoulder, Lydia discovered, he was more than a match for her. Besides, she told herself, she was breathless from all the horseplay and dunking. All the same, when he finally released her she could only stare at him wide-eyed for a long, long moment, because she had in fact stopped fighting him for other reasons...

Such as the electric feeling of fitting perfectly into his arms and the lovely shock of their wet bodies touching. The miraculous way he'd made her feel tall and slim but happy to be so, even though she was nearly as tall as he was and there had been times in her life when being five feet eleven had been a handicap. But not with Joe Jordan.

Because he'd made everything about her feel as if it had been expressly designed to please him, to feel gloriously attractive to him, and the way he'd kissed her once she'd started to feel this way had been sensationally arousing. The way he'd held her and handled her, so that she could feel his strength, but only to glory in it at the same time as she felt special and cherished. So much so that to be released had brought a pang of disappointment, and she'd only just stopped herself from reaching out to him...

'So,' he said quietly, and touched a finger to her wet cheek, 'we are in this together, Lydia, despite your assertions to the contrary.'

'I...you...' she stammered, on the brink of telling him that he could have given Casanova lessons.

He waited attentively.

She sighed. 'I knew it was too good to be true, Mr Jordan.'

CHAPTER THREE

HE DIDN'T ASK her to explain immediately.

She went behind a clump of bushes and changed back into her shorts and blouse. When she reappeared he was lighting a small fire on the sand. There was a tripod over it with a blackened can hanging from it.

'Genuine billy tea,' he said conversationally as she hesitated with her towel in her hand.

'Oh.' She gave her hair a final rub dry and hung the towel on the bull bars of the buggy. Then she ran her fingers through it a couple of times and let it settle, and started to plait it again.

'Here.' He pulled a cushion forward. 'Take a pew. I thought tea and a piece of your cake first, then, when we feel hungry again, I brought a couple of steaks.'

He hadn't changed, just added a shirt over his damp shorts.

They said nothing until the billy boiled and he threw in a handful of tea leaves. Lydia got the ginger cake out of the esky, discovered some butter and buttered some slices, one of which she gave to Meg. Joe poured the tea into thick china mugs.

'This cake is delicious,' he pronounced. 'Did he teach you to cook?'

'Brad? No, my aunt Chattie was mostly responsible, but I

think one really teaches oneself to cook, don't you? Either you have the interest or you don't.'

'True,' he conceded, 'although in my case it was a survival technique too. My mother was just like Sarah, so we grew up with a series of disastrous cooks—you learnt to fend for yourself.'

Lydia looked at him, slightly interested. 'Did your parents carve Katerina out of the wilderness, so to speak?'

'They did. They came here as a young couple very much in love. They survived drought, flood, pestilence, and gradually built up a herd. It was all the more remarkable because my mother was an English schoolteacher, born in the country and mad about horses, but there's a big difference.'

'What about your father?'

'He grew up in outback Queensland. He was from a grazing family.'

'Why don't you...' Lydia paused '...carry on the tradition?'

Joe stretched out on the sand and leant on his elbow, his good side. 'I was always torn between Katerina and the big smoke. So when Rolf arrived on the scene, proved his worth and—later, of course—married Sarah, it seemed like an opportunity to go out and try to make my name in another field. In this game you're always hostage to so many imponderables: weather, beef prices and so on. It's not a bad idea to have a couple of strings to your bow. But part of me will always live here.'

'Did you expect to succeed as well as you did?'

He was silent.

Lydia smiled. 'You did.'

He shrugged a shade ruefully. 'Perhaps, but not in the field I have succeeded in.'

'Tell me,' she invited.

'I majored in political science and English at university. I intended to become a journalist, a serious journalist. It was quite by accident that a bit of a talent for sketching saw me go down another road—although it is a form of journalism.'

'So you don't...' she paused '...paint or sketch or draw for any other reason?'

'No. I'm good at drawing funny faces to go with pithy captions; that's about it.'

'You, as well as Sarah and Rolf, need some strong sons to help you carry on the tradition here,' Lydia commented.

Joe hesitated. 'It's probably Sarah's place to tell you this, but she's had a few problems in that area. That's why they're taking this break. It's not exactly a holiday; they're joining an *in vitro* fertilisation programme.'

Lydia blinked and sipped her tea. 'I hope they're successful.'

He sat up. 'Otherwise it will be left to me to provide heirs. Just think what Daisy could have robbed Katerina of.'

Lydia glanced heavenwards.

'Have you heard how she is?' he asked.

'Away on a Musica Viva tour. No, I haven't been able to catch up with her personally.'

'Then should we discuss how Daisy didn't appear to even cross your mind not that long ago?' He gestured towards the pool.

'Let's not,' Lydia murmured.

'OK.' He looked quite obliging. 'I'm all for banning Daisy from looming up between us, but you said you knew it was too good to be true. What did you mean?'

'I...spoke without thinking.'

'Lydia,' he murmured, 'did you also kiss me without thinking?'

The sun was starting to set and the shadows of the trees were lengthening across the series of pools. Since they'd come out of the water the birds had gradually returned from the trees and were stalking through the shallows. The sound of the waterfall was oddly soothing.

'I've never,' she said slowly, 'been kissed against my will before. So I didn't really think. I...got carried along, I guess. That's all.'

He was silent again, and much as she would have wished otherwise she couldn't resist the flow of something between them that forced her to look into his eyes at last. And she had to flinch inwardly at the scepticism she saw in their hazel depths.

'All right,' she said abruptly. 'When I said I knew it was too good to be true I meant that I'd found it hard to believe you had given up all aspirations towards me. Men—'

'That was Plan B,' he broke in. 'But go on. Men...?'

'Can be extremely annoying,' she said through her teeth. 'But the most annoying thing of all, if you must know, was to find that I was even thinking about it. Although before you get your hopes up, Mr Jordan, most *women* suffer from—well, we're just human, I guess, and I couldn't help wondering why, or how, you could switch off me just like that!'

He raised an eyebrow. 'That's rather honest.'

'It doesn't mean to say I still wouldn't have given you the flick,' she answered with irony.

'So you don't mind being desired—?'

'It means,' she pressed on, disregarding, 'one would prefer to think one was desirable as opposed to as forgettable as an old shoe. End of story.'

'I see.'

She could see he was trying not to laugh, and she made a disgusted sound but was annoyed to find herself feeling hot all over. Possibly the result of making a fool of herself and *not* being entirely honest.

'I think I'd better tell you about Plan B,' he said gravely. 'When you explained about your husband, as well as your sister—who is not in love with me, by the way, but let's not digress—I realised that I'd been clumsy and heavy-handed and it might be a good idea for us to get to know each other better before I made any more—moves.'

Lydia's dark blue eyes widened.

'However, your legs bowled me over,' he said apologetically. 'Then, to see you frolicking like a mermaid, so naturally and joyfully, compounded things. But what really brought the worst out in me was being treated like a horse and—manhandled again.'

'I—didn't.'

He smiled wryly. 'Well, you are a vet, and you have a singular knack of making me feel like a piece of horseflesh when you're manipulating my shoulder, and you can't deny you've pushed me around a couple of times.'

'So that was revenge?' Lydia said incredulously.

'Not exactly. It was more like beating my manly chest to warn you that you may have taken me by surprise a couple of times but not to depend on getting away with it for ever.'

He said it quite seriously, but Lydia knew he was laughing at her, and to her amazement she found herself smiling reluctantly, then actually laughing at herself.

'I feel like an Amazon,' she said ruefully, at last.

'Don't,' he advised. 'You are talking to a slightly wounded ego, I have to confess. But...' He paused, and all of a sudden she sensed that he was completely sober as he went on, 'Proving that I *could* kiss you, whether you were willing or not, is not quite the same thing as wanting to kiss you.'

She swallowed.

'Or you enjoying being kissed by me,' he added.

She looked down at her hands, still clasping her mug, and put it down carefully. 'How not to feel a fool,' she murmured. 'Yes, I enjoyed it, but then I think I always knew I'd enjoy being kissed by you.'

She saw the flicker of surprise in his eyes.

'Put it this way,' she went on with a little shrug, and flicked her plait back. 'I didn't think it was that easy to define when we first met, but—I guess you exude a certain amount, if not to say rather a lot, of sex appeal, Joe. And I could suddenly see what Daisy obviously saw in you. As well as many others, no doubt.'

'Crikey,' he murmured, and stood up.

'Most men would be delighted to hear that.'

'I'm not most men,' he said witheringly. 'If I'd said something similar to you—'

'What's so different about you telling me you had this curious desire to see me without my clothes?' she countered, stung. 'If we're discussing being made to feel like an object!'

'Rubbish,' he retorted. 'All I'm trying to do is admit that we've had a "curious" effect on each other from the moment we laid eyes on one another.'

'And all I'm trying to do is point out why. But I'll put it plainer, if you like,' Lydia said dangerously. 'As I said at the time, your reputation preceded you, Mr Jordan. On top of which, Daisy thought enough of you to want you for the father of her child—who would *not* have wondered about you? But what you really thought of me was encapsulated in your cartoon.' She stopped abruptly and eyed him narrowly. 'You wouldn't have had a bet with yourself, by any chance?'

His sudden stillness gave him away.

Lydia made a disgusted sound and stood up to walk over to the edge of the pool.

He didn't follow suit, but watched her thoughtfully as she stared into the water with her arms folded. With that long-legged, coltish grace and her hair in a plait she looked about sixteen, he thought. But she hadn't kissed him like a novice teenager and one couldn't doubt she had a sharp brain and a mature outlook. He said quietly, 'Was that a stab in the dark?'

She looked over her shoulder at him. 'It obviously hit home.'

'OK. I did have a bet with myself.' He shrugged. 'But if we're talking about honest reactions, that's the way men tend to think, and is it any different from enjoying being desired rather than discarded like an old shoe—by *anyone*?'

'What was the bet?' Lydia enquired in arctic tones.

'That you would like to come to bed with me one day.'

She swung around and gazed at him fiercely. 'Take me home, Joe Jordan!'

'Not before we've sorted something else out, Lydia Kelso,'

he drawled. 'Could you be so worked up because you've found you're coming out of the shell of grief and missing your Brad and don't know how to handle it?'

'With a man who talks about making "moves" on me, has bets with himself about me and has bedded my sister? You couldn't be more right!'

'I—'

'Just take me home.' Her shoulders slumped. 'I don't want to talk about it any more.' She shivered suddenly.

'Here.' He pulled a jacket out of the buggy and handed it to her.

She accepted it reluctantly. It was his jacket, a khaki battle jacket, and she draped it over her shoulders, then went to sit in the buggy.

'Lydia,' he murmured, 'you're wasting your time.'

'What do you mean?'

He was unpacking the esky, which she suddenly saw contained a lot more than she'd realised. He straightened and gazed at her. And her nerves tightened unexpectedly. She recognised an easy finality about him, and not only that, a very adult masculinity, and he was, damn him, the only man who had intrigued her since Brad.

He said, 'We're not going home. In fact we're going to spend the night here. I tossed a couple of swags into the back.' He gestured at the buggy. 'We're going to cook steak and sausages, have a singsong and tell stories around the fire. We won't discuss anything you don't want to discuss and you don't have to worry that I'll take advantage of your person. That's what we'll be doing.'

'You can't! You can't just...do this!'

His lips twisted and he patted his pocket. 'I can. I happen to be in possession of the keys.'

'But I might not have wanted to do this ever before... before...' she stammered.

'Before we fell out? I think there are a few things you *think* you might not want to do, Lydia, but this one I'm sure you'll enjoy. Look, I'm not going to touch you, so you can sulk there, if you wish, or you could help me cook these steaks.' He bent down to continue unpacking the esky.

As the sun cast its first rays over the horizon the next morning, Lydia sat up and looked around dazedly. Then she went still, because there was a kangaroo drinking at one of the pools and some strange, tall birds she couldn't identify in another. She put her hand on Meg's collar and they watched and listened to the ·dawn and its chorus in sheer wonder—at least on Lydia's part.

She turned her head at last to see that Joe was awake and watching her. 'Brolgas?' she mouthed.

He nodded.

An hour later she was drinking hot coffee and eating a heated-up sausage in a roll. Despite having slept on the sand in a swag, she was not stiff. Joe had scraped out hollows for them, but she'd also had another swim. The water had been freezing, but marvellously refreshing, and she felt, she reflected, as good as she'd ever felt in her life.

She cupped her mug and glanced sideways at Joe Jordan. For she was wondering how to thank a man who had basically kidnapped her, for such a night to remember.

He hadn't laid a finger on her, but after they'd eaten their steaks, washed down with some red wine, he'd brought out a battered old mouth organ, and, soothed by food and wine, who would *not* have put aside their slightly chilly demeanour and relaxed beneath the stars with the fire built up to some bush ballads? Even joined in with her rather husky contralto?

She blinked suddenly as she realised he was looking back at her, and said, 'I know what you meant.'

He raised an eyebrow at her.

'About not taking advantage of my *person*. It was my soul you...' She stopped and looked away.

'Stole?' he suggested.

'Not quite, but soothed. Thanks. You were right; it was great.'

Joe ran his fingers over the shadows on his jaw, then through his hair, causing it to stand up in peaks. She was wearing his jacket again, but he didn't seem to feel the cold, nor did he have the look about him this morning of a man who would plot and plan to hold someone against her will. He looked disarmingly relaxed, even boyishly charming, bare-legged in the same shorts and shirt of the day before, which was to say that he looked quite harmless.

Then he stood up and stretched, and his physique caused Lydia's heartbeat to alter subtly. His legs were long, his waist and hips lean, his shoulders wide and powerful. And it occurred to her that all she'd seen him do over the past week—as good as any man on the property but more than that, with a particular ease and grace that made him a pleasure to watch on a horse—must have represented quite some will-power and toughness if his shoulder was still hurting him.

So he was something of an enigma, Joe Jordan, she was musing, when she realised he'd said her name. And realised her eyes were still on him, and that another plane of her mind was still registering all the things, all the physical things about him, that appealed to her.

She swallowed, and admonished herself for allowing herself to be affected in any way by the physical aspect of this man. And managed to say calmly, 'Yes?'

'I think it might be an idea to pack up and go. It's still early and we can beat the Simpsons home.'

She got up with sudden alacrity as a vision of his sister Sarah's curiosity at what might have transpired here in this delightful place overnight took hold of her. 'I couldn't agree more—and if no one asks I don't intend to tell them we spent the night here.'

He grinned, but said, 'It's what I had in mind as well. The protection of your fair reputation, Ms Kelso, although—'

'I know, I know.' She waved a hand. 'But people tend to imagine all sorts of things, so let's get this show on the road.'

They did. They were all loaded, Lydia was seated beside him in the front, Meg was perched in the back with her tongue lolling out happily, but when he put the key in and turned it, nothing happened.

Half an acrimonious hour later, they'd worked out the problem. On the journey from the homestead they must have hit a rock that had caused a fuel line to spring a fine leak, thereby gradually draining the tank along the way, and they must have coasted into the clearing around the pools and waterfall on the last drops of fuel in the tank.

'I don't believe this!'

'You've said that before,' Joe responded. 'By the way, where did you learn about mechanics?'

'What does it *matter*,' she replied impatiently. 'How could you not have noticed what was happening from the fuel gauge?'

'The fuel gauge hasn't been working for the last couple of days. That's why I filled it up.'

She stared at him frustratedly.

'Lydia, it's just one of those things,' he said serenely. 'And you've got grease on your chin. We'll be found, believe me.'

'The object of the exercise was not to be found! Now, not only will people be wondering all sorts of things but we'll be the laughing stock of the place—what are you doing?' she demanded as he took the esky out.

'I'm going to make you a cup of tea just now. There's more ginger cake.'

'I don't suppose you thought to bring more fuel,' she said witheringly.

'Assuming I had, which I didn't, to make space for the swags, we'd still have the problem—unless you're that good you can fix a fuel line in the middle of the bush? Were you proposing to wrap it up in your hanky?'

'Oh!' she groaned, in the most heartfelt way. 'Why are men so superior?'

'Now, Lydia,' he recommended, 'perhaps we shouldn't get on to that topic, because it could lead to other things about men. For example, we're hot, bothered and dirty, so I intend to have a swim—so should you, incidentally—and then I could recommend the perfect way to…ease your frustration. Were you to allow yourself to be thoroughly kissed, you'd find yourself feeling much better.'

Her mouth dropped open and stayed open for a moment, until she said feebly, 'How old do you think I am, Joe Jordan?'

'I know how old you are; you told me yourself—twenty-six, going on sixty.'

'I didn't say that,' she protested, and stopped.

'You didn't have to.'

Lydia put her hands on her hips and tossed her hair. 'What are you implying now?'

'Nothing.' He shrugged and pulled his shirt off. 'But come in,' he invited. 'At least this part of the cure comes with no strings attached.' And he waded into the water.

'How do I know you're not going to beat your manly chest again?'

'You don't.' He sank beneath the surface and came up with his hair plastered to his head, then started to wade towards her. 'Are you coming in or not?' he asked dangerously.

'Stay there,' she commanded, but not quite as forcefully as she would have wished. 'I… I've got to change first.'

They were drinking their tea when the Bell 45 flew overhead, then came back to hover over the clearing. Pete leant out and gave them the thumbs-up, but there was not enough clear space to land. Joe gestured to the bull buggy and gave the thumbs-down sign. Pete waved and flew off.

'See?' Joe said to Lydia. 'Help will be with us shortly. He'll radio through to the homestead.'

'Help in the form of horses?' she enquired.

'No, a truck that we can load the buggy on to, with a tow line and a winch.'

She sipped her tea. 'I didn't really believe you'd do it.'

'Do it?' He raised an eyebrow at her, causing her to bite her lip with annoyance, because Joe Jordan had not laid a finger on her, yet again, and, worse, found her obvious wariness amusing.

'Kiss me,' she elucidated gloomily.

'Is that an invitation?'

'No.'

'You weren't about to take the risk, however?' he hazarded.

She shrugged.

'Never mind,' he said comfortingly. 'I don't think any the less of you.'

Lydia frowned. 'What do you mean?'

'That I don't think it was wimpish of you to decide discretion might be better than valour in the circumstances but rather wise, that's all. If that's what was worrying you.'

She stared at him with her lips compressed, as much with annoyance towards herself as him. Because he'd spelt out her vague feeling of dissatisfaction with herself and, in doing so, had made her feel ridiculous. 'You are too clever by half, Joe Jordan,' she said bitterly.

'It's how I make a living,' he replied flippantly. 'But you're not half bad yourself. Where did you learn to strip an engine like that?'

She breathed deeply and took hold. If there was a way to counter the unsettling effect this man was having on her, it certainly wasn't the way she was going about it. 'The boy next door,' she said wryly.

He laughed. 'A boyfriend?'

'No. We grew up together because we were neighbours and the same age, and he was mad about motors. I used to help him. Eventually we progressed from lawn mowers to cars, although along the way we designed and produced a motorised go-cart.'

She grinned. 'When we nearly killed ourselves in it, we were banned from using it.'

'How did you nearly kill yourselves?' he asked, looking genuinely entertained.

'Well, the brakes failed as we were tearing down the drive, a long, sloping drive, and he ended up in the gutter and I came to rest in the hedge. He broke his arm. I just suffered cuts and bruises. His mother was particularly mad with me. I can remember her yelling—"Boys are bad enough, Lydia, you expect them to do crazy things, but girls should know better..." She got an awful fright.'

'So,' he said slowly, but with an assessing glint in his eye, 'a bit of a tomboy?'

She shrugged. 'I baked her this wonderful cake to say sorry for all the trauma we'd caused her. But, yes, I was always more interested in how things worked and, of course, animals rather than clothes, et cetera. That came later.'

'I think I'd like to have known you when you were growing up,' he said thoughtfully.

'What were you like?'

He raised his eyebrows and stroked Meg's head. 'A bit of a handful, I see now in hindsight. I didn't get on that well with my father. Possibly because while Sarah has never had any ambition to be anywhere else but Katerina, I did.'

'I'm sorry,' Lydia said sincerely.

He glanced at her narrowly, as if seeking an explanation for her sincerity.

'It's just, well, I've often wondered how my mother, who was a lot like Daisy, apparently, would have coped with a changeling like me.'

'You don't really see yourself as a changeling, do you?'

'No, not exactly. What I meant was, I'm different, and I think that can be hard for one's same-sex parent to cope with, but especially, perhaps, for fathers, who want to be able to pass on what they've carved out to their sons.'

'That's rather like—hitting the nail on the head,' he said ruefully, then paused with his head raised.

Lydia heard it a moment later: the sound of a truck.

He looked back at her. 'Rescue, salvation, whatever you like to call it, is at hand, Lydia.'

She swallowed, but couldn't tear her gaze away, and she felt her skin prickle because of an awareness of this man on several levels, now. Not only the physical, but an inkling of the currents that flowed beneath the surface and had helped shape him into something of an enigma. A feeling that there was more depth to Joe Jordan than some of his attitudes implied, as well as the uncertainty he provoked in her—he might not have touched her against her will after that first kiss, but she wasn't sure she could always rely on it.

They were still staring into each other's eyes when the truck laboured down the causeway, with Rolf at the wheel.

When they got back to the homestead, Sarah, as it happened, was not immediately curious about her brother and Lydia's night out under the stars. True, there was a slightly narrow look cast in Lydia's direction but that was the extent of it. The reason for this abstention might have been the result of Sarah finding herself on the receiving end of a pointed look of his own from Joe. Or it might have been because she'd come home from Dunoon full of plans to organise a 'B&S' ball the following Saturday night.

'A ball!' Joe said exasperatedly. 'We're in the middle of the mustering season, Sarah! And it gives you less than a week.'

'I don't need a week. And it can be our farewell party before we go away. It'll also give Lydia a chance to meet some of our neighbours.'

'Are we talking about a Bachelor and Spinster Ball?' Lydia asked.

'A synonym for any excuse to have a bash,' Joe said cynically. 'More than fifty per cent of the invitees will be married.'

'Who cares?' Sarah said blithely. 'Joe, be a darling and get in touch with Lefty Murdoch and his mates, for the music. Rolf is going to clean up the small shed—aren't you, my sweet? And I've arranged for the Dunoon cook to handle the food. We've just got to provide barbecues and spits—and, of course, the meat.'

'Thank heavens for one small mercy,' Joe intoned.

Causing his sister to say, 'You're not in a very good mood, beloved. Why don't you go and create a cartoon?'

He went, muttering beneath his breath.

That was when Sarah chose to voice her thoughts about the night Lydia and Joe had spent together. 'Keep knocking him back, Lydia. It's about time some woman did,' she said, with a conspiratorial smile, and she waltzed off leaving Lydia blinking dazedly.

'I didn't bring anything to wear to a ball, Sarah,' Lydia said several days later.

Sarah laughed. 'Well, we do try to be innovative and dressy, and most of the men wear dinner jackets even if it's with jeans, but let me take a look at what you did bring and I'll pass judgement.'

'My dear Lydia,' she said a few minutes later, holding up the only dress Lydia had brought—and then only because she'd been quite sure Brad's parents would take her out to dinner in Townsville. 'What do you mean you don't have a dress?'

'But it's short. It's not really a ball thing; it's—'

'Divine,' Sarah said of the simple black silk georgette dress studded with silver metal embroidery. She looked at the label. 'Ah. No wonder! No, its beauty will lie in the fact that it's not a ball dress, but I can just picture you looking stunning in it—stunning enough to sock Joe right between the eyes.'

Lydia sat down on her bed. 'Sarah, Joe has not addressed two words to me for the last few days.'

'I know, he's been going around like a bear with a sore head, but that generally is because he's either been thwarted or he's finding it hard to get inspiration.'

'Daisy said he could be moody...' Lydia realised she'd spoken without thinking.

Sarah raised an eyebrow. 'Your sister?'

'The same.'

'Well, she's right. But if you just ignore it, it doesn't last. Look, I've got to dash. Rolf is complaining mightily about all the time he's spending on the shed, so I said I'd give him a hand. Would you be sweet enough to do dinner for me tonight?'

'Of course,' Lydia murmured, and stood up to hang up her dress.

She was having an easy day because the men, most of them, were setting up portable yards in a new paddock for the next muster. In fact the next two days until the ball were going to be easy for her—one of the huge road trains used to transport the mustered stock had broken down and would be delayed, so the muster itself would be delayed.

Not that she'd sat around doing nothing. She'd also helped with the shed, helped a mare with a difficult foaling, and spent some time on the team that was educating the weaners so that in future musters they would be easy to handle and know what was required of them before they were returned to the herd.

She went to the kitchen and started dinner. When the roast lamb was in the oven, the potatoes and pumpkin peeled and the green vegetables prepared, she poured herself a glass of wine and went to sit on the back step to watch the sunset. Meg immediately joined her, indicating that Joe must be home, although she hadn't heard him come in. It caused her to smile faintly to think that he could be avoiding her.

Was this Plan C? she wondered.

But almost as soon as she'd wondered it he wandered out onto the verandah—with a beer in his hand, and there was an air about him that she instantly recognised, a relaxed air.

'So it *was* a lack of inspiration rather than—' she said, and stopped ruefully.

He sat down on the step beside her. 'If you're referring to my uncommunicative attitude for the past few days, yes, but how the hell could you tell and how can you now tell it's over?'

'My father,' she explained. 'He goes through the same thing. Mind you, I wouldn't call it uncommunicative, downright moody is a better description—but when he's over it he has this rather beatific, relaxed air about him. That's exactly how you look at the moment.'

He raised an eyebrow. 'I apologise for being so transparent, but what was your second scenario?'

Lydia bit her lip, because she'd been hoping he would ignore what she'd left unsaid. Faint hope with this man, she mused. 'Just something your sister said,' she murmured.

'Don't tell me,' he drawled. 'Sarah is even more transparent than I am. She thinks I'm in a mood because I'm not getting my way with you, no doubt.'

'Just goes to show how wrong you can be, even a sister,' Lydia remarked, not without some complacency.

'She's not wrong at all.'

The sun had set, but its rays were still illuminating the sky with streaks of orange, and a living, fleeting rose-pink that almost made you want to catch your breath it was so beautiful was colouring the dusty countryside beyond the garden fence.

Lydia watched it fade before she turned her head to Joe Jordan. 'I don't know what to say.'

'Obviously.'

'So did it have anything at all to do with not being able to create?'

'Sure.' He shrugged. 'A double whammy for me again—I really don't know what I've done to deserve it,' he added plaintively.

'Well, tell me about the other one,' she said a little helplessly.

He looked at her with some irony before saying, 'OK. I am

in fact on official leave at the moment. Someone else has taken over from me. But in the event of Sarah and Rolf having to spend more time down south, which is a possibility, then I'm going to have to spend more time up here. So I thought I'd have a go at doing things at long distance, so to speak. It's almost impossible.'

'But you said technology, et cetera, made it possible to pursue your career up here.'

'I was hoping it would. But I need to be right there, with my finger on the pulse.'

'I see.' Lydia blinked at the growing dusk. 'You couldn't get in another manager?'

'It's not easy, and I want Sarah and Rolf to be able to relax and give this shot at having a baby a real go without having to worry about Katerina. They deserve it.'

'So,' she said slowly, 'what were you looking so relaxed and beatific about?'

He grinned. 'Well, it wasn't some devilish plan to have my way with you, Lydia. No, I've made a decision. I'm taking the next nine months off.'

'Will—*can you*, without prejudicing your future?'

'Time will tell. In the meantime I'm going to transfer my creative skills to something a bit different. A weekly column about the outback.'

'That's very...very decent of you,' Lydia said.

'Ah, but it is only you, dear Lydia, who has doubts about my decency,' he countered, and raised his beer can.

Lydia glanced sideways and saw the smooth muscles of his tanned throat work as he swallowed some beer. For some reason it caused her to shiver noticeably, and when he asked if she was cold, and she said she was, she was miserably aware that she was telling a lie. Worse, she was also aware that she might not have deceived him, judging from the glint of something in his eyes that was at the same time amused and faintly sardonic.

But he made no move to stop her when she got up and went inside to tend to dinner. Nor did he offer to help.

She tossed and turned in bed for a while that night before she could get to sleep as she examined her feelings about Joe Jordan. Especially in light of what he'd done for Sarah and Rolf. And not only that, he was right, she mused. There was an undoubted attraction about him for her, and she was forced to face the fact that she could be coming out of her shell of grief and loneliness for Brad, and didn't know how to handle it.

But a physical attraction was one thing, she reflected. Being soul-partners with a man was another. Having once had it, she could never settle for less... And, of course, pertaining to the point was—what was he looking for? Just the settlement of a bet he'd had with himself?

She flinched as she thought of it and reflected that there was a lot to be wary about regarding Joe. Then she sighed and reminded herself there was more than that. There was Daisy.

Two nights later she dressed for the ball.

The shed, open on two sides and strung with gas lights, streamers and kerosene lanterns, no longer resembled a rather rusty iron structure with a concrete floor. Square bales of hay had been set about and draped with colourful covers. Trestle tables had been erected and Sarah had produced a wide variety of cloths to cover them. Green boughs tied with ribbon had been hung up, and several barbecues and open fires just outside the shed were glowing in the darkness.

All afternoon a steady stream of light planes and four-wheel drives had been converging on Katerina, and the trestle tables were starting to groan beneath an array of food. Joe and Rolf had already started the spit roasting of the meat, but the Dunoon chef had arrived now and taken over.

Lydia had been down with Sarah to put the last touches to things. Whilst some people were staying over at the homestead, a lot were camping under the wings of their planes, or in tents beside their vehicles. Lydia had looked around in some amazement, because it was as if a small community had grown up around the small shed—a misnomer, actually. It was a large shed, just smaller than the others.

And she'd complimented Sarah on achieving all this in less than a week as they'd walked back to the house.

'Oh, we're all old hands at this. Not that we do it that often. But you have to make your own entertainment up here. I'm feeling very happy,' Sarah had confided. 'Joe told me he'd mentioned to you why Rolf and I are going away?'

'He did.' Lydia had taken Sarah's hand and squeezed it gently. 'I hope and pray it will be successful for you.'

'You're sweet, Lydia. And I can't help feeling—I know it sounds stupid—but with this kind of a send-off, we might be. It's also such a load off our minds to know that Joe is happy to stay and look after things, should we need to be away for longer. They did advise me I'd be better off closer to civilisation.'

All the same, Lydia reflected as she dressed, she was curiously reluctant to go to this ball.

No, not curiously reluctant, she amended. She knew exactly the cause of her reluctance. It had a name. Joe...

CHAPTER FOUR

HE WAS THE first person she bumped into as she stepped out on to the verandah from her room. He was doing the same.

And because the homestead was lit up like a Christmas tree, they could see each other with extraordinary clarity.

Lydia had started to say something, although she had no idea what it was, but she closed her mouth and found herself unable to do anything but accept his scrutiny.

The black silk georgette was simply styled, a vee-neck, cap sleeved, waistless panelled style that hugged her figure to the hips then flared slightly about her knees. The silver metallic embroidery was dotted over the material like tiny bursts of star-light and swirled into a denser cluster down one flank. With it she wore a pair of elegant, closed-toe sandals with small heels.

It was a dress that showed off her legs to advantage and her figure in a way that brought it into its own—her long, slender waist and unexpectedly feminine hips.

She'd also put her hair up in a smooth pleat and stroked some mascara on to her lashes. She wore a silver bangle in place of her watch, and Brad's signet ring, which she'd had made smaller, on her little finger, as always.

Joe Jordan looked up into her eyes at last and murmured, 'You should have warned me.'

'I...what do you mean?'

'When I saw you in your togs it occurred to me that I could dress you far better than you dressed yourself—'

'Now don't start, Joe,' she broke in wearily.

'No, I mean...' he looked rueful '...choose a style of clothes for you to wear that would make you look stunning rather than hiding your figure in mannish suits.'

She breathed exasperatedly. 'That was the only time you've seen me out of work clothes or shorts!'

'All the same, I wasn't to know you could dress like this. My apologies—unless this dress was an accidental choice?' he said gravely.

'You're...you are impossible!' she accused.

'Perhaps. But why *do* you hide behind those suits?'

'Hide what?' She stopped and tried to recover her composure. 'That I'm a bit of a beanpole?' she asked with amusement. 'And not fashioned in the least like my sister Daisy?' The last bit slipped out less amusedly.

He put his head on one side and allowed his hazel gaze to travel up and down her figure again. 'No, you're not, but in fact you could be classier than D—' He stopped as her hand flashed out and struck his cheek.

'Don't you dare insult my sister,' she breathed at the same time, then stopped, both shocked and amazed at what she'd done. Her lips parted. 'I...'

But she couldn't go on, and Joe Jordan touched his cheek then took the hand she'd used in a hard grip. 'I think I'll keep this weapon in my possession while I say what I'm going to say. I was only talking about a certain elegance you display that is less obvious than your sister Daisy's charms, therefore all the more surprising, and, yes, classier, to my mind.'

Lydia tried to pull free but he wouldn't let her.

'I haven't finished, Lydia,' he murmured dryly. 'And if your beloved Brad didn't make you aware of this, then he may not have been the man you took him for.'

She gasped, coloured brilliantly, and her eyes darkened to midnight-blue. 'Oh, yes, he was, Joe Jordan. He used to tell me he adored my hips and legs and every beanpole inch of me. He made me feel wonderful in his arms and what was more, he gave me the courage to dress for comfort when I wanted to and not give a damn about what other men thought,' she said proudly. 'Will you let me go?'

He released her hand abruptly and she turned on her heel and left him standing where he was.

Meg wandered up to her master, and after a moment he bent down and patted her head. At the same time he said, 'What is it about her that brings out all the worst in me, Meg?'

Predictably, Meg didn't answer.

Why, why, why?

It was something Lydia asked herself over and over during the rest of what turned out to be a very long evening. Why had she allowed herself to be taunted into making personal statements of such a nature? Why had she resorted to slapping his face when she'd never done anything like that in her entire life? But who wouldn't take offence at being told they didn't know how to dress, that their sister was not classy and that their beloved husband might not have been much of a man?

Not to mention the mere fact that *he* was a man who *could* comment on her sister's figure, she thought bitterly at one point.

Throughout this internal dialogue with herself she was introduced to a lot of people. She danced to Lefty Murdoch's band, she talked, laughed and ate, and at one point got quite cross with herself for not being able to give this unique experience her all. Her being furious just below the surface would always colour this version of a Bachelor and Spinster Ball, way up in the VRD of the Northern Territory, where a lot of the men *did* wear evening jackets with jeans and boots and tall, wide cowboy hats and where part of the food was a roast pig on a spit.

Some of the gowns were magnificently formal—despite the fact that their wearers had dressed in a tent or under the wing of a plane—and her own dress came in for plenty of compliments on its sheer, simple elegance. And Joe Jordan was obviously delighting his neighbours with his presence, although he hadn't followed the dinner jacket and jeans fashion, but wore a blue long-sleeved shirt with button-down pockets, a dark red tie and bone-coloured moleskins.

She sat down on a bale of straw at one point and fanned herself with her hand, then discovered Meg beside her. 'It's not fair,' she said to the dog. 'You're so gorgeous and your master is a complete pig!'

Meg lifted her paw gravely. Lydia shook it, smiling reluctantly and saying, 'Oh, well, I don't suppose you can agree with me—what's that you've got on your collar?'

It turned out to be a note tied to the dog's collar with a piece of string. What was more, it had her name on it. She untied it with a frown and opened it. It was a cartoon. A Joe Jordan look-alike was banging his head against a wall in despair. A Lydia Kelso look-alike, even to the dress she was wearing at that moment, was walking away from him. The caption was 'HOW CAN I SAY I'M SORRY? I AM, TRULY.'

She gazed at it, then, as a shadow fell across her, gazed up at the author and moistened her lips. 'How did you know Meg would get it to me?'

'I have unlimited faith in Meg. She even forgives me when she shouldn't. When I've been a complete pig.'

Prepared to see amusement lurking in those hazel eyes, Lydia was amazed to find none.

'May I find you something to drink and somewhere a bit quieter to drink it?' he queried.

She hesitated.

'Lydia,' he said quietly, 'there seems to be some confusion between us on one point at least. I never slept with Daisy; I never even gave her cause to think I would.'

* * *

'Why didn't you tell me this straight away?'

They were back up at the homestead on their own, having found no quiet spot around the shed. When he'd looked at her with a question in his eyes she'd agreed that she'd had enough of the B&S ball.

And once again they were sitting in the garden, with the sounds of revelry carried to them faintly through the chilly night air. Lydia had gone to her room and put on a long silver cashmere cardigan. Joe had made them coffee laced with whisky to counteract the chill, especially after the frenzy of the ball. The homestead was still lit up like a Christmas tree.

To say that she was still feeling dazed was true. Because she hadn't known what to say until this moment.

'Why didn't Daisy tell you?' he murmured.

She shrugged. 'Daisy has a habit of clamming up about things like that. But I was pretty sure. That still doesn't explain why *you* didn't, on one of the several opportunities you had to tell me yourself.'

He crossed his hands behind his head and gazed up at the stars. 'I think,' he said slowly, 'I was waiting for the right opportunity to give it the most impact. Mind you, I did start to tell you a couple of times, but on the last occasion at least, you cut me off.'

She started to speak several times then, said, 'Would you explain what you mean by "the most impact"?'

'Before I do that...' He frowned. 'I was not to know what Daisy *had* told you.'

'I took it as read, I'm afraid,' Lydia said. 'I... I...well, Daisy's walking around listening to her biological clock ticking. She seems quite obsessed with it and she did say a couple of things that—well—led me to think—and then there was your reputation.' She stopped a little helplessly.

He grimaced, but made no comment.

'You are fairly renowned for escorting beautiful women around the place,' she pointed out.

'If you're asking me whether I sleep with them all, no, I don't, although I can't deny there have been a few relationships down the years. So, no, I don't sleep around on a casual basis, Lydia. I do possess a few scruples, not to mention a sense of self-preservation, and that's why I didn't fall in with Daisy's suggestion.'

He paused, then went on, 'As a matter of fact, I like Daisy. She's fun and I think she'd be a good friend.'

'But you must have had some idea that she was wanting to be more than a friend,' Lydia objected.

Joe Jordan sighed and looked up at the starry heavens with, to Lydia's surprise, a distinct air of remorse. 'I may not have given it a lot of thought.'

She made a slight sound.

'I know,' he went on. 'I can be like that at the best of times, and this was not one of them.' He looked down and across at her. 'I had this situation looming.' He gestured to encompass Katerina, and Rolf and Sarah.

Poor Daisy, crossed Lydia's mind. She said, with some irony, although Joe was not to know it was mostly self-directed, 'Tell me about this "most impact" bit, then?'

He frowned. 'It's a little hard to define—'

'You wouldn't have been waiting to use it when it was about the only thing left that would redeem you?' she asked with some cynicism.

He said soberly, 'I asked Meg what it was about you that brought out the worst in me... I'm sorry, it was unforgivable. But, no, I don't think it was that, although that's undoubtedly how I used it. I guess I was hoping to use it to remove the last traces of doubt you may have had about what we do to each other.'

Lydia was struck silent.

'All the same,' he added 'when you're unfairly painted the deepest black, you tend to be defiant—that is, if you're me.'

Lydia couldn't help the shadow of a smile touching her lips. 'I believe you,' she murmured, and sipped her coffee.

He sat up. 'So, having removed Daisy for once and for all, where do we stand now?'

'I...look... I don't know if we have. I gave her some advice that I'm heartily regretting now, because I think she may be practising it—towards you.'

'Lydia, you struck terror into my heart when we first met,' he said ominously, 'so—'

'I did not!'

'Yes, you did. You told me your sister was planning to use me as a stud and that your father was liable to come and harangue me, if nothing else. So what's in the wind now?'

Lydia sighed. 'I suggested, in the most general way, that perhaps she should play hard to get instead of being so...so generous towards the men she was sure she was in love with before she'd really had time to, well, know what it was.'

'So? That's good advice, I would have thought.'

She cast him a frustrated little glance. 'I think she's playing hard for *you* to get, Joe.'

He swore softly. 'Look, so long as you don't slap my face again, I admire your desire to save your sister from herself, if I may put it like that.' He stopped and their gazes caught and held.

Lydia bit her lip. 'I'm sorry for that, and it's not likely to happen again, but—'

'Yes,' he interrupted, 'there were other things said. But before we go into those, surely you must absolve me now from any of Daisy's—uh—problems?'

'I do,' she said, after a long pause. 'The one thing I can't get around is that she may be genuinely in love with you.'

'Oh, no,' he said grimly. 'No, Lydia. That's carrying your generosity towards your sister a bit too far. In fact it's more. It's cowardly, and I think you know why.'

'Here we go again,' she said, but with genuine distress in her voice as she put her mug down on the lawn and stood up. 'More insults, Joe? Well, I'm not going to listen to them. Goodnight.'

But as she went to walk away from him he was on his feet like a flash, then she heard his indrawn breath and saw his hands clench into fists before he deliberately relaxed and let them hang at his sides, and took a step backwards.

Surprise held her quite still, on two counts. The sheer intensity he'd conveyed before harnessing it, and the invisible cord of something flowing between them that refused to let her move away.

A cord that became a painfully searching moment as they stared into each other's eyes, and the power of knowing that he'd stopped himself from touching her against her will held her hostage, unable to move from the spot, she realised.

Then he said, barely audibly, 'Insulting is the last thing to describe my state of mind towards you. The fact that I seem to have two left feet is, in fact, an indication that I've been thrown off base from the moment I laid eyes on you and I don't seem to be handling it too well.'

'Oh, Joe.' She said it softly, on little more than a breath, and discovered she was moved by this admission, moved to a feeling of tenderness that made her reach out and put the tips of her fingers on the exact spot where she'd slapped him earlier.

He didn't stir for a long moment, but then he took her hand from his cheek and kissed the palm, and looked up into her eyes again. And she began to experience the unique sensation of drowning in that clever hazel gaze. Not only that, she thought with the edges of her mind, but drowning in a sudden surge of desire to be held and caressed and warmed by this surprising man who could also infuriate her like no other.

He did it slowly, as if testing her reaction bit by bit. He took the two steps that would bring them together but he was still only holding her hand. And the edges of her mind were slowly turning inwards, and everything else on it was dissolving into a feeling of helpless intimacy, a yearning to know again a man's hard strength against her, *this* man's. A yearning to be gathered close, and at the same time, a curiosity about how he would kiss her...

She should have known, she was to think later, that he would do it expertly and with finesse. She should have known that he would not rush but make sure she was following where he led with the lightest of touches that were at the same time devastatingly sensual. Even the way he slid her silver cardigan off and laid it over the chair involved the running of his fingers down her arms in a way that made her shiver with a kind of rapture.

Then he released her hair, and she shook her head so that it flew out in a cloud, then settled to its usual tousled unruly mane.

But there was no way she could have known the things he would say. No way of preparing herself to have her eyes, as he kissed her closed lids, her skin, as he laid his lips lightly on her slender neck, her hair, as he ran his hands through it luxuriously, or her body, as he ran his hands down it, described so richly and beautifully in his deep murmur.

Nor could she have predicted that beneath the weight of his words and his hands, she would feel like an exquisite creature instead of a rather gangly vet, with skin that felt like velvet and had the glow of crushed pearls, sapphire eyes, a graceful, slender figure that was beckoning him from behind a sheer veil of star-dusted georgette without the benefit of its satin lining.

'You kissed the Blarney Stone somewhere along the line, Joe,' she whispered once, in an effort to keep her feet on the ground—speaking metaphorically? she wondered at the same time.

'No, I'm kissing you, Lydia,' he murmured. 'Did you know your skin has a perfume all of its own? *Fragrance Lydia*, I'll call it. And I love the fact that you're tall enough not to give me a crick in my neck when we do this...'

'This', when they'd stopped smiling, was to come together again, so she was deep within his embrace with her breasts crushed against him as they kissed once more, and the stirrings of desire were flowering within her as she slid her arms around his waist and moved against him.

What would have happened to them from there on she couldn't doubt, because amidst the embarrassment that ensued there was also the cruel little feeling of a cold, empty space within. But the fact of the matter was the homestead party chose that moment to return, and she and Joe Jordan were surprised, if not exactly *in flagrante delicto*, certainly in a telling embrace.

As a chorus of whistles erupted his arms hardened around her and he swore beneath his breath. Then he took one arm away, but kept her close, saluted the revellers leisurely and drew her around the corner of the house out of sight.

'How... ? Oh, no,' she said, distraught, with her hands to her hot cheeks. 'What will Sarah think?'

'She's probably cheering. Don't be upset. Let's look on the funny side—'

'You may be able to; I can't see a funny side,' she broke in, then, to her amazement, started to smile, and finally they were laughing together. But as they sobered he took her hand and said her name.

She swallowed and shook her head, as if to clear her mind, but voices and footsteps were approaching and her nerve failed her.

'Goodnight, Joe,' she murmured, and fled.

The next morning her cardigan was folded neatly on a chair outside her verandah door with a spray of wild flowers resting on it.

But Lydia had had a night to come to her senses. She picked up the flowers and rested their soft, dewy petals against her cheek for a moment, then sighed and went to confront Joe Jordan, as well as his sister.

It didn't prove as awkward as she'd feared—Joe was already out on the run and Sarah was in such a fluster about leaving Katerina that the surprising events of the previous night seemed to have escaped her mind.

Finally, when Rolf was starting to look impatient and Pete was making remarks about them missing their Darwin connection because whilst he *was* flying them there it was not in a Lear jet, Lydia said to Sarah, 'Just go, Mrs Simpson! I'll look after the house, I'll clear up the shed, and between us Joe and I can fill in for you and Rolf.' She put her hands on Sarah's shoulders and added softly, 'Good luck.'

But when she wandered down to the shed it was to discover that Katerina's neighbours, now heading home either by road or air, had been very neighbourly. It was all tidied up.

Lydia leant against a metal upright and marvelled at the transformation. In the harsh daylight, and stripped of its streamers, music and greenery, its colourful revellers and the rich aroma of food, it was an ordinary, not particularly attractive tin shed. Was there an analogy there for her own situation? she wondered.

Had she been transported to a rich, sensuous wonderland by a clever man who could not be unskilled at pleasing women? Had he made her feel like a silken creature from the pages of an exotic *Arabian Nights* kind of story, which, of course, bore little resemblance to her down-to-earth, practical self? Not even Brad...

She stopped on the thought and put her hand to her mouth with something like anguish piercing her heart. How could she compare them? How could a physical attraction take the place of that sense of belonging, that ease she and Brad had had? That feeling of knowing Brad through and through, whereas Joe Jordan was an enigma and sometimes a dangerous one.

To complicate matters, she mused, after staring into the distance rather blindly, she couldn't now blame him for assuming she was a willing participant in the sensual games they'd played last night—and she was stuck on her own with him for the next three weeks.

She moved at last and decided there was only one thing she could do at the moment, and that was to concentrate on earning her keep.

The gelding she usually rode was in the horse paddock, and as she whistled and produced the couple of sugar cubes she always put in her pocket it pricked its ears and trotted up obligingly. Stock horses were a breed in their own right in the outback, and although they'd suffered a decline in popularity when, for a variety of reasons, helicopter mustering had all but taken over, they were now coming back into their own, as were experienced ringers or coachers—quality riders skilled in handling mobs of cattle from horseback.

And Billy, her chestnut gelding, was a joy to ride. She could never compare herself in skill or quality to most of the ringers she'd seen on Katerina, but with Billy's help, his training and stamina, she'd managed not to disgrace herself. It had been Joe who'd picked Billy out for her and recommended her to put herself in his hands... 'He knows what he's doing,' he'd said, with a glimmer of a smile.

She'd later discovered that Joe himself had broken Billy in. One of the many surprising discoveries she'd made about the man she'd labelled as 'trendy' on first impressions, she reflected, as she put the heavy stock saddle on and tightened the girth, then crammed her felt hat on and swung herself up on to the horse. Another being the fact that he could ride like the wind with the best of them and was obviously respected, not only as an owner of Katerina but for his skills.

She guided Billy out of the paddock, opening and closing the gate without having to dismount, and set him at a canter towards the portable yards that they'd erected for the latest muster.

After a while she was able to drag her mind from Joe Jordan as her body rose and fell to the rhythm of the canter, the saddle creaked and a light breeze lifted Billy's mane. She gazed about as she rode and noticed that the countryside was drying out noticeably as winter slid towards the wet season. A swirl of dust on the horizon showed her that the delayed road train was crawling along a rocky track towards another swirl of dust— the temporary yards. She slowed Billy to a walk, not that keen to arrive, and not only because of Joe, but because of a sense of wonder at her environment.

Despite feeling like a dot in the vast sandy-pink landscape, she didn't feel intimidated. Which was a little strange, because she'd lived all her life in a city. Of course her father had taken both she and Daisy on pilgrimages to the bush, and perhaps his preoccupation with it had encouraged this attraction for her. But that still didn't explain the feeling she'd discovered since coming to Katerina of a better understanding of what life was about, although how or why she wasn't sure.

Did it mean she felt more at peace with herself because of these surroundings? Was it the challenge she enjoyed? It certainly wasn't always comfortable. Despite most modern amenities at the homestead there was still the heat, the dust, there were still the flies, the loneliness of the wet months when roads were impassable and the only way in and out was by air.

She shrugged and clicked her tongue and wondered, as Billy lengthened his stride, whether it was all much simpler. She was restless because of the lack of focus in her life...

As soon as she arrived at the yards, it was plain to see things weren't going well. The cattle truck, a monster with two double-decker trailers, had somehow managed to jackknife in its attempt to back up to the loading ramp and jam one of its couplings. Fortunately, it was a smallish muster, this one, and the drafting process had gone smoothly, so it was only the sale cattle still yarded. But the dust and the delay were making them restless, and, not long after she arrived, they broke through the fence.

She thought later that Billy had acted instinctively, and it had to have helped that she'd been the only one mounted whilst all the other men had been labouring over the truck. All the same it took her breath away when the horse took off at a gallop and began to round up the errant cattle.

She regained her breath and had the sense to simply sit tight for a while, but then she began to participate, to move with him, to rip her hat off and use it as well as the whistles and hand signals she'd learnt over the previous weeks—a whole language of hand signals that were vital when you were working as a team. And there were others on their horses now, helping as they attempted to calm and collect a mob of cows bent on stampeding to freedom.

When they were all back in the yard, and Lydia was breathing raggedly and feeling exhausted, it was one of the ringers who said to her, 'Well done, missus! We'd'a lost 'em without you.'

She patted Billy's steaming neck and slid off him. 'I think it was my horse, but thanks.'

Joe strode up to her as she hit the ground and found herself curiously unsteady on her legs. He put his hands around her waist, smiled into her eyes, and murmured, 'I could kiss you for that, Ms Kelso. I haven't been having the best of days, as you can see.' And he did.

Whereupon everyone cheered and someone called out, 'I'd ride her straight to the altar if I were you, Joe. Word's around you two got something going, and it's 'bout time you got hitched, anyway.'

'Steak, eggs, chips and a salad?'

'Why not?' Joe responded to her query re dinner. 'But only if you promise to sit down first and tell me what you're thinking.'

They hadn't come back together. Joe had insisted she hitch a ride on a vehicle bound for the tool shed not long after her daring feat of mustering, and had promised to lead Billy home himself. So she'd spent the rest of the day making sure the vet station was in good order, then she'd walked up to the homestead and, as she'd promised Sarah, tidied up there.

He had only just come in when she'd posed the question of dinner to him. So that while she was showered, changed and looking cool and clean in a pair of grey trousers and a warm blue long-sleeved shirt, he was the opposite. His khaki shirt was sweat-soaked and clinging to his back, the golden hairs on his arms were invisible beneath a layer of dust, and his hair, as he took his hat off, was plastered to his head.

'Nothing very much,' she responded casually, with a friendly smile. 'Well, I just thought I'd check your preferences for dinner so you can go and have a heavenly shower while I get started. I'm sure you're dying for a beer, but it will go down much better when you're cleaned up.'

He stood in the middle of the kitchen, staring at her narrowly. Then he said slowly, 'Is this what I think it is?'

She looked at him blankly.

'Get back into your box, Fido, in other words?'

'I don't know what you mean—' She broke off and closed her eyes briefly, because of course she knew exactly what he meant. She'd also underestimated her capacity to deal with him in what she'd hoped would be a friendly but firm manner.

'Lydia?'

She moved towards the stove, unable to think of a thing to say and unable to meet the challenge in his eyes.

'All right,' he drawled, 'but I not only need a shower, I need about an hour to make some calls and send some faxes. If you'd like to have dinner ready then, I'll join you.'

He strode out of the kitchen, leaving Lydia so angry she could only stare after him, speechless. What was going through her mind was quite articulate, however. How dared he treat her as if she were only the hired cook?

It was because she desperately needed something to do that she did in fact cook dinner, although with an angry reluctance as she pondered his sheer high-handedness. It also occurred to her that she should have known he could assume this manner. She'd seen it with her own eyes today down at the muster yards, although she'd failed to take heed. But with Rolf gone, Joe had gone up a notch, in a manner of speaking.

His authority had always been there, she reflected, but in a low-key way so that his manager, who also happened to be his brother-in-law and a shareholder, was his equal. Now he deferred to no one, and if she hadn't been dazzled by him on another plane, as well as trying to sort out philosophical questions to do with her own life, she would have taken heed of his manner today down at the yards—very much the boss and respected for it.

But not by her, she thought, as she dished up dinner, set it out in the verandah room, called out that it was ready, and sat down to start without waiting for him.

He came within a few minutes, and, without consulting her, opened a bottle of wine and poured two glasses.

She stared at the glass he'd placed in front of her. 'Don't imagine this will soften me up, Joe.' And she raised deep blue hostile eyes to his.

He shrugged and sat down. 'All right. Let's have a good row, Lydia. If we're going to spend the next three weeks together, we might as well clear the air now.'

He'd changed into a green and white checked viyella shirt and fawn corduroy trousers. He looked aggressively clean and scrubbed and exuded the faint tang of soap. He also looked attractive in that lean-hipped, broad-shouldered way that was a trial to many woman, she had no doubt, and looked dangerous at the same time—as only he could.

'You can go first,' he added casually, and started to cut his steak.

'No, I've a better idea. Why don't you? I haven't got much to say—how *can* you?' she added, as if genuinely offended, with her gaze on the tomato sauce bottle he'd just upended over his chips.

'I may be a gourmet in some respects but that's how I like

my chips, Lydia. With tomato sauce.' He put the bottle down with a small thump.

'My apologies,' she murmured dryly.

He looked at her sardonically.

'You may not realise this, Joe,' she said through her teeth, 'but I am not the hired household help. I'm doing this out of the goodness of my heart, so don't think you can order me around as to when I deliver meals because you might just find yourself getting your own!'

'And you may not realise *this*, Lydia, but when you kiss someone the way you did last night, it is then unacceptable to treat them as if it never happened, with a pat on the head and—'

'Joe, nevertheless,' she said with an effort, 'we need to put it into perspective. I'm just not prepared to carry on mindlessly. Nor do I appreciate the whole world linking me with you.'

He raised an eyebrow. 'A very small world. And have I asked you to carry on *mindlessly*?'

Lydia helped herself to some salad. 'Well, no...but you did kiss me without my permission in front of a lot of people today,' she finished, with more spirit.

There was so much irony in his hazel gaze when she looked across at him at last that she bit her lip and looked away immediately, knowing she was perceptibly flustered.

'Other than that, then, is there anything about me...' he paused, then continued in a leisurely way which she found insulting '...that tells you I can't understand the dilemma you're facing?'

'What do you mean?'

He smiled without amusement. 'The dilemma of how to say goodbye to an old love and start a new one.'

Shock made Lydia stare at him with her lips parted.

'And is that because you've decided, for some reason, that I'm particularly insensitive?' He posed the question blandly.

She swallowed and could think of nothing to say.

'If it's not that,' he murmured, looking at her narrowly and with sheer arrogance, 'are you clinging to the Casanova view of me for a very good reason—you're afraid you'll go overboard otherwise?'

'If you don't stop making fun of me you're liable to find yourself not only without a cook but without a member of the mustering team,' she said sharply, and clashed her knife and fork together over her unfinished meal.

'Then let's talk, Lydia. What is the problem?'

'If you must know, you hit the nail on the head twice. I *was* thinking of Brad today, and I *don't* know whether you're a Casanova—but you seem to have got to thirty-two with no commitments, and you do some things most professionally, so—'

'Would you rather I was clumsy and mauled you?' he asked with dangerous irony.

Lydia chose to ignore this taunt as she looped her hair behind her ears. 'And you also told me you had no intention of marrying anyone at the moment, least of all my sister.'

'Well, why the hell can't we discuss these things?' he said grimly.

'Because what I felt for Brad was very special and very private.' She stopped abruptly.

'Go on.'

'And what I feel for you...' Her shoulders slumped. 'It doesn't seem to be the same kind of thing. I don't know you through and through; I don't even know if I can trust you.'

'If you're expecting me to leap on you and have my way with you without your permission, Lydia, it's a vain hope, my dear. I don't operate that way,' he drawled.

She tightened her lips, then managed to say smoothly, but with obvious scorn, 'That's the other thing. That kind of superficial cleverness doesn't appeal to me in the slightest. In fact you annoy me much more than you...than the other thing.'

'One wouldn't have thought so from your performance last night.'

Lydia pushed her chair back and stood up. 'Go to hell, Joe Jordan,' she whispered. 'And don't expect me to do the dishes!'

The next few days were spent in a sort of armed truce.

They had a bit of breather before the next muster but that didn't mean there was any idleness on Katerina Station. Running road repairs were made with the huge grader, fences and dams were checked—all sorts of maintenance work was carried out, and carried out quickly and competently for a boss who was, visibly, not in the best of moods.

Lydia took the time to devote herself to the horses, most of which were turned out for a few days' rest. She treated them for internal parasites, checked them for any sign of lameness, loose teeth, and operated on one to remove a malignant sun spot. She was also able to cure a case of colic, which could lead to a twisted bowel and be fatal for a horse.

She also got to know a bit more about the running of Katerina homestead as well as the station. Because the nearest shop was a day and half's drive away, it was critical to ensure not only foodstuffs but fuel and so on were kept up. This had been Sarah's responsibility, listing and ordering the supplies by the fortnightly truckload.

Of course they had their own meat—an unlimited supply, if you could stomach beef every day of the week—which was killed on the property, and there was a retired ringer who looked after the homestead garden and, according to the seasons, produced vegetables and had a flock of chickens he guarded with his life from snakes and dingoes. All the rest had to be brought in.

Although they didn't say much, she felt again the growing respect of the men she worked with, although there were occasions, when Joe was being extra terse, that she was on the receiving end of some odd little glances. No one on Katerina seemed to have any doubt as to what the cause of his unfriendly mood was.

She also exercised Sarah's two jumpers daily, and in any spare time she had looked after the homestead, probably giving it more attention than Sarah did. And she consulted with Sammy, the retired ringer, because she was a gardener at heart, and this little oasis in the middle of the bush fascinated her.

When they did meet on their own, she and Joe, which was only at meal times, and only rarely, because he left the house before sunrise and returned late so most of his meals were kept hot for him and he ate them in his study, she was as normal as she could be whilst uttering the least she could. Although polite, he in turn contrived to make her feel as if she didn't exist. Apart from one occasion…

One of the cattle dogs cornered a wild pig and got itself severely gored. Sammy came to get her, but when she arrived at the vet station Joe had made the decision that the kindest thing to do for the dog was to put it out of its misery.

'Oh, no you don't,' she said coolly. 'I can handle this.'

'Lydia—'

She straightened from her examination of the dog. 'Joe, you could help if you want to or you could go away, but don't tell me how to do my job!' She opened her own bag and took out a McGill tube with an inflatable cuff to insert into the dog's windpipe, a respirator bag, and prepared an anaesthetic. She scrubbed up, pulled on gloves and set out her pre-sterilised instruments.

Joe was still there.

'If you're going to stay, I'll tell you how to use the respirator bag if we need it. Please do exactly as I say.'

An hour later she'd repaired a tear to the animal's abdominal wall and trimmed and sutured a lung as well as stitching some superficial gashes. Joe had followed her directions while she'd been working on the lung to the letter.

'There.' She wiped her brow with her sleeve, stripped off her gloves and scrubbed her hands again. 'In a few days he should be as good as new.'

'I'll nurse him.' Sammy stepped forward. 'Just tell me what to do, but I got a good hand with crook animals.'

She told him, but promised to check him out herself frequently. She then eyed Joe Jordan, who was watching her broodingly, and walked out.

She didn't see the way he noted how she looped her hair behind her ears, a trademark gesture she always made when under any kind of pressure, and had no way of knowing what was going through his mind.

Girl, woman, married *woman,* Joe found himself thinking. *Cool, dedicated vet, deadly with your tongue but sometimes, when you walk away from me with that boyish stride, so slim and serious, I don't know what the hell to make of you, Lydia Kelso. But if you still want war, if you still like to think you're in charge, so be it!*

And their polite but armed truce continued.

Despite the incongruity of it, and despite asking herself why she stayed on and telling herself it was for Sarah's sake, Lydia couldn't help wondering whether she was holding out for a moral victory of sorts. As in trying to make the point that he was being ridiculous?

But, being on the whole honest with herself, she was aware that she'd been the one to force this kind of impasse on them. She just hadn't expected him to take her at her word so literally, which was not a comforting thought to take to bed with her.

Four days after their initial fall-out, she had to admit that she, her nerves, or something, had been worn down, to the extent that she was possessed of the desire to scream at him that she was not a complete stranger who cooked his meals and looked after his animals.

Whether she would have done it she was never to know, because they bumped into each other that evening as she was on her way to bed and he was coming out of his study.

It was a particularly cold night and she had on warm pyjamas under her violet velvet robe. She was also clutching a hot water bottle wrapped in a towel.

He said nothing after a searching glance up and down her, and stood aside for her to pass.

But it struck Lydia that he looked particularly grim, even slightly pale beneath the overhead light, and she didn't move. 'Is...is something wrong?' she asked tentatively.

Once again that hazel gaze dwelt on her. And it was so unreadable and his mouth so hard she tensed and wondered what kind of a put-down to expect.

What came was the last thing she expected. He said, 'I've just had a call from Sarah. She and Rolf are splitting up.'

CHAPTER FIVE

'BUT...BUT *WHY*? I thought—I thought they...' Lydia stopped helplessly.

'Thought they were the ideal couple?' he supplied.

She stared at him, with her mind reeling. Then she said, 'Would you like a cup of coffee?'

His leant his head back against the wall and she saw the lines scored beside his mouth. 'Thanks,' he said after a moment.

She made a pot of coffee and they sat in the kitchen, which was warmer than the rest of the house. She warmed her hands on her mug and shook her head dazedly. 'I suppose I didn't really stop to think about it. He's not that easy to know, Rolf, is he? He doesn't say much and I guess I thought if he wasn't overtly demonstrative it just wasn't his nature—did you expect this?' she asked directly, with a frown. 'I remember you saying something now—about Sarah thinking she had him house-trained—but...' She shrugged.

Joe sighed. 'I've been afraid for a while that it was in the wind.'

'Because of her inability to conceive?' Lydia said, and looked shocked. 'But that's why they went away—oh, the poor thing,' she whispered.

'No—well,' Joe amended, 'it may have been a factor, but for

quite some time I've been aware of another worm of discontent niggling away at Rolf. He likes to be his own boss. He's not happy with a half-share in Katerina; he would like he and Sarah to have the lot. Unfortunately, we had differing opinions on a couple of critical issues, and Sarah voted with me.'

'Oh.' It was one little word she uttered but it conveyed a wealth of understanding.

'As you say,' he agreed.

'Why did she? I mean, were they such contentious issues and was Rolf...wrong? He seemed like the consummate cattleman, if you don't mind me saying so.'

Joe grimaced. 'It wasn't a question of being right or wrong about cattle *per se*. It was a question of expanding Katerina. It was a question of perhaps getting out of our depth financially. That's how I saw it, anyway, and so did Sarah, who can be quite shrewd at times.'

'So—but why did it all boil up like this?' Lydia asked.

'I don't know if he picked his timing deliberately; I don't think so. Perhaps the reality of the *in vitro* programme hit him all of a sudden. But anyway, the state of play is, either I buy their share, so they can get a place of their own, or we dissolve the partnership and he sells his share elsewhere and leaves Sarah.'

'But you were so good with him!'

He raised an eyebrow at her.

'I mean, I was only thinking the other day that you were a team, you and Rolf, whereas on your own you're a different matter.' She paused.

'As in how?' he asked.

'Very much the boss,' she said flatly, after a moment.

He smiled fleetingly. 'I take it you don't approve?'

She favoured him with a straight, give-nothing-away gaze, then shrugged as if it were neither here nor there. 'So, when Sarah married Rolf, did she—did either of you—have any inkling this was likely to happen?'

'Women in love, certainly in the first flush of love, are not renowned for their intuition. No,' he said, as Lydia made an abrupt movement, 'let me finish. Sarah *was* madly in love with Rolf, and quite blind to the fact that she might not be able to handle him in this kind of situation. I know, because I tried to point it out to her.'

Lydia subsided, although reluctantly. Then she thought for a bit and said finally, 'Could—is there any way they could buy you out?'

'They'd have to borrow heavily. But that's assuming I want to be bought out.'

She glanced at him. 'I just thought—you do seem to be in two minds about whether you're a cartoonist or a grazier.'

'Perhaps,' he responded. 'And, sure, I've had the best of both worlds for quite a while now, but to a certain extent that was to accommodate Sarah and Rolf. I've never had any intention of giving up Katerina, however.' He got up and walked over to the stove to refill his cup from the gently bubbling percolator, then leant against the counter.

Lydia shivered involuntarily, because there was something quite implacable about Joe Jordan at that moment, although he'd spoken evenly and without emphasis. Not only implacable but tough, as he leant negligently against the counter with his legs crossed and his arms folded. She wondered if it might be his olive-green military-style ribbed pullover with elbow and shoulder patches and his khaki trousers that contributed to this impression, but immediately doubted it from the set of his jaw.

'What is going to happen, then?' she asked.

He shrugged. 'It's up to Sarah. She says she's told Rolf she can't agree to what he wants. I told her to think again. Men are... It *can* be hard to play second fiddle. And if Rolf is that kind of man, she won't be able to change him. That doesn't mean to say all the other things she loves about him, or did, count for nothing.'

'It's a choice between Katerina or Rolf for her, then,' Lydia said abstractedly. 'She does seem to love this place.'

'Yes,' he agreed, 'but whether it will be the same when she's on her own, without Rolf, is another matter. And Katerina, while I'm here, will always be here for her.'

'Could you buy them out?'

'With a bit of manoeuvring, yes.'

She blinked at him. 'Is cartooning that well paid?'

A spark of amusement lit his eyes, although he said gravely, 'It's very well paid, as it happens, when you make a name for yourself, but I—er—happen to have other resources.'

Curiosity made her say without thinking, 'Such as?'

This time he laughed softly. 'Are you compiling a dossier on me by any chance, Lydia? If so, one has to wonder why?'

She bit her lip. 'Sorry, that was—I was just curious, but that was unforgivably nosy.'

He eyed her, still looking amused. 'I've been lucky enough to make some profitable investments and read the stockmarket fairly accurately.'

'So did Brad—' She broke off, and then, perhaps because she'd been so curious, added, 'Due to which I've been left rather...well off.'

'I'm glad,' he said simply.

She moved restlessly. 'It wasn't much consolation.'

'No.'

'What do you think Sarah will do? You know, now I come to think of it, I did notice Rolf looking impatient with her a couple of times.'

'I don't know what she'll do,' he said sombrely. 'You can never know exactly what goes on between a man and a woman, even if she's your sister. We'll have to wait and see.'

'You could be more tied to the place than ever,' Lydia said slowly.

'Sometimes these things have their chronological place in life.'

She looked at him with sudden interest. 'Do you mean Balmain and that kind of trendy life was starting to pall?'

He ran a hand through his hair and stroked his jaw thought-fully. 'Perhaps. On the other hand there may always be a "Balmain" side of me, as you put it.' A glint of something lit his eyes—irony? she wondered. Because she'd misread him initially?

'But when you find yourself stopping what you're doing,' he went on, 'and missing your dog madly, when you find yourself picturing a sea of grass waving in the breeze and brolgas dancing beside a creek—a creek you've caught a barramundi in—and you can smell and taste and feel the bush as if it's singing to your soul—when that starts to happen fairly regularly it could be a message.'

'That's lovely.'

He smiled wryly at her. 'You may be more of a bushie at heart than you realise, Ms Kelso. You've certainly taken to it like a duck to water.'

'I know. I was asking myself only the other day what it was about, well, this life, I guess, that's so appealing.'

'Did you come to any conclusion?'

She was silent for a long moment. 'Not really, other than lacking a focus in my life.'

'Why don't you make me a focus?'

There was an even longer silence, during which the only sound was Meg, changing her position in her basket.

'We've just been through the kind of domestic war for the last four days, Joe, that would make life hell for us, don't you think?'

He studied her comprehensively. From the fall of her hair, the lines of her face, that delicate yet stern mouth, down her velvet robe to her hands lying on the table. Upon one of which she always wore a man's signet ring. Brad's? he wondered.

He said, 'I don't know about you but that's because I'm as *frustrated* as hell.'

'And you don't think that could happen every time you don't get your own way?' she asked very quietly.

'There's only ever going to be one way to find out if we're

soulmates, Lydia, and that's to get a bit closer,' he answered obliquely, but, of course, it was a telling comment.

She went to stand up, but stilled as he spoke again.

'If I've been difficult, you've been deliberately obstructive. You opened your heart just a little to let me kiss you, because you couldn't help it, then you closed all channels of communication like a clam. You even—' he smiled briefly '—decided to take issue with how I like my chips, as if I were untutored, uncultured and about ten years old. You know, there are times when you look about sixteen and times when you *do* act sixtyish.'

She licked her lips. 'Perhaps it's the only way I feel I can handle you, Joe.'

She saw his gaze narrow, then he pushed himself away from the counter almost carefully.

She didn't move as he came round the table slowly because she couldn't. It ran through her mind that the admission she'd made might not have been wise, and she might regret it, but at least it had been honest, and she couldn't help but feel she owed Joe Jordan that at least. If she'd hoped they could talk about it first—not that any of this had occurred to her as she'd spoken— she knew, as her heart started to thud irregularly, that it had been a faint hope at best, for them both...

Because something more powerful than talk was gathering them in faster than she could even think straight. His gaze had never left her face as he moved around the table, so it was with a slightly unsteady movement that he pulled out the chair beside her and sat down next to her, but facing her. All the same, he did talk.

'Don't look so wary,' he murmured. 'I'm neither the dentist nor a big bad wolf.'

She breathed unevenly, then had to smile. 'That makes me feel quite—silly.'

'Not at all. Wise girls take precautions. Don't give too much away; you never know what it can do to callow, impressionable people of the male sex,' he said gravely, but reached out and covered her hand with his.

'Joe, you're having me on!' But she was laughing a little now.

'Would I kid you?'

'Oh, yes,' she answered, 'but that's because you're rather—sweet.'

He looked instantly injured. 'I'm not that callow and impressionable!'

'Don't I know it.' Her eyes were dark blue and very bright.

'Then may I take another approach?' he said consideringly. 'Having once kissed you without your permission—'

'Twice.'

He shrugged. 'OK, twice, but anyway, may I have your permission now?'

'I guess I did ask for this,' she murmured, and leant forward to finger the lapel of his shirt.

'I wouldn't put it quite like that, but...' He released her hand and drew his fingers down her cheek. 'You did say something that made me a little mad with—hope? However, if you—'

'Joe Jordan, kiss me before I change my mind,' she advised, still laughing at him.

He did.

'That may have been a record,' he said solemnly, quite some time later.

Lydia brushed her hair with her fingers and tried to control her breathing. She was still standing within the circle of his arms, they were still in the kitchen, and although there was no enchanted garden around them, no star-spangled silk georgette dress between them, if Meg hadn't made a belated although timely intervention by getting out of her basket and coming over to investigate what they were doing, she would have been lost, she knew.

As it was, although they hadn't made the ultimate union, they'd come dangerously close. They'd imprinted the feel of their bodies on one another, he'd explored secret, sensitive sites and she'd melted beneath his lightest touch to a quivering rapture that she could no more disguise than fly to the moon. Because even beneath her pyjamas and robe he'd contrived to celebrate the slim, smooth planes and curves of her body in a way that made her feel unique.

She remembered saying once, 'If this is what you can do in the middle of a kitchen, the mind boggles at the thought of a bed.'

To which he'd responded gravely, but with a sheerly wicked little glint in his eyes, 'I was also thinking how well we do this on our feet.'

'I...yes, that was quite something,' she murmured disjointedly, coming back to the present—and the realisation of how little control she had of herself in his arms.

He smiled fleetingly and touched a finger to her lips. 'Come.'

'Joe,' she whispered, and stopped.

He looked into her eyes, then took his arms away and tidied the top of her pyjama jacket, redid the sash of her robe around her waist, causing her to tremble because, with her tacit permission, his hands had found their way beneath both her robe and pyjamas and had wrought the most devastating delight on her bare breasts.

'I was only going to suggest we find somewhere more comfortable than the kitchen to sit down, and I was going to recommend a brandy to restore us to normality,' he said very quietly. 'That's all.'

She swallowed, then breathed more easily. 'That's...that would be nice.'

'So you see, Lydia,' he continued seriously although with a smile lurking in his eyes, 'I'm actually easier to handle in these circumstances than others.'

They went into the lounge and she sank into a comfortable armchair while he poured two balloon glasses of liqueur brandy. He also switched on a heater and brought it closer.

'Know what I think?' he said, after handing her a glass and sitting down on a footstool in front of her.

Lydia studied him, the slight hint of freckles, the way his brown hair fell and the loose, twisted grace of his body hunched on the stool. 'No. What do you think, Joe?'

She was lying back in the chair with her head pillowed against the headrest and her glass cupped in her hands at the level of her slender waist. There were very faint blue shadows beneath her eyes, and still a slightly dazed air about her that caused him to grimace inwardly and wonder whether she was comparing him to her beloved Brad...

'I think we should go about this very carefully,' he said, studying his glass now, with his head bent, then lifting his hazel gaze to hers suddenly. 'I think there's only one criterion we should apply—that it exists in its own right, what we feel for and do to each other.'

'Yes,' she said after a long pause.

'I'm glad you agree.'

She sipped some brandy.

'All the same, I sense you have reservations,' he murmured.

She smiled briefly. 'I must be very transparent.'

'Tell me.'

'Joe...' She hesitated. 'How would you react if I told you it would be very easy to make you the focus of my life, especially in this setting?' She glanced around. 'But I can't help wondering how much the magic of the bush and Katerina is contributing to things.'

'You don't think that down in Balmain we would achieve record-breaking kisses?' he asked wryly.

She closed her eyes. 'Possibly.'

'So?'

'I can't think straight.' She moved her head restlessly against the back of the chair.

'Well, that's why I suggested we take things one at a time.

And my next suggestion is that you drink up and go to bed. You look exhausted.'

Lydia was silent for quite a while, then she said with a little glint of mischief dancing in her eyes, 'Is this Plan C, by any chance?'

He said gravely. 'Yes and no. It's certainly a device not to rush you or crowd you, as well as a way to get me to my own bed before I become—hard to handle. I guess Plan C is as good a name as any for it.' He shrugged.

She drained her glass and handed it to him. 'Then let us abide by your good intentions, Joe. Goodnight.' She stood up, but he remained still, although he watched her every move.

She hesitated, then kissed her fingers and touched them lightly to his brow, and went to bed.

Sleep didn't come easily, however. Memories of being in his arms, of responding to his touch, made her twist and turn restlessly. Memories of the extreme passion that had gripped them to the exclusion of all else—a man and a woman set alight by each other—but also memories of his forbearance and humour were on her mind. Such a change from the polite but cold stranger of the past four days, she thought.

At one point it was even hard not to admit that her lonely bed was lonelier and colder than she would have thought possible—lonelier and colder without a man who was not Brad.

Nor was she to know it was curiously prophetic that she should finally fall asleep with something her sister Daisy had said about Joe Jordan on her mind— *He's something else.*

Because, the next morning, who should fly into Katerina in a chartered light plane but Daisy herself?

Lydia was working in the garden when the plane buzzed over the homestead. She hadn't seen Joe that morning; he'd left before the crack of dawn. She got up off her knees and frowned, because it wasn't the station plane, she could tell by the markings, and it occurred to her that it might be Sarah. Because all the men were working on a new dam, she drove the utility down to the airstrip to pick up whoever it was, not for one moment expecting Daisy.

But Daisy it was, in jeans and a white silk blouse with elegant high-heeled boots, her dark hair loose and glorious and her violet eyes alight with love and laughter.

'Daisy!'

'I just couldn't resist surprising the life out of you, Lyd!' her sister responded joyfully, and flung her arms around her.

'You've certainly done that!' Lydia hugged her back. 'But—how come?'

'The Musica Viva tour! We've come to Darwin. I was so mixed up before you left, I hadn't even checked the itinerary properly. Then, when I got up here and discovered we had a couple of free days, I rang Chattie and got the details from her, and I chartered this little plane.'

She waved a hand towards the two-seater she'd climbed out of and explained she'd arranged with the pilot to fly her back to Darwin if there was any problem with her staying, otherwise he'd come back tomorrow to pick her up. 'Do you think they'll mind me staying a night, Lyd? I am your sister,' she finished anxiously.

'No. No! But…but there is one thing, Daisy.' Lydia stopped as the enormity of explaining hit her.

Daisy linked her arm through Lydia's as they walked towards the utility. 'Don't tell me I have to sleep rough; the house looked huge.'

'No. No, you won't. Daisy—Joe Jordan's here.'

Daisy stopped as if she'd been shot. Then she said breathlessly, 'How? Why? Does he have anyone with him? Lydia, I can't believe this!' And she was absolutely radiant.

'It turns out that he owns the place. Daisy, I have to confess something. I went to see him before I left, to make sure he wasn't playing fast and loose with you.'

Daisy blinked, then broke into spontaneous laughter. 'Darling, if you had any idea what lengths I went to—unsuccessfully—to get him to, well, take me seriously—' She broke off and shook her head. 'I can't believe you did that for me, but thanks. And I took your advice. I decided to play hard to get with him. Now I'll be able to tell whether it's worked. This is— amazing! I've got the feeling it must have been meant. The thing is, I can't stop thinking about him,' she added simply.

Neither can I... Lydia didn't say it, but the words seemed to burn themselves into her brain as she started the utility and prepared to drive her sister up to the homestead.

But she had to say something, and she had to say it soon. So her mind was working furiously while Daisy was obviously unaware of her preoccupation as she chattered about their father and Chattie and all the news from home.

Nor had any simple way of telling her sister the truth presented itself to Lydia when she drew up outside the garden fence and, to her horror, saw that the bull buggy was parked there, just arrived from the opposite direction, with Joe climbing out and Meg jumping off the back.

'Daisy,' she swallowed, 'Daisy—'

But Daisy forestalled her with a sigh of sheer wonder as she said, 'He *is* quite something, isn't he?' and opened her door to get out.

'Daisy,' Lydia said desperately.

But Daisy said over her shoulder, 'Don't worry, darling! I'm still playing hard to get. Just watch me.'

So Lydia watched helplessly as her sister put on a bravura performance.

She advanced on Joe Jordan, who had stopped dead in his tracks, and put out her hand. 'Joe, I had no idea,' she said with obvious sincerity. 'I came to surprise Lydia because I'm in Darwin doing some concerts—you were the *last* person I expected to find here!'

Joe took her hand, although his gaze flicked briefly to Lydia, standing behind Daisy. All Lydia could do was shrug helplessly and make a negative gesture with her hands.

'I guess I could say the same,' Joe replied, shaking Daisy's hand. 'I thought it might be my sister Sarah flying in, that's why I came back, but—welcome to Katerina, Daisy. I'm sure Lydia is thrilled to see you.'

'Yes,' Lydia said, a touch belatedly although Daisy seemed not to notice.

'I'm only staying the night, if that's OK with you,' Daisy said charmingly to Joe. 'Truth to tell, a bit of a break from music is just what I need. We can...' She paused and looked at him seriously. 'We can still be friends, can't we?'

'Of course,' Joe Jordan murmured.

'Oh, good!'

It wasn't until Daisy had gone to bed that night that Lydia and Joe got the opportunity to talk in private.

They'd given Daisy a royal tour of the property. A flight over the next paddock to be mustered, a drive out to the waterfall and pools for a swim, then a barbecue under the stars with the mustering team. During it all Daisy had been her own delightful self: bubbly, interested in all she saw, charming everyone she came in contact with but showing not the slightest sign of any personal interest in Joe.

Lydia had taken her a hot water bottle and stayed to chat as Daisy got into bed, but it had not been for long as her sister had yawned prodigiously several times and laughingly admitted to being exhausted.

Joe was waiting for her in the kitchen when she went back to it.

She pulled out a chair and sank down exhaustedly herself.

'Here.'

'Thanks,' she murmured as he put a cup of tea in front of her. 'Do I need this! What is it about tea in a crisis?'

He smiled faintly and sat down opposite with his own cup. 'Is it such a crisis?'

'Yes,' she said baldly. 'I just couldn't find any way to tell her.'

'But she genuinely had no idea she would find me here?'

'None at all. I hadn't spoken to her, and I didn't mention it in my letters or when I rang Chattie.'

'Well, what is the crisis, then?' He watched her narrowly. 'She would appear to have given up on me.'

Lydia raised her dark blue gaze to his. 'It's as I feared. She's playing hard to get. She can't stop thinking about you.'

'Lydia—she *told* you this?'

Lydia nodded and sipped her tea.

'Then we'll just have to be honest.'

Lydia blinked a couple of times. 'That's easy to say, Joe, but—'

'No.' He slid his hand across the table and covered hers. 'This has gone on long enough. There is only one problem: that she's your sister. Believe me, Lydia, for all my sins, apart from wining and dining and escorting Daisy around a bit, I did not give her any reason to believe that there was more between us than friendship. I never laid so much as a finger on her intimately.'

'Joe—' Lydia held his gaze steadily '—don't you realise that wining, dining and escorting women around, even just a bit, leads to—expectations?'

'Of course.' He looked suddenly grim. 'But—and I've never told you this, because I know how defensive you are of Daisy— she was the one who did all the inviting. She was the one who rang me each and every time and suggested we do this, that or the other.' He gestured impatiently.

'You could have refused. Don't tell me you don't *know* the effect you have on women.'

'Yourself included?'

It wasn't the response she'd expected, and although she could tell that she'd angered him with what had been, perhaps, an unfair question, she felt her hackles rising all the same at the sheer

arrogance of his expression as he sat opposite her, his hazel eyes
supremely mocking and his mouth hard.

She pushed her cup away decisively and stood up. 'I'm not
going to argue with you, Joe. Nor am I going to fall out with
my own sister over a man I'm not even sure I like. Goodnight.'

'Before you go, Lydia, liking and loving are two different
things. And there are some things I do to you that you actually
appear to adore.'

'I'd hate to think how unchivalrous you could be if you really set your mind to it. I'm only surprised you haven't put it
into a cartoon,' she said bitterly.

'Unchivalrous?' He raised an eyebrow at her. 'I was merely
being honest. Think of it this way, though. Was it lonesome in
your single bed last night? It sure as hell was in mine, and really,' he continued, softly but lethally, 'all the rest is insignifi-
cant, were *you* to be honest, Lydia.'

She walked out, but not before he'd seen the rise of rich colour in her cheeks.

She took a tea tray in to Daisy the next morning.

Her sister stretched luxuriously and propped herself up on
the pillows. 'I slept like a log! Must be the country air. Thanks,
you're a sweetie, but, hey!' She sat up and regarded Lydia with
a frown. 'You don't look too bright—as if you didn't sleep a
wink.'

'I did, but not many,' Lydia confessed, and sat on the twin
bed as she poured the tea. 'There's something I have to tell you,
Daisy, but first of all could you tell me this? Did Joe ever give
you *any* hope that, well, something might come of your friendship, something more?'

Daisy blinked dazedly. 'You're not still worried about him
playing fast and loose with me, Lyd? I—'

'Daisy, please, just tell me.'

Daisy pulled up the strap of her exquisite pearl silk night-
dress, shrugged and gave the matter some thought. 'No,' she

said finally. 'I mean I kept thinking he wouldn't want to go out with me if he didn't—well, you know, but...' She sighed suddenly. 'I was always the one who asked, and he was always the one who managed to turn it into a crowd.'

'So,' Lydia said slowly, 'when you thought to yourself that this guy was something else and perhaps you should hang on to him, not just use him to father a child for you, he had never even—for example—kissed you?'

Daisy eyed her sister ruefully. 'No. I know what you're going to say. Am I mad or what? But the thing is—'

'I wasn't going to say that at all, because you see...' Lydia looked at her sister steadily, although she also swallowed a little painfully. 'He has kissed me.'

Daisy nearly dropped her cup.

And Lydia, with complete honesty, told her exactly what had happened between herself and Joe Jordan.

'Why didn't you tell me this yesterday?' Daisy whispered. 'I would have flown right back to Darwin there and then.'

Lydia rubbed her face wearily. 'I couldn't find the words. I'm so sorry—'

'No.' Daisy cast aside the bedclothes and came to sit on the twin bed beside her. 'I'm not blaming you for...anything, but I...even if I hadn't flown away I wouldn't have raved on about him. I...can't think straight,' she said.

'He's had that effect on me too,' Lydia commented with some cynicism as she recalled saying those exact words just two nights ago.

'So we've both fallen for the same man. No, no,' Daisy immediately corrected herself, 'there's no question of me *really* having fallen for him. It was just a bit of a pipe-dream—yes, that's all it was,' she assured Lydia.

Lydia put her arms around her. 'Is that why you couldn't stop thinking about him?' she asked gently.

'I will. I definitely will now,' Daisy promised. 'Look, you know me. I fall in and out of love at the drop of a hat. But you're different, and if you're finally getting over Brad and falling in love again then I'm the last person, the *very* last person, not to be happy for you! How can I make you believe it?' she asked with supreme anxiety.

Lydia hugged her again, and was silent for a time, hoping desperately that if nothing else the scales might have fallen from Daisy's eyes in regard to Joe. Then she said carefully, 'The thing is, he might not be the right man for either of us.'

'What do you mean?'

'I—' Lydia broke off, then started again. 'I don't know if it isn't just a physical attraction. There are times when I find him impossible. It's so different from how it was with Brad. We fight a lot.' She flinched inwardly, because it sounded awfully immature if nothing else.

Daisy said quietly, 'If a man wants to fight you and still make love to you, it's because there are obstacles he can't seem to overcome. And I would say Joe hasn't had a lot of opposition put in his way.' She grimaced. 'You have, sitting next to you, a perfect example. Would one of the obstacles you've been throwing up have been me, Lyd?'

'Of course. I've felt incredibly guilty. I tried, I really tried not to have anything to do with him, but—'

'Then things will be different from now on without that to worry about.'

'Is—the oboe player on the Musica Viva tour?' Lydia asked tentatively.

Daisy turned and smiled at her. 'No. But he sends me flowers every time we open in a new town. Now that I've Joe out of my system, who knows? I know!' She brightened. 'I shall tell Joe Jordan about him.'

'Daisy—'

But Daisy suddenly cast a wise little glance at her younger sister. 'No, I won't, but listen, kid.' They both smiled at the term Daisy had used over the years, then sobered. 'I need you to make me a promise. Don't hide behind me any longer. Whatever reservations you have about him, make sure they're genuine. Because I've retired completely from the lists—I was never in them in the first place, other than in my imagination.'

'But—'

'Lydia,' Daisy said, 'if you value me at all as a sister, if you understand that there are times when I'm rash because I can't seem to help myself but I'm *not* a complete fool who can't admit I do some crazy things, will you promise to banish all thoughts of me in the context of Joe Jordan?'

Lydia sniffed and blinked. 'I do value you as a sister. That's how I got myself into this in the first place,' she said huskily.

'So you promise?'

'OK. I promise.'

'Good. Because I'll tell you something else. I can't think why it didn't occur to me at the time—well, yes, I can—but I think he's just what you need...'

Daisy flew off after lunch.

Joe had come back from the dam to have lunch with them and no one would have guessed at all the dramatic strands threaded between them. Not that there had been anyone else to share their light-hearted lunch. Nor had Lydia any inkling that in the short time Joe and Daisy had been left alone, while she'd been dishing up the apple pie she'd made in the kitchen and whipping some cream, Daisy would turn the tables on her.

In fact, Joe was called away to a burst pipe they were trying to connect from a bore to the dam as the plane was taking off, so she went back to the homestead alone and spent an uncomfortable afternoon wondering just how she was going to handle Joe Jordan, and be handled by him, in light of their 'words' of the previous evening.

Because, although she'd promised not to hide behind her sister any longer, she was not about to drop her other reservations about him. And while in her heart she could no longer hide behind Daisy, she wasn't at all sure that Joe deserved to know it.

She cooked roast beef and made a large pot of pumpkin soup. But it was quite dark and later than normal before she heard the bull buggy pull up, and then she nearly didn't recognise Joe when he loomed up on to the verandah because he was coated in a mixture of dried mud and grease.

'What...?' she began, but couldn't go on because he looked so funny, and she started to laugh.

'You may well laugh, Ms Kelso,' he remarked bitterly, 'but if you'd spent the entire afternoon crawling around a burst pipe and a faulty bore engine that repeatedly spouted when it wasn't supposed to and failed to operate when it should have, you might be more sympathetic!'

'I'm entirely sympathetic, Joe. Entirely,' she protested. 'Just one thing, though. How are you going to get clean without reducing the bathroom to a sea of mud and grease?'

He threw his hat on to a chair and put his hands on his hips. 'I have no intention of doing that to a bathroom. What do you think I am?'

'I won't answer that.' She grinned. 'So?'

'For my sins—all sorts of sins I've never committed, by the way—I shall have to use the tank shower. Which, you may or may not know, is cold. Freezing, to be more accurate. Would you mind, if it wouldn't be too much trouble, getting me a towel and a piece of soap?' He removed his hands from his hips and started to unbutton his shirt.

'On the double, sir!' Lydia responded smartly, and disappeared inside.

When she returned he'd dispensed with his shirt and the overhead verandah light was mellow on the clean skin beneath it, on the smooth flow of muscles across his shoulders and the sprinkling of golden hairs on his chest that turned darker and became thicker towards his waist.

He stopped with his fingers on the waistband of his trousers, she stopped on the doorstep almost as if she'd been shot and for about half a minute, they made a frozen little tableau with their gazes clashing—once she'd been able to tear hers from the sleek, beautiful proportions of his body.

Then Lydia came to life and advanced towards him. 'Soap, a towel—two towels actually—and—this.'

The last thing she handed him was an open bottle of beer. Their fingers brushed as he took it and she took her hand away rather quickly. 'Just thought it might help,' she murmured, 'while you're out there in the dark, showering under the tank stand.' She stopped speaking, because it sounded more like babbling than coherent speech to her, and she retreated to the doorstep.

Joe studied the beer bottle, then raised it to his mouth and took several long swallows. He shuddered as it went down, then looked across at her. 'You were right. You never know, I might even be able to sing during this bracing experience.' He turned away, vaulted off the verandah and disappeared into the darkness.

Lydia stood where she was for a moment longer experiencing several reactions. Relief that the ice had been broken was one, but the comfort that brought to her was tempered somewhat because she'd been reduced to feeling like a starstruck girl on a very physical level.

Then she heard him—singing in a deep baritone that carried clearly as the sound of water rushing could also be heard. Although—and she guessed this was as he came into contact with the tank water—the baritone rose to a distinct yodelling falsetto for a moment, before continuing rather breathlessly.

She laid her cheek on the doorjamb and laughed until tears sprang to her eyes. Then she went away to co-ordinate dinner.

CHAPTER SIX

IT WAS AN almost frighteningly alive Joe Jordan who sat down to dinner presently.

If she'd been struck by him on the verandah without his shirt, she was doubly struck, she thought ruefully, by the impact of his clean, vigorous masculinity as he sat opposite her in the verandah room. He'd put on a grey tracksuit, his hair gleamed smooth and neat, and just below the surface lay all the power of a strong man in his prime plus that sheer sex appeal.

Was he altogether aware of it? she wondered. What was it precisely—and how many times had she asked herself that? A tall, supple body, to be sure, but there had to be more. A vitality about him and his sense of humour. The undoubted and, much as she hated to admit it, clever arrogance he could exhibit at the same time as you sensed that the single-minded attentions of Joe Jordan could be the pathway to a certain kind of heaven—as she not only sensed but now knew to be true.

She dished up the pumpkin soup as all this passed through her mind and passed him the croutons.

'I'm starving,' he announced. 'And if that's roast beef, my dear Lydia—' he gestured towards the sideboard and a covered dish set on a heating pad '—you have won my heart.'

Lydia sat down and picked up her soup spoon. 'You seem

to be in a very good mood, Joe,' she murmured, then winced to think she could have made any reference to their dispute of the previous evening. 'For a man who's been battling wayward bores and pumps.'

He glinted her an enigmatic little look that told her all the same that he'd noticed her movement of regret. 'As a matter of fact I'm a man in a unique position.'

'Oh?'

'Yep.' He continued to drink his soup.

'So you're not going to tell me,' she said.

He looked up, and this time his glance was entirely readable; it was about as wicked as she'd ever seen. 'You may not approve,' he warned.

She pushed her plate away and asked ominously, 'Have you been having bets with yourself again?'

'No, ma'am! I learnt that lesson the hard way.'

Lydia plucked her napkin from her lap and dropped it on to the tablecloth from a height. 'Joe, that is not true!'

He looked surprised. 'I can assure you it is—'

'You know very well what I mean—you were the one who— stopped.' She stopped herself, appalled at the admission she'd made, then tossed her head as if to stand by what she'd said.

Something—could it have been oddly tender?—lit his hazel eyes for a moment before he said, 'Meg was the one to take any credit the night before last.'

'A lot of men would have pressed on.'

'They may not have heard about Plan C.'

A smile trembled on her lips. 'You're impossibly...nice sometimes, Joe.'

'Well—' he shrugged '—that's a relief. I thought you were going to say something else. Impossibly sweet.'

She laughed openly, then said curiously, 'So what was it if not a bet?'

He finished his soup and stood up. 'Would you like me to carve?'

'Please,' she murmured, and gathered the soup plates.

He lifted the lid on the roast, inhaled luxuriously and passed the carving knife over the steel a couple of times before he said, 'I'm in the unique position of having been warned by each of the Kelso sisters to be on my best behaviour towards the other sister.' He cut the beef expertly and placed a faintly pink slice, a perfect example of rare roast beef, on a plate.

'I...you... Daisy *told* you!'

'Daisy warned me that if I hurt you I would have her to contend with,' he corrected. 'By the way, I admire your courage in coming clean with her. I know I recommended it, but I never for one minute thought it would be easy, although there was never any question of you stealing me from her.'

Lydia swallowed several times, then accepted a plate from him and took the lid off the vegetables. 'What exactly did she say?' she asked in a strangled sort of way.

He sat down again with his own plate and helped himself to gravy. Then he looked at her completely soberly. 'She didn't tell me anything I didn't know, except, perhaps, to underline what a perfect couple you and Brad Kelso had been. And how difficult it was for you to forget him.'

'Oh.'

'She also gave me a few words of wisdom to do with myself.' He raised his eyebrows.

'Such as?'

'"Don't imagine you're the best thing since sliced bread, Joe Jordan."'

Lydia gasped. 'Daisy said that to you?'

'Uh-huh.' He cut some beef into a triangle and studied it before putting it into his mouth.

Lydia stared at him dazedly. 'Was she joking, was she angry, or what?'

He finished his mouthful then reached for a glass of water. 'It would appear she's suffered a complete reversal of feeling for me. No—' he grinned fleetingly at Lydia's expression '—she was very honest. She said she'd been a fool and she'd caused unnecessary complications between you and I but it was all over for her. All the same—' he gestured '—that's when she mentioned the sliced bread bit.'

'What did you say to her?' Lydia asked, with a mixture of dread and fascination.

He looked over her head, as if trying to recall his exact words. 'I said it had been an honour to know her because in her own way she was unique, and if I hadn't known her, I wouldn't have known you. I think Daisy and I understand each other now.'

'Oh.'

'That's the third time you've said that, Lydia.' He looked at her wryly.

She shook her head. 'I feel as if I'm lost at sea without a chart.'

'So do I.'

Lydia blinked at him.

'The thing is…' He paused and looked at her reflectively. 'If you really want to dedicate your life to the memory of Brad, I wouldn't be so crass as to take issue with that.'

Lydia licked her lips. 'Was that something else Daisy indicated?'

'No. In all conscience, though, I felt I had to say it.'

'Thank you,' Lydia whispered, then cleared her throat to go on normally. 'The thing is, I don't know. Yes, I do,' she contradicted herself immediately. 'Although there'll always be a corner of my heart for him, I've made no pact to dedicate my life to a memory.'

'Is that,' he said slowly, 'a go-ahead, Lydia?'

She tried to compose her thoughts. 'It's an admission,' she said at last, 'that you intrigue me, annoy me, set me alight—but more than that? I can't say at this stage.'

He grinned ruefully. 'Very succinct,' he commented. 'It just about sums up how I feel about you, too.'

Lydia suffered the sensation of having the wind rather taken out of her sails, and gritted her teeth on a tart retort. He'd be quite entitled to point out that what was sauce for the goose was sauce for the gander, and being Joe Jordan no doubt would, should she give him the opportunity.

'You were going to say?' he asked innocently, right on cue.

'Nothing. Except this is one of the moments when you're annoying me, but I'll leave you to work out why. Have you heard anything from Sarah?'

He registered the deliberate change of subject with the flicker of a smile but said soberly, 'No. I'm going to try to get hold of her tonight. I really thought she was Daisy, if you know what I mean, and I didn't know whether to be happy or sad for her.'

'Joe, I don't want to add to your problems, but I took six weeks' leave from my job in Sydney and there's only a few weeks left now. Not that I've been much help over the past few days, but—'

'Not your fault,' he broke in. 'And we've only got a few more paddocks to muster. With some help from above we may get it done in a fortnight.'

'I noticed the other day how the country was drying out,' she said.

'By the time the monsoon starts in November or December we're generally desperate for rain,' he commented. 'That's how it goes in this part of the world, a feast or a famine. Talking of which, did I see a lemon meringue in the kitchen?'

'I'll get it.'

But he wandered through to the kitchen himself as she was serving up two portions of the lemon meringue instead of bringing it out to the table. And he put his hands on her waist from behind.

She stilled, then put the cake slice down and turned to face him. 'What?' she breathed.

'Don't you know?' He raised a hand and trailed his fingers down the side of her neck.

She shivered, but not because she was cold. She had on her

warm blue long-sleeved shirt, with jeans. 'Yes, I know,' she said barely audibly. 'And I have been lonesome the last two nights.'

'But it's a big step?' he suggested.

She swallowed, and nodded.

He touched his lips to her forehead, then said into her hair, 'It is for me too.'

Surprise held her rigid for a moment, then she put her hands on his upper arms and he looked down into her eyes.

'You can't mean that, Joe?'

'Why not?' he murmured. 'I feel like a rookie upstart with you sometimes, Lydia.' His hands were on her waist again. 'A playboy, a rather shallow sex object, slickly clever, definitely lightweight in the commitment department having reached the grand old age of thirty-two—'

'I didn't put it all quite like that.'

'You gave me to understand it, however.' He shrugged and stroked her hair, confusing her all the more. 'Then there was the way you amazed me when you got up here. You showed an awful lot of courage for a city girl, you are obviously a very professional vet and I know enough about vets to know you need an awful lot of brains to get into it in the first place. Whereas all I demonstrated was that I could be a very volatile artist of sorts. So, yes, that added to my feeling of inferiority.'

Lydia could only stare at him with her lips parted.

He smiled slightly and traced the outline of her mouth with his forefinger. 'But most of all,' he said very quietly, 'and this is why it would be a big step for me, Lydia, you've known—perfection. I never have. Not the kind that's locked me to a lover both mentally and physically.' He paused. 'Even in the relationships I've had, I was always—it was as if I was standing on the outside, waiting for it to happen.'

She blinked dazedly.

'Which has left me wondering,' he went on, 'whether the lack is something within me.'

'So you don't think you've ever been in love?' she asked huskily.

'Not properly, not completely, no.'

'The lack could be to do with not finding the right person yet,' she suggested.

He shrugged. 'Or it could be to do with how often that perfection comes. Perhaps not to all of us.'

'What if you and I don't achieve it?' she asked, and discovered her heart beating rapidly because that was tantamount to saying she would go to bed with him. Yet this honesty from Joe Jordan had broken through her defences more than anything else could have, she realised.

'We'll be a little older and a little wiser,' he said gently. 'And perhaps there will be a corner of your heart for a bloke who wanted you desperately but—fell down in other areas.'

'I never thought I would go to bed with a man I wasn't sure about, Joe, but at this moment, and although it may not last, you have a corner of my heart. Come.'

And she led him out of the kitchen.

His bedroom had the luxury of a double bed beneath an elegant fitted beige and white patterned spread

It also had a lovely old cedar wardrobe with brass handles, its doors lined with oval mirrors, a beige wall-to-wall carpet and white curtains tied back with ties made from the bedspread material. The walls were painted a soft ochre, two white marble lamps stood on the bedside tables and there was a comfortable russet velvet-covered armchair. It was the only room in the house that looked as if someone had decorated it to a plan and created a harmonious effect.

Lydia stopped on the threshold, she'd never seen this room before, and turned to him with a raised eyebrow.

'We decided to get the house redecorated a couple of years ago but we never got beyond this bedroom and Sarah and Rolf's.'

'It's nice.' She was still holding his hand, but she dropped it and went into the room to stroke the lovely lines of the cedar wardrobe.

'I'm glad you approve,' he murmured, looming up behind her so they were both reflected in the mirrors, 'but I hope it hasn't deflected us in any way.'

Lydia paused, and experienced a trill of sensation running through her at the way he was looking down at her in the mirror. 'No,' she murmured, turning to face him. 'My mind is made up.'

His lips twisted, and this time he took her hand and raised it to his lips.

'Unless...' she hesitated '...I'm being too bossy?'

'Believe me, I couldn't approve more.'

She stared at him, suddenly wary. 'No, Joe, I mean, I know I *can* be, and—'

'I see there's only way to resolve this impasse, Lydia.' And he took her into his arms and started to kiss her.

From there on being bossy was the last thing on her mind. And the magic of what they did to each other was heightened by their reflection in the mirror. It created a new dimension for Lydia, to see herself in his arms, to see the colour fluctuating in her cheeks as well as feel it as he drew her blouse off and stared down at her grey velvet bra with roses etched into the soft, silky pile.

'I often wear it,' she said breathlessly.

'Which means you didn't put it on especially to drive me wild tonight?'

'No, I didn't know—' She broke off and bit her lip, because it sounded as if she was defending herself. 'No,' she amended. 'But the briefs match.'

He laughed softly and put his hands on the waistband of her jeans. 'So Ms Kelso, veterinarian extraordinaire, has a secret passion for gorgeous undies?'

'She does,' she agreed.

'I hope she won't object to me taking them off?'

'Please do,' she murmured, with a smile trembling on her

lips. 'But before you do, Ms Kelso also has a passion for equality. You were rather breathtaking without your shirt earlier.'

He took his hands from her body and stripped the top of his tracksuit off speedily. 'How's that?'

She grinned and laid her cheek against his chest, then started to laugh.

'That's not very kind,' he objected.

'I'm not laughing at you like this. I'm thinking of how your voice changed when you stepped under the tank shower.'

'Ah. I was hoping you hadn't heard that!'

She lifted her head and her eyes were dancing. But something else came to them as he slid his hands around her back and undid her bra.

It dropped with a whisper to the carpet, and although he made no move to touch them his eyes were on her breasts, small, close mounds that lay sleekly on her slender torso, in perfect proportion with it and tipped with natural velvet.

Perhaps it was something in the intensity of his gaze, perhaps it was the cool night air, but those velvet tips flowered, and he drew in a suddenly uneven breath and covered each one with the palms of his hands.

'OK?' she asked barely audibly.

'Exquisite. May I see the briefs?'

She could only nod.

And, still in front of the mirror, they helped each other to undress.

The briefs caused a smile to touch his mouth, but they soon met the same fate as her bra, and then they were glorying in being in each other's arms with no impediment between them.

There was also a tempo building up between them of rhythmic desire as they touched each other, fitted into each other and savoured the different textures of their skin, the different shapes and lines of their bodies. And finally, with her arms around his neck, he cupped her hips and lifted her, as she wound her legs around him, and carried her to bed.

The tempo became like a drumbeat as she lay beneath him, so skilled was he, so patient at times, gentle and funny, yet never letting her doubt for a moment that he wanted her desperately. And her reintroduction to sex after nearly six years of chastity came in waves of sheer desire she could only marvel at and savour with extreme pleasure, until the final peak of pleasure claimed them both.

Then he wrapped her in his arms, cocooned them in blankets, and stroked her hair until she fell asleep.

Dawn was just rimming the horizon when she woke, to find him dressed and sitting beside her on the bed.

She stretched luxuriously, then pulled the blankets up under her arms and said, 'Good morning. You didn't have to wait to go to work until I woke.'

'Yes, I did,' he replied. 'I'm not going to work just yet.'

Unaware that her skin, in the lamplight, was like ivory satin, and her eyes as blue as sapphires, she looked her fill of him for a long moment, then reached for his hand and kissed the knuckles. 'Thanks,' she said huskily.

'No thanks are due,' he said softly. 'It was mutual.' But he held her gaze compellingly.

Aware, immediately, of what he was asking her—had it existed in its own right?—she said, with complete honesty, 'Yes.'

Something flickered in the hazel depths of his eyes that she thought might have been relief, but it was gone as he said, 'Then I've had rather a good idea. I got up about an hour ago and made some preparations. All you have to do is get dressed.'

'What for?'

'Ah, I know what you mean.' His gaze skimmed down her figure beneath the blankets and her bare shoulders above them. 'Well, we could do that instead, but—'

Her fingers tightened on his briefly. 'That wasn't what I meant, Mr Jordan. Should I get dressed to go to work or stay at home is what I meant!'

He grinned. 'I knew that. Just couldn't help testing you out. Uh—going out, but not to work. My horse and Billy are saddled up and tied to the garden fence, I thought a gallop to the waterfall as the sun comes up, and a swim...' He stopped quizzically as Lydia drew in a breath. 'Like the idea?'

She sat up, uncaring of the blanket slipping down to her waist. 'You're a genius, Joe Jordan!'

It was a magical gallop through a world waking up to a new day.

At one stage they flushed out two emus with their striped chicks, the adults keeping pace with them for a short while before turning back to the chicks.

Lydia tore off her hat and yodelled with sheer exhilaration beneath a dome of blue streaked with lemon and apricot as Billy flew, in his sure-footed way, across the sandy-pink, sage-green dotted earth. The air was chilly but as clear as glass, so every breath hung on it and the tip of her nose was freezing. Then the lemon and apricot faded from the sky and the sun appeared over the edge of the earth—or so it seemed to her—and tiny droplets of dew on low bushes and bare branches radiated the light, and spider webs trapped moisture on every filament so that they looked like snowflakes.

They slowed their horses to a walk eventually, as they made their way down to the water holes, and there was another marvel to greet them. Flocks of white, sulphur-crested cockatoos and pink and grey galahs, rising in squawking surprise—so many of them she could only gasp in wonderment.

'They weren't here last time!' she exclaimed as she slid off Billy, looped the reins over his head and patted his sweating neck appreciatively.

'We probably scared them away, and we did have a fire. There was also more water in other places,' Joe remarked, and stripped off his gloves.

He looked, she thought, the consummate bushman in his flat-brimmed hat and distinctively caped Driza-Bone oilskin coat, over a red and white checked flannel shirt, jeans and boots.

She said, involuntarily, 'You look like *The Man From Snowy River*.'

He grinned. 'This ain't much of a river, ma'am, and a long way from Kosciusko, but I can guarantee it'll be snowy!'

She shivered inside her yellow thermal jacket, and laughed. Then she watched him untie his saddle rolls, and did the same to those that were attached to her saddle.

When everything was laid out, she murmured, 'You were busy, Joe, while I was fast asleep.' And shook her head again in wonderment. Because laid out on the sandy bank were the billy and tripod, mugs, plates, milk, tea and sugar, honey and butter and, the *coup de grâce*, a round golden damper. There were also a couple of nets of lucerne hay for the horses.

'I cheated a bit,' he said modestly. 'I cooked the damper in the stove at the home; it should be done in the coals of a camp oven.'

'I'm not complaining. And we can keep it warm in the coals.'

'Good thinking,' he said gravely. 'Shall we water our horses, then I'll make a fire, start the billy and we can decide whether to swim first—or afterwards?'

'I'll look after the horses; you can concentrate on the fire.'

'You really are a woman after my own heart, Lydia!'

She didn't reply as she led both horses down to the pool, but she shot him a laughing little look.

'We're crazy!' she said later as they stood beside the same pool half undressed—they were both stripped to their shirts and underpants. 'I'm blue with cold.' The fire was going and the horses, tied to trees, were munching their lucerne contentedly.

'Just think how nice it will be when we come out and sit around the fire—and there is another factor to consider.'

'I can't think of one!'

'Well, freezing water is renowned for freezing certain ambitions of the masculine variety, so you'll be quite safe from me, in certain respects, for a time. I can't specify how long, but—'

'Oh, well,' she broke in, 'when you put it like that I have little choice!' And, taking a deep breath, she pulled off the rest of her clothes and plunged in. He followed suit.

'Not only crazy, stark, staring *bonkers*,' she spluttered about five minutes later. 'Why didn't you tell me there were crocodiles?'

They were back on the bank and Joe was rubbing her down vigorously with a rough towel. He had pulled his jeans on but she, as yet, wore nothing.

'I thought you knew; you mentioned them the first time we swam—'

'Yes, but I didn't expect to come face to face with one!'

'Lydia, they're Johnson River crocs, they don't attack people, we were quite safe. Mind you, I got a bit of a surprise myself.'

Her teeth chattered as she said with extreme frustration, 'But I got such an awful fright—I could have drowned!'

'Here.' He dropped the towel and picked up her undies. She grabbed them and stepped into her briefs and clasped her bra on, a different one, lacy and white with a navy blue satin bow that matched her briefs.

'That's the other thing! Being naked didn't help!' she told him tartly.

'I'm sure it didn't,' he murmured soothingly, and helped her to put on her thin white woollen pullover. 'Not that a swimming costume provides much of a deterrent for a crocodile with serious man-eating on his mind,' he added.

She shot him a withering look, but he merely provided himself placidly as something to hang on to as she hopped into her jeans, one leg at a time, and wriggled vigorously to eliminate the resistance her cold skin was offering to the denim. He also helped her, gravely, to give them a final tug up.

'You give new meaning to being poured into a pair of jeans, Lydia,' he offered respectfully.

She let go of him suddenly. 'That's only because I'm still damp!' she retorted arctically as she pulled on her yellow jacket and sat down abruptly to reach for her socks and boots.

She was still brooding on the sheer, heart-stopping terror of coming face to face with a crocodile—admittedly a startled one. All the same, she'd been unable to move a muscle, and had started to sink before Joe had grabbed her and, with the lifesaving technique that she'd experienced before, towed her to the bank whilst the creature had swum away in the other direction and disappeared into the next pool.

But with her boots zipped up, she crossed her legs and turned her attention to Joe Jordan.

He now had his shirt on as well as his jeans, and with a wry little glance at her he came to sit down opposite her, also cross-legged, so that their knees touched, and started to button up the shirt.

Lydia maintained her disapproval for a good minute as they stared into each other's eyes, until she looked down first and realised he'd got his buttons crooked.

'Let me,' she murmured, and he surrendered them to her, saying nothing, although his gaze was quizzical as it rested on her bent head.

When she'd finished, she looked up into his eyes again, austerely, but she also straightened his collar with one hand then slipped her hand round the back of his neck. And as their foreheads touched, she said on a gurgle of laughter, 'I feel such a fool!'

They laughed together until she was almost crying. Then she pulled a hanky from her pocket to wipe her eyes and nose, and he said, 'That's my girl.'

'But if you had a romantic, naked tryst beneath the waterfall in mind, Joe, I couldn't have ruined it more effectively.'

'That water was too cold to be romantic, and that croc had other ideas; it wasn't one of my better plans,' he admitted ruefully.

'It was a lovely one,' Lydia contradicted. 'I'll cherish the ride, the sunrise, even the croc and half freezing.' She looked around and it was plain to see the magic that the spot, and the morning, was reawakening in her.

'And I'll be content with that—for the time being,' he murmured.

She waited until he'd retrieved the damper, wrapped in foil, from the coals, and poured the tea from the billy, before she said, 'About last night.'

He paused to look at her briefly, then went on buttering the damper he'd sliced.

'Can I just make some observations as they come to mind?' she asked with a faintly puzzled frown.

'If you want to.'

She studied him for a long moment. 'Don't you think it should be talked about, Joe?'

He shrugged. 'It could be difficult to put into words.'

'I'm entirely in agreement, about some of it. But if you're worried I'm going to put you through a "Was I any good?" kind of routine, I'm not.'

'You were. You reminded me of the *Song of Solomon*.'

'Oh, Joe,' she whispered, 'you don't have to say that.'

He handed her a slice of damper dripping with butter and honey on a tin plate, and for an instant his hazel gaze held hers and it was completely serious.

So much so that she was shaken to the core, and she'd finished her damper and tea before she came out of her reverie. Nor did he intrude on her thoughts, but when she did come out of it, he raised an enquiring eyebrow at her.

She shook her head. 'No, you're right; I can't put anything into words.'

He smiled slightly and held out his hand to her. She took it and he drew her to her feet, then slid his arms around her beneath her open jacket. And for at least five minutes he demonstrated how unnecessary words were between them.

She was breathless, flushed and had stars in her eyes when they stopped kissing each other passionately, causing him to tell her that she was a sight for sore eyes.

'Oh, dear,' she said decorously.

He grinned and reached for his coat to shrug it on. 'What does that mean?'

'I've got the feeling I actually look all starstruck and girlish.'

He took her in his arms again and rested his forehead on hers. 'Not exactly like the Ms Kelso who arrived on Katerina, or bearded me in Balmain, no,' he said barely audibly.

Her lips trembled, but she said gravely, 'Quite a dragon she must have appeared to you.'

He considered. 'All the same that was when I first experienced the desire to see you without your clothes. As I mentioned so disastrously when we remet.'

'Your choice of words did leave a lot to be desired,' she agreed. 'But I have to admit you were the first man to intrigue me for a long time.'

He kissed her mouth lightly. 'I'm glad. Should we head home?'

'Let's.'

They rode home more sedately and via a different route, stopping once on a rise at a boundary fence where they could see the Victoria River as it flowed in a series of curves towards some distant mountains, now browsing in golden sunlight, on its journey to the sea and the Joseph Bonaparte Gulf.

And Joe told her a bit about Augustus Gregory who, in 1855 and 1886, had discovered the vast grazing lands of the Victoria River Basin as well as the rugged, virtually inaccessible country around it.

Lydia sat on her horse, drinking it all in, and was unaware that he was watching her rather intently as her expression radiated her delight in the vast Top End panorama.

* * *

They were to have three more days on their own.

Sarah rang to say that she and Rolf were still trying to talk things through. Joe put the phone down and stared into the distance thoughtfully; the call had come in just after they'd got back to the homestead from their ride and swim.

'How does she sound?' Lydia asked.

'Distracted. Jumpy. Very tense,' he replied.

'Would it help if you were there with her?'

'I don't think so. I'm a large part of Rolf's problem, so to speak.' He shrugged. 'No, I think this has to be between them.'

Lydia went up to him and put her arms around his waist. 'I can see you suffering for her, though, and I know what it's like.'

He looked into her eyes and his lips twisted. 'Fate seems to have decreed that you and I bear the responsibility of our sisters.'

She touched his cheek with her fingertips. 'I'd love to be able to help.'

He caught her hand and kissed her fingers.

'I mean, I know I can't actually help with Sarah and Rolf,' she continued after a moment. 'But with the other dislocation of your life. It has to be a huge step for you, giving up your cartooning to come back to Katerina, even although you love it.'

'I didn't think you approved of my cartooning,' he said with a fleeting smile.

'I was determined not to approve of anything to do with Joe Jordan at the time,' she said wryly. 'Obviously you've won me over to a certain extent since then.'

His eyebrows shot up. 'Only to a certain extent?'

She maintained a calm expression, although their proximity was creating havoc with her senses. They'd shed their jackets and she was able to feel the warmth of his body against hers, inhale the heady scent of a mixture of sweat after their ride back and strength. She wondered as she stood against him how it could be described as strength, but that was how it struck her;

that was the difference between the perfume of her skin and his, and that was what made it so heady and exciting.

She swallowed suddenly, remembering his question, and was struck by the fact that although she'd been teasing him she was in fact gloriously if not foolishly won over.

'To a large extent, then,' she said airily, still trying to keep it light.

He looked amused. He said, however, 'Well, this evening I have to pound out a two-thousand-word article for the paper. You might like to give me your assessment of it.'

'I'd love to,' she responded, although looking genuinely surprised.

'Good. But now I have to do some work, much as I'd love to—do something else with you.'

It was her turn to look amused. 'Can I come? Is there anything for me to do?'

'You may, with pleasure,' he responded. 'Like to do a bit of mustering from the chopper?'

'I'd love to! But who...are you flying it?'

He nodded. 'Pete's had to go into Timber Creek to pick up a part for the grader. And this next paddock has some rough country in it.'

'But I didn't know you flew!'

'I may have mentioned before that I was modesty personified?'

She looked into his wicked hazel eyes and said a little helplessly, 'Nobody else mentioned it either.'

'Probably didn't cross their minds. We employ Pete because Rolf doesn't fly, and although a lot of stations use contract helicopter mustering, it's handy to have your own, if you can fly one.'

'I see. Don't they cost a small fortune? And you also have a plane.'

He grinned. 'I picked both of them up secondhand, Ms Kelso, and, together with Pete, renovated them.'

She shook her head. 'There's no end to you, Mr Jordan!'

'In that case—come fly with me, Lydia!'

She did.

* * *

So she spent the next few hours diving down ravines and up gullies, clinging on and shutting her eyes at times, as they chased cattle out on to the plain into the waiting arms of the mustering team. The noise was tremendous, despite her earphones, but Joe's cool daring and complete understanding of the limitations of his machine were wildly impressive.

'That was tremendously exciting but I'm exhausted!' she confessed when they returned to the homestead after dark. 'I feel as if I've been pounded and battered and I've got a headache.' She grimaced. 'How feeble!'

He grinned down at her. 'Not feeble at all. It takes a bit of getting used to. Why don't you soak in a hot bath and I'll make us a drink? You deserve it.'

She sighed. 'That sounds wonderful, but I only have a shower in my bathroom.'

'Lydia.' He caught her wrist as she went to go past him. 'Use mine. It's got a proper full-length bath.'

'Well—may I?' But she sounded suddenly hesitant.

He released her wrist and traced the outline of her mouth. 'Of course. Because we are going to use my bedroom tonight, aren't we?'

She distinctly felt herself go weak inside, and could only nod.

She didn't soak for long, although she did lie back and apply a hot facecloth to her brow for about five minutes, which seemed to cure her headache. As she got out of the bath, Joe came in.

He pulled a towel from the rail and murmured, 'You have no idea what will-power I exerted this morning when I dried you off, Lydia.'

Her lips parted as she stood before him, naked and dripping. 'I… I mean, I assumed…' she stammered like an inarticulate girl, and couldn't go on.

Tiny lines crinkled beside his eyes as he smiled wryly. 'You mean you were so mad at me you failed to notice that, freezing water and a Johnson River croc notwithstanding, I was seriously stricken with desire for you?' he teased.

'Well, yes,' she confessed. 'But you also told me what the effect of the water was likely to be!' She breathed in deeply as he started to towel her.

'Just think...' he lifted her arm to dry her side '..how powerful your attraction must be, then.'

She closed her eyes, because all she could think of was the effect his gentle yet thorough towelling was having on her. Then she said softly, although with her eyes still closed, 'Hang on.'

His hands stilled where they just happened to be, cupping her hips through the towel. 'Lydia?'

She lifted her lashes at last and there was a spark of devilry in the deep blue of her eyes, as well as desire. 'I'd just like to assess how powerful it is now.'

'I'll tell you,' he replied plaintively. 'If you don't take me to bed pretty soon, I shall be lost.'

'You started this,' she reminded him.

He gazed down at her quizzically. 'Ah, but only you can complete it.'

Her lips curved. 'All the same, I'd much rather you took me to bed, Joe.'

'Why?'

She shrugged, and he dropped the towel and moved his hands round to her breasts. He also said, 'Do that again.'

'What? Shrug?'

'Please.'

'No, Joe—'

'It's—breathtaking, the way they move, that's all,' he said seriously.

'Joe, I'm not going to stand here shrugging all—oh, all right! Come to bed, Joe Jordan!' She took his hand and led him out of the bathroom.

CHAPTER SEVEN

WHEN THEY GOT UP, Lydia donned her pyjamas and dressing gown and said she'd make them bacon and eggs, if that was all right with him.

'Mmm, sounds perfect.' But he put his arms around her.

He'd pulled on a tracksuit, and while she'd kept her hair dry as they'd showered together his was still damp, and standing up in spikes from the towelling he'd given it. She resisted the urge to tame them by combing her fingers through his hair, then gave way to it, causing him to smile gravely.

'How was that?' he asked.

The corners of her mouth dimpled. 'I thought we weren't supposed to talk about it.'

He considered. 'That was this morning. It seems to be different this evening, but I did—'

She put her fingers to his lips. 'I know, you did make the most wonderful reference to it. How was it tonight?' She paused and her mind roamed back to the pleasure he'd brought her, the soaring climax so that her spirit as well as her body had been transported to a peak of perfection... 'It was exquisite,' she said huskily, and trembled suddenly in his arms.

He kissed her lightly and with extreme gentleness. 'I couldn't have said it better myself.'

'Why don't you go and exercise your way with words, then, while I do the cooking?' she suggested.

He laughed, and she caught her breath because there was something so alive and devastatingly attractive about him it caught at her heart.

She not only cooked bacon and eggs, she fried tomatoes and made a lot of chips. She set it all out on a warming trolley, complete with a bottle of tomato sauce, and wheeled it, with a flask of coffee, into his study.

He looked up from his computer and held out his hand to her.

'How's it going?'

'Nearly done. Wow! Chips and tomato sauce. I must have been doing some things right lately.' He drew her down on to his lap.

'As you very well know, Mr Jordan,' she murmured, with her head resting comfortably on his shoulder, 'I like your study. I liked your other study, as a matter of fact. I even...' She paused.

'Go on,' he invited.

'No, nothing. Well,' she said at his quizzical expression, 'you might get a swollen head, so I won't say it. Shall we eat?'

He gazed at her enigmatically, giving her to understand, by making no movement and keeping his arms around her, that she wasn't going to get away with being mysterious.

She clicked her tongue with humorous frustration, but secretly she had other reasons for changing tack and not going on to say that she'd very much liked his Balmain house, even to the extent of wanting one like it herself. In case he realised just how far overboard she'd gone? she asked herself.

'Lydia?'

She came out of her thoughts with a little jerk. 'Uh... Joe, it may not exactly be a gourmet meal, but we shouldn't waste it.'

'I'll make a bargain with you, then. We'll eat now if you promise to tell me what you were going to say over coffee.'

'That's blackmail,' she protested.

'I have a further string to my bow, although I'd hesitate to use it,' he drawled.

'Such as?' she enquired dangerously.

'Well, I know you've overpowered me a couple of times, but in the normal course of events, and fully prepared, I'm stronger than you are, so...' He shrugged.

'Joe Jordan, put me down.'

He grinned satanically.

'I mean let me go!' she commanded.

'Only if you promise.'

'This is childish!'

'I'm a big kid at heart; look how I like my chips,' he murmured.

She looked into his eyes instead, which was a mistake, because there was so much laughter in them once again she went breathless at the impact of him. 'All right, Tarzan,' she said unsteadily, 'I'll promise—to think about it.'

'That's not—'

'Joe!'

'Yes, ma'am! Just doing it, ma'am.' He released her.

'Now you've made me feel like a schoolmistress.'

He lifted her to her feet and stood up himself, kissed her, and took her hand to lead her towards the trolley. 'As a mistress you're sensational, even when you comb my hair for me and do up my buttons. I'm starving,' he continued as her lips parted. 'Thank you so much for providing this feast.' And he drew up two stools and started to unload the trolley on to a table.

Predictably, Lydia subsided, then started to smile, and finally burst out laughing. She said, 'I've got the feeling you could charm a block of wood.'

He smothered his chips with tomato sauce and looked at her ruefully. 'So long as you don't hold it against me.'

In the event she didn't have to tell him anything, nor did she get to read his article, because before they'd had a chance to drink their coffee a call came through from the head ringer out on the plain. The mob that Lydia and Joe had mustered by chopper had been settled for the night, preparatory to moving them to the portable yards tomorrow for drafting. But one of the ringers keeping watch had been thrown from his horse when it had been startled by a snake and had broken his leg: a nasty compound fracture, apparently, that would require the attention of the Flying Doctor.

He'd also hit his head and didn't seem to know where he was.

Before Lydia's eyes, Joe went from laid-back, teasing and relaxed to ice-cool and very much in command.

There were a couple of supply vehicles at the scene, fortunately, and one of them was bringing the ringer in. So the main concern was to get the airstrip lit so the Flying Doctor could land, and provide palliative care until he arrived.

'I can help there,' Lydia said. 'I know I'm not a doctor, but—'

'Good,' Joe interrupted briefly. 'Thanks.' Then, as his gaze rested on her, it softened. 'I'm sorry. You were already exhausted—'

'It doesn't matter. I'm fine. Let's go.'

By sunrise the next morning she fell into bed, her own bed, and slept for six hours. During the dark hours of the night she'd not only helped to build fires and prime lanterns to light the strip, but she'd monitored the ringer's condition and been patched through to the doctor via satellite telephone, so she'd been able to keep him stabilised. The Flying Doctor had just commenced the return trip to Darwin.

Joe had gone back to the muster. She'd offered, but had been told gently but firmly to go to bed.

She swam up from deep layers of sleep just before lunchtime, stretched, and found her gaze dwelling on Brad's picture on the dressing table. Something like a shaft of pain pierced her heart, because it had been a couple of days since she'd thought of him, and not only that, she'd given herself to another man under the weight of an attraction so strong it had driven him from her mind.

Or had it? she asked herself as she sat up and reached for the silver-framed photo. Could it be that Joe and Brad would always occupy different parts of her heart? Could it be a blessing of Brad's that she could now go forward to love again because she was able to draw on the things he'd taught her and shared with her?

She blinked a couple of times, then held his image to her heart for a long moment, before putting it back on the dressing table.

Although, of course, she mused, neither she nor Joe had discussed being in love with each other, or where it would lead. But perhaps this release she felt, to go forward with Brad's blessing, would...what? she wondered. It had to make it easier for her, if nothing else. Unless she should still be very wary about falling in love so quickly. But that was how it had happened for her *with* Brad. The difference being, though, she thought, with an odd little tremor running through her, she and Brad had both been of one mind, whereas Joe...

'Is still something of an enigma.' She said it out aloud and frowned as she remembered his disinclination to talk about it. And there was something else, she realised, that she couldn't quite put her finger on, except to think *was* he more manageable than she'd expected? She shook her head immediately, because it wasn't that, but...

Finally she gave up and got up. Although as she showered she made one decision. She would just go with the flow for the time being.

It was in this spirit, the following evening, that she barred Joe from the kitchen and prepared a special meal: a delicate zucchini soup, veal with mushrooms in a cream sauce, and *crêpes Suzette* to finish. She set the rarely used table in the main dining room with Sarah's best linen, found some candles, put on a heater and retired to her room.

Half an hour later she emerged, lit the candles and dished up the soup, calling him from his study. Although they'd spent the day together it had always been amongst others, and the night before had seen Joe so tired they'd slept together but 'most chastely', as he'd put it with a wicked little grin.

He came as soon as she called, but paused on the threshold, taking in the candles, the bottle of wine, the soft music in the background, the warm room, and her. 'You should have warned me,' he said at last, and looked down at his jeans and navy jumper.

Lydia moved forward in her black silk georgette dress, and took his hand. 'I just felt this dress...' she smoothed it '...didn't get to—didn't *quite* get to realise its full potential the last time I wore it,' she murmured.

He smiled faintly, his gaze examining her discreet make-up and shining loose hair.

'Besides which,' she continued softly, 'Sarah told me you have to make your own entertainment in this part of the world, so I thought I would not only cook you a special dinner, I'd dress up for you.'

'I see,' he said at last. 'I can only approve.'

'I'm glad,' she murmured gravely, and led him to the table.

'You wouldn't also be laughing at me?' he enquired.

'Why would I do that?'

'Because I may have looked completely bowled over?'

'You did look satisfyingly stunned,' she conceded.

'You do know what's going to happen after dinner, Lydia? Assuming I can wait that long,' he said.

They were standing very close and she could see the shadows on his jaw, those little lines beside his eyes and what was lurking in their hazel depths: a preoccupation and fascination with her that caused her to breathe unsteadily.

'Oh, yes,' she said huskily, and touched those shadows, feeling the roughness of his skin with her fingertips. 'Oh, yes, Joe. And I can only approve...'

They made love later with an intensity that shouldn't have surprised her, because all through her special meal, or as far as they'd got, the tension had grown—the tension of trying to be good company and make conversation, of according her food the respect it deserved—when really the last thing either of them had wanted to be doing was eating and talking...

Nor had they got to the dessert stage, because before she'd finished her veal she'd put her napkin on the table and looked across at him rather helplessly.

He'd risen, come round to her and drawn her to her feet, then clasped both her hands in his between them, level with her breasts. 'Would I be terribly uncouth if I also declined dessert?' he'd murmured, his eyelids half lowered, his voice deep and quiet.

'Yes. I mean, no... I mean, I was going to agree that...dessert could wait. That's what I meant,' she'd said lamely.

His lips had twisted. 'Then it seems we're of one mind.'

'Yes...' She hadn't been able to think of a single thing to add, had barely been able to breathe, as her pulses leapt and a flame of desire swept through her. And this time it had been he who led her to his bedroom.

All the same, he'd started slowly. He'd kissed her thoroughly first, then undone her lovely dress so that it had slithered down her thighs with a silken hush. Her underwear was black lace tonight, and the removing of it had involved touching her intimately. She hadn't helped, powerless, she'd discovered, other than to accept being undressed and thrill to the sensations he'd been inflicting on her.

It had struck her once, dimly, that if she'd set the scene for this seduction, he was carrying it through in a way that was killing her slowly, with love and a yearning of the most physical kind.

She'd also felt as if she should make a stand of some kind, play some part, but when she'd been free of her clothes, and he'd dispensed quickly with his, she had still been standing in the middle of the floor, with her arms at her sides, unable to move because she'd never felt more slender, or vulnerable suddenly, at the power of the attraction of his tall, sleek and strong body, and the way he handled hers.

Then he had come to her, and, after one brief, searching look into her stunned eyes, said very quietly as he touched her mouth gently, 'Don't look like that; it's mutual.'

That had been when it became not only mutual but extremely urgent as they'd claimed each other with an intensity that hadn't allowed them to reach the bed.

Hours later, after they'd made love again, but much more decorously, on the bed, she stirred and laid her cheek on his chest. He stroked her hair. 'All right?'

'Mmm...'

'Want to talk?'

'What about?' she murmured.

He paused, slipping strand after strand of hair through his fingers. 'How well we do some things on our feet?'

A smile curved her lips. 'I knew you'd make some reference to that, Joe.'

'Did you, now? In point of fact, that's the first time it's happened that way for me.'

'In point of fact, me too, and I feel...' it was her turn to pause '...slightly embarrassed about it.'

'I can't agree there.' His fingers drifted down her cheek to her chin, which he tilted so he could see her eyes. 'It was marvellous. It was spontaneous combustion, you might say.'

'It was certainly that.'

'So I don't see why there should be any regrets, but if you prefer I shall desist from the upright position in future.'

She blinked at him. 'You were...' She stopped.

'Lydia, you still have one other thing you started to say then refused to enlighten me about, and it's unlikely that anyone is going to fall off their horse and fracture their leg again so soon.'

'Is that a threat, Joe? Anyway, I... I thought you'd forgotten.'

'Not at all, on both counts.'

'So why make the point?'

'Because I could keep you in bed with me for days. But would you see that as a threat? Or a penance?'

She leant up on one elbow and observed him dryly. 'Yes. Well, not a penance exactly...'

'Not exactly?' he teased.

'Damn. I should never get into an argument with you, Joe— you know what I mean!'

'I do now, and if you'll just tell me what you were going to say earlier, I'll get up and make us a midnight snack.'

'I was going to say you were the one who initiated the spontaneous combustion!'

'Ah, I'm not so sure about that. Your black dress is actually renowned for the effect it has on me.'

Lydia stared at him, then suddenly dissolved into laughter. 'I didn't expect quite such an effect, though.'

He kissed her hair and hugged her. 'Why was that so hard to say?'

'I don't know,' she murmured, after some thought. 'Did you say something about a midnight snack?'

'Just going.'

She lay in his bed and could hear him in the kitchen, talking to Meg and producing the snack. And she wondered why it had been so hard to say, and what she'd *really* been trying to say anyway? But all she could define was that it seemed to be linked with something on her mind to do with Joe Jordan that refused to make itself clear to her, something worrying.

She sighed, pulled the blankets up to her chin and contemplated the fact that she felt wrecked in the most wonderful way, so it was an odd time to be having doubts about the man who had achieved this—unless it was to do with just how good he was at it?

She sat up abruptly as things suddenly slid more into focus for her. Had she been subconsciously congratulating herself on handling things between them to her satisfaction and at her pace? Had she secretly liked to think he was quite manageable when in fact he'd only been allowing her to think it?

But why, she asked herself, did this occur to her now? What had unlocked this growing conviction that she'd managed nothing, but had been led with great subtlety and charm along a path that she wouldn't have had a hope in hell of resisting anyway? Was it the way she'd melted tonight and seemed to lose all will? So that her planned seduction after a good meal, intelligent conversation, music, candles and all the trimmings had been overpowered by something she'd had no control over?

Was it the knowledge now that he was irresistible and she was no better at being immune from him than Daisy had been? In fact, had she been lured into being as notoriously generous as her sister could be on very few grounds for anything permanent likely to develop from it?

She swallowed, and remembered something he'd said two nights ago, when she'd told him she suspected he could charm a block of wood—*So long as you don't hold it against me.*

'Lydia?'

She looked up, startled, because she hadn't heard him come in, and he was standing beside the bed with a tray in his hands. 'Oh. That...that looks great.'

There were toasted cheese sandwiches and a pot of tea on the tray.

He put it down on the bedside table. 'What were you thinking about?'

She hesitated, and couldn't help wondering how he would prise it out of her if she refused to tell him. 'I was feeling lonely, I guess,' she said a little sadly, which was true, but not quite as he might imagine.

He sat down on the side of the bed and kissed her forehead. 'It was lonely out in the kitchen.'

'At least you had Meg,' she murmured.

'You know how I adore Meg, but it's not the same thing at all. May I come back in?'

'Joe...of course!' But it had not been what she was going to say. Joe, you don't fool me any more, she'd been going to say. You've got me literally eating out of your hand, but I'm no longer the only one who didn't know it...

'I thought you might have been having second thoughts.'

They'd eaten their sandwiches, drunk their tea, and laughingly remade the bed, getting rid of the crumbs. They were now lying in the dark, she with her head on his shoulder but wide awake.

'I'm probably a bit dazed,' she said at last.

'Lydia—'

'And wondering whether I'm a control freak.'

She felt his jolt of laughter. 'Because your beautiful dinner, *et al*, didn't go quite according to plan?'

She nodded gratefully, because he'd understood immediately—although that was only half of it, and the least important part of it.

'We could do it again tomorrow night. I promise to behave myself.'

'I don't think so, Joe.'

'How would it be if we slept on it and made any momentous decisions to do with it tomorrow?'

'We do…we do need to talk,' she said, a little unsteadily. Then added hastily, 'But you're right. Tomorrow.'

He kissed her hair. 'I don't mind talking now. But I thought you might be a little highly strung at the moment. So, turn over, and I'll see what I can do about it.'

She hesitated, uncomfortably aware that he'd read her state of mind accurately and feeling foolish in consequence. Then she did as she was bid and he started to stroke her back gently.

And, quite helpless beneath the rhythm of his hand, she felt herself softening and relaxing, even starting to feel sleepy. 'I thought I was the one with the magic hands,' she murmured drowsily.

'You are, but this is a pleasure compared to a chore.'

She fell asleep with a smile on her lips.

There was a note on the pillow when she woke to say that he was down at the main yards to take delivery of a breeding bull they'd purchased, and also that Sarah had rung and Pete, who'd been in Darwin to pick up supplies, was bringing her home to Katerina. They'd be back later in the morning. It finished with a query—would she like to come down and inspect the new bull?

Lydia brushed her hair out of her eyes, glanced at the bed-side clock, then scrambled out of bed. It was already nine-thirty and she'd slept through not only Joe leaving but the phone ring-ing; she'd slept on despite the remains of a meal and an untidy kitchen to deal with, but also having taken up residence in Joe's bedroom, and now Sarah was due home shortly, with all the at-tendant unhappiness that might bring.

And he thought she had time to go down and see a bull?

She smiled briefly as she headed for the shower, amused at herself mostly, and her housewifely concerns, when she had far larger issues hanging over her head, but nothing seemed to dent her determination to hand Sarah's house back to her spick and span. Not even the question on her mind of whether Joe

Jordan was standing on the outside of *their* relationship and feeling a lack...

Because she'd succumbed like every other woman he'd known? Had he been hoping, when he'd allowed her to think she was calling the tune, that she'd call a different tune? Was that what he'd meant—Don't hold it against me when you find out you're no different from the others?

It was quite by accident that she heard Sarah before she saw her.

Pete flew over the homestead as usual, but there was no vehicle up at the house so Lydia assumed Joe would pick Sarah up from the airstrip. And she suddenly decided she would give them some time on their own before she intruded, so she put on her hat and went for a walk beyond the garden environs.

As she walked through the bush she pondered the new thoughts that had come to her as she'd showered. Was that why they'd neither of them simply said last night—I love you? He, because it hadn't happened; she, because of a fear of what she would hear if she said it?

Hear that they needed more time before they made any decisions. Sensible, of course, she told herself, particularly in light of her new understanding that she was virtually like putty in his hands, but...

She was coming back and was just on the other side of the garden fence behind a stand of bushes when Sarah's clear voice and good enunciation wafted on the still, hot air, and she realised Sarah and her brother must be walking in the garden. To talk privately, perhaps, thinking Lydia was in the house?

She froze, then heard Sarah say, 'Joe, if you and Lydia were to make a go of it, that would be perfect! I needn't feel guilty about leaving you alone here; it's about time you settled down anyway, and she's so right for this place.'

'Beloved,' Lydia heard Joe drawl, 'those are not reasons to marry, much as I would like to accommodate you, and, to a lesser extent, Rolf.'

'But you have—I mean you and she have—got together, haven't you?'

'What makes you think that?' Joe sounded abrupt.

'Pete,' Sarah replied. 'He reckons it's happened.'

Lydia flinched as Joe swore. Then he said, with a clear warning in his voice, 'Sarah, what has happened between me and Lydia is our own business entirely. Don't trample about on it!'

'All right! But you can't deny if you're going to run Katerina you need a wife, and you need someone like Lydia. And Joe,' Sarah said firmly, 'love and all the rest of it may not be all it's cracked up to appear. Far better to have someone sensible by your side and let it grow.'

'Are you talking from your own experience?' Joe enquired cynically.

'Yes. What I love about Rolf now are not the same things I thought I saw in him when I was so madly attracted I couldn't think straight. I've been lucky,' she added soberly. 'I've got another chance. You know what your problem is? You're too darned independent.'

'Do you think marriage will solve that?'

They must have moved away, because Lydia didn't hear Sarah's reply, but Joe's question seemed to brand itself on her brain. She sat down on a rock and took off her hat to fan herself, not only because she was hot from the sun but because her heart was beating uncomfortably and another question posed itself to her.

Would she wait to discover whether Joe Jordan would offer to marry her because he needed a wife? Or would she acknowledge the truth of what Sarah had said, as Joe had, and get out before she broke her heart completely?

They were sitting in the garden, Joe and Sarah, on the other side of the house when Lydia ostensibly came back from her walk and managed to look suitably surprised as well as making her explanation of where she'd been.

Sarah got up immediately and hugged her enthusiastically.

'Sit down and have something to drink,' she said. 'I've got a lot to tell you!'

There was a tray on the grass with a pitcher of cold lime juice. Joe smiled at her and said, 'I won't embarrass you by kissing you without your permission, Lydia, but it seems the whole world knows we "got together", so you don't need to worry about covering anything up from Sarah. On the other hand, why not?' he murmured, and, taking her in his arms, kissed her lightly. 'You were a sleepyhead this morning,' he added, with his eyes wicked, teasing and warm all at the same time.

Then he released her and pulled up a chair for her, and she wasn't sure if she was furious with Joe Jordan or the opposite, but she did know that she was blushing furiously.

'Yes, well,' Sarah commented airily, 'I've been told not to trample about on this turn of events, so I won't, except to say—'

'Sarah.'

She turned to her brother and pulled a face at him. 'You won't always be there, Joe! But all right. Rolf and I have resolved our problems,' she said eagerly to Lydia. 'We're going to sell our shares to Joe, and Rolf has in mind a place in Queensland, out from Cooktown. It'll be a battle but instead of feeling like the meat in the sandwich at times, I shall—*we* shall have a common purpose from now on.'

'I don't know what to say,' Lydia conceded honestly. 'Except if it's what you truly want, I wish you all the success and happiness in the world.'

'Thanks. There's another piece of news I haven't even told Joe yet. They never could find out why I couldn't conceive, but I've seen a new specialist and he's of the opinion I don't need the *in vitro* program, I need, above all, to relax about it. I just didn't realise how tense I was, not only about a baby but seeing Rolf slipping away from me.'

Both Joe and Lydia leant forward and said, 'That's wonderful!' then grinned at each other and Sarah.

A little later Lydia got up to make lunch, protesting that she didn't need any help and they must have a lot to discuss. And she left them together after lunch, locked in critical business discussions by the sound of it, and took herself down finally to inspect the new bull.

'Would this be where I find the veterinarian, ma'am?'

Lydia looked up to see Joe standing at the door of the vet station, hat in hand.

'Perhaps.'

He came in. 'Then you're not the lady with the magic hands?'

A smile touched her mouth. 'I could be. But I also know a man with good hands.'

'Are you cross with me?'

'What makes you think that?' she asked.

'A certain sternness about you,' he replied. 'A certain air of preoccupation.'

'How long have you been watching me?'

'A minute or more. You were staring at the wall for all that time.'

Lydia glanced around the small room devoted to veterinary equipment that was built into the main shed. She'd come in with the idea of making an inventory of the sprays and drenches used for internal and external parasite control in cattle and horses, so she could pinpoint which stocks were low and perhaps suggest more updated alternatives. But her list lay on the table next to her pen and it was quite blank.

'You shouldn't watch people without their permission, Joe.'

'As in kissing them? Is that it?'

She looked up and found a certain irony in his gaze as it rested on her.

'No—I mean, it's sneaky—is that *what*?' she asked disjointedly.

'The reason for your mood?'

'There is no mood!' she denied.

He continued as if she hadn't spoken, 'Because I not only spilt the beans to Sarah but kissed you in front of her?'

'You could have consulted me first!' Lydia stared at him proudly.

'She already knew. The whole damn station knows. You may not have heard about the bush telegraph,' he said dryly, 'but even without it, for the last three days you've been going around like a woman in love, Lydia.'

She gasped.

'Not that there's anything wrong with that, it's been lovely to see, so why worry and get all uptight about Sarah knowing?'

She took several deep breaths. 'Because I can't say the same thing for you, Joe. I have, I've discovered, no idea whether you feel the same way.'

'No idea?' he said softly but lethally. 'Have you forgotten what happened to us only last night?'

'No. But I also haven't forgotten that we put off discussing it until today, and I happen to know that today may have brought a whole new complexion to things.' She stopped abruptly and bit her lip.

His eyes narrowed, and she flinched as she could see him making the connection—her walk, he and Sarah talking in the garden... 'You heard,' he said flatly.

'I... I didn't mean to,' she stammered. 'I went for a walk in the first place so you and Sarah could have a bit of time on your own, but I was just on the other side of those bushes...' She stopped helplessly.

'And you're now convinced I either need a wife, especially a sensible one like you, who's also right for Katerina, or I'm too independent to fall in love properly?'

'Joe, whatever and why ever...' she twisted her hands in obvious distress '...you are still something of an enigma to me. But it's worse. I thought... I thought I was handling this well—'

'Us?' He smiled briefly.

She nodded. 'That's what you let me think, though, isn't it?'

'Perhaps.'

Her eyes widened.

'Lydia,' he said, 'what should I have done? Trampled all over your memories of Brad or let you feel unthreatened and unpressured whilst I tried to be as manageable as I could?'

She licked her lips as several expressions chased through her eyes. 'Joe, that still doesn't tell me if you think we could be united, body and soul.'

He didn't move. 'Yes, I think we could,' he said quietly, 'but there's one thing I'm very afraid of. The pressures I may bring to bear whilst I get to grips with changing my life the way I'm about to.'

CHAPTER EIGHT

'JOE...' SHE STOPPED, supremely frustrated, as Pete rapped his knuckles on the door and stuck his head around it.

Joe himself said shortly, 'What is it now, Pete?'

'Uh...if this isn't a good time for you two,' Pete temporised, 'I can come back.'

But Lydia could clearly see the curiosity and amusement in the pilot's eyes. And she could feel herself getting hot at the thought of the whole station realising she was a woman in love and discussing it, perhaps laughing about the ups and downs of it, making predictions, even having bets?

She said, although in a strangled kind of way, 'Not at all, Pete. I was just about to go up to the house anyway.' And she walked out.

Joe made no attempt to follow her.

Nor did they have any further private communication until after dinner.

Over dinner, Sarah continued to be enthusiastic, and it emerged that Rolf, who had been a bit unsure of his brother-in-law's reaction, apparently, since upsetting the apple cart so thoroughly, would be coming back tomorrow. And that he and Sarah would stay on at Katerina until the end of this season's muster.

Lydia glanced at Joe. He'd obviously assured Sarah that Rolf would be welcome, which was only the sensible thing to do, but she couldn't help wondering what his inner feelings on the subject were, and closed her eyes briefly. Because, of course, she herself wasn't too good at reading his inner feelings, let alone sorting out her own.

He came to seek her out in her bedroom after Sarah had gone to bed.

She was standing in front of the door to the verandah, staring out into the night with her arms folded. She hadn't changed out of her khaki pants and dark green pullover. She didn't turn at his light knock and he didn't wait to be invited in. There was no reason that he should, she reflected. He had seen everything there was to see about her.

At the same time, when he put his arms around her from behind, she couldn't stop herself from leaning back against him with a sigh, and blinking a couple of ridiculous tears from her lashes.

'I think I can guess how you feel,' he said quietly.

'Can you?'

'As if everything that should be essentially private between us has been laid out and trampled on from here to Darwin.'

'You're so right,' she murmured. 'I even wondered whether they'd been laying bets. Talking of which, you won *your* bet hands down, Joe.'

'I'm not rejoicing. I wish I'd never made it. Lydia, can I look at you?'

He let her go and she turned slowly. And something inside her ached at what she saw. A man too good with women for his own good, perhaps. She winced inwardly to think that on first impressions she'd wondered what Daisy had seen in him—not that it had lasted long. Only moments, perhaps, before the impact of Joe Jordan had started to make itself felt.

The impact that now saw her standing in an unremarkable

bedroom with twin beds, horribly pink chenille covers and furniture that didn't match, knowing he could make love to her anywhere and it would be heaven. Knowing that she loved everything about him. From his brown hair, that sometimes stood up, to his freckles, his sense of humour, his body, his hands, even the darkness of his moods, at times. But also knowing she hadn't made the same impact…

'If there are doubts,' he said gently, 'it's because I'm not the easiest person to live with at the best of times. Which is not to say we mightn't make it. But I think there needs to be a longer run-up. I think you need to see the really…the times when I know I'm being impossible but I just can't seem to help myself. The times when I'm going to curse Katerina for the hold it has on me and long for Balmain. When I get desperately sick of cows and yearn for bright lights and clever conversation, even though I know they won't hold me either.'

Her lips parted but he went on. 'I guess it's like a crisis, or a crossroad. I don't know how I'm going to react to it. I—'

'You could always find a manager. You could spend the wet season down south…' She stopped abruptly.

'Perhaps,' he agreed. 'But that's an example of the kind of decision I'm going to have to make. Give up journalism completely or try some other form of it, some part-time form of it? Try my hand at politics?' He shook his head. 'The only thing I know at the moment is, it's not going to be easy.'

'So, what do you propose we do?' she heard herself asking from what sounded like far away.

He took her hand. 'Come and live with me until you can really say whether you love me or hate me.'

'That sounds so sensible, Joe,' she whispered, 'but—'

'I know. It's also asking you to give up your job and your life down south. It's asking a hell of a lot, in fact, but I wouldn't even think of it if I didn't know you loved Katerina.'

'I wasn't going to say that.' She looked away and bit her lip.

He ran his fingers down her cheek. 'Tell me.'

'Well, the other side of me finding out if I could live with you is *you* finding out whether you are locked to me mentally and physically or—still standing on the outside.'

'I am—locked to you both mentally and physically—'

'No, Joe. If you were you wouldn't be proposing this. This very sensible, sane solution—I'm sure a lot of people would no doubt agree it is. But I don't see it that way. And, because of that, when Pete goes to pick up Rolf tomorrow I'm going with him.'

'Lydia—'

But she managed to smile at him through her tears. 'Joe, there's only one thing you failed to understand about me. You read me right in so many ways, you let me think I was dictating terms and going at my pace, and all of that got me over the final hurdle of laying Brad's memory to rest. But there's one thing you missed. The one thing you didn't see was that you led me all this way only to offer me second best. I can't accept it.'

'Would you seriously prefer a rush to the altar?'

'No. I'd seriously prefer you to know your own mind, but since you don't, and can only offer me something that's a sort of "mostly marriage" compromise but not the real thing, so we can cop out when the going gets a bit tough—'

'Lydia,' he said grimly.

'Since you can only do that,' she persisted, 'I'm going to say thank you for everything and please don't subject me to a Joe Jordan who's been thwarted. And just remember, when the right one does come along for you you'll know it, when where you live or what you do pales into insignificance beside not being *truly* together.'

'You don't think you're in control freak mode, do you, Lydia?' he said harshly.

She drew a breath. 'I'm not sure which one of us is a control freak, Joe, but it could just as easily be you. Goodnight.' She turned away decisively.

He went.

* * *

'So it finished just like that?' Daisy said two days later when she returned from the Musica Viva tour to find her younger sister back at home. 'He didn't try to stop you the next morning or—'

'No. Not that he'd have succeeded,' Lydia said. 'We were exceedingly polite. We'd had a bit of practice at that, which is just as well because Sarah was wildly curious. In fact Meg and I had a more emotional parting than Joe and I...and I don't regret it.'

'Say that again?'

This time they were in Daisy's bedroom as she unpacked.

Lydia shrugged after a moment. 'Of course I do.' She blinked a couple of times and sniffed. 'I feel as if I'll never be the same again, but...' She sighed and pleated her hanky. 'I wasn't the right one for him. It's as simple as that.'

Daisy glanced at her bent head and working fingers. 'I told you he could be moody and sarcastic. Perhaps you shouldn't take too much notice of it? I mean—'

'Daisy, this was different.'

'OK, but all the same—'

'No, tell me about you!' Lydia insisted.

Daisy sat down on the bed rather abruptly. 'I'm engaged.'

'What?'

'The oboe player,' Daisy said a bit dazedly. 'He—his name is Simon, by the way—he was waiting for me in Darwin when I got back from Katerina.'

'Daisy—'

'No, this is different, Lyd,' Daisy assured her. 'This really is different...'

Three months later Lydia had to acknowledge Daisy was right as she walked down the aisle behind her sister. Because it was hard to imagine two people more in love than her sister and Simon Hart, or more suited to each other, despite the age difference—which Daisy seemed to have long since disregarded, anyway.

After Daisy's wedding ceremony, at the reception in a chic

restaurant, it was Chattie who took Lydia aside and looked her up and down in her beautiful champagne silk gown. 'How's it going?'

'Fine.' Lydia looked comically perplexed, as if this was a strange time and place to be asking that.

'I just wondered if this was a bit hard on you,' Chattie said.

Her aunt was looking supremely elegant in a navy suit, but she also looked determined and had a *you don't fool me for a moment* air about her.

Lydia sighed. 'Because it's made me think of my own wedding? Sure, but—'

'Because you're eating your heart out for a man who may not be perfection personified,' Chattie said baldly.

Lydia licked her lips. 'How do you know that?'

'You've lost weight—that dress has had to be taken in twice since the dressmaker started to make it—and I happen to know all about Joe Jordan.'

Lydia sighed. 'Daisy, I suppose.'

'Daisy,' Chattie agreed.

'This is still an odd time to choose. I'm sure Daisy spilt the beans a while ago.'

'She did.' Chattie paused and sipped her wine. 'But I thought, OK, let's see how you handle it. You obviously had your reasons for walking away from him. What I can see *now* is that you're not handling it very well—'

'This is still an odd time to choose,' Lydia insisted, with a spark of anger in her eyes.

'You aren't the easiest person to get through to, Lydia, so I thought I'd choose a time when you might be lacking some of your usual defences,' her aunt replied blandly.

To her horror, Lydia discovered she had tears in her eyes, because no one could know how difficult this wedding had been for her except her intuitive aunt.

'The thing is,' Chattie said gently, 'we're a lot alike, you and I. But I wouldn't like you to make the same mistake I made.

Here, pet.' And she handed Lydia a lace-edged handkerchief from her pocket.

Lydia swallowed a couple of times and blew her nose. 'What was that?' she asked hoarsely.

'I turned my back on a man because I felt I loved him more than he loved me. It made me feel...vulnerable. It made me scared that I'd break my heart. I now know,' Chattie said slowly, 'that if I could have my time over again, even heartbreak would be preferable to this feeling I have to take to my grave that I should have given it a go.'

'Is...is it too late?' Lydia stammered, tears for her aunt now starting to well.

'Far too late. He's married to someone else with a teenage family.' She gestured.

'I think I need to sit down,' Lydia said.

When they'd found themselves a quiet spot in a couple of armchairs, Lydia said intensely, 'He manipulated me.'

Chattie raised an eyebrow. 'He must have known you well to be able to do that. How did he manipulate you?'

'He let me think I could manage him. He let me believe I made the decision to go to bed with him. That's the other thing. He knows *women* too well. There I was—' Lydia stopped, with a strangely futile expression in her eyes. 'Being superior about Daisy, and how she'd keeled over for him, only to find myself doing the same.'

They both glanced towards the bridal table, where Daisy and Simon were staring into each other's eyes and James Kelso was looking on indulgently. True to form, although he'd added a tweed jacket and a tie to his khaki shirt, James still wore jeans.

Then they looked at each other with identically wry smiles. And Chattie said, 'At least we don't have to worry about Daisy and what her biological clock may have got her into.'

'No. Thank goodness.'

'But he did ask you to live with him?' Chattie queried.

'Yes. For all sorts of good reasons, but not the best.'

'That may have been wiser than you think,' Chattie commented. 'Look, I'm not going to say much more, just this. The way it happened for you with Brad may have been the best and the easiest way. That doesn't mean to say it always happens that way. If you can't get this man out of your heart and mind, give it another go, my dear.'

'There's…what about…? My pride seems to be involved,' Lydia said unhappily. 'Not that I'm…' She stopped helplessly.

'I've always thought that a bit of pride is a good thing,' Chattie said. 'Too much is the opposite.'

A couple of days after the wedding Lydia was striding out along the walkway not far from home, across the cliffs that linked several beaches. It was overcast and showery, although not cold. There were storms out to sea and slanting pencil lines of rain on the horizon.

She'd been walking for a couple of hours and was on her way back when she sat down on a bench and pulled off her raincoat. Her hair was damp but she was hot, and there looked to be a break in the showers. She stared at the silvery patches of light on the dull pewter surface of the ocean, where thinner cloud was allowing the sun to admit to a slight presence on this otherwise grey and drizzly Sydney day.

Daisy and Simon were in Fiji on their honeymoon, her father was in Melbourne at a writers' conference, and her aunt was about to launch an exhibition of her work, so she was extremely preoccupied and had made no further comments on Lydia's love life. It was a weekday, but because she was on weekend duty at the vet practice Lydia had a couple of days off. Days that she was finding extremely hard to fill.

She'd tried to blame Chattie for this in her mind, but honesty had prevailed. Her whole life had been extremely difficult and hard to fill for the last three months. But of course Chattie *was* responsible for throwing down the gauntlet, so to speak. Responsible for making her face the growing conviction that she might have made an awful mistake. Why else would it be getting harder rather than easier to live without Joe? Why else were her thoughts always elsewhere? Precisely, up in the VRD of the Northern Territory.

Had the wet season commenced? she wondered. Had Rolf and Sarah moved out? Was Joe in residence at Katerina or Balmain? Had she been so self-engrossed she'd walked out on him when he'd really needed her? Had she accused him of manipulating her when in fact what he'd said was true? She could never have got over Brad any other way than to think *she* was shaping her life.

She sighed. One could be forgiven, she mused, for thinking he needed no one. But then, hadn't she been through a stage in her life when she'd thought she needed no one?

And how to give it another go, as Chattie had suggested? How to cope with rejection if Joe had decided he could live without her?

She closed her eyes as all these questions went round and round her mind. Then opened them as she heard a dog barking excitedly and saw two people walking towards her with a pale golden Labrador that looked just like Meg. Before she could blink the dog raced up to her and sat down in front of her to extend its paw lovingly.

'Meg?' she whispered. 'Is it you? No, it can't be.'

The couple, a middle-aged man and woman, had also stopped, and were smiling at the dog's antics.

'She's lovely,' Lydia said huskily. 'I knew another dog just like her; she also used to shake my hand. You've trained her well.'

'Oh, she's not ours,' the man said. 'She just appeared out of the blue. She's got a note tied to her collar, addressed to someone called Lydia—would that be you? She seems to know you. She didn't offer to shake our hands.'

'Meg, it *is* you.' Lydia swallowed, and with shaking hands she untied the string attaching the note to the dog's collar and smoothed it open. It was a cartoon. A look-alike Joe Jordan on his bended knees. The caption said 'HAVE I BURNT MY BOATS?'

She looked around and he was there, standing tall and straight only a few feet away, as the middle-aged couple melted away. A different-looking Joe Jordan, in a grey suit with a white shirt and navy tie, although the jacket was hooked over his shoulder. But not only different because of that. A more serious, sombre person than she'd ever seen him.

'Joe?' she said dazedly. 'I... I...' She was shaking all over, she realised.

'Hello, Lydia,' he said, and walked towards her.

She started to get up, then stopped, and he stopped, and closed his eyes briefly. 'Don't run away from me, please.'

'I...' She swallowed, because some instinct had prompted her to flight. Some sense of self-preservation, perhaps, some fear that this couldn't be real.

'Can I sit down and talk to you?' he asked quietly.

'I...how did you find me, and...?' But she couldn't go on.

He sat down beside her and she thought there were new lines scored beside his mouth, and that he looked thinner. 'Your aunt told me where I'd find you. She also updated me with Daisy's news. You must be very happy for her.'

'I am. We all are—what else did Chattie tell you?'

He glanced at her. So far he'd made no move to touch her, and there was about six inches of clear space between them on the bench. Close enough, though, for Lydia to be acutely aware of him through all her senses. 'Nothing, other than that your father is in Melbourne. Should she have?'

Lydia breathed a little easier, although her pulses were still beating erratically. 'No.'

'How are you?' he said.

'Fine,' she lied. 'Uh—how are things up on the VRD?'

'Very wet.'

Lydia realised she was smoothing his cartoon almost franti-cally and willed herself to stop. 'This…is a bit of a surprise, Joe.'

'I know.' Once again he glanced at her, taking in the black vee-necked body suit she wore with jeans, her hair, her lips… 'Can I tell you about it?'

She could only nod.

'You asked me once whether I'd missed Daisy when she wasn't there. I told you no. But it wasn't the same with another girl. A tall, serious girl with a boyish stride, who shot from the hip—when she wasn't laughing and making me laugh. A girl who seemed to develop an almost mystical affinity with my home. A girl who strode the back roads of my mind even when I…tried everything to make myself forget.'

'Such as?' There was the faintest quiver to her lips that might, or might not have been a smile.

'Working myself to exhaustion. Fighting with myself over trivial things. That's all.'

'So you didn't try to forget this girl in the traditional man-ner?'

'No, Lydia. That would have been impossible, if you mean finding myself another girl to take her place in my bed.'

'Joe…' Lydia paused and licked her lips. 'You may have been wiser than I realised at the time.'

'That was one of the disputes I had with myself.' He put his arm along the back of the bench behind her. 'Along the lines of who does this twenty-six-year-old girl think she is? A pillar of wisdom on these matters? And all because she happens to have been married once?'

Lydia moved abruptly, but his fingers rested lightly on the point of her shoulder and she stilled, because even through the black stretch knit of her top it was electric to feel his touch again.

'As with the other disputes I had with myself,' he continued, 'well, her point of view won hands down when I finally stopped and realised what I'd done.'

Lydia turned her head to look at him properly for the first time since he'd sat down beside her. 'Do you mean...' she asked huskily, but couldn't go on, and closed her eyes because she was still afraid to hope...

'I mean...' he said, and leant forward to kiss the tip of her nose, and then it seemed as if *he* couldn't go on.

'I mean,' he said at last, this time against the corner of her mouth, 'what we had was so special—where I lived, what I did, all those big decisions that I thought were going to be so difficult to make, they turned out to be nothing compared to the pain of thinking I might have lost you, and that, for good.'

'Joe...' Her lashes fluttered up and her eyes were wet. 'It's been three months.'

'I know,' he said bleakly. 'But I persisted in trying to sort some kind of a life out of the chaos, and I persisted in the belief that until I did I shouldn't drag you through the process, assuming I hadn't turned you off me completely.'

'So what changed your mind?'

'It was Meg, really.' Meg was now lying contentedly at their feet.

This time Lydia did smile. 'I know she's a charming and intelligent dog, but can she talk now?'

'No. Not in so many words. It was when I realised I'd alienated even her while I was tilting at imaginary windmills, so that she no longer sought me out or appeared to get any pleasure from my company...' He stopped and put both his arms around Lydia.

'This sounds absolutely bloody stupid,' he went on harshly, 'but perhaps it's a good idea to remember it, because that's what I can be like—that's when I realised what I'd done and that there was one simple key to my whole life, and it was you.'

'Thank heavens for Meg.'

He lifted his head and looked into her eyes. 'Do you really mean that, Lydia?'

She sighed a shuddering little sigh. 'Oh, yes.'

'So these three months haven't...?' He paused.

'They've been sheer hell,' she confessed, and put the palm of her left hand to his cheek.

He covered it with his hand, then took it away from his face and looked at it. It was the hand she always wore Brad's signet ring on, but it was bare.

'When?' he asked.

'When did I take it off? When I got home from Katerina. Because although I'd convinced myself,' she said, 'that I loved you more than you might ever love me, and although I thought I had succumbed like every other woman you'd known, I also knew I'd been released at last from the pain of losing Brad and was able to love another man.'

'You weren't like any other woman I'd known, Lydia. And you turned the tables on me completely. You let me love you then you left me because I didn't come up to scratch.'

'Joe—' she blinked at him '—I thought it was the other way around...'

'No, sweetheart,' he said definitely. 'I've been such a fool.' He released her hand and cupped her face. 'Because I can't begin to tell you how many ways I love you. I can't begin to tell you how arid not only my life has been but my soul has felt.' He paused and she saw him swallow, and realised he was speaking from the heart. 'But other things about me haven't changed. Such as the way I let you leave Katerina because I was convinced I was right when I was quite wrong.'

'I may have contributed.' Tears were slipping down her cheeks now and he smoothed them with his thumbs. 'I may have laid down the law occasionally myself. It wasn't easy for me to admit you were irresistible, Joe Jordan.'

He closed his eyes and leant his forehead against hers, and she felt the shudder of relief that went through him. Then he kissed her wet, salty lips gently. 'Will you marry me, Lydia? I still haven't worked out what I'm going to do, but at least half our lives will be spent on Katerina, if that's OK with you.'

'I don't think you need to worry about that. I love Katerina. As a matter of fact—and I started to tell you this once, then never did say it because I thought it may have been an indication that I'd gone overboard for you, and I had difficulty admitting that to myself, let alone you—'

'Ah. The night the ringer broke his leg?'

'Yes.' She laughed a little. 'It sounds ridiculous now, but I was going to say that I loved your Balmain house even to wanting one like it myself.'

'Not ridiculous at all. The list is building up,' he said with a wicked little glint in his eyes. 'You like my homes, you like my dog. Could you see your way clear to liking me enough to marry me?'

'Yes, thank you, Joe, I can.' And they laughed together until he started to kiss her...

It was Meg's growl that drew their attention from their passionate embrace to some walkers approaching.

'Perhaps we ought to go somewhere more private,' Joe suggested.

'What a good idea—how did you get here?'

'I flew myself from Katerina then drove from Balmain,' he replied. 'I didn't want to subject Meg to the indignity of a cargo hold, especially since I was sending her on such an important mission.'

'So you've never brought her down here before?'

'No.'

'Thank you,' Lydia said softly. 'But why are you looking so formal?' she asked as they rose and she pulled her raincoat on and he donned his jacket. It was starting to rain again.

'I had planned to approach your father and ask for your hand, having been threatened with him on at least two occasions.'

'Who—? You didn't tell me Daisy had also threatened you with Dad!'

'It must have slipped my mind,' he said wryly.

Lydia's lips curved. 'He's in Melbourne.'

'I now know that. It's not funny either,' he said gravely as Lydia gurgled with laughter.

'Yes, it is,' she insisted. 'My father is the worst dresser in the world. He never wears anything other than bush shirts, jeans and odd socks.'

'I see.' Joe Jordan stopped in the middle of the path. 'So I could have made a right fool of myself?'

'Not with me,' she disagreed. 'Somehow, the thought of you dressing in a suit to impress my father lends a whole lot of authenticity to this.'

'What about this?' he asked, hours later.

They'd driven to Balmain and gone to bed, where they still were after making love.

Lydia stirred and looped her hair behind her ears.

'I love the way you do that,' he murmured, 'but it's often a sign that something's bothering you.'

She pulled a pillow under her head and ran her fingers across his bare shoulders. She said nothing as she took in everything about him. The sandy-brown hair that often stood up in spikes. The faint hint of freckles, his hazel eyes—serious and with a question in them. And her emotions suddenly boiled over. The months of thinking she'd lost him and the cold ache inside her that that loss had produced claimed her. Tears welled, but she said simply, 'Nothing's bothering me—I was moved beyond words, that's all.'

'So it also had the stamp of authenticity?' he said into her hair, gathering her close. 'Don't cry—I could kill myself for being such a fool.'

'I'm not really crying. Well...' She paused. 'I felt like it so often, but never did—perhaps I need to get it out of my system.'

'Do you remember,' he said softly, 'taking issue with me over the way I eat my chips?'

'I...yes.' She started to smile. 'But what's this leading up to, Joe?'

'Two things—are you sure you really want to take on such an uncivilised idiot?'

'I...what's the other one?'

'Before we get on to that, I'm just trying to point out some of my deficiencies.' He stopped as she moved, then quietened in his arms.

'For example,' he went on gravely, 'how many men do you know who've taken you for an early-morning swim in a freezing, crocodile-infested pool?'

She dissolved into laughter.

He kissed her gently. 'That's what I was really trying to do, make you laugh. It's one of things I missed so dreadfully, not having you to laugh with.'

She sighed, but because of the sheer warmth that flooded her. 'Now,' she murmured, 'whilst your lovemaking left me feeling exalted, uplifted and wrecked—' her lips quivered '—*that* makes me believe you do love me, Joe. I don't know why, but it really does. How do you feel?' she asked.

He lifted the sheet aside and stared down at her body, then buried his head between her breasts for a long moment. 'Luckier than I deserve to be,' he said at last, with an effort. 'And not only that but locked physically and mentally to a lover who will very soon be a wife—and, for the first time in my life, no longer standing on the outside.'

'Oh, Joe.' She smiled at him gloriously and smoothed his hair down. 'Thank you for that.'

* * * * *

The Constantin Marriage

CHAPTER ONE

ALEX CONSTANTIN RIFLED a hand through his dark hair and glanced at his watch. It was his first wedding anniversary and the time for the celebrations was approaching fast.

He pushed his chair back and swivelled it so that he could watch the sun set over Darwin and the Timor Sea as he thought about the evening ahead. His wife, uncharacteristically, had been more than happy to allow his parents carte blanche in organising the festivities—she was only now due to fly into Darwin.

His mother, not uncharacteristically, had been delighted to take on the task and the family home, one of them, would be polished to within an inch of its life and glowing with flowers. Mountains of delicious food would be in the last stages of preparation for the buffet supper and the long veranda would be cleared for dancing.

So far so good, he thought drily. What his mother had not dreamt, and what he'd only become aware of when she'd blithely dropped by the invitation list earlier in the day, was that she'd invited his ex-mistress, whose name was known to his wife, to be amongst the hundred or so people celebrating his first wedding anniversary...

A discreet knock on the door interrupted his reflections and his devoted secretary, Paula Gibbs, came in with the last of the dictation he had given her—and the slim, colourful gift box he'd asked her to get out of the safe before she left for the day.

'Thanks, Paula,' Alex said, and motioned her to sit down while he signed the letters. He pushed them back across the desk to her and his hand hovered over the present. 'Would you like to see it?'

'I'd love to!'

Alex opened the box, studied the contents for a moment, then with a shrug pushed it across towards Paula.

She picked up the box and let out a little gasp. 'It's beautiful! I knew it would be pearls, but diamonds as well! And Argyle pinks if I'm not mistaken.'

'You're not,' Alex said wryly, and added in answer to the query in his secretary's eye, 'Giving her Constantin pearls would be a bit like giving coals to Newcastle. At least she'll know I had to buy the diamonds.'

Paula closed the box after a last lingering look at the pearl necklace with its beautiful diamond clasp. Then she said firmly, 'But Mrs Constantin isn't like that, I'm sure.'

He replied, after a moment's thought and with a fleeting smile, 'No, Mrs Constantin is not like that at all, Paula.' But he was suddenly and insanely tempted to add—*Would the real Mrs Constantin please stand up?*

He stood up himself instead, because Paula was an ardent fan of his wife, and, anyway, his problems were his alone. But the question was still on his mind as he drove the short few blocks home to the apartment that faced Bicentennial Park and Lameroo Beach. It had been a cause of some amusement for his wife that the Sultan of Brunei was reputed to own the penthouse in the same building. 'Are you in the same class wealth-wise as the Sultan of Brunei, Alex?' she'd asked with a gleam of sparkling fun in her blue eyes.

He'd denied the charge in all honesty, adding that the Constantin family fortune, added to the Beaufort fortune which she herself had inherited, would probably be less than small change to the Sultan of Brunei and, indeed, the Paspaley family which had pioneered cultured-pearl farming in the Northern Territory and the Kimberley region of Western Australia.

'But you've also done very nicely out of pearls, thank you, haven't you, Alex?' she'd remarked, and added, 'Plus the cattle stations, cruise boats *et al*?'

He'd agreed, but pointed out that she had also done very well out of her family's fortune.

'True.' She'd glanced at him with a question in those stunning blue eyes.

'I only make the point because you seem to hold my family fortune in a certain sort of low esteem,' he'd said. 'Is it because I'm only a first-generation Australian of Greek descent whereas the Beauforts go back to the pioneering roots of this part of the country?'

'Darling,' his wife had said, 'I never make those kind of judgements. The Beauforts may have been around these parts for a long time but your family is a model of propriety compared to some of my ancestors.'

'So why do you look condescending at times?'

She'd shrugged. 'Sorry. Didn't mean to. But perhaps some of your Greek family's customs don't entirely impress me. I'll leave you to work out which one in particular.' And she'd flitted away before he'd had the chance to remind her that her own mother, who had Russian blood in her, had actively participated in the custom she was referring to...

All this was still on his mind as he took the lift to their apartment, and all the illuminated rooms told him that his wife had arrived back from Perth on schedule. In fact, as her bedroom door was open and Sibelius was pouring out *Finlandia* from her CD player, he was able to observe Tatiana Constantin née Beaufort unseen and at his leisure.

She was dressed and applying her make-up. Her dress was long, strapless, and clung to her figure. It was the same cornflower-blue as her eyes and her dark hair was in a loose, shining bob to her shoulders. At five feet two, she was petite with a delicate figure and smooth, pale skin.

But his wife always had an air of vitality about her, often even suppressed excitement. He'd taken it for a girlish attribute at first—she was only twenty-one now—with not a great deal of substance behind it.

Then again, he'd taken a lot about Tatiana Beaufort on face value when he'd allowed his parents and her mother to manoeuvre them into an arranged marriage. So it had come as something of a surprise when she'd told him unemotionally on their wedding night that she was aware of its orchestration. She was even aware that he had a mistress, she even knew her name. And he'd had to revise his opinions of his wife further when she'd suggested that a year's grace for them both might be a good idea. A year, at least, for her to make up her mind whether to make it a real marriage.

He had agreed and, a year later, was still revising his opinions. Yes, there was something irrepressible about Tatiana Beaufort, there probably always would be, but he'd been wrong about the lack of substance. Just how to quantify it was not so simple, however.

There was no doubt she'd made the best of this first year of their 'marriage in name only' or *marriage by contract*, as she'd called it. She'd relished the role of mistress of his several homes, breathing life and comfort and colour into them. She'd entertained with charm and originality. She'd travelled extensively with him and given the appearance of being a proper wife to the outside world, and she'd been genuinely interested in the process of cultivating pearls.

She had also added stature to the Constantin family by means of her charity work. She was a born social worker and she spent a lot of time working unpaid in a legal aid office. The only thing she hadn't done to date to completely fulfil his parents' expectations was to present them with a grandchild. Which, of course, was what it had all been about in the first place.

His parents were deeply family oriented, and it had been a cross to bear that they'd only been able to have one child. Therefore all their hopes rested on him, and they took an abiding interest in every aspect of his life. Occasionally this was claustrophobic and exasperating, but mostly he bore it with equanimity and did his own thing anyway. But when he'd reached thirty and shown no inclination to marry and provide the dynasty with heirs his mother had decided to take matters into her own hands.

From the first suitable girl she'd paraded in front of him, he'd been quite aware of what was going on. He'd even been slightly amused at her ingenuity. Then he'd grown exasperated by her persistence and gone into evasion mode. But this had hurt her feelings and then two things had happened simultaneously—he'd felt guilty and she'd come up with Tatiana Beaufort, the daughter of an old friend of hers. And there was one aspect of the Beaufort girl that had been impossible to ignore. Her family had been pioneers in the Kimberley district of Western Australia—it was a very old, respected name, and she came with two vast cattle stations.

Not that he gave a damn about the old, respected name, although he'd known his mother would like nothing better than to add a Beaufort to the Constantin family. But the cattle stations were something else... Between them, should he and Tatiana Beaufort marry, they would own a fair slice of the Kimberley and beef prices were in the process of doubling.

He'd still had no plans to actually do it, though, until it had become obvious that if his mother was a matchmaker of some skill, Tatiana's mother, Natalie, was even better. Cool and subtle, she had presented her daughter beautifully, and it was, Alex had decided, rather like sparring with an accomplished business rival. Perhaps, he reasoned, this was why he'd become determined to find out why Natalie Beaufort, whose daughter could have married anyone, had seemed equally determined it should be him.

And finally she'd put her cards on the table. Tatiana, she felt, had been left extremely vulnerable to fortune-hunters since her father had died. Moreover, before her father had died, she'd led a very sheltered life. He'd been a strict, old-fashioned father, apparently, and the result was that Tatiana, although well-educated and very expensively 'finished', had had a mostly convent education with little contact with the real world.

'She could so easily fall into the hands of an unscrupulous man, Alex,' Natalie had said, and shuddered delicately.

Reviewing her daughter's air of breathless anticipation as he had known it at the time, Alex had agreed—although tacitly. 'What about love, though? I'm sure girls like Tatiana believe in love,' he'd added with some cynicism.

Natalie had waved an elegant hand. 'Is there anyone less wise than a young girl who believes herself in love for the first time?'

He'd raised his eyebrows and agreed with her again, but this time he'd said, 'Maybe, but how do you propose to make her think she's in love with me? In other words, would she agree to an arranged marriage?'

Natalie had taken her time in answering. She'd looked him over comprehensively, then murmured, 'If you couldn't make a young, impressionable girl fall in love with you, Alex Constantin, who could?'

Alex had met her eyes impassively and she'd laughed softly. 'Sorry, but I'm sure it's true. The other thing is, you have your own cattle stations—who would be better placed to take over the running of Beaufort and Carnarvon than you?'

'Mrs Beaufort,' he'd replied rather grimly, 'this is your daughter's future we're talking about, not a couple of cattle stations.'

Natalie had shrugged. 'Your own mother shares my...belief that a well-arranged marriage has as much chance if not more of success than...what else might befall Tatiana.'

'My own mother,' he'd stated, 'has been parading a series of girls before me in the hope that I'll fall in love with one of them.'

'But all of them eminently suitable, I have no doubt.'

'It is still not the same as cold-bloodedly choosing a husband for your daughter,' he'd retorted.

'Then I'll tell you this, Alex. Tatiana is already a little in love with you.'

This had pulled him up short, although he hadn't allowed Natalie Beaufort to see it. And, as he sometimes did, he'd mentioned the matter to his father. George Constantin had handed the reins of the Constantin empire over to him several years previously but he still liked nothing better than to be consulted. Yet it had come as something of a surprise to Alex to learn that his father was as keen as his mother for him to marry Tatiana Beaufort.

'I didn't even know you were aware of what was going on,' he'd told his father with a lurking smile.

George had shrugged and confessed that he'd left all the details up to his wife, but of all the girls she'd found he had to confess that he thought none could hold a candle to Tatiana. She had looks, she was well-bred, apparently virtuous, and she was young enough to accept a gentle moulding into being a suitable wife. 'And,' he'd added, 'your grandmother actually suggested and campaigned for me to marry your mother—look how well that turned out.'

'It's a different day and age now.'

'Maybe.' George had studied him keenly. 'But would I be wrong in assuming that since Flora Simpson returned to her husband marriage has not been on your agenda?'

Alex hadn't replied and George had gone on. 'Your mother and I aren't getting any younger, Alex. We'd given up hope of having children and thought we were past it when you came along. I think nothing means so much to your mother than to see you happy and with a family. Me too. And, if love has...

disappointed you, maybe this is the best way. But the decision has to be yours, of course.'

Alex had glanced at him wryly and thought of telling him that due to his connivance he, Alex, now had a breathless girl a little in love with him, he was being pursued by the queen of all matchmakers and he was actually cherishing unworthy thoughts for a man of integrity—Beaufort and Carnarvon to be precise, to add to the Constantin empire.

But it was only human nature, he had assured himself, to wonder what would happen to Beaufort and Carnarvon if they were left to the mercy of a twenty-year-old girl with a mother who had a reputation of having only one use for money and that was to spend it—perhaps that was why they hadn't been left to her in the first place?

Whatever, he thought, coming back to the present as he watched his wife brush her hair vigorously then pause and conduct a few bars of *Finlandia* using her brush as a baton. He'd had to do nothing but go with the flow from that point on. Tatiana had appeared to welcome his attentions and enjoy his company.

On the lovemaking front he'd learnt that she was rather shy. He had strongly suspected she was a virgin and would like to remain one until she was married. But as their relationship had progressed he'd found that she trembled in his arms and enjoyed his kisses. By the time they'd got engaged he'd been sure that, whatever his feelings were, Tatiana Beaufort was more than a 'little' in love with him.

So what had happened? he wondered, not for the first time. She had consistently refused to explain where she'd gained her knowledge of his mistress, and if she'd known all along it was an arranged marriage, why leave it until then to tell him? Had she ever been even a 'little' in love with him?

Finlandia, and Tatiana, still armed with her brush, came to a stirring conclusion, then she whirled round and saw him leaning against the doorpost. And in the moment before she spoke he saw the rush of colour that came to her cheeks and the momentary look of vulnerability that came to her eyes. Because she'd been caught conducting an imaginary orchestra, he pondered, or because of him?

'Alex! How long have you been there?' she asked laughingly, almost immediately recovered.

'Long enough to be impressed by your conducting skills.'

'Oh, that's not fair!' she protested. 'I had no idea you were home.'

He straightened. 'Don't be embarrassed, Tattie. I have the urge to do the same sometimes. How was Perth?'

'Lovely.' She sighed. 'Lovely and cool! I had great fun getting out all my winter clothes and sitting in front of a fire. What have you been up to?'

'The same.' He shrugged. 'By the way, happy anniversary!' And he put the gift box into her hand.

She sobered and looked up into his dark eyes. 'I... Alex, you didn't have to get me a present.'

'No,' he agreed.

'Then...why?'

'I'm quite sure your mother and my parents will be dying to know what I bought you. And I'm quite sure they believe you merit a present for being such a good little wife to me, and you have—for the most part.'

Tattie swallowed visibly. 'You're angry,' she said quietly.

'Not angry,' he denied. 'Puzzled. And wondering what is in store for the second year of our marriage or—if there is to be one?' He looked down at her with a thoughtfully raised eyebrow.

Tattie looked away and turned the box over in her hands. 'The thing is, I...haven't made up my mind...yet.'

He smiled satanically. 'Are you asking for another year, Tattie?'

'No.' She squared her shoulders and looked up at him. 'But I would like to discuss it with you and I don't think now is the right time. For one thing we'll be late.' A smile touched her mouth. 'Think how anxious that would make your mother!'

'Very well,' he said after a long, searching moment, and took the gift box out of her hands. 'In the meantime, allow me to do this.' He drew the necklace out of the box and she gasped much as Paula had done as the river of stunning pearls ran through his fingers and the intricate white and pink Argyle diamond clasp caught the overhead light and reflected it radiantly. 'Turn around.'

'Alex,' she breathed, 'it's *beautiful*, but I don't—'

'Tattie, just do as you're told,' he commanded.

'But I'll feel a fraud, Alex,' she protested.

'You are a fraud, Mrs Constantin,' he reminded her, and grinned wickedly as she opened her mouth to accuse him of the same thing. 'No, don't say it. You shouldn't have agreed to this party in the first place if that's how you feel.'

She subsided, then looked frustrated. 'You may be able to twist your mother around your little finger but I can't. She... she just flatly insisted on a party.'

'My dear, if I could twist my mother around my little finger, not to mention *your* mother, neither of us would be in this mess. Since we are, however, I intend to put a good face on it and so should you. Turn around, Tattie.'

She stared at him with her lips parted and confusion in her eyes for a long moment, then did as she was bid.

'There,' he said, and felt her tremble as his fingers touched the skin of her neck. 'Mmm.' He turned her back. 'Perfect,' he murmured. 'Have I told you about strand synergy, Tattie?'

He traced the lie of the pearls down her skin and across the top of her breasts beneath the blue material of her dress and back up to her neck, and he saw her take an unexpected breath.

Then she began to recite, as if it was a lesson she'd learned, 'The art of choosing the right pearls to put together and drilling and knotting them so the strand drapes like a piece of silk rather than dangling around the wearer's neck.'

'You've done your homework,' he said humorously, and

turned her again, this time in the direction of her dressing-table mirror. 'What do you think?'

Tattie took another breath as she studied the pearls in the mirror, but he thought that the whole picture was absorbing her more than the pearls themselves, the two of them close together in the mirror.

She closed her eyes suddenly and said, 'Yes, quite perfect. Thank you *so* much.'

But, as her lashes fluttered up, their gazes caught in the mirror. And he saw the surprise in her eyes as he said softly, 'You're quite perfect too, Mrs Constantin, and your skin is a perfect background for these pearls, it has its own beautiful lustre.'

This time he traced the outline of her oval face and looked down her figure in the lovely dress and thought that she really was exquisite in her own way. Like a delicate figurine, smooth and softly curved but at the same time full of life and laughter.

'Give me ten minutes to shower and change,' he said then, wresting his mind from his wife's physical perfections, and went to turn away but paused. 'Tattie, there's one other unfortunate aspect to tonight's party.'

She was standing quite still, as he'd left her, and she blinked a couple of times as if she was having trouble redirecting her attention. 'There is?' she asked a little blankly.

He grimaced. 'I only saw the guest list today when my mother dropped it into the office. Leonie Falconer is on it.'

He stopped and studied her narrowly but perceived no reaction—at first. Then a dawning look of comprehension came to Tatiana.

'You mean...you mean your mistress?' she stammered.

'My ex-mistress,' he replied harshly. 'How that bit of information escaped my mother I'll never know, but—'

'Perhaps she took it for granted that you had reformed since you married me?'

'Quick thinking, Tattie,' he parried swiftly, 'but you yourself gave me to understand you didn't expect me to live like a monk while you made up your mind about this marriage.'

Tatiana flushed and closed her mouth.

'Even so,' Alex went on, after a tense little moment, 'whatever else I am—' he looked fleetingly amused '—parading my mistresses in front of my wife is not one of my vices. But Leonie has chosen to make herself unavailable today—she's not at her office, she's not home and she's not answering her mobile phone—so I felt…honour bound to warn you that I haven't been able to warn *her* off.'

Tatiana drew herself up to her full five feet two. 'How kind of you, Alex,' she said with all the famed Beaufort hauteur she was capable of but hadn't allowed him to see until after she'd married him, 'but Ms Falconer is welcome to do her damnedest!'

He raised a wry eyebrow. 'Bravo, Tattie! See you in ten minutes.'

CHAPTER TWO

DARWIN, THE NORTHERNMOST city in Australia and named after Charles Darwin, had only two seasons—the wet and the dry. The wet season coincided with spring and summer on the rest of the continent and the dry with autumn and winter, but, since the temperature rarely fell below thirty degrees Celsius during the day, winter was an inappropriate term.

It was early in the dry season as Tatiana Constantin rode beside her husband to her first wedding-anniversary party, reflecting as she sat in the plush cream leather comfort of his blue Jaguar that things could have been worse. It could have been the height of the wet season when the humidity was legendary, flooding and violent storms were common and cyclones often a threat.

How would she have coped, she wondered irrationally, with that kind of weather on top of the cyclone-like disturbance of mind she was experiencing at the moment? With the kind of weather that, in the few short steps from an air-conditioned car to air-conditioned premises, left you bathed in sweat with your make-up melted and your hair limp?

She glanced at Alex through her lashes. Unlike her, he had been born and bred in Darwin and the ravages of the wet season never seemed to bother him. But men, she reminded herself, didn't have to worry about looking limp and bedraggled. Indeed, men, she added bitterly to herself, had more powers than were altogether good for them. Such as being able to command a mistress to do this or that.

Mind you, always assuming the mistress hadn't gone to ground, she reminded herself with a touch of black humour!

Tattie had never met Leonie Falconer, design jeweller with her own business who did quite a bit of work for Constantin, although she'd had her pointed out a couple of times. There had to be an element of luck in this, Tattie had reasoned, because, although she didn't think Alex would parade his mistresses in front of her, Darwin was not a big city.

And, although she couldn't think favourably of his mistress, a small part of her applauded the woman's bravado. She had obviously accepted the invitation, then put herself out of Alex's reach at least on this the last day that he might have been able to 'warn her off'. But why accept it in the first place? Tattie was forced to ponder. And why would Alex's mother invite her? Not to mention—how lately had Leonie become an *ex*-mistress?

So many imponderables, she thought wistfully, but the greatest of them all was sitting right beside her, driving his beautiful car with such ease and flair towards his parents' Fannie Bay mansion.

Of course he had always been a huge imponderable, if not to say the biggest challenge of her admittedly young life. And she'd cautioned herself from the moment she'd known what was going on to keep her wits about her. Right up until about half an hour ago she'd thought she'd succeeded in this ambition.

A pearl necklace, the feel of his fingers on her skin and her breasts and the shocking discovery that the mere mention of the word *mistress*, ex or otherwise, had caused all her careful strategies to come tumbling down. To the extent that she wasn't sure whether she loved Alex Constantin to distraction or hated him exceedingly.

She clenched her fists in her lap and wondered how much

she'd given away this evening. Twelve months of such self-control, she marvelled, quite possibly lost in a matter of minutes. She visualised again the picture they'd made in the mirror, he with his dark head bent towards her, she still stunned beneath the impact of his personality, and all that usually leashed masculinity in his tall frame flowing through to her.

Had it been her imagination, she mused a little painfully, or wishful thinking? Because he normally kept that side of him very much leashed in all his dealings with her but she had the feeling tonight had been different. If only, she went on to think, the subject of his mistress had not come up in almost the same breath she would have been more sure...

But really—she glanced at him covertly again—there was only so much of the masculine impact of Alex Constantin he could leash from her. Just to be sitting beside him in his austere dark suit and blue shirt, watching him drive his car, was a bit like a body blow.

Not especially good-looking, he was nevertheless vitally attractive. He was tall, fit and athletic, he could be wickedly amused and amusing, he could be quite kind yet devastatingly scornful when the mood was on him. Above all, he could be the quintessential enigma, so that the reason he'd agreed to an arranged marriage with her when he could have had any woman he chose remained a mystery to her.

Unless, his reason had been her reason—two vast cattle stations that went by the name of Beaufort and Carnarvon...

'We're here, Tattie.'

She came back to the present with a little jump, to see that her husband had made his statement with false gravity.

'So I see,' she commented, looking at the house blazing with lights and the stream of cars parked in the street. 'Oh, well, what do they say? "Onward, Christian soldiers"! "Fight the good fight"—or, something along those lines.'

He laughed and put his fist beneath the point of her chin.

'You are a character, Tattie,' he said affectionately, and added, 'If it's at all possible, just be yourself and have a good time.'

With your mistress in attendance, your mother, who never fails to drop delicate little hints and tips about how to fall pregnant, and *my* mother there, and *you* treating me like a kid you pat on the head—of course!

She didn't say it, but only by the narrowest of margins. She couldn't prevent the serious irony of her fronded blue gaze as it rested on him fleetingly, however. But before he got the chance to remark on it she opened her door and slipped out of the car.

'That is quite a statement, Tatiana,' Natalie Beaufort said to her daughter when they found themselves alone in the powder room together after the fabulous seafood buffet.

Tattie squinted down at her pearls. 'It is lovely, isn't it?'

'It is, but I was thinking more along the lines of the comment it makes on the success of your marriage.'

Tattie observed her mother and spoke without thinking. 'How do you know it's not conscience money?'

Natalie's sculptured eyebrows shot upwards. 'Is it?'

'I could be the last to know—aren't wives supposed to be?'

'You don't seriously believe Alex is being unfaithful to you so early on?' Natalie asked with a frown.

Tattie thought of pointing out that, although she was behaving herself beautifully, Leonie Falconer was amongst the guests tonight. Leonie, who had been reliably revealed to her as Alex's mistress before he'd married her—and she'd had no reason to believe, until tonight, that things had changed.

But although Natalie was her mother—or perhaps because of it—Tattie knew only too well that her mind moved in mysterious ways sometimes. Such as the number of times Natalie had brought her to Darwin over a year ago, ostensibly to catch up with her old friend Irina Constantin but really to position her daughter firmly in Alex Constantin's sights.

Such as Natalie's decision to move to Darwin herself after

Tattie's marriage, like some sort of guardian angel, even though she basically considered the place a far-flung outpost of civilisation. And she decided to hold her peace.

'Just kidding,' she said mischievously, and was relieved to see her mother subside. She couldn't keep herself from thinking that there was irony everywhere she turned these days, though. It was her mother who had advised her before her marriage that there were times when men would be men and it was often wiser to ignore the odd fling they might have...

And she found herself watching her now, curiously, as Natalie expertly touched up her make-up. Whereas Alex's mother was dumpy and not greatly into fashion, but with such a warm personality you couldn't help loving her, Natalie was very slim and very trendy. She was also artistic and played the piano beautifully and adored what she called 'café society'.

Whereas George and Irina Constantin rarely left each other's side, Natalie had frequently sought the solace of their Perth home, away from the lifestyle of Beaufort and Carnarvon and Austin Beaufort, taking Tattie with her.

To be honest, Austin Beaufort had not been an easy man to live with, and Tattie could clearly remember asking her mother passionately once how she coped with him.

Natalie had smiled ruefully and replied that there was an art to coping with men, as she would no doubt discover for herself one day, but walking away from them was something they disliked intensely, and it generally brought them round.

And her mother was undeniably quirky, if not to say downright eccentric at times. She was one of the few people who always used Tattie's full name, but when Tattie had asked her if she'd been named after a Russian ancestor her mother had replied that she hadn't. And she'd gone on to say, 'There's no doubt pregnancy brought out the Russian in me, however.'

'Why? How?'

'Well, it can be very heavy-going at times, with lots of ups and downs and a distinctly 1812 cannon-like flavour to it for the finale. I guess that's why the name Tatiana came to mind.'

Only her mother could say things like that and believe she sounded quite logical.

For all this, though, when she was not fencing with her mother on the subject of Alex and her marriage, she mostly loved her mother's quirkiness. And she knew, even if she disagreed with the means, that Natalie had genuinely thought she was protecting her daughter from the dreaded prospect of fortune-hunters, and had genuinely thought she was in love with Alex.

As for disagreeing with her means, that wasn't entirely true, Tattie forced herself to acknowledge. Because what her mother knew, but few people suspected, was how much of Austin Beaufort there was in his daughter beneath the gloss. And how much of that pioneering Beaufort blood ran in Tattie's veins, so that Beaufort and Carnarvon meant an awful lot to her, and she'd inherited his almost mystical affinity with the Kimberley country they spread over.

Natalie knew how it had affected Tattie to see both properties start to run down during the last few years of her father's ill-health before his death, and had sensed the moment of panic that had come to her daughter to discover, on her father's death, that the responsibility for them now rested squarely on her shoulders. Mystic affinity was one thing. Running two cattle stations that covered the size of the United Kingdom was another.

From that point of view Alex Constantin had been an inspired choice on her mother's part. It had also been, Tattie knew, why she'd gone along with the charade even after she'd realised she was being steered into marriage with a man who wasn't in love with her. It had not had anything to do with the fact that she'd been more than a little in love with him. She would never do anything as essentially wet as marrying a man in the hope that she could make him fall in love with her...

'Penny for them, my sweet?' Natalie patted her fashionable bronze hair and stood up.

Tattie blinked. 'Uh…she's very attractive, Leonie Falconer, isn't she?'

'Certainly very golden. She's a brilliant jewellery designer, I believe, but since she works with Alex you probably know more about her than I do.'

Yes and no, Tattie replied internally. I seem to be the only one tonight who knows she is—or was—his mistress. What I don't know is why I should be alone in the possession of this knowledge. Perhaps I should be applauding how discreet they've been instead of worrying about it?

Her internal monologue was interrupted as her mother gave her hair one last pat and moved towards the door, saying, 'I wouldn't be surprised if she designed the clasp of your pearls—why don't you ask her?'

One of the things Tattie loved about Darwin was its cosmopolitan population. In the space of half an hour she danced with a Danish boat-builder, met a Chinese couple who owned a popular restaurant and a New Zealander who made stainless-steel carvings, as well as a Japanese woman who designed clothes.

Nor could she fault her mother-in-law's party-giving talents. Now the food had been disposed of, the long veranda glowed beneath fairy lights, and the air was fragrant with the heady perfume of what must have been a truckload of roses and orchids in all colours. The guests were colourful and, having wined and dined superbly, were set to dance the night away. It was an extremely successful party.

At all times, however, it was as if Tattie possessed an unseen pair of antennae tuned in exclusively to Alex and Leonie. So far her antennae had picked up no communication between them at all. Then she looked around and found Leonie standing directly behind her, apparently admiring the clasp of her pearls.

'Oh. Hello,' Tattie said brightly. 'We've never met but I know who you are—do I have you to thank for my clasp?'

Leonie Falconer possessed hazel eyes, long gold hair and a

statuesque figure presently clad in a beautiful gown of gauzy fabric shot with all the colours of the rainbow. She too wore pearls—Constantin? Tattie wondered—and a chunky, very lovely gold bracelet.

But all this was on the periphery of Tattie's mind as she watched those hazel eyes narrow with a slight wariness then relax as she finished speaking.

'No,' Leonie said in a husky, transatlantic voice. 'Not my work, but rather nice all the same.'

'Thank you!' Tattie looked around and, observing Alex nowhere in sight, added quietly, 'Why did you come tonight, Miss Falconer?'

Leonie Falconer resumed her wariness rather abruptly. She was in her late twenties, early thirties, Tattie judged. She was also several inches taller than Tattie, but none of that prevented Tattie from eyeing her severely and imperiously.

A tinge of colour ran beneath Leonie's honey-gold skin, then she shrugged. 'Curiosity, I suppose. Why would I be invited in the first place? Also—'

'I can tell you that,' Tattie interposed swiftly, 'Irina organised this party. Alex was unaware until today that you had been invited. So was I. And Irina was definitely unaware of who you were, otherwise she wouldn't have touched you with a bargepole.'

'I see.' Leonie looked fleetingly amused then oddly bitter. 'Well, there's no reason I shouldn't be here, as it happens. I got my marching orders some time ago. And marching orders they were too—*Any fuss, Leonie, and Constantin will cease to do business with you.* I'm sure I don't have to tell you how deadly Alex can be when he sets his mind to it. But when his brief infatuation with you ceases, *Mrs Constantin*,' Leonie added silkily, 'I'll get him back.' And she turned on her heel and walked away.

'What was all that about?'

Tattie jumped and found her husband standing beside her. 'Probably an age-old ritual between mistress and wife, Alex,' she said coolly, then her lips trembled and she laughed softly. 'But how bizarre that you should use me to extricate yourself from her.'

'What do you mean?' he said rather grimly.

Tattie opened her mouth then caught sight out of the corner of her eye of his mother, radiant in pink silk that didn't suit her at all but didn't manage to dim her personality either, approaching them with a slight limp. She sighed inwardly and said, 'Don't worry about it, Alex, but I think you should dance with me in a very husbandly way now, if for no other reason than to let your mother think her party is a real success!' And she melted into his arms.

Surprise kept him rigid for a moment. And he said barely audibly, 'You're going to have to explain later, you know, Tatiana.' Then he drew her into his arms and, despite the implicit threat in the use of her proper name that always told her he was in a dangerous mood, kissed her lightly before swinging her round to the music.

'I think I'll go to bed now, Alex,' Tattie said at two-thirty in the morning, after a swift silent ride home at the end of the party.

She had preceded him into the lounge, a lovely room she had created in their apartment—the apartment he had bought and presented to her as a wedding present in accordance with the contracts he and her mother had agreed upon—with a view through the wide windows to the terrace. The view was dark now, of course, but the oil rig anchored in Darwin Harbour for maintenance was lit up like a Christmas tree.

'Oh, no, you don't, Tattie.'

She stopped in the middle of the lounge and turned to look at him. She had her shoes in one hand, her pearls in the other and her face was shadowed with weariness. 'Alex, this is no time—'

'Sit down, Tattie,' he ordered, and came across to her with two tall glasses in his hands.

'What's this?' she queried as he handed her one.

'Something long, cool and delicious for someone who has partied as vigorously as you have. Don't worry, I'm not planning to make you drunk and seduce you.' He looked down at her wide eyes and slightly apprehensive expression.

Tattie took the glass from him, drank deeply as if she was very thirsty, then in a stiff little voice recounted her conversation with his mistress. And she sat down abruptly.

Alex lounged against a pillar and merely twisted his glass in his hands. 'What she told you is not an accurate representation of the events.'

Tattie went to wave her hand and realised she was still clutching her pearls. She put them down carefully. 'It doesn't matter one way or the other to me, Alex.'

'I would have thought it might in the light of how we go on, Tattie. You did say you wanted to discuss that with me.'

'Well. Yes. But...' She trailed off, looking almost ashen with weariness and strain now. 'I can't think straight.'

He took his time. He sipped his drink then he said quietly, 'My suggestion is that we stop fooling around and get this marriage off the ground.'

Tattie's mouth fell open as she sorted through this. 'Fooling...?' she said incredulously, picking on perhaps the least startling aspect of his advice.

'Or whatever you like to call it.' He looked briefly quizzical.

'You know what I like to call it, Alex.'

He lifted an eyebrow at her. 'You also gave me to understand that you knew what you were getting into, Tattie. But, for what it's worth, your suggestion of a year's grace was a good one. At least we know now that we can get along pretty well.' His mouth quirked. 'We don't appear to have any habits that drive each other up the wall.' He looked at her with a question in his eyes.

'That's...assuming we were brother and sister, Alex. Lovers could be a different matter.'

He put his glass down on a beautiful, inlaid pedestal table

and came over to her. She stared up at him wide-eyed as he removed her glass from her fingers then drew her to her feet.

'My dear Tattie,' he murmured with his hands resting lightly on her shoulders and his gaze summing her up from head to toe, 'I feel quite sure that it could only enhance our relationship to become lovers. Trust me.'

His fingers slipped from her shoulder to trace the line where his pearls would have lain and, despite her tiredness and confusion, she couldn't help the reaction that came to her again, that trembling sensation any close contact with him brought to the surface.

'But sleep on it,' he suggested.

'I...' She bit her lip.

'I'm off on a tour of the pearl farms early tomorrow,' he continued. 'I'll be away for a few days. So you'll be able to do more than sleep on it.' He kissed her lightly on the top of her head. 'I thought, after that, we could spend a little while at Beaufort. I have some ideas for it.'

Sheer blackmail!

Tattie sat up, saw it was nine o'clock in the morning and clutched her head as the blackmail thought raced through her mind.

Tired as she'd been, sleep had been difficult, and when she'd achieved it weird dreams populated by Leonie Falconer resembling some sort of smug sun goddess had plagued her. So why had she woken up with blackmail on her mind?

Because apart from her mother only Alex knew how close to her heart Beaufort especially was. How could he not? True, she'd been fascinated by the cultured-pearl side of his business—she would have loved to be visiting the farms with him—but it was his cattle stations and how he handled them that she had attempted to absorb like blotting paper. All for the purpose of applying that knowledge to Beaufort and Carnarvon should she ever have to run them on her own.

But, more than that, perhaps only Alex guessed that twelve months had not been long enough for her to have the confidence to run them on her own and that was why he'd applied the sheer blackmail of promising her some of his time at Beaufort and mentioning the ideas he had for the station. What else could she think?

'You could ask yourself why he wants to stay married to you, Tatiana,' she murmured, and lay back with a sigh.

Had the impossible, the wonderful, the dream within a dream that she hadn't dared to allow herself to dream, come true? Had her husband finally fallen in love with her? Or had the time come to amalgamate her inheritance with his into one big cattle operation, something that had not happened to date?

Why, she pondered gloomily, did that seem much more likely?

And she answered herself tartly, he made her feel like a kid, not—apart from one fleeting moment yesterday and she wasn't even sure about that—a woman he found desirable. It was as simple as that.

On the other hand—she sat up again, struck by a new thought—why had he divested himself of his mistress? Because of a growing but *hidden* attraction to her—or so she would have no ammunition with which to continue the stalemate or base a decision to leave him on?

Her bedside phone rang. She stared at it, then lifted it reluctantly.

'Hello?'

'Tattie?' her mother-in-law said down the line in a slightly overwrought way. 'My dear, that was the best party I've ever given and all thanks to you!'

Tattie frowned. 'No way, Irina. I didn't do anything; you did it all.'

'But you were there, you were so lovely, and the whole world could see that you and Alex are perfect for each other—I just wanted to tell you! Perhaps next year,' she added, 'we will have a little addition to the family to celebrate? Tattie...' There was a slightly awkward pause down the line—an indication of a bull being taken by the horns as it turned out. 'Are there any problems in that direction? Because I have the best gynaecologist in the country, the most understanding, most gentle, most kind, and he has performed miracles for several of my friends' daughters.'

This time Tattie grimaced, then drew a deep breath. 'Irina...' But she couldn't do it. She simply couldn't dent her mother-in-law's enthusiasm and her old-fashioned belief that her arranged marriage concept had worked blissfully—although it did cross her mind to say, Perhaps you should have found a Greek girl for Alex. A girl who would understand these things and know where her duty lies...

She cleared her throat. 'Uh—Irina, no, no problems that I know of, but this is between Alex and me, I feel... I *really* feel, don't you?'

There was silence, then, 'My dear, forgive me,' Irina said a little tremulously down the line. 'Of course it is. It's just that I have such a longing for grandchildren and, sadly, I'm not getting any younger.'

'Irina...' What to say? Tattie thought desperately, because in every other respect Irina had been a lovely mother-in-law. Nor *was* she getting any younger, and she was also plagued by a troublesome hip, but kept putting off a hip replacement because of her fear of hospitals and operations.

She was saved by Irina herself, who said bravely, with less tremolo, 'I promise not to mention these things again, Tattie. I just... Last night...seeing you and Alex... I got carried away. Forgive me?'

'Of course,' Tattie said warmly. 'Tell you what, why don't we have lunch? I'll ring Mum and see if she can make it as well and we can have a gorgeous gossip about the party. How about Cullen Bay?' She named a restaurant.

She put the phone down eventually, wondering as she did if she wasn't digging a deeper grave to have to climb out of one day. Then she lay back and switched on her television, only to be arrested as she flicked through the channels by a programme about an Indian family in Mauritius. What arrested her was the fact that the patriarch still chose husbands and wives for his family, even sending to India for them, and the whole family laughingly agreed it was still the best way to go.

She tightened her mouth, switched off and got up to take a shower. While the shower refreshed her body the circles of her mind ran around a familiar pattern. Why *hadn't* the Constantins sought a Greek girl for Alex? She knew enough about the continental community in Darwin to know that it wasn't only amongst Mauritian Indians that this practice was common. She could even see a certain sense to it. Same culture, same background—possibly the same expectations.

But Alex was about as cosmopolitan as they came—or, to put it another way, he was as Australian as they came. So perhaps he wouldn't have stood for it?

A smile crossed her lips at this point in her reflections but it was gone almost before it was born—Alex did exactly as he pleased, she knew, despite his affection for his parents. So had they been, as she'd long suspected, rather clever? Had they found the one lure he'd been unable to resist in their quest to further the dynasty?

A little dialogue ran though her head, *no matter that the girl is not one of us. She still looks to be pliable, and she does have Beaufort and Carnarvon—could he resist that?* Could he?

'Perhaps not,' she answered herself, and started to dress.

It was yet another bright, cloudless July day, but it passed by in a bit of a blur for Tattie.

Her cleaning lady arrived as she was having her breakfast

coffee, and together they went through the apartment, deciding what needed to be done. Then Tattie went back to her coffee, but the apartment stayed on her mind and she looked around with new eyes.

She'd chosen pastels, light, airy colours that were above all cool. There were no curtains but wooden louvers at the windows, and she'd made simple but effective statements—a glorious oil painting on a feature wall; a pair of waist-high porcelain urns hand-painted in soft pinks, gold and royal blue; an intricately carved solid silver bowl it was hard to take your eyes from, so perfect were its proportions and soft old glow as it sat on a small sea chest; a vast, comfortable cream couch lined with pink and pewter cushions.

Mysteriously, she thought with a sudden pang, it had all become home. Yes, of course the lure of the Kimberley region where her ancestral home was, a sprawling, rambling country homestead, still held pride of place in her heart—or did it? And if not, why not?

Because this was her own creation? she wondered. Because this was where she and Alex spent most of their time? There was also a house in Perth, another house in Darwin and an apartment in Sydney, but, even though she'd added her own touches to those, this apartment in Darwin was all hers—and Alex's.

She took up her cup and wandered into his bedroom. Not that he'd known until their wedding night that this room was to be his and the main bedroom would be reserved for her exclusive use. And what kind of a gamble had that been? she paused to ask herself as she remembered how her wedding day had passed in a fever of nerves. Nerves and the terror that she might have made an awful mistake, only to discover that the equanimity with which he'd heard her out and accepted her proposal had killed a silly little ray of hope in her heart...

Nor would she forget the humorous quirk to his mouth and the glint of devilry in his eyes as he'd surveyed this bedroom on that night. Because, luxurious though it was, it contained a single bed—a king-size single not much smaller than a double, but nevertheless, perhaps a ridiculous gesture on her part, she brooded. Not to mention a sheer nuisance, since she'd had to get all its bedding custom-made, king-single linen to match her dusky-blue and pearl decor being impossible to come by.

She grimaced. Young and stupid she'd been, but was she only now about to discover just how young and stupid? She'd certainly had an inkling, as the milestone of her first anniversary approached and she'd found herself unable to come to any decision about her marriage, that—what? She was staring down the barrel of a gun? That she'd foolishly expected *something* to crop up, some resolution to present itself, only to find that she was still at square one?

If only she could find the key to the enigma that was Alex Constantin, she thought a little wildly, and walked into the room. The bed was unmade, but otherwise it was fairly tidy. He'd hung up his suit from the night before, his shirt was in the linen basket; only his tie was carelessly discarded over the back of a blue velvet chair. She picked it up and sat down on the bed, running the length of silk through her fingers.

Other than an exquisite pearl shell on the bureau, Alex had brought nothing to this room. No photos or memorabilia from his pre-marriage days. And his study in the apartment was the same. Functional, sometimes untidy, but essentially impersonal—so much so it was she who had added some blown-up photos of the beautiful bays and rivers that housed his pearl farms. Was he just that kind of man or were his treasures and mementoes stored elsewhere? At the Fannie Bay house of his parents? At—she shivered suddenly—a separate residence he maintained for entertaining his mistress?

I won't do it, she thought abruptly, and got up to hang his tie on the tie rack in his cupboard. I won't agree to a real marriage with Alex Constantin until I know without doubt that he is...*madly* in love with me!

She stared at his ties rebelliously, then went to change for her lunch date with his mother.

CHAPTER THREE

FOUR DAYS LATER Tattie was no further forward in her deci-
sion-making process and not sure when to expect Alex back.
He'd gone on to Broome, apparently. But she'd kept herself
busy, spending most of her days in the legal-aid office where
she played the role of receptionist but spent a lot of time listening to other people's problems and trying to give sound advice.

It was a Wednesday morning before she left for work when
she discovered an invitation in her mailbox from a friend who
was having an impromptu luncheon at a popular café in Parap
that day. It had been hand-delivered. It crossed her mind to
wonder why Amy Goodall, whom she'd been to school with in
Perth and was now living in Darwin, hadn't simply rung her,
but she shrugged as she tossed the colourful little invitation on
the hall table. Amy had always been unconventional and given
to springing surprises on people, and an hour of her stimulat-
ing company and others' would be fun.

So she dressed with a little more care than normal for work
in a stunningly simple sleeveless white piqué dress, black and
white sandals and a loop of black and white beads. She brushed
her hair vigorously and drew it back into a white scrunchie, and
with a lighter step descended to the garage and her racy little
silver Volkswagen Golf convertible.

At twelve-thirty she drove to the Parap shopping centre with its leafy boulevards, parked the Golf under a magnificent poinciana tree and stepped out to be confronted by a man who appeared from nowhere.

'Mrs Constantin?'

'Yes,' Tattie said uncertainly, and with a strange feeling at the pit of her stomach. He was tall, he looked as if he hadn't shaved for days, and he had angry blue eyes and matted curly hair. He was also completely unknown to her.

'Just do as I say, Mrs Constantin,' he recommended, and pulled a small gun from the pocket of his jacket.

Her eyes dilated and her heart leapt into her throat. 'What on *earth*—' she began.

'Come with me nice and quiet so I don't have to use this, which I will if I have to.'

'I... I...' But as she stammered and felt like fainting he took her elbow in a hard grasp and began to lead her towards a battered utility parked two spots away from the Golf.

She stumbled and tried to pull her elbow free but he growled an obscenity into her ear. She sucked some air into her lungs and opened her mouth to scream, but she felt the gun poke into her waist—and nothing came out of her mouth. Then all hell broke loose.

A car screeched to a halt in the middle of the road only a few feet from them—a blue Jaguar—and Alex jumped out without bothering to switch off the engine.

Her attacker immediately pulled her in front of him and swore viciously but Tattie buckled at the knees, wrenched her elbow free and threw herself sideways. Alex leapt on the man and punched him to the ground in a hail of devastating blows.

Tattie got to her knees as they rolled away from her, saw the gun on the ground and fell on it, but her assailant was no match for Alex—he was being mercilessly subdued in a show of brute strength that made Tattie blink. Then there were sirens and police swarming around them. Finally Alex, still breathing heavily, was helping her to her feet.

'What...? I don't understand... Oh, you're bleeding!'

'It's nothing, Tattie. Are *you* OK?'

'Yes, I think so, but...why...what?' she gasped.

He held her close for a moment then said gently, 'Come, I'll explain when we get home.'

Three policeman had accompanied them and now listened intently to Alex's explanation.

'When I got home today I noticed this invitation on the hall table.' He lifted Amy's colourful little card. 'But it so happens I ran into Amy Goodall at the airport this morning and we had a bit of a chat. I was on my way home from Broome, she was on her way to Sydney, so it made no sense that she would be inviting my wife to lunch today. I also noticed that the invitation had been hand-delivered.' He proffered the envelope. 'And it occurred to me that someone might have deliberately lured my wife out on a false pretext.'

Tattie made a strange little sound of disbelief.

'And that's when you rang us,' the detective in charge murmured. 'Only you got there before us. Mrs Constantin, did you recognise the man at all?'

'No! I've never seen him before.'

'Did you find this invitation at all strange?'

Tattie shrugged. 'I wondered why she hadn't rung, that's all. But she is that kind of person, prone to springing surprises.'

'So it would be fair to say the gentleman we've taken into custody must be aware of Miss Goodall's quirks. How well do you know her, incidentally, Mrs Constantin?'

Tattie told him.

'And you don't think she could have had anything to do with this?'

'Good heavens, no! Anyway, she's on her way down south.'

'Yes,' the detective said thoughtfully, and looked at Alex. 'The obvious thing that springs to mind is kidnapping for ransom.'

Tattie gasped, and if she hadn't already been sitting down would have collapsed.

Alex said then, 'I think my wife has had enough for the moment.'

As soon as the police had left, Tattie said one of the sillier things she'd ever said as she looked at Alex wide-eyed and still stunned.

'Why would anyone want to kidnap me?'

He came to sit down beside her. There was a darkening bruise on his cheek, his shirt was torn, his knuckles grazed, but the cut on his arm had stopped bleeding. For that matter, her lovely white dress was stained, her knees were grazed, her scrunchie was hanging by a thread of hair and her face was dirty.

He half smiled and gently removed the scrunchie. 'Why? I have rather a lot of money, Tattie.'

She swallowed. 'Thank heavens you came home and saw the invitation. Thank heavens you bumped into Amy! I didn't know what to do. Part of me was thinking, surely he wouldn't shoot me in broad daylight in the middle of Parap, but the other half couldn't be sure. It... I...'

'Tattie.' He took her in his arms. 'I can imagine. And if it's any consolation I doubt whether he would have shot you in the middle of Parap, but he's safely under lock and key now.'

'Maybe there are more of them!' She shivered in his arms.

'I doubt that too.' He stroked her hair. 'I suspect he was a loner and it wasn't a very well-thought-out plot.'

'Maybe,' she conceded, but couldn't stop shivering.

'Hey,' he said quietly, 'it's over. I'm here.' And he kissed her.

As an antidote to extreme nervous tension, it worked well. The shivering started to subside as his mouth closed on hers, and the incredible events that had befallen her gave way to something else.

How good it felt to be in his arms, how safe—and how ruth-less he'd been in her defence, as if she meant an awful lot to him. Then even those thoughts receded and sensations began to take their place. She no longer noticed that she was in a mess. She began to be aware of herself on a different plane altogether, very much as a woman with all the needs and desires of one, most of which he was attending to with his hands and his lips.

He stroked her arms with his long fingers and she shiv-ered quite differently, with delight. He kissed her lightly, then those cool, firm lips sought the soft hollows at the base of her throat while his wandering fingers combed through her hair. But not only was it what he was doing to her, it was the feel of his strong, hard body against hers that filled her with a lovely, special feeling of excitement.

Then he started to kiss her more deeply and she responded, shyly at first, then more and more freely. They drew apart once and she stared at him, suddenly overwhelmingly aware of the sexy side of Alex Constantin as she'd never been before. The mouth-watering masculinity of his wide shoulders and lean hips, the planes of his face, and what being under the gaze of his faintly amused eyes did to her.

It was one thing to be sitting beside him in a car and feel his presence like a body blow, she realised. It was one thing to have been kissed by him during their engagement—most chastely, she now realised. It was entirely another thing to have him fo-cused squarely on her and kissing her with all that latent sexi-ness very much unleashed. Oh, yes, she thought a little wildly, this was another matter altogether.

'This' brought out the strangest thoughts in her. How glad, for example, she was to be wearing a minuscule but very fetch-ing pair of white lace bikini briefs and a matching bra. How her skin would feel against the cream textured velvet of the couch when he undressed her; how hot, erotic and sexy she felt herself, so that the couch, the carpet, anywhere would be OK for him to make love to her, because she might die a little if he didn't...

Then he slid his hand beneath the hem of her dress and stroked her thigh, and she made absolutely no protests of any kind—and the phone rang.

She thought he swore under his breath. She thought she made a husky little sound of sheer frustration, but in the next moment he'd released her and she was sitting very properly, with her hem tucked around her legs, while he went to answer the phone and the door.

'The police,' he said, coming back to her with his lips twisting to see she hadn't moved a muscle. 'I need to go down to the station but you don't have to come. And you don't have to worry about being alone. The apartment has been put under surveillance just to be on the safe side.'

Tattie licked her lips but found herself with nothing to say.

'Why don't you have a long shower and a rest?' he suggested. 'Or would you like me to call your mother or my mother?'

'No! Uh...no, thank you.' She tried to smile. 'I'd rather not be fussed over at the moment.'

'Tattie.' He sat down beside her and put his arms loosely around her. 'You look as if you've been in an earthquake, and I don't mean physically, although there's that too. But the fact that we both enjoyed that very much has got to help in our marriage, wouldn't you agree?'

Her lips parted but again no sound came.

'Anyway—' he smiled faintly '—think about it. I'll be as quick as I can. And I am going to call your mother and my parents—we can't leave them to hear about it on the radio and I don't think you should be alone.'

He waited until George, Irina and Natalie arrived. It didn't take long for them to rush over. He suffered their concern—his mother thought he might need stitches in his arm—and admiration with a wry little smile.

And for a time after he'd gone Tattie was glad not to be alone. So she let them ply her with tea and cake and generally fuss over her, especially her mother, who kept folding Tattie in her arms. And she went through it all again with them, unaware of how her eyes shone as she described how magnificent Alex had been in her defence.

But all of a sudden she knew she had to be alone, and she told them she was going to have a sleep. It took some determination to persuade them—again, especially her mother—that she would be fine, but finally they left.

She took a bubble bath in the huge, raised marble bath that was fashioned in the shape of a shell in her *en suite* bathroom. The marble was champagne-coloured and all the towels, the soap and bottles were a soft jade-green. It was normally a most relaxing place but, even smothered in bubbles to her chin and with two fragrant candles burning as she soaked away the unusual events of the day, she felt far from relaxed.

Really, she thought, it was too much to be almost kidnapped then subjected to her husband at his dangerously sexy best—a first for her—all in the space of a few hours!

Was it any wonder she couldn't think straight?

And was this why Leonie Falconer was determined to get Alex back? Because his dangerously sexy best was irresistible?

She looked at the pads of her fingers and discovered they were wrinkled. So she got out of the bath before she resembled a prune all over, but her thoughts continued like a string of pearls with synergy—one set of thoughts leading smoothly to the next. No, not smoothly, she contradicted herself, not synergy at all, really, but jumping about like fleas, with all sorts of possibilities for this turn of events presenting themselves...

How long had Alex deliberately deprived himself of his mistress, and did that have anything to do with him needing not necessarily her but any woman?

She would have to put it to him, she felt, although she quailed inwardly at the prospect. Because it was all very well to take these developments at face value, but what protection did that offer her against spending the rest of her life in love with him while he had a series of mistresses once he'd secured her, heirs for the dynasty and, of course, two cattle stations?

She dressed in a long fuchsia skirt, to hide her grazed knees, and a pale rose silky knit top. And, because she didn't have anything else to do, she started to prepare dinner. It was a beautiful evening with the sun setting over Mandorah, so she set the glass table on the veranda—a yellow candle in a glass, frosted yellow wine glasses, and white Rosenthal china with ice-blue place mats and napkins. And her stir-fry beef with oriental rice and a salad was just about ready as Alex came home.

He looked her over, and the meal, forked some of the stir-fry from the pan, told her it was delicious and that if she could give him five minutes for a shower he'd really appreciate it.

'Of course! Take as long as you like; I can keep this warm—'

'Five minutes, Tattie,' he murmured, and kissed her lightly on his way past.

She leant back against the counter and swallowed, because it was all happening to her again: the accelerated pulse, the ragged breathing, patches of dew on her forehead and the deep inner trembling even though his lean body had barely brushed hers. In fact she had to go outside and sit at the table to compose herself.

He brought the meal out and opened a bottle of wine. He'd changed into fresh jeans and a white shirt.

'So?' she said, having fought a stern fight with herself and told herself not to be such a wimp. 'Have they found out who he is and why he did it?'

Alex poured some golden-green liquid into the frosted glasses, then propped the bottle in a wine cooler. 'Yep. He went to water. He was an employee of mine, although we'd never met—a diver. He got sacked for drinking. Then he met Amy Goodall at a party, she let slip that she knew you, so he— cultivated her, you might say. They had a brief affair, but long enough for him to discover how wacky she could be and how that could be used to further his obsession with revenge against me for his sacking.'

'And Amy has confirmed all this?' Tattie asked, wide-eyed.

'Amy has told the Sydney police that she did have an affair with him, but she had no idea how he was using her.'

Tattie sat back. 'Does this mean,' she asked with a frown, and sipped her wine, 'I'll have to be on guard against this for the rest of my life?'

Alex lifted the covers from the stir-fry and the rice and inhaled the fragrant steam. 'If you stay married to me, Tattie, we will need to take precautions, but that could be the least of our problems. Will I dish up?'

She nodded dazedly after a moment. 'What do you mean?'

He wielded the stainless-steel serving spoons and handed her a plate. 'If you stay married to me I'll be able to put all the necessary precautions in place. If you don't, you'll still be Tatiana Constantin.'

'Only on my own...oh!'

'Mmm,' he agreed. 'But that is certainly not the only reason for you to overcome your reservations about this marriage.' He sat down. 'And don't tell me there aren't some.'

'How...how did you know?'

A corner of his mouth quirked and the look he sent her was full of irony. 'Tattie, in some respects I have to admit you're a closed book. But when you're concerned or undecided about something I can tell.' He paused and contemplated his meal, then raised his dark eyes to her with a glint of sheer devilry. 'Although that wasn't altogether the case just before the phone rang.'

A slow tide of colour burnt its way up Tattie's throat and stained her cheeks, but she wasn't a Beaufort for nothing. 'How long is it since you've had a woman, Alex?'

'Ah. A Beaufort counter-attack, I take it?' He laughed softly. 'I never did meet your father but I've heard he was a hard man. I wonder if he realised you inherited some of his famed…quickness on the draw?'

'Perhaps he did,' she said evenly. 'Perhaps that's why he left me Beaufort and Carnarvon. But I have to tell you, Alex, that, while I may have got a little…carried away before the phone rang, it doesn't stop me from pondering your motives. Out with your mistress; in with your wife—why?'

'I'll tell you, Tattie,' he said pleasantly. 'Leonie became obsessed with replacing you as my wife, despite the provenance of our relationship, which was to begin with, and before I ever met you, that she had no desire to marry anyone.'

Tattie absorbed this. 'And…and you didn't threaten her with taking all the Constantin business away from her?'

'Yes, I did. In fact, I have now done so.'

'W-why?' Tattie stammered.

He looked at her meditatively. 'She shouldn't have come to our anniversary party.'

'Isn't that a little…hard and unfair?' Tattie postulated.

'Are you taking her side?' he countered. 'Could there have been any reason for her to come other than to make mischief?'

'Of course I'm not taking her side, but she might not have known I knew about her!'

That silenced him for a moment, then, 'How *did* you come to know about her, Tattie?'

Tattie ate the last of her rice and pushed her plate away. 'I have a friend who worked for her. She…thought she was doing me a good turn.'

'I see. And did your friend tell you the whole story?'

Tattie lifted her blue gaze to his. 'I thought so—are you going to tell me she wasn't your mistress?'

'No.' He shrugged. 'But she was not my mistress at the time of our marriage.'

Tattie's mouth fell open.

'Quite so,' he said with a tinge of mockery.

'So what…what…? How…?'

'I'll tell you in the hope that we can put Leonie behind us once and for all, Tatiana,' he murmured.

But he got up and cleared their plates first, poured them some more wine and studied the darkening waters of Darwin Harbour—which, as the locals were so fond of pointing out, was bigger than Sydney Harbour.

'When Leonie set up shop in Darwin a couple of years ago I was impressed by her skills and ideas. One thing led to another and we got into a relationship, but on the basis that we *both*,' he said significantly, 'had no wish for any further entanglement. She was passionate about her career and couldn't visualise herself as a wife and mother. Then, not long after our engagement, she decided to go back to America for some time and we parted.'

Tattie stared at him, wide-eyed.

'She didn't close her business but handed the reins to her chief assistant,' he continued. 'When she came back you and I were married, but she got in touch—ostensibly to show me some of the work she'd done overseas and the ideas she'd picked up. They were brilliant, and once more she started to work for Constantin as a freelance designer. However...' He paused and looked at her. 'Well, you know the state of our marriage, Tattie.'

'But why didn't you tell me this when I...when I—?'

'Delivered yourself of your ultimatums on our wedding night?' he drawled, and smiled faintly. 'I thought you had a point. I thought it would be less than right to force myself on you and I guess it seemed like a good idea to keep my options open. You did also give me your blessing.'

His last words fell into a pool of silence like stones dropping to the bottom of a well, and seemed to Tattie to contain an unmistakable undertone.

'Are you saying I forced you back into her arms?'

He grinned wickedly, but sobered almost immediately. 'Tattie, I know you're very young and quite naïve, but a year is a long time,' he said abruptly.

She sat back and drained her wine in a single swallow. 'I

suppose so,' she replied at last, and could have kicked herself for feeling so particularly young and naïve at that moment—something she would normally have denied hotly. 'Uh—what happened then?' she asked.

'It became apparent that Leonie had revised her opinions on marriage and motherhood,' he said simply.

'How inconvenient for you,' she countered tartly.

His lips twitched. 'Another Beaufort thrust? Yes, it was,' he agreed, although blandly. 'But, whatever my sins are, Tattie—and I'm not trying to deny them—you would not have approved of Leonie Falconer in what one could only describe as "haggling mode". And, for your information, her true colours turned me right off.'

'She...she gave me to understand you'd become infatuated with me and that's why you'd cast her off. Was that true?' She gazed at him.

'Tattie, what you and I feel for each other is our own affair entirely,' he answered a little grimly. 'I have never discussed you with her or anyone else. Other than your mother,' he added drily.

'I see.'

'Talking of your mother...'

He paused and moved his shoulders in an impatient gesture, reminding Tattie of his ambivalence towards her mother—she was never quite sure whether he liked Natalie or viewed her as seriously nutty. 'Was that how you came to know ours was an arranged marriage?' he asked.

Tattie folded her hands in her lap and found an opportunity to refute the 'young and naïve' allegation, on some fronts anyway.

'I'm not quite stupid, you know, Alex,' she said finally. 'No, she never actually said it, but I know how her mind works.'

'So was it finding out about Leonie that convinced you?'

'It didn't help,' Tattie conceded. 'That, and the strong impression that you weren't in love with me.'

He favoured her with a darkly amused gaze. 'You thought you could tell?'

'I not only thought it, I could,' she stated stubbornly.

'What about you?'

Her lips parted and her eyes widened. 'What about me?'

'Your mother gave it to me as her considered opinion that you were in love with me.'

Tattie closed her eyes in frustration at her mother's machinations, even if they happened to have hit the nail on the head...

'There was a bit of a crush,' she said, and tried to shrug fatalistically.

He grinned. 'Only a bit? So why did you do it, Tattie?'

Time to lay her cards on the table? she wondered with a little flicker of panic. What else could she do? None of what had just passed between them gave her the hope that Alex Constantin had fallen madly in love with her.

'I...' She gazed at the oil rig with its mantle of lights, then looked at her husband directly. 'I didn't know what else to do. Beaufort and Carnarvon were going downhill fast. Mum has always been like a displaced person out there and—' she sighed suddenly '—I didn't have the expertise or authority to run them myself, although I have this almost mystical tie to them and this perhaps ridiculously strong sense of...being a Beaufort.'

He said nothing for an age, and she watched his long fingers twirling the stem of his glass and his hooded eyes while she nerved herself to find that she was the object of his amusement.

But when he looked up at last there was no mirth in his gaze, no patronising disbelief. In fact he said quietly, 'We could be two of a kind, Tattie.'

'We could?'

He smiled absently. 'Both realists. Look, thanks for coming clean. However, if Beaufort and Carnarvon mean so much to you you're going to have to stay married to me.'

She swallowed something in her throat. 'Before I ask you why,' she said on a tremor, 'was that why you married *me*, Alex? To get them?'

He considered for a moment, then gestured wryly. 'They

played a part, yes. I kept thinking of the—sorry!—mess they could get into with only you at the helm. It sort of…went against the grain with me, especially at a time when beef prices are going through the roof.'

'Oh.'

He looked at her intently for a long moment, at the gentle, slender lines of her figure beneath the pale rose silky knit of her top, the sweep of her dark hair against her throat and the shadows of her absurdly long lashes against her cheek as she looked down—in disappointment? he wondered.

'But I must tell you, Tattie, that I fully intended to make this a real marriage before you…said your little piece.'

Her lashes flew up and her deep blue eyes were suddenly surprisingly cynical. 'A marriage without love?'

'A marriage that would grow *into* love, respect and mutual expectations,' he said steadily. 'You may not think it can work but I've seen the evidence of it.'

'But—'

He overrode her. 'But living like brother and sister is not going to achieve it, Tattie. I hesitate to do this, but…' He paused. 'How you felt earlier on the couch is a prime reason to…go forward.'

'Alex—' She put her hands to her hot cheeks. 'I was in shock and horrified at what had happened to me. Don't you think that might have accounted for a lot of it?'

He smiled suddenly. 'Let's put it to the test again, now some of the shock and horror has receded.'

She stumbled up. 'No—I mean, no,' she stammered. 'Let's not.'

'What are you scared of, Tattie? How much you'll give yourself away?'

'Alex,' she said desperately, and dredged through to her soul to find an answer for him, 'I have one *very* good reason for not wanting to change our marriage at the moment. Maybe I'll tell you what it is one day, maybe I won't, but it's *there* and I can't help it.'

'Another mystery?' he said with considerable irony, and frowned.

'Another man?' he asked incredulously after a moment. 'But one who doesn't have the ability or the money to save Beaufort and Carnarvon for you—is *that* it, Tattie?'

She opened her mouth to pour supreme scorn on this supposition, then closed it, almost biting her tongue in two. 'There has been another woman in your life,' she pointed out.

'Who is he?'

'I didn't say that! I'm only... I don't see why you of all people should be so surprised if it were the case but...well, that's all I'm saying!'

'And do you honestly think I'd hand you over to another man to enjoy, along with two cattle stations I've rescued?'

There was something unusually grim in his dark eyes as they flickered over her.

'If you don't love me that can only be because you want them yourself or your macho Greek background is coming to the fore, Alex. Perhaps it's both,' she surmised, 'but either way it doesn't impress me.'

'Who the hell do you think you are, Tatiana?' he said softly, and added, 'I wouldn't trade on being a Beaufort too much with me, because I couldn't give a damn about that.' He stood up and reached for her.

Surprise was her downfall. It rooted her to the spot, it even opened her mouth for her, and he took advantage of it all to sweep her into his arms and bend his head to kiss her.

It was a hard, merciless kiss but, to her horror, it still ignited some of the fires he'd lit in her earlier in the afternoon. How could that *be*? she wondered helplessly, then knew—intuitively?—that sometimes between a man and a woman a release from their demons only came this way. But it didn't end that way...

When he had her helpless and aroused in his arms he lifted his head and, looking supremely macho, dark and dangerously attractive, said softly, 'You've been playing with matches for the last twelve months, Tatiana Beaufort. Don't be surprised when you get burnt.'

And he left her to stride away to his study, closing the door behind him.

'Pearling in northern Australia has a colourful history,' Tattie said, slowly and clearly.

She picked up a handful of lustrous free pearls and let them slip through her fingers into a velvet-lined porcelain bowl.

'"That elusive pearl, the one bigger, brighter and more beautiful than all the others",' she quoted, 'has drawn men like a siren song, and they've described them as teardrops of the moon or a full moon rising...' She paused. 'Here at Constantin we produce the finest cultured Australian South Sea pearls, and I'd like to show you how.' She stopped and the camera clicked off.

'That was quite good, Mrs Constantin,' the director of the video said. 'Not too bad at all.'

But not good enough, Tattie said to herself, and looked around. It was two days after her attempted kidnapping, but even more importantly two days after Alex and she had come to a monumental misunderstanding. So monumental that she'd forgotten, until reminded yesterday, that she'd agreed to, and even looked forward to, making a video on the Constantin pearling operation, to be played in their stores.

And she'd looked forward to it because there were segments to be filmed at the actual pearl farms, as well as in the luxurious Darwin showroom where she was now, in a beautiful dusky-pink linen dress that shouted couturier, and wearing her own pearls.

Trouble was, Alex was there too. Alex, leaning his broad shoulders casually against a wall, out of the way of the cameras but all the same—to her—an enemy in a war, even if she wasn't sure what the precise nature of the war was.

She'd hardly seen him over the past two days, but when she had she'd been treated to cool uninterest. She'd been told that their visit to Beaufort would have to be postponed—he'd also forgotten about the video, apparently, so it was a legitimate excuse, but she had no doubt he would have made some other.

As for her feelings, they ranged from boiling indignation through a certain sense of mystification and some mortification to a nervous speculation about what she'd brought on herself. She'd had time to reflect, and regret bitterly, that she herself had driven him back into Leonie's arms, even if she'd had little idea at the time of what she was doing. All in all, she reflected, more than enough under that dark gaze to become tongue-tied and afflicted with stage fright.

'Uh...if I could just have a glass of water? Thank you.'

'Tattie.' Alex straightened and came over to her. 'I think you look a bit too solemn. You're supposed to be a gorgeous young woman full of the mystery and romanticism of pearls, alive and warm and vital—which you normally are.'

There was an embarrassed huffing and shuffling around the room as everyone avoided looking at anyone—apart from Tattie and Alex, whose gazes were locked.

'Alex...' Tattie licked her lips. 'This may sound crazy but I think I'd find it easier if you weren't here. You're making me self-conscious.'

'Uh...' The director interposed, and cleared his throat. 'That's not unusual. Acting is often easier in front of people you don't know. But I think you've made a good point, Mr Constantin. What we're striving for is exactly what you described.'

Everyone held their breath, including Tattie, but Alex looked amused, if anything, and with a shrug said, 'My dear Tattie, I would hate to discomfort you in any way, so I'll leave, but I'll meet you for lunch.' He left the showroom.

Why did that sound like a threat? Tattie wondered. His tone

had been light and casual. Had she imagined the insolent flicker in his eyes in the last moment they'd rested on her? She didn't think so...

'When you're ready, Mrs Constantin,' the director said. 'Just take your time.'

Tattie turned away and took a deep breath. And she let her mind wander down the ages of pearl diving in the area since the 1850s. The hard-hat era of cumbersome brass helmets, the many Japanese divers who had made Broome and Thursday Island their home. The lovely but really remote bays and rivers of north-west Australia, the Northern Territory and far-north Queensland that were so suitable for the farming of cultured pearls. All places where the scenery was spectacular and unspoilt, remote, tropical Australia in all its wild glory.

And she thought of the technology associated with cultured pearls. Diving for the wild shell, the delicate seeding operation, the care of the shells in those tropical waters as the oyster deposited layers of nacre around the minute seed to form a pearl.

She looked at the bowl of pearls beside her, all with an exquisite lustre or the quality of light being reflected from the surface of the pearl and at the same time refracted from within the nacre. At their different colours: white, white-pink, silver, gold, fancy and yellow. And their different shapes—circlé or baroque in this case. And she felt the magic of it all seep into her psyche...

She turned back to the cameras. 'I'm ready,' she said simply.

CHAPTER FOUR

'REALLY RED-HOT sex liberates not only the body but also the mind—you should try it.'

Tattie faltered with her hand on a chair as she was about to sit down, and couldn't help but look round at the source of this advice. Alex had chosen the Darwin Sailing Club for lunch, a pleasant spot with tables outside under shady trees overlooking Fannie Bay and the flotilla of yachts anchored in it. It being a weekday, it wasn't crowded.

But there was a bearded, tattooed man with a Crocodile Dundee hat holding court a couple of tables away, and the advice had been offered to a woman companion who was looking singularly unaffected.

'Did you think that was directed at you?' Alex murmured as he pulled out her chair and waited politely for her to sit down.

'I didn't know what to think,' Tattie confessed.

He sat down opposite. 'Have you ever indulged in really red-hot sex?'

She bit her lip. 'I'm sure you have.'

'That doesn't answer the question.'

'Nor do I intend to.' Tattie fussed over the placement of her calfskin handbag that was dyed exactly to match her dress and added, 'I feel a little overdressed for the sailing club.'

'I wouldn't worry about it,' he drawled. 'I felt like being out-doors. And you don't have to look so embarrassed, we'll leave sex—of any kind—off the menu for the moment. As is your obvious preference.'

She shot him a fighting little look this time. 'Thank you. I'd appreciate it,' she said arctically. 'But if you've brought me to lunch in order to insult me—'

'Not at all,' he interrupted with his lips twisting. 'It came up out of the blue. How did the rest of the shoot go?'

She waited until their drinks had been placed—a glass of wine for her, a beer for him. 'I've been reliably informed by the director that I'm a natural once I get over my nerves. Not that I agree with him.' She wrinkled her nose. 'It wasn't really acting.'

'You must have managed to instil some more life into it than you were while I was there.'

'I did.'

'How?'

'Does it matter?'

'Yes. I'm really curious, Tattie.'

She eyed him, but could see only a genuine enquiry in his eyes. She sipped her wine and sat back. 'I love this part of the world, I love the Kimberley, as I've told you, and that's where a lot of the pearling history is, as well as the farms. And de-spite this being your company, Alex, it's…it's been fascinating to learn all about it, so I just made myself think about all that.'

'I'm glad something about your association with me has been fascinating. Shall we order?'

'Before we do that,' Tattie said in a swift undertone, 'I gather I'm in some kind of disgrace with you. Well, that's fine with me, and don't expect me to grovel, Alex! We know why we married each other, and in light of it I am still not prepared to be a dutiful little wife.'

'Or indulge in red-hot sex? It was getting pretty hot the other day,' he said lazily. 'I got the distinct feeling you could no more help yourself than I…might have been able to.'

She looked around a little wildly. 'I can't believe you've chosen a place as public as this to have this kind of conversation with me!'

He raised a dark eyebrow and smiled satanically. 'Would you rather we were home alone?'

The most acute memories flooded Tattie, of that never-to-be-forgotten day, so that she had to drop her gaze and by a huge power of will block the vibes that were coming her way even with a table between them and the amount of discord that existed in the air.

In a light beige linen jacket, a cream shirt and khaki trousers, with his dark hair ruffled, Alex Constantin was the stuff to dream about. But the reality was turning out to be more sexy, more dangerously fascinating and less easy to handle than *she* had dreamt, and she'd been married to him for a year.

The knowledge awakened two things to be confused about. She might be in love with him, but would she ever be able to come up to what he needed in a woman? A twenty-one-year-old virgin who, thanks to her old-fashioned father and her mother's paranoia about fortune-hunters, had never really been let off the leash...

The other troubling point was how safe she felt with him in almost every other circumstance. As if there were suddenly two Alexes and she was unable to fuse them.

She clicked her tongue, shook her head, and said at random, 'I'd never seen so many beards and tattoos in a city until I came to Darwin. I guess it's the "outback" influence, because really, in the Northern Territory, even in the middle of Darwin, the outback is only a few miles down the Stuart Highway.'

He blinked, and said gravely, 'How true, Tattie!' Then he started to laugh. 'I take it you've given up?'

Her shoulders slumped. 'I'm not too sure what I'm fighting about,' she said honestly. 'It's all got very confusing.'

'It needn't be.'

'Alex...'

She stared at him and for a moment was unbearably tempted to let down her guard and place herself, body and soul, in his hands, but a sudden golden image of Leonie Falconer flashed before her mind's eye.

'Alex,' she said again, 'all my life I've been told what to do by people who believe they know what's best for me.' She shrugged. 'While I appreciate their love and concern, I need to make my own decisions now or I could become frozen in that mode. Do you—could you understand that?' she asked anxiously.

He stirred and broke his narrowed, intent study of her to look across the bay. 'Within limits,' he said at last. 'If you need more time—OK. Breaking up this marriage is not what I have in mind, however. But we don't have to make such heavy weather of it.' He smiled at her suddenly and nearly took her breath away. 'As soon as the video is finished we'll go to Beaufort.'

The next two weeks were busy and satisfying for Tattie.

She flew out to a pearl farm with Alex and the film crew and enjoyed not only filming the farming operation but also just being there. The Constantin mother ship was anchored in the Kimberley bay, with accommodation on it, and when they weren't filming she and Alex went fishing by dinghy up the Drysdale River.

Not as grand as the King George or the Berkeley, nevertheless the Drysdale had a timeless beauty of its own. Red cabbage-tree palms soared above the bushy, rock-strewn banks and the sand on the shores was pale gold. There were red-tailed black cockatoos with their large, lazy wingspan and their distinctive call. There were magnificent white-breasted sea eagles working the waters and a pair of brahminy kites with their white heads and tan feathers, always in the same spot, that she nicknamed George and Georgina.

There were crocodiles.

Often when they stopped to fish she looked at a rock or what appeared to be a log in the water, only to see it move and reveal itself as a knobbly, prehistoric crocodile. Or, as they were cruising along, what looked like a log on the bank would come to life and slide swiftly and silently into the water.

They caught barramundi, the holy grail of Australian fish, and her first catch was intensely exciting as she realised from the black-fringed flash of silver that leapt from the water what she had on her line. She refused any help from Alex, and after a magnificent fight managed to land it and collapse exhaustedly but delightedly with her catch—an eighty-centimetre fish.

One day they took a picnic lunch and steered the dinghy to the head of the river between rock walls that made her think of a Roman amphitheatre. It was as far as any boat could go anyway, before the river became a series of rapids and freshwater rock pools. There was a flat shelf along the bank and they climbed out and sat in the shade of the rock overhang to enjoy their picnic.

Tattie wore a green blouse and shorts over a blue bikini, a racy peaked cap with her hair tucked through the back, and sunglasses. It was a clear, warm day—they all were at this time of the year in this part of the world—and she stared up at the blue sky and breathed deeply. Beyond Napier Broome Bay and the Drysdale River, the Timor Sea extended towards East and West Timor and Indonesia, and the equator wasn't that far away.

'It's like a last frontier, isn't it?' she said a little dreamily. 'So wild, untamed and wonderful.'

He nodded. 'I see what you mean.'

Tattie raised an eyebrow at him, because it seemed like an odd reply.

He poured two cups of tea from a Thermos flask. 'You really do love this part of the world—and it shows on the video now.' His lips quirked. 'You've also endeared yourself to everyone on the pearl farm with your infectious enthusiasm.'

She grinned impishly. 'It's nice to know I'm earning my keep. In a very small way.'

'Perhaps I ought to fly you up here on a regular basis. Staff morale is important in these out-of-the-way places, and with jobs still dangerous despite modern technology—like diving for the wild shells.'

She shivered suddenly. 'I was reading about King Sound the other day, and how many hard-hat divers it claimed with its treacherous deep-water drop-offs. I believe the area is still known as "The Graveyard"'.

'Pearling was a very hazardous occupation in those days. Decompression, drop-offs and squeezing were big problems, not to mention above-water catastrophes like cyclones that wiped out whole fleets before they had today's weather-forecasting technology. And all for buttons.'

'Buttons?'

'Uh-huh.' He unwrapped two slices of fruit cake and handed one to her to have with her tea. 'Mother-of-pearl for buttons was the mainstay of the pearling industry up here in those days. Gem pearls were very rare, but everyone needed buttons. Then plastic took over and the bottom fell out of the mother-of-pearl market. That's when the cultured-pearl industry was pioneered.'

Tattie was sitting cross-legged, enjoying her fruit cake. 'It's funny how the world turns. One door closes and another opens.'

Alex stood up and brushed his crumbs away. He had on a pair of khaki shorts and a grey T-shirt, which he now pulled over his head.

'Time for a swim. You know, Tattie, talking of things like that—how the world turns and earning your keep—there's another very good reason for staying married to me. You've taken to all this like a duck to water. You are an asset, and to have a wife who is as vitally interested in what one does as you are provides a very good framework for a marriage.'

She blinked behind her sunglasses.

'Take your mother, for example,' he said quietly. 'Word— gossip, possibly, but all the same—has it that she and your father did not have that in common, and you yourself told me she was like a displaced person at Beaufort. Did that help their marriage?'

'N-no, but...' She stopped and could only gaze up at him helplessly. This was the first time any discussion of their marriage had surfaced since lunch at the Darwin Sailing Club. And since that day Alex had gone back to being the Alex she'd known up until their wedding anniversary, apart from their brief and, she now realised, essentially chaste courtship.

Oh, yes, she'd conceded to herself several times lately, he had been able to make her tremble in his arms when he'd kissed her in those days, but that had been nothing to how he'd affected her when he'd really set his mind to it...

There was something else his words aroused in her. She would dearly love to prove to him that she was not just the trendy, social-butterfly daughter of her mother he might have taken her for. She would really like, she realised, to have the opportunity to prove her intelligence and substance to him, and taking a more active part in his business could be the way to do it.

But that was all he said or did. After waiting a moment for her reply he strolled over to the rock pool and lowered himself into the water with a groan.

'It's bloody cold,' he called to her.

'Go on, you're being a baby!' she responded, and stood up to strip off her blouse and shorts.

'Wait and see!' He disappeared under the water.

But she hesitated for a moment as she contemplated what she was up against now. No more red-hot sex? she thought with a tinge of humour that disappeared as fast as it had come. Logic instead, it seemed to her—sane, sensible realism. And, of course, he had a point—and one that struck right to the heart of her home—because he was also diabolically clever, Alex Constantin.

He was also right—the water was cold, so that she yelped as she slipped in and he laughed at her. But their trip back to the mother ship after they'd dried off and warmed themselves in the sun was quiet and swift.

'Tatiana, you're looking wonderful!'

Her mother had come round for coffee the first morning after Tattie's return.

'Thanks!'

'That light tan suits you,' Natalie said enthusiastically. 'Did you have a wonderful time? I believe the video is sensational.'

Tattie looked down at herself in filmy chalk-blue trousers and a matching loose over-blouse. 'Yes, I had a wonderful time, and everyone seems pleased with the video, but I don't know about sensational. I haven't seen the edited version yet.' She poured coffee from the percolator and sat down.

'I'm sure you're being modest,' Natalie said complacently. 'And I can't help wondering if that...sort of bloom you've got and the clothes you're wearing mean anything else?'

Tattie stared at her mother over the top of her cup, mystified. 'Bloom? Clothes?'

'As in needing a bit more space in your clothes. As in the stork being on the way, darling.'

Tattie put her cup down with a little clatter. 'Don't *you* start, Mum! I've been out in the open a lot, that's all. As for clothes, it gets hot up here, in case you haven't noticed, even at this time of the year!'

Natalie grimaced. 'Sorry! I just wondered. Who else has been bugging you—Alex?'

'His mother,' Tattie said darkly. 'She never lets an opportunity pass, but for your information, Mum, there is no problem; it's entirely up to Alex and me when we start a family.'

Natalie looked thoughtful. Then she said, 'I could always come back, of course.'

'What for? Come back from where?'

'Tatiana...' Natalie hesitated then took a deep breath. 'I'm getting married again. I hope this doesn't upset you; I hope you don't feel as if I'm deserting you or being unfaithful to your father's memory—although the truth of the matter is he...we...it wasn't an easy marriage...and I... I...' She stopped and looked, for once in her life, terrified.

Tattie got up swiftly and went to put her arms around her mother. 'Mum,' she said softly, 'why are you scared of telling *me* this? I know how it was; I was there. And all I want for you is happiness!'

'Oh, Tattie,' Natalie said—one of the few times she'd shortened the name, 'there's a lot of Austin in you. Sometimes I see a glint of steel in you and it's made me wonder...but forget about that; I was so afraid you'd disapprove of me falling in love.'

'Tell me about it,' Tattie urged.

Ten minutes later she had it all. Natalie had fallen in love with a widowed artist who had been up in the Territory for the last six months painting Kakadu. They planned to live in Perth. There was such a glow about her mother as she spoke of the man in her life; Tattie saw a new and softer side to her that amazed her a little.

'But why would you feel as if you were deserting me?' she asked after they'd had a comfortable chat about this turn of events.

'Well, I brought you to Darwin, and I introduced you to Alex.' Natalie stopped and looked at Tattie a shade self-consciously. 'But it is all going well with you and Alex?' she asked intensely.

'Why shouldn't it be?' Tattie replied with what she hoped was just the right amount of unconcern.

'I...' Natalie hesitated and sighed. 'You know that glint of steel you inherited from your father that I mentioned earlier? I sometimes can't help wondering if you didn't have your own agenda for Alex Constantin, Tatiana.'

Tattie knew suddenly—inexplicably, but knew all the same—that she couldn't and didn't want to fence with her mother any longer. Perhaps it had something to do with this new, softer

Natalie, or perhaps for the first time she felt on an equal foot-
ing with her.

'I did,' she said, and told her mother the truth about her marriage for the first time.

'Now I feel really terrible,' Natalie pronounced. 'Now I know
I can't leave you!'

'Nonsense,' Tattie said, but affectionately. 'I went into it with
my eyes open. No amount of matchmaking would have pushed
me where I didn't want or didn't need to go, Mum. So you may
go to Perth and start your new life with my blessing! It's not as
if it's the other side of the world anyway.'

'Talk about role reversal!' Her mother looked at her ruefully.

'All the same, I'm so happy for you,' Tattie said softly. 'When
do I get to meet him?'

Natalie sat back, as if relieved of a huge burden. 'Tomorrow
night, if you and Alex would like to come to dinner.' She sat
up suddenly. 'About Alex...surely I could—'

'Mum,' Tattie said firmly, 'you leave Alex to me—I mean
that,' she warned.

Natalie blinked a couple of times. 'You've got even more of
Austin in you than I thought. I wonder if Alex realises what
he's up against?'

And for some reason they laughed quietly together.

Tattie was not so sanguine when she was alone, however.

So far as she could see Alex held all the cards and was determined to use them. Whilst she was holding out for him to
fall madly in love with her but was seriously concerned that she
might not be woman enough for him if he did.

She grimaced, shook her head and wondered if she was
mad...

'Well, well,' Alex said that night when she told him about her
mother's impending marriage.

'What does that mean?' Tattie enquired, suddenly prepared

to defend her mother to the death. 'I don't think I've ever seen her so happy.'

Alex threw his jacket over the back of a chair, pulled off his tie and pushed up his shirtsleeves. He'd been in a series of conferences all day, he'd told her, and he wasn't looking relaxed.

'It means what it says,' he replied. 'Surprise—because I thought her life revolved around you, I guess.'

'You don't like her,' Tattie stated tautly.

'When you bargain with someone over their daughter, liking them is not an emotion that comes into play. I suppose I don't relate to her, that's all.'

'She can be…' Tattie started again. 'She really thought it was best for me.'

'She certainly protected your interests like a tigress.' He looked around the apartment reminiscently.

Tattie swallowed awkwardly. 'I didn't know about that until it was a *fait accompli*.'

'I know. I mightn't have married you otherwise.' He moved across to the bar and poured himself a Scotch. 'Want one?'

'No, thank you.' She sank onto the cream settee and pulled a pewter cushion into her lap to hug. 'Sorry to be repetitious—but what does *that* mean?'

Alex finished mixing his drink and cast himself down in an armchair. 'A mother out to get all she can for her daughter is one thing. A wife out to get all she can from her husband is another.'

'Agreed,' Tattie said coolly. 'But I was bringing you two cattle stations.'

'That remains to be seen. The marriage contract stipulates that, unless by mutual consent, what is yours remains yours and what is mine remains mine, with our children being the beneficiaries of our estates.'

'All the same, don't you feel you might have got your morals a little twisted, Alex?'

He put his drink down on a side-table and contemplated her out of cynical dark eyes. 'I'll tell you how I feel, Tattie—sick and tired of all this. I'll tell you what I'd like to do. Have a nice, relaxing meal, perhaps a stroll through the park, and then I'd like to bring my wife home and take her to bed.'

Tattie stared at him over the top of the cushion with her lips parted.

'I'll tell you something else,' he went on drily. 'You would feel much less aggressive, combative and scratchy if you allowed me to do that.'

'Scratchy?' It came out hoarsely.

'As in wanting to scratch my eyes out over an innocent remark about your mother,' he elucidated.

Tattie cast the cushion aside and stood up. 'You're wrong—I'd rather die—'

'No, you wouldn't.' He stood up swiftly and reached for her. 'But if you want to go on playing girlish games with me, how about this one?'

She refused to allow herself the indignity of trying to struggle out of his arms. But her eyes were bright with anger at his gibe—because it had hit home, no doubt exactly as he'd intended. What he didn't know was that it had also ignited a spark within her, fast becoming a flame of desire—to show the world, Leonie Falconer and particularly Alex Constantin that she was not to be underestimated in any way but in this regard especially.

'Girlish?' she breathed. 'Perhaps that's one of the areas of me that's a closed book to you, Alex? So let me show you otherwise.'

She slipped her hands around his neck and offered him her mouth at the same time as she moved her body sensuously against his. She was still wearing the filmy chalk-blue outfit, so there was not a lot between her skin and the hard, warm feel of his body against hers.

Nor did she allow herself to rush or be rushed. When his mouth came down hard on hers she resisted, and went to trail a line of butterfly kisses down his throat. And she opened a few more buttons of his shirt so she could slide her hands beneath it and smooth the skin of his shoulders.

'Mmm…nice,' she said huskily, and opened her blue eyes at him.

'Tattie…' He said her name in a low growl and his eyes were hard but hot.

'Perhaps you should call me Tatiana,' she suggested impishly. 'I always know you're cross with me when you do that. Although why you should be cross is a bit of a mystery.'

'Tattie…you're playing with fire,' he warned.

'You may kiss me now, Alex,' she replied.

He held himself in check for one long, tense moment, then he did so, and she gave herself up to his mouth and his hands on her, sure and devastatingly adept at seeking her most sensitive areas.

So when she discovered herself back on the couch, but in his arms this time, and minus the bottom half of her outfit, her nipples were aching in the most divine way, her mouth was bruised and she was shivering with desire, uncaring if she'd lit a fire she now had no control over.

Because all her senses were alive and drinking in Alex Constantin: the rough feel of the end-of-the-day stubble on his jaw against the smoothness of her skin; the hard strength of his body; the heat of his desire. So much so, she was ready to surrender her virginity to him, even though she'd started this as a lesson. How ironic, she thought as he slipped her shirt off and looked down at the pale blue bra that matched her briefs.

But there was a serpent in paradise. And the irony of *that* was—she had introduced it.

He slid his fingers between her thighs, then looked into her eyes. 'So,' he said barely audibly, 'my wife may not be the virgin I was promised. Who is he, Tattie?'

If someone had thrown a bucket of cold water over her the effect could not have been more punishing. She gasped and sat upright incredulously. 'That was *not* in the marriage contract!' she denied.

A cool, absent smile twisted his lips. 'It was what I was given to understand, and quite important in this kind of marriage.'

'What do you mean?' she asked in a deadly undertone.

He shrugged. 'In the context of being able to mould you into a wife who would suit me.'

Tattie sprang off the couch with her hair flying like rough black silk. 'I knew it,' she fumed. 'Don't think this has come as any surprise to me—I hate it!'

She planted her hands on her hips, then made the mistake of looking down at herself, clad only in three triangles of pale blue silk. She closed her eyes briefly, and snatched her shirt and pulled it on. Then she looked around for the other half of her outfit and, with as much dignity as possible, fished her trousers out from beneath the coffee-table. But it was hard to maintain a lot of dignity as she stood on one leg, then the other, and wriggled into them.

It was just as well that her sense of outrage was enormous, and once again she was able to plant her hands on her hips, this time fully dressed, if slightly awry.

Alex remained sprawled out on the settee and eyed her as he ran his hand through his hair and fingered his jaw. 'Hate what?' he enquired gravely, but in a way that barely hid a restrained spark of humour. 'There didn't seem to be an awful lot of hate going on just now.'

'Your Greek background,' she said fiercely, 'and this whole business of arranged marriages to virgins you can *mould* into suitable wives!'

'Oh, that. What about your own mother, who didn't seem to think it was such a bad idea?'

'She might have thought she was arranging a highly suitable marriage for me, but *I* never had any intention of being a virgin bride you could *train* to suit your tastes.'

He grimaced. 'Are you a virgin, Tattie?'

'Why? Are you having doubts now that I might be? A pity, because it's something you may be destined never to know.'

He folded his arms. 'That is throwing down the gauntlet, Tattie.'

'Oh!' She ground her teeth.

'On the other hand, let's forget about moulding, training and all that—'

'*You* brought it up!'

'Perhaps I was taken by surprise.' He raised his eyebrows quizzically. 'Uh—on the other hand, how badly do you want me to go on rescuing Beaufort?'

'What...what do you mean?'

'I mean it's come to the stage where a significant cash inflow is required. Of course you could do it yourself—if you sold Carnarvon.'

Something clicked into place in Tattie's mind, something he'd said to her a couple of weeks ago, but in the heat of *that* moment she'd forgotten to query it. Something about not being able to run the stations without him, anyway...

She sat down on the coffee-table unexpectedly. 'Sold Carnarvon?'

'You have plenty of assets, Tattie, but not a lot of cash.'

'But... I thought beef prices were going through the roof.'

'They are. Your beef, however, is thinly spread over two huge stations in a way that's going to require a massive mustering operation, the cost of which alone will eat away most of your profits this year.'

'I know that. We've been through this before, Alex.' She swallowed. 'I told you that's what I was very much afraid of. There hasn't been a proper muster for a couple of years and a lot of the stock has gone feral. You said—'

'Tattie,' he interrupted, 'what I've done for you is this: during the last dry we mustered what we could—not a lot, but all the same—and with the proceeds spent the wet season improving as much of the facilities as we could. The bores, yards, equipment, et cetera. But what we were not able to do during the wet season was improve the roads, particularly on Carnarvon, which have since suffered some bad wash-aways during the last wet. It's almost impossible to get a road train through there now, Tattie.'

She was silent, counting the cost of it mentally.

'On top of that,' he continued, 'you know what a big muster means. Extra ringers and horses, helicopters for the really difficult terrain and the wilder stock, freight costs and all the rest.'

'So—this may sound like a silly question,' she said at last, and looked anxious, 'but where are we at? Am I in hock to you already?'

'A new road into Carnarvon would put you there.'

'I'm sure I could get a loan.' She bit her lip, then suddenly looked around the apartment. 'Or I could give you this! I haven't really done anything to earn it.'

'You could do that.' He shrugged. 'Or you could form a real partnership with me.' He looked at her significantly.

'I got the impression you might not want me, assuming I was "soiled goods", Alex.'

'I didn't say that,' he countered. 'Although you would have to put away any aspirations you had towards having another man in your life.'

'Like you put away Leonie Falconer, and whoever her replacements might be?' she asked innocently.

He stood up. 'Those are my terms, Tattie. Take it or leave it. In the meantime, the dry season is progressing and there's a strong chance Carnarvon won't get mustered this year.' He reached for his jacket and slipped it on.

'Where are you going?'

He looked at her mockingly. 'Out.'

CHAPTER FIVE

NOR HAD HE come home that night, Tattie discovered the next morning.

Of course there was the house at Brinkin, a new home right on Casuarina Beach, a home with big grounds to bring up children in, ironically.

So it didn't automatically follow that she might have driven him back into Leonie's arms, she reasoned, but shivered all the same.

Then she got a call from her father-in-law, who asked if he could come and have a cup of coffee with her. Of course, she told him, but it was an unusual enough request to make her frown at the phone before she put it down, and to wonder what it was all about.

More pressure to start a family? Little did George know…

But she dressed with care in a three-quarter-length denim skirt and a cap-sleeved fine white rib-knit top, tucked in, a patent turquoise belt around her waist and turquoise mules on her feet. She also took pains to be perfectly groomed and her hair gleamed with vitality.

'Pretty as a picture!' George Constantin beamed at her. He sniffed the air. 'And your coffee smells gorgeous!'

Tattie thanked him and reflected that if the advice about

looking at a girl's mother before you married her held good for a man's father, any wife of Alex Constantin would be reassured. George Constantin was grey now, but still reminiscent of his son in his tall, only slightly stooped bearing, still, really, a fine figure of a man. And his manners were courtly, he had a nice sense of humour and a way of making you feel at ease.

Well, she amended as she poured the coffee and offered him a plate of homemade shortbread, not as at ease as he usually made her feel.

'Irina is not with you today, George?' She sat down and took her own piece of shortbread.

'Sadly not, Tatiana. Her hip is playing up a little—we may have to consider a replacement soon, if only I can persuade her out of her fear of hospitals. This is delicious!' He helped himself to another biscuit. 'Did you make it?'

'I was hoping you wouldn't ask me that.' Tattie wrinkled her nose. 'I cannot tell a lie! My cleaning lady, who often helps me out with dinner parties, also keeps me in a constant supply of goodies like these. She's a gem. But I'm sorry to hear about Irina. Is there anything I can do?'

George waved a hand. 'No, thank you, my dear, but it's so kind of you to offer. By the way, I ran into Alex last night.'

'Oh.' Tattie went still for a moment.

'Mmm,' her father-in-law said, and hesitated for a long moment. 'And that's why I wanted to see you today, Tattie,' he finished.

She stared at him. 'Where...did you run into him?'

'In a pub. There was a Bledisloe Cup match on last night—rugby union, between the Wallabies and the All Blacks,' he explained, and looked mischievous. 'I have some mates I always watch those games with, have a few beers and so on, but Irina hates me filling the house with them so...' He shrugged.

Tattie smiled understandingly on several fronts. Despite the millions he'd made, George was renowned in Darwin for his common touch. And her mother-in-law was exceptionally house-proud as well as a teetotaller.

'But there was Alex,' George went on, 'alone—don't think he even knew the game was on—and—'

'Not in a very good mood,' Tattie finished quietly.

A keen dark glance came her way, although George said, 'Perhaps, although he joined in and appeared to enjoy the game. It's just that I know Alex well; this was rather uncharacteristic and I could tell he had something on his mind, Tattie. But if this is just a little "domestic", my dear, tell me to mind my own business and I'll go home. Not until I've finished my excellent coffee, though!'

Tattie thought for a bit as she stirred her own coffee until it was about to overflow. 'You wouldn't have come here if that's all you thought it was, would you?' she said eventually.

George shrugged. 'No. You see, I wondered—I know this sounds crazy—but I wondered how well you know Alex, Tattie?'

She blinked.

'I've even wondered if this marriage is the fairy tale made in heaven it outwardly appears to be.' He gazed at her soberly.

'How...how did you guess?' she whispered, then closed her eyes as she realised she'd given herself away completely.

'Call me an old fool,' he said slowly, 'but not once have I ever seen a sign of spiritual closeness between you two. I've seen affection and, yes, you laugh together, but I've never seen any spark of real physical tension between you, and I have never seen him look at you the way we men look at the women we desire. For that matter, the same goes for you, Tattie.'

'What did you expect?' Tattie heard herself ask huskily. 'He was never in love with me. Even I realised that. It was all arranged, and forgive me, George, but I can't believe you and Irina didn't have something to do with that.'

'As well as Natalie, your mother.'

'At least my mother thought I was in love with him.'

'Were you?' George asked gently.

Tattie looked away and refused to reply.

'My marriage to Irina was an arranged one,' he said slowly. 'But, while I may slip out to watch rugby with the boys, we couldn't be closer.'

'That's...lovely, but...' She spread her hands helplessly. 'How many years did it take to get that way?'

He stirred. 'A good question. You're saying a year is not a very long time? True. But at least you have to make a start.'

Tattie frowned at him. 'Has Alex been talking to you?' she asked incredulously.

George shook his head ruefully. 'Alex has been a perfect son in many respects, but he's always gone his own way— no, he would never do that. And it was only by accident that I discovered something not even his mother has ever known. Something that just might help you to understand him better, my dear Tatiana.'

Tattie looked at him wide-eyed.

'There was a girl once; Flora Simpson was her name. She and Alex were very much in love. But she was married, and she went back to her husband. You know how oysters coat an irritant with a layer of nacre? That's what happened to Alex; he acquired a hard, protective shell after that.'

'You knew this but you still connived at an arranged marriage for Alex with me?' Tattie asked after it had all sunk in. 'George, forgive me again, but you...your intuition about Alex and me has been astonishingly accurate, but you can't think much of women if you could do that—' She stopped abruptly.

'Do that to you, Tattie?' he said softly.

'I...' She bit her lip.

'If you love him like that, Tattie,' George went on, his dark eyes full of compassion that made her want to burst into tears, 'isn't he worth fighting for?'

'He may *never* forget her!'

'He might think that, but life goes on; things change,' George said wisely. 'Do you have a choice, though?'

That afternoon Tattie flew by commercial airline across the border to Kununurra, Western Australia, and from there she chartered a light plane to take her to Beaufort.

She'd left a note for Alex and she'd postponed her dinner with her mother and the man Natalie planned to marry. She'd also requested Alex not to follow her for a couple of days, if he was so minded, saying she needed a bit of time on her own.

It was the head stockman's wife, Marie, who met her at the airstrip and drove her up to the homestead, apologising all the way for not having had time to spruce the place up.

'Don't worry about it,' Tattie told her lightly. 'I haven't come to check for dust under the beds and I brought some supplies from Kununurra. But could you ask Jim if I can have a horse tomorrow and, if he has the time to show me around, I'd like to see all the improvements that have been made lately?'

Marie agreed to that enthusiastically and then reluctantly, as if she could sense Tattie needed to be alone but didn't approve, left her.

In fact the homestead was in pretty good order, and once the generator was going Tattie had power and hot water. And, since she'd lived in the rambling house on and off all her life, it held no terrors for her to be there alone.

She built up a fire in the lounge, cooked herself scrambled eggs and ate them in front of the fire. It was a huge room, and there were pictures of Beaufort ancestors—one of whom had been a premier of Western Australia—on the walls. But Natalie's was the latest influence on the homestead. Accordingly— and Tattie thought ruefully back to her mother's ongoing battles with her father over this—many renovations had been made and it had a sense of style.

There were decent bathrooms, the kitchen was practical and

modern, there were good beds and fine linen and some lovely furniture.

All the same, she thought as the fire flickered and cast leaping shadows—and this might have frightened her mother—you could never forget how remote you were. You might install air-conditioning but you only had to step outside to encounter the sometimes savage heat, the flies, the torrential downpours of the wet season.

You didn't have to go far at all from the homestead to find yourself in a wilderness where rivers cut deep gorges into the land, where billabongs supported delicately coloured water lilies, paperbark trees, buffalo grass that floated on the water and an amazing array of bird life. You could ride to a burnt-sienna rocky outcrop in a sea of low olive-green scrub, and you could sit on the top beneath a huge sky and feel the heartbeat of a timeless, ancient land as you observed what made this country so special to its traditional owners.

At least she could, she mused, as her father had taught her to appreciate it, as his father had taught him. She could identify a jacana, a tiny bird that hopped about the water-lily pads on feet as long as its body, and all the birds on the billabongs. Lizards, monitors, even snakes fascinated her, as did the little rock wallabies, the wombats and big red kangaroos she sometimes saw.

What she hadn't absorbed so thoroughly—and this was partly due to her mother's wish to keep her as ladylike as possible—were the trials and tribulations of running cattle on this land so that they both flourished.

And that was why she'd willingly lived away from Beaufort for a year now, to try to glean the know-how she lacked from Alex. She'd even enjoyed herself, for the most part, but she knew now that she'd been incredibly naïve.

Was it worse to know why Alex was the way he was? she asked herself with her head resting back and her feet up on a footstool as she stared at the ceiling. How did it help in the equation she was faced with now? The stark knowledge right out in the open that if she wanted his help to save her heritage a proper marriage was what was required of her in exchange.

Why had she closed her mind to the reality that it would have to come to this? she wondered dismally. Why had she allowed herself to play with silly ultimatums, such as she would only consummate this marriage if she knew Alex was madly in love with her?

She closed her eyes and pressed her cheek against the smooth plum velvet of the wing chair. Because she had been too young and too foolhardy to know what she was getting herself into, she answered herself. Because she *had* secretly believed she could make him fall in love with her...

Only now to discover she'd never had a chance.

So, what about the question George had posed? She hadn't answered; she'd only wanted the embarrassment of it all to end as soon as possible. She'd tried to tell herself she wasn't even sure what he'd meant. Did she have a choice regarding Beaufort and Carnarvon?

But all the time a sinking certainty had presented itself— if she was that much in love with his son, would leaving him make it stop?

Was she that much in love with Alex? she wondered suddenly. She'd lived with him like a sister for a year. How had she done that if she was so madly in love with him?

Another sinking certainty presented itself to her—he had made it impossible for her to be any other way than sisterly. But things had changed, hadn't they? she reminded herself. Things had got to a stage where she only had to be in the same room as him to be conscious of him in a most unsisterly way...

And suddenly she was crying at the terrible sadness of it all. Of Alex loving a woman he couldn't have, of herself dying to be truly loved by him.

She took herself to bed eventually and woke up with her mind clearer.

Tatiana Constantin née Beaufort was a new person as of

today. Gone was the social butterfly, gone was the naïve girl who'd thought she could make a very experienced man fall in love with her. Gone was the innocent, the *ingénue*. And from today she would be assessing how she could save Beaufort and Carnarvon without having to spend the rest of her life married to a man who couldn't love her.

'So, Jim.' Tattie took her hat off and wiped her brow as she sat on a well-mannered brown mare. 'Beaufort looks to be in pretty good shape...the new yards and loading ramp, the six-mile bore et cetera—but what about Carnarvon?'

It was a clear blue day, the temperature was thirty degrees and the dust from a mob of cattle being moved to the main holding yards hung in the air. Air that was alive with whistles and hoofbeats, moos, the occasional yelp of a cattle dog—and lots of sticky little flies.

'Miss Tattie,' Jim said, 'things aren't so good over there, mate.'

He was dry and wiry, and he'd known her since she was ten. He looked into the far blue yonder. Beaufort and Carnarvon were adjoined, but their common border was one of extremely rough terrain for the most part, almost impenetrable rock-strewn gullies and sheer cliffs. Which meant a long way round getting between the two stations.

'The last wet played havoc with the main road in, and the stock last time I did a recce was all gone bush and needs a damn good weeding out anyway,' he continued laconically.

She raised an eyebrow at him.

'Because Carnarvon is a lot rougher country than Beaufort generally, it's always been a problem to get rid of the shorthorn influence. There are a lot of wild scrubber bulls lurking in them gullies—used to annoy the hell out of your dad, may he rest in peace.'

'Jim,' Tattie said slowly, 'would it be fair to say Carnarvon is becoming—unviable?'

'As is, sure,' he responded. 'But I thought… I mean Alex…' He stopped and looked at her. 'What I mean is, with a bit of work and the way beef prices are going, Carnarvon could be made to pay its way. Your dad would never have parted with it and—'

'I know,' Tattie interrupted. 'It was just a thought.'

'The last time he was here on his own,' Jim said thoughtfully, 'Alex, I mean—we flew over the boundary and we found one spot where he thought you could make a road to join 'em up. I tell you what, Miss Tattie, it would make both of 'em a hell of a lot more viable. If we could get that stock over here we could have one main operation rather than two separate ones. But it would take a bit of dosh to build that road.'

It stuck in Tattie's throat, fortunately, the frustrated urge to enquire at large why her husband had seen fit not to share this news with her. But perhaps those were the ideas he'd mentioned to her? And would have confided to her if she'd been a good little wife in *all* respects?

Then Jim looked up and shaded his eyes at the same time as Tattie became aware of a buzzing above.

'Speak of the devil,' he said.

'That's Alex?' she asked incredulously as a light plane flew over them.

'Sure is. Recognise that beaut little bird anywhere!'

'So I'll thank you never to do that again, Tattie,' her husband said grimly.

She'd ridden back to the homestead to arrive just as Marie had dropped him off from the airstrip. And she supposed she should be grateful that he'd waited until they were inside and alone before he'd commenced to tear strips off her for allowing him to wonder whether she'd been kidnapped again.

'But I left you a note!' she protested.

'You should be more careful with your notes in future. It fell down behind the hall table and I only found it because I dropped my car keys—three hours after you'd apparently disappeared off the face of the earth. But that's not all.'

'I… I—'

He overrode her. 'Tattie, I never wanted to scare the daylights out of you but, since it—almost—happened once, you need to adopt a bit of caution. Buzzing off on your own without any consultation is not on, do you *understand*? Surely you're mature enough for that?'

Tattie breathed in and exhaled deliberately. It didn't help. Nothing helped her in this confrontation with her tall, angry husband. And it mysteriously added fuel to the fire because he so much looked the part of a cattleman, lean and tough in jeans and a bush shirt, whereas she felt like a girl desperately trying to *play* a part.

'What's the problem, Alex?' she said. 'The next time someone tries to kidnap me you could tell them to go ahead, because I'm not the wife you want, am I? It could even solve a few problems.'

'What the hell are you talking about?' he ground out.

Tears were starting to create dark rivulets down her dusty cheeks and she wiped her nose on the back of her hand. 'I'm talking about not being Flora Simpson, or whatever her name is. I'm talking about— Alex—' She broke off on a breath and winced as he took her by the shoulders and his fingers dug in hard.

'Who…?' He didn't finish, but stared down at her with such a blaze of anger in his eyes she literally felt herself shrink beneath his hands. Then he blinked and seemed to get himself under better control. 'My father?'

She swallowed, and would have given anything to keep her mouth shut.

'It had to be,' he said and swore.

'I think he was only trying to help,' Tattie offered tentatively.

'When was this?'

She told him haltingly.

'So that's why you scuttled home to Beaufort, Tattie?'

All the bravado of a few moments ago had drained out of Tattie, but she couldn't let this pass entirely. 'You had a bit to do with it yourself, Alex.'

He stared down at her searchingly, then seemed to make a decision. 'All right, go and wash your face and I'll make us a drink. It is lunch time.'

'Perhaps we should eat rather than drink?'

He smiled slightly. 'I'll see what I can do. Off you go.'

When she got back it was to find that he'd made some substantial ham sandwiches and poured them each a gin and tonic.

And he waited until she'd had a sandwich and sipped her drink before he said, 'You'd better tell me the whole story.'

She didn't, of course, but she offered him the gist of his father's concern.

He looked heavenwards and commented bitterly on the trials of being an only son. Then he looked at her directly and said, 'That was six years ago, Tattie, and I sent Flora Simpson back to her husband when I discovered she liked to have her cake and eat it.'

Tattie looked at him wide-eyed.

'I am not pining for her,' he added, and shook his head in a rather weary disclaimer. 'I got over it all years ago.'

'So why does your father think...?'

He grimaced. 'They're both desperate for a grandchild.'

Tattie frowned, but decided to hold her peace—for the time being anyway. 'Why didn't you tell me about the possibility of a road between the two stations?'

'That's a switch of topics! Not that a break from the tortured course of this marriage isn't welcome... Uh, it would cost, that's why. I think it would be worth it in the long run but—'

'It brings us right back to the tortured course of this marriage, doesn't it?' Tattie suggested sweetly, then sat back, suddenly mentally exhausted.

Alex watched her for a long moment—the way she sipped

her gin and tonic, then put it down as if she wasn't enjoying it at all, the way her hands clasped then unclasped in her lap, the shadows he suddenly noticed beneath her eyes. More vulnerable, he thought, than he'd ever seen her...

'Let's take a break,' he said suddenly.

She looked a question at him.

'Would you like me to fly you over the area where I think a road is a possibility this afternoon?'

There was no mistaking the sudden eagerness in her eyes, but then her shoulders slumped. 'I couldn't afford it so it may be better not to get too worked up about the idea. Alex—' she took a deep breath '—I really came here, and I intend to stay here, to try to work out a way I can run at least Beaufort without having to depend on you in any way.'

'It means that much to you?' he said slowly.

No, *you* mean too much to me for me to put myself through a loveless marriage to you, and I haven't discounted the Flora Simpson scenario yet, she answered him in her mind.

She said instead, 'I thought it was about time I...got a bit mature about all this.' The faintest smile lit her blue eyes. 'I've made quite a few mistakes, obviously—'

'The biggest being marrying me?'

'As it's turned out, yes. So—'

'You really thought a year with me would give you the expertise you lacked?' he asked probingly.

'Obviously,' Tattie said again. 'Now I know otherwise there's only one thing for me to do, and that's get stuck into it myself.'

Alex sat back and continued to watch her as she tilted her chin Beaufort-style, and resolutely squared her shoulders. And it came to him that whatever he felt for Tatiana Beaufort he would not rest easy until he'd discovered what made her tick. He'd let her have her way for a year, he reflected. Then he'd applied a bit of pressure to get their marriage going, only to come to this.

So what if he used more subtle measures? he mused. Not such a hardship, really. While it was her fighting spirit he found fascinating, she was also rather gorgeous. And, he reflected, there was the curious fact that barely two days ago her trim little body had been warm and pliant and as sexy as hell in his arms—but now this.

'What are you thinking?' She broke into his reverie, looking slightly nervous.

He shrugged. 'I was wondering if I could give you a crash course in cattle-station management, seeing you're so determined to leave me,' he said casually. 'I have the next week free.'

Her long dark lashes fluttered and her blue eyes were wide and startled. 'Just like that? I mean...with no strings attached?'

It passed through his mind to think—Got you, Tattie Beaufort!—only to wonder immediately what kind of a bastard he was. But he reminded himself that it had always been her intention to use him; OK, she might have been very young and not known what she was getting herself into, but all the same...

'No strings attached. And no guarantees I'll be successful. But we can try.'

'Oh, thank you!' she breathed, looking suddenly radiant. 'Can we start now, today?'

Another thought crossed Alex Constantin's mind. What effect would it have on him were she to look as radiant about *him* rather than a damn cattle station? But he dismissed it. 'Sure. I'll give you an aerial tour of Carnarvon this afternoon, so you know just what you're up against.'

But it was rather a glum Tattie who sat down to dinner with him that night. She'd cooked them steak, egg and chips, and they'd had to push a lot of paperwork aside to be able to eat at the dining-room table.

She'd seen for herself the diabolical state of the main road into Carnarvon, the way the stock was thinly spread over tortuous country, the shorthorn influence that they'd been able to eradicate from Beaufort in favour of Brahmin or Brahmin-cross cattle. He'd taken her through the bookwork Jim had provided, and she was looking exhausted again.

'Enough of this,' Alex said when she went to look at the paperwork again after they'd eaten. 'You relax; I'll make the coffee.'

But when he came back with it she was asleep in the wing chair.

He looked down at her for a long time. At the absurdly long lashes lying on her cheeks, at the twisted grace of her lithe body—and he wondered again at what he thought he was doing in the moment before he picked her up gently and carried her to bed.

Breakfast was steak again, cooked this time by Alex.

'Sorry you had to put me to bed,' Tattie said as she looked at her steak and remembered waking up in her shirt and briefs, having been divested of her jeans. 'I must have been out like a light.'

'You were. So I thought we might take it easy today. Are there any special places on Beaufort we could ride to?'

She forgot about the indignity of being partially undressed and looked at him eagerly. 'There's my favourite billabong; it's only about an hour's ride away.'

'Should we take a picnic?'

'I'd love to!' She picked up her knife and fork and looked much more enthusiastic about her breakfast. 'I'm sure Jim will have a horse for you.'

Jim did, a raking chestnut gelding that eyed Alex and gave every indication of taking exception to his weight on its back. Five minutes later, though, it was behaving itself impeccably.

Tattie tipped her hat to Alex. 'Didn't take you long to let him know who's the boss!'

He looked over to her seated on her mare. 'Best to get it over and done with in my opinion.'

'In more walks of life than one,' Tattie said mischievously.

'But not with you, Tattie,' he responded. 'Shall we go?'

'Follow me!'

Several hours later they were eating their picnic lunch beside the billabong and Tattie was pointing out the wonders of it all to him. 'I've been coming here since I was six,' she told him, 'on my first pony. It was also the year I got a puppy, now I come to think of it. This darling little blue heeler Dad found for me.'

'What happened to him?'

'He went to the great hunting ground in the sky a bit prematurely.' She looked sad.

'Did you get another one?'

'No. Dad wanted me to but I was away at boarding-school most of the time so there didn't seem much point.'

'So...' He leant back on his elbow. 'You got on pretty well with your father?'

She grimaced. 'Yes, but not always. I know he would have loved to have a son, but Mum fought tooth and nail not to have him turn me into a son by proxy, so I often felt like the meat in a sandwich.' She shrugged. 'I often wonder if life wouldn't have been easier if she'd let him have his way—he turned out to be extremely strict with me as a daughter.'

'I think he'd be very proud of you as a daughter.'

'Do you? Why?' Tattie asked interestedly.

'You're feisty, you're interesting, most people light up when you're around and—you're lovely.'

Tattie nearly dropped her tin mug and splashed hot tea all over her jeans.

'I've surprised you,' he murmured.

'A bit,' she conceded. 'I guess because I somehow manage to be—all froth and bubble when I'm with you.'

He looked amused. 'If I thought that at first, I've revised my opinions. And you have been—other things with me.'

She coloured, but said valiantly, 'With disastrous consequences, Alex. I didn't think you approved at all!'

'Perhaps I'm having trouble putting my finger on the real Tattie Beaufort,' he said after a moment. 'Not that it's a problem now.'

'No,' she said slowly, and stood up to begin putting the picnic things together. 'Your parents...' She paused and looked at him with a comically rueful expression.

'Not to mention your mother, Tattie.' He sat up. 'But we married each other, not them, so it's our business.'

'Of course,' she agreed in a businesslike way, but spoilt the effect completely by tripping over a root and landing on her bottom virtually in his lap.

'Tattie—' His arms closed around her and she thought he was smothering some laughter. 'Are you OK?'

'I'm fine! I'm...fine.' But she was not. She was far too conscious of his arms around her. She had not the slightest inclination to leave them—and she wasn't at all sure, she realised abruptly, that she liked being given such an easy way out from their marriage.

'Tattie?' He tilted her chin so he could look into her eyes.

An almost overwhelming longing came to her to run her fingers through his hair and offer him her mouth. In fact she could picture herself going a whole lot further, such as removing her clothes and having him tell her how lovely she was in an entirely *personal* way, rather than the impersonal way he had done so earlier.

She swallowed visibly and got extremely flustered just in case this husband she was about to part with could read her thoughts.

But he stilled her restless movements with a faint smile and her heart started to beat heavily, because she thought, she really thought, he was going to kiss her. He was certainly taking his time about something. He was certainly not attempting to put any distance between them, so she was resting against him and getting all hot and bothered again at the feel of him...

Then he said lightly, 'I'll go first.'

Her lips parted and her breath came raggedly, but all he did was ease himself away and stand up. Then he helped her up and—as if it was not adding insult to injury, did he but know it, she thought darkly—he dusted her bottom off.

'There. OK? Shall we head home?' He raised an eyebrow at her.

'Oh, definitely!'

There was a plop as a fish broke the surface of the billabong; there were ibis wading in the shallows, and an exquisite little kingfisher with turquoise wings sitting motionless in a bush. There were lush pink water lilies against the far bank. But all this faded from Tattie's consciousness because, despite her bright agreement, she could not stop staring into Alex's dark eyes.

And she had the terrible feeling that he *had* read her mind, that her awful confusion had given her away—if only she could tear her gaze away from his! It was not as if she could read what was in his eyes, but then, when had she ever been able to?

Perhaps this put some starch into her, because she finally found the will-power to turn towards the horses, and, after loading up, they rode home.

Two days later she found herself in Alex's arms once more, and once again in the most innocent way. She'd taken him to a rocky outcrop from where you could see forever over the station. They'd climbed to the top, and she'd pointed out all the landmarks to him: the gorge at the head of a tributary that wound its way into a mighty river; the mesa, or tabletop mountain, at the base of which her great-great-grandfather had camped when he'd taken up what would become known as Beaufort; the waterhole that had originally been the lifeblood of the station.

It was on the way down that he reached up and swung her down from the last rock—although she was perfectly capable of climbing down herself—and kept his hands on her waist.

She looked a question at him, but he merely studied her from head to toe—the sweat on her face and the tendrils of damp hair stuck to her cheeks, despite her hat, the outline of her mouth. The place where her slender neck disappeared into the V of her checked shirt and the soft hollows at the base of her throat. The swell of her breasts beneath her shirt.

'I could have done that,' she said huskily—anything to break the tension that was building up inside her.

'I know.' He smiled slightly. 'It just seemed the gallant thing to do.'

'Gallant!' something cried within her. If only he knew what a trial his being gallant was to her.

'Thanks,' she mumbled. 'Let me know when I can be gallant back.'

He laughed this time. 'We have a slight weight-ratio problem in that line, Tattie.'

'I don't doubt it.' She looked up at him and tried to block his tall proximity from her senses. 'In that respect you probably need a wife a little taller than five feet two...' She stopped and blinked rapidly, appalled at even mentioning the subject.

'Oh, I don't know. They say small packages can be very... sweet.' He looked her up and down again—comprehensively and, she thought, significantly, as if he was assessing her sweetest points, in fact.

'Oh. Well.' Aware that she was babbling, but unable to help herself, she ploughed on, 'I'm sure there are other ways of being gallant than swinging people off rocks.'

He moved his hands on her waist. 'Possibly. I'll let you know when I think you're being particularly gallant, Tattie.' But his eyes were *particularly* dark and wicked.

And he let her go and brought her horse to her.

Tattie managed to mount without any mishaps, considering the hammering of her pulses and the confused state of her mind. But all the way home she was asking herself a question—what was going on?

* * *

There was a surprise waiting for them at the homestead.

Marie and the farrier's wife had had a spring clean and Marie was engaged in cooking dinner.

'This is very nice of you, Marie,' Tattie said, 'but you didn't have to.'

'No problem,' Marie replied airily. 'I know how nicely you and Mr Constantin do things in Darwin—I saw a spread of your apartment in a magazine. And your mother used to do the same here when they had important visitors, so I thought… it would be nice, that's all. I got the good silver out and polished it up.'

Tattie hesitated, then went into the dining room to take a look.

The old oak table was set for two with the best china, shining silver, gleaming crystal and candles.

She came back to the kitchen. 'It looks lovely, Marie, but—'

'You've got plenty of time to have a soak in the tub and get changed,' Marie said. 'I won't be ready to dish up for another hour.'

Tattie eyed her as she moved busily from the stove to the counter, and knew she would disappoint her dreadfully if she didn't at least change—something her mother had always encouraged for dinner.

But she took the thought with her to the bathtub that Alex was responsible for this, she just knew it—what she didn't know was why.

She hadn't brought a lot of gear with her, but she had a pair of ivory stretch cotton trousers, a ruby silk-knit cowl-neck top and a pair of little-heeled patent ruby shoes.

Would have to do, she thought as she surveyed herself in her bedroom mirror and swung her newly washed hair. Then she rummaged through her dressing-table drawers and came up with a pair of flower earrings, roses edged in gold—she hadn't worn them since she was about sixteen but the main colour matched her top. She put them on, tucked her hair behind her ears and nodded at her reflection—Marie would appreciate the touch, she thought.

They met in the lounge and she wasn't surprised to see Alex had changed into a blue and white striped shirt with navy trousers.

'So this was your idea,' she said as she accepted a glass of sherry from him.

His eyebrows rose. 'Not at all. I merely got told you would be dressing for dinner. I gathered I'd better do likewise.'

She frowned. 'I still feel I'm being conspired against.'

'What's that supposed to mean?'

'Nothing,' she said hastily, and sipped her sherry. 'Well, it was you who probably got Marie all hepped up.'

'Why would I have that effect on her?'

She was sorely tempted to tell him he had that effect on all women but desisted—even in irony it wasn't an admission she cared to make at the moment.

'Whoever's idea, perhaps it wasn't such a bad one,' he said tranquilly while she battled with her demons. 'You look very nice, Tattie.' His gaze lingered on the ruby top and the flower earrings. 'One thing I can never take exception to is your dress sense.'

'What *do* you take exception to?' She regarded him, a true Beaufort beneath all her Beaufort ancestors.

He looked her over again. 'Not a lot. Shall we dine?'

It might have been roast beef—and you could get fairly sick of beef on a cattle station—but Marie had excelled herself. It was tender, faintly pink, melt-in-the-mouth beef, accompanied by Yorkshire pudding and all the trimmings. There was a brandy pudding to follow. And it was only after she'd served the pudding that Marie left them alone and retired to the head stockman's cottage.

'I feel exhausted,' Tattie said as she heard the back door close at last. 'As if I've been under a searchlight, expected to come up to all Marie's *House & Garden* expectations or be instrumental in her living the Constantin lifestyle vicariously.'

Alex grinned and looked around. 'We have nowhere near the history the Beauforts have, so don't blame the Constantins, Tattie.'

'I feel like blaming them.' She pushed her dessert plate away and rose to pour the coffee. 'Shall we have this in front of the fire?'

He agreed, and when they were settled Tattie said thoughtfully, 'Alex, I don't know a great deal about you, your father's right.'

'I hope you're not going to harp on Flora Simpson; there is truly no more to be said. In more ways than one, now.'

Tattie rested her cheek on the plum velvet of her favourite wing chair and studied him. He was stretched out in an armchair on the other side of the fireplace, watching the fire, and he hadn't turned his head to her as he spoke. There had been a dry, unimpressed note in his voice too.

'No,' she said slowly, 'I'm not going to harp on Flora Simpson. You're right, there's no point. It's just that when I see you being the quintessential cattleman and grazier I can't help wondering how it fits in with your pearling background.'

Alex looked at her at last. 'When I was about seventeen my father decided to diversify and he threw me in at the deep end. He bought Mount Cookson, in the Territory, and told me it was mine to sink or swim with.'

'Of course you swam with it,' Tattie supplied with a tinge of bitterness in her voice.

He looked amused. 'I very nearly sank it. It was only buffalo that saved me.'

She looked interested. 'Go on. I know there's a bit of a market for buffalo meat, but not that much, I would have thought.'

'Strangely enough there's now a market for buffalo from whence they came—Indonesia and south-east Asia. I started exporting them, but as breeding stock. I still export buffalo from Cookson, as a matter of fact, although I've got back into cattle there as well.'

'The boy wonder.'

'Not really; there was a lot of hard work involved. And it helps to be able to turn your hand to a few things. For instance, I was always interested in mechanics, even as a kid.'

'So motors hold no mysteries for you, you only have to look a horse in the eye for it to know who's boss, you're a lot stronger than I am—all this is very depressing, Alex.'

He reached for his coffee. 'I've seen women who can strip a motor, prime a pump, stand no nonsense from a horse and throw a calf.'

'Big, tough women?' she hazarded.

He grinned at her. 'Generally, but not always. And you do ride beautifully, Tattie.'

'Thanks,' she murmured humbly. 'Alex, why do I get the feeling this week is designed to…give me a crash course in how *unsuitable* I am for the task I've set myself?'

He raised his eyebrows. 'I'm sorry if that's how it's turned out. I was only trying to help.'

'But you don't think I can do it?'

He grimaced.

'You can be honest, Alex.'

He sat forward with his cup in his hands. 'Tattie, no, I don't think you can do it.'

'And you're hoping, now that I've more or less seen it for myself, I'll pass the reins over to you and stay married to you?'

Alex put his cup down and stood up. He wandered to the fireplace, put another log on, then stood staring down at it with his hands shoved into his pockets. 'I take it that goes against the grain, Tattie?'

She shrugged. 'I don't have much option.'

'Then I have a suggestion.' He told her what it was.

CHAPTER SIX

SHE STARED AT him with her mouth open for a long moment, then sat up suddenly. 'Say all that again!'

'The market for tourism is huge in this part of Australia.' He repeated himself patiently. 'Visitors flock from all over the world to see the Kimberley region and the Northern Territory. And many cattle stations are going into tourism as a sideline. They're offering accommodation—they're offering the cattle-station "experience" as well as the "top end of Australia" experience. The fantastic scenery, the Aboriginal culture, the fishing, the crocodiles—and I think Beaufort, and you, would be ideal for such a venture.'

'Why me?'

He looked around and shrugged. 'You're a Beaufort down to your socks, and you have your pioneering ancestors on the walls to prove it. People love that kind of history and authenticity. You have a lot of taste and discrimination when it comes to providing accommodation.' He gestured. 'This house is almost ready to go as it is—'

'That's my mother's taste and discrimination,' she said rapidly. 'But go on.'

'And you have a real feel for the country, Tattie. Few guests, even if they were paying through the nose for the experience, would fail to be moved by how much you love this place.'

She blinked several times. 'They needn't all pay through the nose. We could have some bunkhouse guests.'

He smiled. 'Of course, you'd have to assess how you would feel about a lot of people visiting Beaufort.'

She looked around at her ancestors. 'If it would mean I could save Carnarvon, I wouldn't feel as if I'd let them down,' she said intensely. Her shoulders slumped and she swallowed. 'But it could take years to get going. I'd have to get a loan—'

'Or take me on as a partner.'

The words hung in the air.

She gazed at him warily.

He shrugged. 'It makes good business sense, Tattie. We already operate cruises between Broome and Wyndham; we have an advertising campaign well in place all over the world. We have access to a lot of people already coming here. We could give Beaufort a lot of promotion.'

'It's just...' she began.

'And you could pay me back every cent I put into this operation, as well as anything I spend on Carnarvon to get it out of the red.'

'What—' she licked her lips '—what about our marriage?'

'It stays as is.'

'Why?' she whispered. 'I thought you were ready to wash your hands of me.'

'I've changed my mind,' he said simply. 'Perhaps I've come to a better understanding of you, Tattie. Perhaps I'm still curious to know the *very good reason* you had for not wanting to change our marriage. Who knows?'

'I... I...' She closed her mouth frustratedly, then, 'How do you mean, a better understanding of me?'

He paused. 'You've got much more spirit than I gave you credit for when I married you. And I don't know why but I've got the feeling you would love to prove yourself to me.' He put his head on one side and watched her narrowly.

She gasped. 'How did you know?'

But he only looked at her enigmatically.

'What if I don't want to stay married to you once I haven't got a cash-flow problem and Carnarvon is running well again?'

'We can reassess the situation then.'

Tattie discovered several emotions running through her. A sense of mystification, a sense of excitement, but also a little thread of relief. You're still hoping, aren't you? she asked herself. That he'll fall in love with you...

She looked away and trembled inwardly. It would seem she just couldn't help herself, but she hadn't been helped by these last few days. Days when she'd wondered if it mightn't be happening for him?

But there was nothing to indicate that now, she thought as she switched her gaze back to her husband, standing so tall and thoughtful beside the fire. No way to know, for her anyway, what was going through his mind.

'All right,' she said at last. 'I'll do it. Thank you.'

'I think this calls for a celebration.' He looked down at her. 'Shall we crack a bottle of champagne? To seal our—business— partnership?'

'Why not?' She went to get up.

'Stay there. I'll do it.'

She was seated exactly as he'd left her when he came back with the champagne and two glasses.

He popped the cork, handed her a foaming glass and pulled up the footstool. 'Cheers.' He sat down in front of her.

'Cheers.'

'I thought you'd be more excited. You were earlier.'

She tried to smile. 'I feel quite...stunned.'

'Drink up,' he suggested.

She drank half a glass, then he took it from her and stood up to pull her to her feet and into his arms.

'Alex?' she breathed.

'We may be business partners now, but we're also married, Mrs Constantin.'

'I thought you said we'd continue as is?'

His lips quirked. 'This is not something we've never done before, Tattie.' And he bent his head to tease her lips apart at the same time as he moved his hands down her back, sculpting her figure beneath the ruby silk jersey of her top and the thin cotton of her trousers.

He tasted of champagne—fresh and slightly tart—so did she, she guessed—and he felt hard but warm against her. Then he slipped his hands beneath her top, unerringly unclipped her bra and cupped her breasts.

She shuddered against him and slid her hands up to his shoulders, every inch of her body alive and urgently in need of his hands on it. Then she was kissing him and moving against him with a fire of desire surging through her.

And he led her to even more pleasure as he plucked her nipples and caressed her hips, all the time kissing her and allowing her the freedom of his body. To touch and stroke and marvel in his strength against her own small softness.

But just as her breathing reached a ragged crescendo and she was about to beg him to take her he brought their embrace down from the clouds and to a conclusion whereby there was a foot of space between them and no contact other than his hand on her elbow to steady her.

'What...?' she whispered uncomprehendingly.

'I don't think we should do anything—you might regret, Tattie,' he said.

'You... I...' She stopped and wildly sought for some understanding. But all she could see in his eyes was irony, and then she understood.

She took a deep breath. 'You're right. Goodnight, Alex.'

* * *

For a long time before she fell asleep her emotions defied description. What kind of a fool had she made of herself? How could she have let herself go like that? What game was he playing with her? Well, she thought she knew that. He was trying to show her she had no self-control when he really set his mind to arousing her, and forcing her to face the irony of it in the light of her refusal to consummate their marriage.

Which led her directly to an old question she'd asked herself at least once before…

Did she love or did she hate Alex Constantin?

By morning, when she woke in a mess of twisted bedclothes, all her questions seemed to be academic compared to the problem of how to face him again.

But when she forced herself to get dressed and appear at breakfast he had a surprise waiting for her—a puppy, the most adorable blue heeler with black-tipped ears and tail, and he simply put it in her arms.

'Oh! Where…? How…?' She gazed at him incredulously.

'One of the ringers' dogs had this litter six weeks ago and Jim just happened to mention it to me yesterday. So I went to have a look and picked him out myself. I hope he brings you a lot of joy and companionship.'

Tattie felt the warm little body squirm against her, got her nose licked, and was subjected to the anxious gaze of a baby removed from its mother and its siblings and not at all sure what on earth was going on.

'Oh… Oh, sweetheart,' she crooned, and hugged it. 'You're gorgeous!'

The puppy wriggled ecstatically, then closed its eyes and fell asleep.

Tattie raised a blue gaze full of wry amusement to Alex, and just about everything she'd planned to say to him flew out of the window. *What kind of game do you think you're playing with me,*

Alex Constantin? I no more want to be involved in a business partnership, let alone a marriage, with you than I want to fly to the moon. I not only don't like you, I don't approve of you...

None of it got said, and then he took her further by surprise.

'Your mother and Doug Partridge are flying in today, to spend a few days with us, Tattie.'

'I... You've met him? The man she's planning to marry?' Tattie said, again incredulously.

'I have,' he agreed. 'I liked him. And I thought you'd enjoy having your mother help you with plans for the new project.'

'I would. That is to say...' She trailed off and gazed at him helplessly. Then, 'My mother hasn't, been well—' she swallowed '—meddling?'

He raised his eyebrows. 'Not as far as I know. Why?'

'Uh...it doesn't matter. What was I saying?'

'I got the impression you might have been trying to tell me you've changed your mind after last night?' He looked at her alertly.

Tattie closed her eyes, then looked down at the puppy in her arms. What did you do with a man who kissed you witless, left you almost crazy with desire then got you a puppy?

'No,' she said at last, 'I guess not.'

'Wise thinking, Tattie. Shall we have breakfast?'

The next few days were quite hectic.

Natalie arrived with Doug Partridge and Tattie took an immediate liking to him. A gentle giant of a man, with a shock of grey hair, he loved painting the outback and therefore was very happy to be at Beaufort. But what really caused Tattie to widen her eyes was the way her mother was suddenly seeing the countryside.

In fact, her mother was like a new person, and thrilled with Alex's idea.

'You don't think Dad would have minded?' Tattie asked her with a frown during their first discussion of it all.

Natalie sat back. 'As I see it, darling, this is your best option if you really want to do things on your own. I mean, since you've explained the position with Carnarvon, I could, in fact, help you out. Your father left me the cash and you the properties, so—'

'No,' Tattie said definitely. 'I do want to do it on my own and I certainly don't want to risk your assets in the process.'

'I take it you don't want Alex to come to the party either?' her mother enquired delicately.

'Well, he is, in a way. We've reached an agreement. We'll stay married for the time being,' Tattie said without a tremor in her voice, which was not a true indication of her feelings on the subject, 'but this will be a purely business partnership between us.'

'I see.' Natalie gazed at her daughter and decided to hold her peace. 'All right. Then let me tell you, Tatiana, that I think this is a far better way for you to express your love and the affinity you have with this place than tearing yourself to pieces trying to be a cattleman. And your father would have done anything he had to do to hold on to Beaufort *and* Carnarvon. So rest easy, my sweet. And go for it.'

One day I'll understand all this, Tattie thought the next day.

They were all seated around the oak dining-room table and ideas for enticing tourists to Beaufort were flying thick and fast. Her mother was using her artistic skills in sketches as she incorporated her and Tattie's ideas for guest bedrooms. Alex and Doug were discussing ideas for a bunkhouse where hardier tourists intent on getting the ultimate cattle-station experience could be housed.

They'd all discussed the vehicles that would be required to show people the wonders of Beaufort, and the horses needed for the hardier. And Alex had briefly run through the more mundane matters, as he put it, pertaining to running a tourist operation—the public-liability policy they'd have to take out, the standards they'd have to aspire to get a five-star rating and the hiring of personnel, since Tattie wouldn't be able to do it all on her own.

But the mystery that Tattie was contemplating through it all was the easy camaraderie that now existed between her mother and her husband. At least, that was one mystery. Her present feelings for her husband were the most mysterious of all. And just as she was about to shake her head in a certain amount of disgust, because she truly did not know where she stood with him and it was killing her, he turned to her.

'This is all very well,' he said with a lurking smile, 'the nuts and bolts. But it's going to be you who gets it off the ground, Tattie. Your touch with people, your feel for the place.'

The puppy, now named Oscar, since Tattie had discovered its mother's name was Lucinda, stirred in her lap and yawned prodigiously.

'Hear, hear!' Natalie said, and clapped her hands, and Doug smiled warmly at her.

Oscar sat up and barked his first bark, then looked surprised, as if he couldn't believe the sound had come from him.

They all dissolved into laughter. 'Thanks,' Tattie said, mysteriously feeling a lot better suddenly.

That night she got up around midnight, as she heard Oscar whimpering, and rushed into the lounge before he woke the whole house.

She'd fixed up a basket for him beside the fireplace, she'd put an old clock in with him, and even a hot-water bottle wrapped in a blanket, but he was sitting up looking piteously unhappy. Then he saw her and placed his paws on the rim of the basket. He experimented with his bark again in joyful recognition of her.

'Shush... Now, look here,' she whispered, kneeling down beside him, 'you've got to learn to sleep on your own. I know it's hard, after having a mum and six brothers and sisters with you, but don't forget you're going to grow up into the best, the bravest dog of them all!'

Oscar wagged his whole body, barked again, and took a flying leap into her lap.

'Oh, dear.' She stroked him. 'What am I going to do with you? I know what you're aiming for, young man! You want to come into my bed, but—'

'Once you start that, Tattie, you'll never get him out.'

They both turned to see Alex standing behind them. Oscar eyed him alertly, then experimented with another sound, a growl this time.

'Oh, the cheek of you!' Tattie marvelled, and hugged him.

'I can see that this might not have been such a great idea,' Alex said wryly.

It flew through Tattie's mind to say that, since no one else shared her bed, most notably not him, why shouldn't she allow her puppy the freedom of it while he was only such a baby?

But she put Oscar on the floor, then picked him up immediately and raced outside with him.

'Whoa! That was a close call!' She came back moments later, shivering from the cold night air with her nose pink and her hair flying.

'OK…' She put Oscar into Alex's arms and said to the puppy, 'Since this bloke gave you to me, I think you need to treat him with a bit more respect. In fact it's all right to make friends with him.'

'Thank you, Tattie,' Alex said ruefully, then addressed himself to the dog. 'Got that, mutt?'

Oscar hesitated, then licked Alex profusely.

'For heaven's sake, have him back.' He handed the dog over. 'I'm not keen on all that much friendship.'

'Don't worry, I know how to train a dog,' Tattie said. 'You see, he'll be a model—when he's a little older. Won't you, sweetness?'

Alex eyed his wife and her puppy and looked sceptical. But he said only, 'I hope you have a lot of fun with him.'

It was then that Tattie realised Alex was still dressed. 'Haven't you been to bed yet? It's past midnight!'

He looked down at his jeans and navy sweater. 'I was just about to go to bed when I heard the dog. There were a few loose ends I wanted to tie up before I go tomorrow.'

'You're going tomorrow? I... I mean, I didn't know that,' she stammered, trying to cover up the surprise, and something else she might have exhibited.

'I was hoping to have a few more days, but something's come up. Your mother and Doug will be here for a while, though.' He looked down at her with a faint frown.

'Of course! I'll be fine, even when they're gone.' But would she? she wondered.

'And I'll be back as soon as I can. You're quite safe here now, Tattie. There are at least five men on Beaufort to protect you in the unlikely event of anyone coming somewhere this remote anyway.'

'Oh, that,' she said a little blankly. 'Do they know about someone trying to kidnap me?'

He paused, as if assessing her unpreparedness for the subject. 'Jim does. All that the others will know is that while you're here they should keep an eye out for you.'

Tattie grimaced.

'That makes good sense in any circumstances,' he said quietly.

'What's happened to Amy Goodall's friend?'

'He's been remanded without bail and will face at least two charges—carrying an unlicenced weapon and attempted kidnapping. You don't have to worry about him. But I have another suggestion to make, purely from a company point of view— company for you, I mean.'

'What's that?'

'Jim and Marie's eighteen-year-old daughter has finished school and may be forced to go to Perth or Darwin to get a job. They think she's too young, but the problem is how to keep her here. I suggested she move into the housekeeper's quarters here in the homestead in the role of trainee housekeeper...'

'Polly?' Tattie stared at him, then started to laugh.

'You know her?'

'Of course I know her! I grew up with her—and if ever there was a tomboy who could run a cattle station, she is it!'

'She seemed quite keen on the idea,' Alex said slowly. 'So's her mother.'

'I'm not surprised. Marie's been trying to tame Polly ever since I can remember.' Tattie was still chuckling.

'Perhaps Marie thinks you might succeed where she failed?' Tattie sobered.

'She reckons that in her heart of hearts Polly would love to be everything you are,' Alex continued.

Tattie blinked. 'I didn't know that!'

He smiled enigmatically. 'Will you give it a try? If you succeed we could put her on the staff.'

'Well, yes. I think Polly loves Beaufort as much as I do, and Jim and Marie have always been wonderful to me. Of course! Just don't blame me if I don't succeed in turning her into a housekeeper.' Tattie hesitated and frowned. 'Alex, you take very good care of me, for a wife you...don't really want.'

There, it was out, she thought, although she closed her eyes and shivered inwardly at her temerity. But she just couldn't allow this unspoken war between them not to have some mention in dispatches before he flew away.

'Tattie?'

Her lashes flew up but he said no more for a long moment while he took in everything about her. Her white flannel pyjamas with their delicate pin-tucking and lace-trimmed collar, her bare feet, her hair, disarrayed but still gorgeous, her shadowed and confused cornflower-blue eyes.

And it occurred to Alex Constantin that his plan was working. She might tell him she didn't want to stay married to him for some mysterious 'very good reason', but one day she would go to bed with him because she couldn't help herself. A day of his choosing, however. And then this arranged marriage would become real whether she liked it or not...

So why, he wondered, did he not feel too good about himself?

'Tattie,' he said again, 'whatever is between us, you *are* my wife. You're also a nice person and my business partner. And your little dog is fast asleep, so now might be a good time to return him to his basket and get some sleep yourself.'

But what he got in return surprised him somewhat. A most rebellious spark entered those cornflower eyes and she drew herself up almost as if she'd love to fling his words right back at him, but at the last moment she turned the rebellion off and smiled sweetly at him.

'If you want to play games with me, Alex,' she said, also sweetly, 'be my guest. Just don't count on getting the opportunity to kiss me and walk away from me again, because I'll make damn sure it doesn't come up. Furthermore, until this dog learns to sleep through the night, he will sleep with me.' She turned on her heel and walked away.

His lips twitched as he watched her go, but for a moment he was almost unbearably tempted to replace Oscar in her arms and her bed—with himself. Well, well, he mused with a mixture of amusement and self-directed irony, that round goes to you, Tatiana Beaufort.

Two months later, Polly dropped a plate, swore, then clapped a hand to her mouth and looked guiltily at Tattie.

'Thought I'd cured myself of that,' she said apologetically, 'dropping things and swearing, but I'm scared stiff, Tattie. There's eight people out there all waiting for me to make a fool of myself!'

'Polly.' Tattie put her hands on her shoulders. 'No one is waiting for you to make a fool of yourself. You can do this. You look terrific, and just think how proud your mum and dad are of you,

THE CONSTANTIN MARRIAGE

not to mention me. And Alex, of course!' An afterthought that would surely do the trick, Tattie thought a little darkly.

Polly looked down at herself in her neat tunic top and long skirt, both professionally made. Then she touched her hair, which Tattie had rescued from blonde straw, bleached and dried by the sun, and persuaded her to get cut into a short bob. And she touched her face, which Tattie had shown her how to make up discreetly—and she took a deep breath.

'I guess I can, thanks to you, Tattie.'

'OK. Now I'm going to join the guests, but if you need me just tell me quietly.'

Polly nodded, and after a last look around Tattie took a deep breath and went through to the dining room, where dinner was almost due to be served.

It was their maiden voyage, in a manner of speaking. Their first group of guests and a most discerning group at that—at least Tattie assumed so, because they'd just come from a Constantin cruise, which would have set them back a small fortune. They were a group of Americans travelling together and they'd arrived two hours ago.

In that time, and earlier, things had not gone smoothly. Marie, who was supposed to be in charge in the kitchen, had developed a bout of hay fever that had to be seen to be believed and had been sent to bed, the only thing she was good for. Natalie was supposed to have flown in earlier in the day but had sprained her ankle. Alex had been asked to stay away and had—when she could really do with him, Tattie thought irrationally—and Oscar had pulled a sheet off the washing line and chewed it up on the front lawn so that it resembled confetti.

Thus it was that only she and Polly were on hand. All the same, the dining table looked wonderful beneath a full complement of the Beaufort silver, crystal and fine porcelain, the guests were happy with their rooms, and it was now up to her to provide them with a wonderful experience.

* * *

Three hours later, she and Polly sat in the kitchen drinking champagne with their shoes kicked off, the door firmly closed and Oscar asleep in his basket.

'What a night!' Polly said enthusiastically. 'But we did it! You know the oldest guy, the one who looks to be in his eighties? He actually pinched me on the bottom and nearly got his dessert poured all over him!'

Tattie giggled like a girl. 'I saw your face and held my breath. Oh, wow! You're right, what a night, but they loved it and you were wonderful.'

'They loved *you*. OK.' Polly looked around at the colourful chaos of the kitchen and groaned.

'I'll help.' Tattie drained her glass. 'At least tomorrow night's a barbecue and your mum might be better.'

'We've got to get through tomorrow's day before we get to tomorrow night,' Polly said ruefully, then looked at Tattie curiously. 'I just wish Alex had been here to see you tonight, Tattie. You looked so...regal.'

Tattie grimaced. 'I asked him to stay away. Sometimes he makes me feel self-conscious.'

Polly smacked her palm on her forehead. 'Know exactly what you mean. Dad has the same effect on me.'

It was midnight before Tattie got to bed, but at least she was secure in the knowledge that everything was as it should be and ready for the day's activities. But Polly's remark about Alex had stayed with her, although her reply had been true to an extent. It was the way things were between her and Alex that would have made her self-conscious did Polly but know it.

Of course, Polly was as crazy about Alex as every other woman he came in contact with, so she had no reason to suspect he could be quite...really *quite* diabolical at times, Tattie thought as she lay down with a sigh and switched her bedside light off.

Such as implementing a truce between them that was a terrible farce. But what option did she have but to go along with her husband, when he came and went from Beaufort, at his charming best in front of her mother, her staff and the whole world whilst keeping an absolutely scrupulous distance from her in private? None, she answered herself. And she'd done it for a whole year so why couldn't she do it now?

'I don't know,' she whispered into the darkness. 'It just tears me apart these days to have nothing resolved, to suspect that he'll wear me down so I'll agree to stay married to him, really married. On top of all that I was the one who threw down the gauntlet,' she reminded herself gloomily. 'Come to that, I was the one who started this whole cat and mouse game in the first place.'

She sniffed, and Oscar, who had been transported fast asleep in his basket to her bedroom, woke up and leapt onto the bed.

'Oh, no,' she murmured. 'We've got an agreement, now, remember? You can sleep in here on the condition you stay in your basket, young man! As a matter of fact, I'm not game to let you sleep anywhere else in case you chew things—which reminds me, I'm still very cross with you! It took us hours to clear up that sheet.'

But Oscar ignored her, possibly because the tone of her voice was not consistent with her words, and he snuggled down beside her.

Tattie sighed. And put her arm round him. 'Just this once, then.'

But at least she fell asleep shortly afterwards.

Two days later she and Polly farewelled their first guests and were on the receiving end of the most ravishing compliments.

Things had gone much more smoothly on day two. Marie had woken clear of her hay fever and able to take over the kitchen. Polly and Tattie had escorted the party on a tour of the property, some on horseback, others in a four-wheel-drive vehicle, and nothing had gone wrong. No horse had bolted or put its foot in a hole—and Beaufort had done the rest.

The barbecue under the stars last night around a big bonfire had been a huge success. They'd sung songs and Polly had electrified them all with her whip-cracking expertise. And now they were going, all swearing they'd be back, and not only that—they'd also tell all their friends about the best 'top end' experience they'd had.

And, possibly because she'd been so inundated, Tattie hadn't heard Alex fly in, so it took her completely by surprise to turn from waving the bus off and almost bump into him.

'Oh! I didn't hear you arrive!'

'So I gathered. Would I be right in assuming you've had an outstanding success?'

'Would you ever!' Polly glowed. 'I've had four invitations to go to America!'

'I take it you've tamed Polly?'

Tattie and Alex were having lunch on the veranda, alone for once, when he made his remark.

Tattie shook her head. 'Not really. Smoothed a few corners, that's all. They just adored her as herself—a dinkum Aussie girl. Alex, if this is a real success, Polly will have to take a lot of the credit.'

'Tell me about it all?'

She did so, making him laugh with the disasters of the first day then the highlights of the rest of it.

But he sobered as she ran out of anecdotes and studied her. 'You're exhausted.'

She couldn't disagree, although she said, 'It's got to get easier.'

'Have you got any bookings this week?'

'No, but next weekend is a big one—a full house and a party of six in the bunkhouse.'

'Come to Darwin with me for a few days.'

Her eyes widened. 'Why?'

'You need a break.'

'I... Not really; I'll be fine, and there's so much to do!'

'Anything Polly, Marie and your mother and the rest of the staff can't handle?'

'Uh... Mum's sprained her ankle.'

'It's better. She rang me this morning to apologise for having to desert you. She and Doug are happy to come for the next influx.'

Tattie looked at her plate of cold meat and salad, then sipped the glass of wine he'd insisted on pouring her. 'There's Oscar.'

At the sound of his name Oscar pricked up his ears and placed his front paws on Tattie's knee.

'Bring him,' Alex said.

'Oh, I don't... I mean, in an apartment—'

'You'll just have to take him for regular walks.'

Tattie stared at him wordlessly.

He held her gaze with his dark eyes unfathomable for a long moment. Then he said drily, 'My mother is having a hip replacement in two days. She's missing you and wants to see you before she goes in. I think she's really nervous about it all.'

Tattie bit her lip. 'Why didn't you say so in the beginning?'

He didn't answer, but his look said it all.

She had a chat with Oscar before she went to bed.

'Sweetheart,' she said seriously, 'I'm going away for a few days. I would love to take you with me but I think it would be really difficult—for both of us. So I'm going to leave you with Polly. Please be good for her, and I'll be back before you know it!'

Oscar gazed at her soulfully.

'I'll tell her to let you sleep on my bed,' Tattie promised, then grimaced. 'Well, maybe not, but rest assured, when I get back it'll be like old times because you and I are a team!'

Oscar crawled into her lap and licked her chin and she hugged him close.

But it was harder than even she had anticipated to leave him the next morning.

CHAPTER SEVEN

AT MIDDAY THE next day she was standing in the middle of the lounge of their Darwin apartment, looking around a little dazedly.

Alex put their bags down and went to open the shutters and sliding glass doors. It was a magnificent dry-season Darwin day, warm and clear with no smoke from bush fires, and two navy boats were steaming smartly towards Stokes Wharf.

'Doesn't feel like home any more?' he queried as he took in her expression.

She opened her mouth to say no, then changed her mind. 'It just feels a bit strange to be back.'

'Perhaps you *should* have brought Oscar,' he said drily.

Tattie grimaced. 'I tremble to think what Oscar could do to this place,' she said, 'if he was left to his own devices.'

But of course the other reason she'd left Oscar behind was for an excuse to get back to Beaufort as soon as possible.

'Is that an admission that you haven't been as successful a dog trainer as you thought?'

Tattie hesitated, belatedly realising that Alex was somewhat annoyed. She wondered why. 'He's only three and a half months old,' she said quietly. 'You... Are you cross with me about something? Other than Oscar?'

He faced her squarely, then shrugged and grinned reluctantly. 'I'm beginning to regret giving you that dog because it's obvious he means more to you than just about anything else. But that is actually rather a "dog in the manger" attitude on my part, so don't worry about it.'

Her lips parted incredulously. 'You...couldn't be jealous!'

He strolled across the carpet, took her chin in his hand and kissed her very lightly. 'For my sins, yes, I could.'

She was transfixed by the glint in his eyes, the feel of his fingers still on her chin, and the whole dangerously exciting experience of Alex Constantin in close proximity with that look in his eye. He wore a bush shirt and jeans, he flew his plane with consummate ease, as he did just about everything, and he was so much pure man her knees felt like buckling at the thought that he could be jealous over her.

But he released her almost immediately, shoved his hands in his pockets and changed the subject completely. 'Look, I'm sorry about this, but I've asked my parents over to dinner tonight. You know how my mother insists on personally supervising an eight-course banquet at home, and I don't think she's up to a restaurant. Could you manage that? The operation is tomorrow, so it will take her mind off it.'

Tattie came down to earth with a bump and swallowed. 'Uh...of course. I've got time to shop and...all the rest.'

'Good girl.' This time he kissed her on the top of her head, most impersonally, and added, 'I've got to go to work for the afternoon, so I'll be out of your hair.'

He turned to go, then turned back. 'By the way, I've got a surprise for you.'

All she could do was raise her eyebrows at him.

'Tonight, Tattie. See you.' And he was gone.

It turned out to be a long, dithery afternoon for Tattie.

She shopped, then had to go out again for the things she'd

forgotten. She prepared dinner, but several times had to stop herself from seasoning dishes twice.

I'm a nervous wreck, she told herself, or, to put it more accurately, I don't know if I'm on my head or my heels—and all because Alex is jealous of Oscar! Unless this is some new direction of the game?

Finally she got things under control and went to have a relaxing soak in the tub. Which turned out to be not so relaxing on account of her churning emotions, and *they* were responsible for her not hearing Alex come home. Thus it was that just as she stepped out of the bath the door opened and Alex stood there.

She froze on the step up to her raised, shell-shaped bath and he stopped abruptly in the doorway.

Then he murmured, 'My apologies, Tattie. Things were so quiet I wondered if you'd run off again, or if someone had kid...' He stopped.

'No. As you see.' She closed her eyes and could have died, because there was absolutely nothing of her that was not on offer for him to see.

'I do. You look like Venus rising out of her shell. I'll bring you a towel.' He plucked a jade towel from the rail and brought it over to her. 'Only much lovelier than Venus to my mind,' he said softly, coming to stand right in front of her.

Their gazes clashed, cornflower-blue and dark, almost black. Then his gaze slipped up and down her sleek, pearly body, from her high little breasts with their velvety tips right down to her toes.

Once again Tattie was transfixed. He handed her the towel and she took it, but the will to wrap it around her seemed to have deserted her. Nor could she tear her gaze from his.

'Tattie,' he said very quietly, deep in his throat and he once again flicked that dark gaze up and down her curves, then paused.

And he sniffed. He definitely sniffed, and half turned from

her, and she was ready to die of mortification—until she caught it as well: the aroma of burning meat.

'Oh, no! My dinner,' she moaned. 'This is just the worst day of my life!' And she wound the towel round her swiftly and leapt down the step, straight into his arms.

He picked her up.

'Alex, no, I haven't got time for this,' she protested. 'I cannot offer your mother a burnt meal!'

'Let's see what we can do, then.' He carried her through to the kitchen, put her down and grabbed a cloth with which to open the smoking oven. When the smoke cleared her piece of roast pork revealed itself as burnt black.

Tattie looked at the temperature gauge unbelievingly. It was far too high, and she put her hand to her mouth in despair.

Alex looked alertly from her to the pork. 'OK. Let's stay calm,' he recommended. 'What else have you got?'

'I've got smoked salmon for the entrée and fruit salad and ice cream for dessert, but I cannot offer them only an entrée and a dessert,' she said tragically.

He tucked the corner of the towel more securely between her breasts. 'I have the solution. There's a take-away I know of that does fantastic spare-ribs. I'll ring them.'

'Your mother would die rather than eat take-away food!'

'That's a good thing,' he said. 'She won't have had any of their spare-ribs, so she won't know it's a take-away.'

'But—isn't it too late?'

He smiled into her deeply worried eyes. 'I've been a very good customer of theirs while you've been doing great deeds at Beaufort, Tattie. They'll rush it here with all the trimmings, and if you just point me in the direction of suitable serving dishes no one will know the difference.'

She breathed a sigh of relief, and the towel slipped a bit as she gestured towards a cupboard.

Once more he tucked the corner more securely between her breasts, but this time his fingers lingered on her skin.

'May I make another suggestion, Tattie?'

She stared a question up into his dark eyes with her breath starting to come raggedly again.

'That you take yourself off and leave all this to me.'

'Yes, all right,' she murmured, but her feet refused to move.

'What's more,' he said softly, but with a most wicked glint in his eye, 'it might be a good idea to wear your least sexy clothes tonight, otherwise I doubt if you and I will get through this evening, and we don't really want to shock my parents rigid, do we?'

His gaze lingered on her throat, the smooth, rounded skin of her shoulders, the valley where the towel was tucked between her breasts, the flare of her hips beneath the jade material.

Tattie swallowed and, although he wasn't touching her, she could feel the graze of his end-of-day stubble on her cheeks, the hard lines of his body on hers and, above all, she could remember all too well what pleasure he could inflict on her with his hands and mouth.

'Tattie?'

'I'm going,' she whispered, and fled for the sanctuary of her bedroom.

Her least sexy clothes!

She surveyed her wardrobe a little wildly and finally came up with a long navy linen dress. It had a Peter Pan collar of off-white Thai silk, cap sleeves and a row of mother-of-pearl buttons down the front. And it was straight, not fitted, although it did have a slit up one side—but a very discreet one. She slipped on a pair of plain navy blue shoes with little heels, then sat down in front of the dressing table to tackle her hair, her make-up, but most of all the still stunned look in her eyes. She couldn't go back out looking like that, she told herself as she brushed her hair and wielded the minimum amount of make-up—a light foundation, the faintest touch of blusher and some lip gloss.

Better—well, a bit, she decided as she studied herself critically, and for the first time in her life longed acutely for a drink. She stood up and sprayed her perfume on, and the door clicked open. It was Alex with a glass in his hands.

'Brought you a Scotch, ma'am, and the information that everything is under control. The ribs have arrived.'

He put the glass on the dressing table and looked her up and down with his lips quirking.

'Now, that dress,' he said gravely, 'makes you look like a nun. Which is a challenge in its own right for any red-blooded man. You've got about ten minutes, Tattie.' And he left, closing the door behind him.

Tattie sat down and murmured several very unladylike epithets her convent school would have been horrified to hear issue from her lips. Then she took a strong swallow of her drink and closed her eyes. Should she change? How did you cope with Alex in this mood? How was she going to get through the evening, and most of all...what awaited her at the end of it?

Then she heard the doorbell chime. It had to be George and Irina. She took another sip of her drink, squared her shoulders and sighed deeply—and went to entertain her parents-in-law as well as cope with her husband.

In point of fact, Alex behaved beautifully.

And Irina, limping painfully and using a cane, was genuinely thrilled to see her. So was George.

'My dear Tatiana, I've missed you so much! I would have loved to come and see Beaufort and what you've done, but as you see I'm an old crock these days.' Irina enveloped Tattie in an emotional hug.

A sliver of guilt pierced Tattie for having run off the way she had—made worse by how nice they were being about it. Unless Alex had coached them...

But dinner progressed without a hitch, and Irina said of the spare-ribs, 'My dear, that was delicious—you excelled yourself!'

Tattie opened her mouth but intercepted a warning glance from Alex, which went along the lines of—*Don't you dare say a word!*

She shut her mouth and went to get the fruit salad and ice cream.

It was while she was pouring the coffee that Alex produced his surprise. He'd suggested they have their coffee in the den, where the television was, and he slipped a video into the machine.

Tattie went on pouring the coffee, then stopped as she, in her pink linen dress, appeared on the screen.

Irina clapped her hands. 'I can't see this often enough!'

'Tattie hasn't seen the edited version yet.' Alex took the coffee-pot from her and told her to sit down.

'My dear, you are excellent,' George pronounced. 'A wonderful advertisement for Constantin pearls.'

'Oh, dear, this is embarrassing,' Tattie murmured, but not long afterwards she lost herself in the video as it brought back memories of the lovely time she'd spent with Alex at the pearl farm and in the Drysdale River.

But her cheeks burned as they all, including Alex, congratulated her again as the video finished.

'You may have to watch this little girl, son,' George said jovially. 'Hollywood could steal her!'

Alex grinned and slipped another video into the machine. 'Now this one is the unedited version of the one we made for Beaufort.'

Tattie sat up. She'd forgotten about the two days they'd had a film crew on the station to make a promotional video. And she blinked as Oscar, with a shoe in his mouth, bounded onto the screen with her and Polly in hot pursuit. Polly could be heard swearing, then was seen clapping a hand over her mouth and saying, 'Sorry, Tattie, strike that!'

Tattie turned to Alex accusingly. 'You didn't!'

He nodded. 'I did. They had their cameras rolling almost all the time. Watch this.'

She looked back at the screen and there she was on horse-back, describing the wonders of a billabong, until her horse got stung by a bee and reared up and took off with her.

'That was take one,' Alex said.

'I don't believe this,' Tattie said.

This time, looking quite windblown as she started her spiel, with Polly holding the horse just to be on the safe side, she said slowly and clearly on the video, 'There are more billabongs in this wonder... That's not right, is it?' And the prompter could be heard in the background correcting her...'there are more wonders in this billabong...'

'That was take two,' Alex murmured, 'but you ain't seen nothing yet.'

In take three she'd only uttered two words when her horse decided to relieve itself at length.

And in take four Tattie had almost got through her speech on the wonders of billabongs when Polly started to do a de-mented jig at the same time as she was heard to say, 'There are also bloody green ants around billabongs and I'm standing on a nest. Ouch!' And the camera panned around to see that ev-eryone was convulsed with laughter.

Tattie had to wipe her eyes in the civilised safety of Darwin as she remembered that hilarious day. 'I think it took seven takes to get it right,' she said, still laughing.

'Oh, look,' Irina said as the video finally rolled to a close, 'I haven't laughed so much for years. Thank you, Alex and Tat-tie. And thank you so much for coming home to be with me during this operation.'

Tattie took Irina's hand in hers. 'I can't wait to show you Beaufort in the flesh. As soon as you've got this little business out of the way you must come and stay. Both of you,' she said warmly to George.

* * *

'A successful evening.'

Tattie turned to see that Alex had come out onto the veranda after seeing his parents off.

'Thanks to you. She really is struggling, isn't she?'

'Mmm… We've been trying to persuade her to have this done for quite a while now, but you know how much she hates hospitals and is scared to death of operations. Hip replacements have a great rate of success, though.'

'Does she…? Do they…? They didn't ask any questions about me leaving Darwin. Did you warn them off, Alex?'

'Of course.'

'How?'

'I told them it was something you needed to get out of your system, that's all.' He shrugged.

Tattie went still. 'Is that what you genuinely believe?'

He glanced down at her and smiled fleetingly. 'Isn't it, Tattie?'

'It's much more than that!'

He shrugged. 'All the same, I'm at a slight disadvantage here, Tatiana. No one can quite understand why I haven't bedded you and got all this nonsense out of the way.'

She made a kittenish sound of pure outrage. 'It is not nonsense, Alex Constantin!'

'*I* wasn't saying it was nonsense. I was only faithfully reporting to you how others, your mother included, view it. And the slightly awkward position it puts me in, that's all.'

'She hasn't—my mother hasn't *dared* to express such an opinion,' Tattie got out, more in sincere hope than from conviction, because the circles of her mother's mind were not always predictable.

'Perhaps not on what I should do about it, but she was the one who told me you needed to get this out of your system—

your obsession with saving Carnarvon like a true Beaufort,' he said drily.

Tattie spluttered something incomprehensible, then took aim at the only thing left in her sights. 'Leaving that aside, it must be a little galling to know that your reputation with women is suffering, Alex.'

But it bounced off him harmlessly.

'I can live with it, Tattie,' he drawled. 'For one thing, they're only our families. For another, they don't know the real story.'

Several sequences flashed through Tattie's brain. The number of occasions he had kissed her and found her not unwilling at all. The occasion he had been the one to call a halt when she had not had the will-power or the desire to do so. Desires quite in the opposite direction, you might say, she thought, and winced. And only this evening, when all that had saved her from giving herself to him had been a piece of burnt roast pork.

But in light of what he'd just told her, even if he claimed it didn't bother him what their families thought, *she* thought she could see a pattern in the game, and that pattern was not that he was falling in love with her or genuinely jealous of Oscar—perish the thought, she marvelled bitterly—but a determination to make this arranged marriage work.

'Alex, I'm going to bed and I'm going to lock my door, because you're still playing games with me,' she told him through her teeth.

He put his hand on her arm to detain her and his mouth was hard, the lines of his face grim. 'Don't bother to lock your door, Tattie. I wouldn't dream of trying to scale your ivory tower tonight. But let's get something straight. All this blew up out of nothing—yes, perhaps I wasn't so tactful but I was honest. Your blow-hot, blow-cold approach is not. If you want me as I want you, at least admit it. And if you don't, you must *really* be an incredible actress.' He released her arm and stepped back.

She gasped as if he'd struck her. Then she ran away from him, and she did lock herself into her bedroom.

She spent the next afternoon at the hospital, after Irina's operation.

She and Alex weren't talking—not in private anyway—and it helped to have something to do, although it wasn't a lot, as Irina slowly came round. But at least she could relieve George from time to time. Alex spent an hour with his mother when she regained consciousness and brought her a lovely spray of yellow cymbidium orchids in a pewter bud vase exquisitely studded with natural keshi pearls.

Tattie watched him during the hour he spent with his mother and found it hard to equate this man with the grim stranger of the night before. He made Irina laugh and he obviously made her feel cherished, so that you could see the terrors of hospitals and operations fading.

After an hour Irina told him to take George away and give him dinner. 'Tattie will stay with me until you bring him back, won't you, my dear?'

'Of course,' Tattie agreed.

'He's so kind to me, Alex is,' Irina murmured when they'd gone. 'In fact, he's a fine man, my son!'

'He is.' Tattie swallowed and wondered what was coming. But Irina fell asleep until George and Alex reappeared.

George whispered to her that he would take over now and Alex would take her home. 'You look really tired, but thank you for everything today and last night,' he added.

She got up and cast an uncertain glance at Alex; she couldn't help herself.

He said quietly, 'Come home, Tattie.'

'You look exhausted.'

They'd just got into the apartment and he put his keys on the hall table and pulled off his jacket and tie.

'Can you eat anything?'

'No... I don't know...' She couldn't go on.

He grimaced. 'Listen, I'm not about to resume hostilities. Go into the den, put your feet up and I'll bring you something. And thank you for being with my mother today.' He turned away.

She went into the den and did as she was told. Presently he arrived with a tray and put before her some toasted cheese sandwiches and a pot of fragrant Earl Grey tea, but he had nothing for himself.

'Don't you want some of this?' she queried.

'No. I ate with Dad.' He moved to an armchair and sprawled out in it. He waited until she'd eaten her sandwiches to say, 'By the way, I heard from Beaufort today. Your mother and Doug have arrived and all is well, although Oscar appears to be missing you. He hasn't chewed a single thing since you left.'

Tattie smiled and sipped her tea. 'Perhaps he's growing up. Either that or I'm a bad influence on him.' Her smiled faded and she looked suddenly desolate.

Alex sat up. 'He's missing you, Tattie, that's all. Look, let's just concentrate on getting my mother over this then you can go back to Beaufort and we'll—' he gestured rather wryly '—come to some arrangement. But it's stupid for us to carry on in a state of armed neutrality at the moment.'

'All right,' she said slowly, and finished her tea. 'But would you mind if I went to bed now? I do seem to feel exhausted.'

'Of course not.' His eyes were alert as he scanned her pale, weary face, and he stood up and came over to her. 'Goodnight, my dear. Sleep well. It's not the end of the earth, you know.'

It may not be for you, Alex, she said in her mind as she leant back against her bedroom door, but I feel as if I've been run over by a steamroller. I don't know what to think. I don't even seem to know myself too well any more. Hasn't that always been the problem, though? What's between us may not be cataclysmic for you, but it is for me...

And, to make matters worse, Irina was transferred into Intensive Care the next morning with post-operative complications. There followed four awful days while her doctors battled to save her life.

'If you want to go back to Beaufort, your next lot of guests are due to arrive shortly,' Alex said to her at one point. 'I—'

'Do you really think I'd do that?' she interrupted.

He looked ten years older, with harsh lines scored beside his mouth, and he was grey from lack of sleep. 'It's not that, but—'

'Alex,' she said more gently, 'between my mother, Polly, Doug and Marie, they can cope. I'm not going anywhere. But I am going to lay down the law here. You must go home and get some sleep. I promise I'll call you if there's any change.'

'Dad—'

She interrupted again. 'I'll be there with him at her bedside.'

Two days later they got the news that, although there was a long road back to full health in front of Irina, she was out of danger. And for the first time they were able to go home together.

It was a balmy evening, and while Tattie made them a meal Alex simply stood on the veranda, staring out over the harbour as the last of the daylight faded with a light show made unique by the dust and smoke from bush fires that were so much part of the Northern Territory at this time of the year.

Nor did he turn, although he must have heard her, and after she'd put the plates down she went to stand next to him at the railing.

He said, 'I was so afraid she was going to die without ever seeing the grandchildren she yearned for. I really felt I'd failed her.'

'Not you—me,' Tattie whispered.

He didn't look at her and shook his head. 'No. It's part of our culture and heritage, Tattie. You'd have to be Greek to understand it. I don't think mostly Anglo-Saxon with a dash of Russian can really give you the same...whatever it is.' He shrugged. 'And you certainly can't be held accountable for it.'

'But you've been a wonderful son to her, Alex. She adores you.'

'I still feel as if I've let her down. I still...' He moved his shoulders restlessly. 'She might have driven me mad at times with the way she tried to run my life but I still...would be devastated to lose her.'

'I know what you mean, and she isn't even my mother,' Tattie said softly. 'There's just something about Irina that you can't help loving. So much warmth, and she's so genuine—she's just one of those people who makes your life better for knowing her.'

He took a deep, shuddery breath and said huskily, 'Thank you for that.'

And something broke within Tattie, something that felt like a knot unravelling, releasing the certainty that, whatever happened in the future, she had never loved Alex Constantin more than she did right now. Was it because she'd never seen him so defenceless before? she wondered. Was it because she had seen real, painful emotion and a very human side to him over the last few days—perhaps for the first time?

She shook her head, unable to answer herself or fight the tide of longing that swamped her to at least bring him some comfort. And she slipped her arm around his waist and laid her head below his shoulder.

He tensed, but she ignored it and rubbed her cheek against his shirt.

'Tattie—no,' he said barely audibly. 'This is very sweet of you, but—'

'It's not sweet. I can't help it, that's all, and I'd appreciate it if you didn't make me feel like a teenager.'

She felt his chest jolt with sudden laughter. But he sobered immediately and there was evident strain in his voice as he said, 'What do you want me to do? Kiss you and walk away from you, Tattie?'

'No. I want you to leave it all to me, Alex, just this once. Come inside.' She took his hand.

'Dinner...' he started to say.

She looked at the meal she'd prepared going cold on the veranda table. 'Dinner can wait.'

Her bedroom was dark, so she switched on a bedside lamp.

Alex was standing in the middle of the room, looking around at the lovely cream and hyacinth decor with a slightly wry expression.

Tattie went to him and put her hand in his. 'I know what you're thinking.'

He looked down at her with his eyebrows raised.

'That this is a little like storming the Bastille?' she suggested.

His lips twitched. 'I was beginning to doubt that I'd ever use this room for its rightful purpose.'

Tattie raised his hand to her mouth and kissed his knuckles. 'At this moment in time,' she said barely audibly, 'it seems very right to be in here, together.'

He touched her hair. 'At this moment in time, Tattie, there's nowhere else I'd rather be, but—'

'Let's just do it,' she whispered, and moved into his arms.

They closed about her, but she could sense he was still holding back, that he was still tense.

'Tattie, there's a point of no return in these matters.'

She raised her eyes to his and they were clear and unshadowed. 'I won't do that to you,' she promised.

He smiled, but there was still a question in his eyes.

'You're wondering if I...know much about it at all?'

'Perhaps.'

'No, I don't,' she conceded. 'In fact, I have no idea where to go from here, so I guess I must have a lot of faith in you, Alex, because I really would like to...go on from here, with you.'

He hesitated briefly and remembered that he had actually planned this, the only difference being that it was to have been a time of his choosing. Was it ironic that she had beaten him to the draw? Was it supremely ironic, he wondered, that he should be worried about taking unfair advantage of her when she herself had opened up the way for him?

Then she stood on her toes and kissed him softly. 'Is this... a good direction to take?' she breathed against the corner of his mouth.

He said her name on a tortured breath and pulled her so close she could barely breathe. 'It's excellent,' he murmured, and started to kiss her deeply.

And in the end he was the one who took control of their love-making; he couldn't help himself. As she clung to him dazedly she was more than happy to surrender the lead. 'Oh—I really don't know how to go on!' she said raggedly.

'Tattie,' he said on a breath, 'do you want to stop?'

'No!' She looked up at him, her eyes horrified. 'I didn't mean that. It's just that it might be an idea if I surrendered the lead to you, in a manner of speaking.'

Her arms were around his neck, his hands were on her hips, her shoes were kicked off, the buttons of the blouse she wore with a long georgette skirt were undone to her waist, and a wicked glint came into his eyes as he looked down at her.

'You were doing very well in the lead, Mrs Constantin, I don't think you have to worry about that.'

'All the same—is it too soon to go to bed?'

He laughed softly. 'No. Any more of this and I could become a basket case.'

Her eyes widened and her lips parted.

He kissed her and picked her up. 'Let me show you.' And he carried her to the bed.

But far from being a basket case, and despite his earlier exhaustion, Alex Constantin went out of his way to make love to her with the most exquisite finesse. He undressed her carefully and told her how lovely she was, until she couldn't help but believe him. And his fingers wrought a devastating trail of fire down her body at the same time.

'I'd like to do the same to you,' she whispered once.

'Be my guest,' he replied, and took his clothes off.

'Oh,' she said huskily when they were in each other's arms with nothing between them. 'I'm sure this isn't really red-hot sex but I don't think I could stand much more.'

He lifted his head; he'd been tugging her nipples gently between his teeth. 'This is as good as it gets, Tattie.'

'Really? For you too?' she gasped.

'Let me show you.' And he eased his weight onto her and all the unfamiliar sensations, instead of frightening her, became a matter of urgency, lovely, rapturous, extremely compelling, and obviously as compelling for him. She was lost for words at last, and she gave herself up completely to Alex's stewardship of her body, following all his leads as he led her to sheer heaven and held her hard in his arms while they both shuddered with the intensity of it.

'OK?' He brushed her hair off her face with his fingers.

She didn't answer because she still couldn't speak.

He grinned and kissed her, and she cuddled up to him with a sigh.

Then she found some words at last. 'I was supposed to be the one bringing you some comfort.'

'You did. I feel like a new man.'

'Really?' She raised her eyes to his a little wryly.

'Yes, really, Tattie. By the way, what did you think *really* red-hot sex meant?'

'Ah. I had visions of, well, doing it anywhere, for example. In cars, on carpets, in hay lofts—'

'I could always arrange that, although personally I'm happier with a bed.'

She ignored him, but with a severe little look. 'I had visions of exotic underwear and strange positions and golden, leopard-like women—'

'Strange positions can play havoc with one's back,' he offered gravely.

'Let me finish—to be honest, really red-hot sex frightened the life out of me.'

He laughed. 'I'm not surprised! But are you trying to say you associated me with all that?'

She went to say yes, then bit her lip. And she said instead, 'I guess you just don't know what you're in for until you do it.'

'No. So how was it?'

She closed her eyes and thought back for a moment, and felt herself go all goosefleshy. 'The most marvellous experience of my life,' she said simply.

He gathered her closer and murmured against the corner of her mouth, 'One day I'll remind you you said that, but thank you.'

Her lashes fluttered up. 'Shouldn't I have said it?'

'You have my permission to say it to me any time you like.'

'So...? Was it too ingenuous or something like that?' she queried, sounding suddenly awkward.

His dark gaze sharpened and she thought he was about to say something. Then he changed his mind. 'No. I'll always remember it.'

Not much later she fell asleep in his arms.

CHAPTER EIGHT

SHE WAS SINGING softly to herself the next morning as she stepped out of the shower.

Then she stopped and told herself that there were a lot of things still unresolved between her and Alex and it mightn't be appropriate to be so happy yet. But he came in as she stood in the middle of the bathroom, wearing only a towel and a smile of sheer contentment.

'Well, now, the last time I saw you wearing only a towel I was thwarted by a crisis in the kitchen,' he said with a lazy smile, and drew the towel away.

'Don't remind me!' She wrinkled her nose and realised he was dressed already, in a white business shirt, dark green tie and charcoal trousers. 'Uh… I'll have the towel back, thanks, Alex.'

'Why?'

She looked down at herself. 'You might not have noticed this but I feel a little undressed in comparison to you.'

'Oh, I noticed it,' he said softly. 'I also heard you singing.'

She grimaced. 'I often sing in the shower.'

'Really?' He lifted an eyebrow. 'So it had nothing to do with what transpired last night?'

'Um…' She chewed her lip. 'Perhaps a bit.' She reached for the towel but he withheld it from her. 'Alex!'

'Only a bit?'

She paused and looked at him with a glint in her eyes. 'What do I have to say to get myself out of the bathroom so that I can cook your breakfast—we did agree we were both starving, having missed dinner last night—and so that you can go to work, which you also told me you truly regretted but it was a necessity?'

'Instead of saying anything, why don't we have some really red-hot sex?'

Tattie frowned. 'I thought you disapproved of that?'

'Not any more. The thought of it with you,' he said softly, 'is more than I can bear.'

'Why did you get dressed, then?'

'I have not the faintest idea.' He pulled off his tie and started to unbutton his shirt.

'I've just had a shower,' Tattie said.

'So have I. But I have the solution to that.' He pulled his shirt off and unbuckled his belt. 'The perfect solution.' And he pulled her into his arms.

Tattie took a shaken little breath. There was so much wicked vitality in his eyes. There was so much about him that was just glorious. The tanned width of his shoulders, his height, the springy dark hair of his chest, the washboard stomach and compact hips, the length and strength of his legs. And memories of the night before began to wash through her...

Memories that caused her to tremble finely all over with the knowledge that no part of her slender body was safe from him and the most intense pleasure of his imprint upon it. It was dangerous, it was exciting, and it was heady to think that she could do the same for him. By the time he'd got rid of his trousers it was not only a heady thought but a reality.

'Oh.' She breathed it into words. 'This is living dangerously, I think.'

He looked into her eyes and slid his fingers between her thighs.

She rocked against him, holding his upper arms, and tilted her head back. 'If you kissed me at the same time,' she murmured, 'I'd really like that.'

'My pleasure.' His mouth closed on hers as his fingers continued to ready her for him with the lightest touch, until she gasped that she was dying of joy. Then he crushed her to him and took her in the moments left to them before they climaxed.

He looked into her stunned eyes and brought her back to earth with gentle humour. 'Vertical sex—we are living dangerously, Tattie. Either that or you've turned me a little crazy. But you must admit I couldn't have chosen a better spot to be a bit crazy.' And he lifted her off her feet, carried her to the shower and turned on the water.

For the first few moments Tattie spluttered and wriggled, then she started to laugh and he was laughing with her as water streamed off them.

They finally had breakfast on the veranda.

A slap-up meal of bacon and eggs, grilled tomato, toast—and champagne and orange juice.

'Here's to you.' Alex raised his glass to her. 'My lovely lover.'

Tattie picked up her glass and touched his with it. 'I am without words.'

He grinned. 'That's most unusual.'

'I'll probably recover.'

'Don't doubt it.' He pushed his plate away. 'What are your plans for the day?'

'I have no idea! Why?'

'I'd just like to be able to picture what you're doing while I'm slaving over a hot desk.'

'Oh! Well, I'll probably go out and do some shopping.' Tattie put her knife and fork together. 'Unless—' her eyes widened '—does it show?'

He sat back with his glass and took his time. She wore slim white trousers and a blue and white striped T-shirt. Her hair

was tied back in a scrunchie, her feet were bare and she wore
no make-up, but her skin glowed.

'Yes.'

She blushed. 'How?'

'There's a new radiance and lustre about you.'

She grew even hotter, and to counteract it said a shade tartly,
'Do you always think in terms of pearls?'

He raised his eyebrows consideringly. 'Can I help it if you
remind me of a pearl of the first water?'

'Look…' She laughed a little. 'I'm flattered, but I think you
may be flirting with the truth, Alex.'

He moved his shoulders. 'Flirting with something. You. But
if you'd rather I got serious?'

'I would.'

'It may be obvious to me, Tattie, but you don't need to worry
that it's printed all over you. On the other hand, does it matter?'

Tattie sobered. 'I suppose not. I'd just like this to be between
you and me for a while, Alex. I guess I don't have to tell you
it's been rather special for me…but it's a very private kind of
"special".'

His dark gaze had narrowed, but now it softened. 'All right.'
He pushed his chair back and stood up. 'I'm sorry about this,
Tattie, but I haven't been into the office for five days now. I'll
get home as soon as I can, though.'

He came round to her and drew her to her feet. 'Take care of
yourself,' he said softly, and kissed her brow. 'Nor do you have
any idea how hard this is to do, I suspect.'

She nestled against him for a moment then looked up into his
eyes. For once they were completely serious and she felt shaken
to the core. 'I will,' she murmured huskily.

They had a week.

And Alex spent most of it with her.

They made love when the mood took them. He flew her to
Cooinda in Kakadu for the day and they hired a dinghy to ex-

plore the wonders of the Yellow Water wetlands on a tributary of the South Alligator River. Even used to Beaufort and Carnarvon as she was, Yellow Water was entrancing for Tattie. This oasis of birdlife, paperbark gums, the lush colours of the billabongs and swamps of the World Heritage listed area in the midst of the sometimes harsh landscape of the Northern Territory, all were astonishingly beautiful.

And instead of flying home that night he flew her to one of the many World War Two airstrips around Darwin. This one was on Mount Bundy Station at Adelaide River, and also offered tourist accommodation.

'Thought you might like to see how others do it,' he told her with a lurking smile.

Of course she was vitally interested to see how others did it, but it caused her a little pang to think how far into the recesses of her mind Beaufort had sunk. She'd spoken to Polly several times, and been assured all was going well, and she would never have dreamt of abandoning Irina through this crisis. But she hadn't spoken of Beaufort since she and Alex had become lovers...

All the same, she fell in love with Mount Bundy and they had a wonderful evening. Their gracious hostess, Fran, suggested they make a party of all the guests and have dinner in the garden of the Adelaide River Tavern, which turned out to be a unique experience, since the buffalo Paul Hogan had "tamed" in *Crocodile Dundee* had lived out its days as a pet at Adelaide River, and was now stuffed in all his glory and took pride of place on top of the bar.

'I don't know why,' Tattie confided to Alex when they were back in their luxurious room at the Mount Bundy homestead, 'but I feel Beaufort lacks something—it could be a stuffed buffalo or, better still, a tame one!'

Alex, at the time, was engaged in undressing her. He paused from this self-appointed task with her blouse in his hands, and withdrew his gaze from her breasts cupped in white lace to look thoughtful.

'I've got buffalo, but I would hesitate to try and do a Crocodile Dundee on any of them. Unless,' he continued, 'you see it as some sort of medieval test you require me to perform for your...favours?'

The last bit was said as he slipped her bra straps down and traced his fingers across the tops of her breasts.

She took a breath. He was sitting on the bed and she was standing between his legs, now only wearing her shorts and underwear.

'That's an idea,' she said gravely. She reached into her pocket and withdrew a clean blue hanky. 'I could even give you this to take into battle with you, tucked into your...helmet or whatever.'

'I suspect I might look a bit silly with it tucked into my helmet.' He took the hanky. 'I could wear it next to my heart, though.'

'It needs to show,' Tattie objected. 'Everyone needs to know that you're performing this dangerous deed for me!'

He tucked the hanky between two buttons of his shirt. 'There. How many people are you planning to invite to my possible demolition by a two-tonne buffalo?'

She gestured widely. 'Heaps. But I have great faith in you, Alex!'

'You do realise Charlie was tame before Paul Hogan got to him?'

She looked down at him, her cornflower-blue eyes alight with laughter. 'I realise a lot of things. A couple of them are that you don't have to go about taming buffalo for my favours, all you have to do is touch me.'

'Like this?' He unclipped her bra, slid it off, abandoned it and spread his hands around her waist. 'I can nearly span this.'

'Mmm,' she agreed. 'Or like this.' And she cupped the back of his head and drew him towards her.

The result was predictable. Before long they were both naked, and he was sculpting her body with his hands and she was shivering in joyful anticipation of his possession of her.

But he paused suddenly, and looked into her eyes. 'What's the other one?'

She blinked. 'Other what?'

'You said there were a couple of things you realised.'

'Oh, that. It doesn't matter.'

'It matters to me, Tattie.'

She looked mischievously stubborn. 'You can't force me to tell you.'

'Yes, I can.' Her arms were around his shoulders and he released them, took her wrists in one hand and positioned them above her head. And he commenced the most devastating assault on her most sensitive spots until she was arching her body in mindless, exquisite desire.

'All right,' she gasped, 'but only after this is over. Alex, I need you!'

'Promise?'

'Yes!'

'Good, because I'm dying here.' He released her wrists and claimed her powerfully.

'This is a little embarrassing,' she said when they'd come down from the heights. 'It's only my opinion, you see.'

He kissed the corner of her mouth. 'Go on. You did promise.'

She moved her cheek on the pillow, her hair spread out in marvellous disarray, and he pulled the sheet over them. 'I was in no position to do anything else,' she told him severely, then laughed softly. 'OK, here goes; I was thinking that I'd taken to this like a duck to water, but again that's only my—'

'You have.'

'My reading of things— I have?'

'Well…' he temporised until she cast him a fierce blue look. 'I can think of a much better analogy, that's all,' he finished with his lips quirking.

'Oh?'

'Uh-huh. A beautiful girl passing into womanhood like a perfect rosebud opening.'

'Alex.' She went to sit up but he pulled her into his arms. 'That's—'

'A bit flowery?' he asked wryly.

They were only inches apart. 'Awesome,' she whispered with her heart in her eyes for a moment. Then she closed them. 'Even if it's not entirely true, I'll cherish those words—'

'Would you like me to show you how true they are?'

Her lashes flew up and her eyes were suddenly wary. 'N-now?' she stammered. 'I don't think I could survive that again. I mean, so soon. I mean—'

He stopped her by kissing her, although he was laughing at the same time. 'If it's any consolation, neither could I. I think we might have done our dash tonight.'

She relaxed and snuggled up against him. She was almost asleep as he stroked her hair, then he said quietly, 'Why did you want me to think there was another man in your life, Tattie? I know now there hasn't been. Not like this anyway.'

She came awake with a slightly chill feeling. 'That…got out of hand,' she said slowly. 'You were the one who suggested it.'

'And you were the one who ran with it.'

'Not really.'

'You didn't exactly deny it.' His hand was still moving rhythmically on her hair, his arm was still around her, but she couldn't help feeling the peace between them was ever so slightly cracked.

'You have to remember your ex-mistress was around the ridges at the time,' she said. 'I was probably suffering from an inferiority complex.'

He was silent for so long she held her breath. Then, 'So there was no man behind your "very good reason" not to want to stay married to me?'

'No, Alex,' she said straightly. 'It just…got out of hand.'

'Good. Sleep well, Tattie.' He hugged her.

* * *

But he fell asleep before she did, as her very good reason for
not wanting to stay married to him came back to her.

Because, although she had no doubt that Alex Constantin
wanted her now, she still didn't know if he was madly in love
with her. He couldn't, for example, have been madly in love with
Leonie Falconer. He surely would have married her otherwise.

All the same, she had done this, she reflected as she moved
ever so slightly in his arms, then froze in case he woke. But he
only pulled her closer and slept on. And it was an entirely different matter extricating herself from a marriage that had not
been consummated.

She closed her eyes and prayed that the situation would never
arise, but in her heart of hearts knew that he was still an enigma
to her.

Breakfast at Mount Bundy was bountiful, and Tattie did her
best to do it justice as well as conceal from all and sundry that
her night's sleep had been patchy.

But something happened as they were setting off to fly back
to Darwin that brought her hope.

She was bending over to shake a stone out of her shoe, and
when she straightened and turned it was to find Alex standing
stock-still behind her with a newly familiar glint in his eye.

She looked him a slightly cautious question, and his teeth
flashed in a wry grin.

'You bend over delightfully, Tattie.'

Some colour came to her cheeks, and all she could say was,
'Oh.'

He flicked a careless finger against her hot cheek. 'Don't
look so surprised. Did you really think this only went on behind closed doors?'

'Well.' She hesitated. He was reaching up to put a bag into
the wing locker of the light plane, there was a slight breeze
blowing and it was flattening the thin cotton of his shirt against

the long muscles of his back. For a moment she was transfixed at the grace and power of his tall body. Then her sense of fun came to her rescue.

'Well,' she said again, 'despite earlier claims I might have made, Alex, I'm a bit of a newcomer to all this.'

He laughed. 'Then you'd better get used to the idea of me visualising you without your clothes—in all sorts of circumstances.'

She swallowed, and this time her whole body felt hot. 'Uh—does that mean I'm not altogether safe, even on this plane?'

'You may not be safe,' he agreed gravely, then relented as her eyes nearly popped. 'Safe from my thoughts. In all other respects I'm a very conscientious pilot.'

'Thank heavens!' She started to laugh. 'You had me worried for a moment.'

'Since you've converted me to red-hot sex, I wouldn't count on always being safe, Tattie,' he murmured as he closed the locker and took her in his arms.

'I converted you! That is a supreme misrepresentation of the facts,' she protested.

'Whatever,' he said softly, with his eyes dancing wickedly, and he subjected her to a long, leisurely but supremely effective kiss.

'I just hope there was no one watching,' she said in a husky undertone when he'd done his worst and was tidying her up—smoothing her hair and straightening the collar of her blouse.

He smiled like the devil and kissed the tip of her nose. 'I don't give a damn how many people were watching. Shall we go home?'

As they flew the short distance to Darwin Airport Tattie examined her feelings.

She discovered she felt more reassured, as if the ripple in their relationship last night, like a cat's paw on the surface of a fish pond, had smoothed over again. Then she found that she felt more than reassured; she felt positively jaunty. Was that the result, she pondered, of having a man fantasise about you without your clothes in all sorts of circumstances, particularly a man like Alex? As a confidence-booster it was rather unique, she acknowledged.

Naturally, it still did not answer the question of whether he was madly in love with her, she cautioned herself, but it made her feel incredibly good…

'Penny for them?' Alex broke into her thoughts.

'No way, not this time!'

He raised an eyebrow at her. Then, as if he understood what had been going through her mind, he put his hand over hers and said no more. And that, Tattie discovered, was the most reassuring thing of all.

Two days later she spoke to Natalie at Beaufort and was able to pass on the news that Irina was doing well and would be out of hospital shortly.

'That's such good news, Tatiana,' Natalie said down the line.

'Yes, it's wonderful. How are things there?'

'Going extremely well, darling. But there's just one thing. Doug and I have to go back to Perth next weekend. He's got an exhibition coming up and he really needs to be there. I would also love to be there. Do you think, now that Irina's so much better, you could come back to Beaufort?'

'Of course. Well…' Tattie hesitated. 'Even if I can't I'll make some arrangements—you go ahead, Mum.'

'Tattie—'

'Don't argue, Mum,' Tattie said humorously down the line. 'Between us, Alex and I will come up with something.'

'How are…things with you and Alex?' Natalie enquired a little diffidently.

'Fine,' Tattie said brightly.

'Is he there with you, listening, perhaps?'

Sensing that her mother was about to embark on an in-depth

discussion of her marriage, Tattie told a lie. 'Yes, as a matter of fact.'

'Oh, well.' Natalie recouped. 'Give him my regards, my sweet.' And not long afterwards they ended the call.

'My mother sends you her regards.'

Alex looked up from the documents he was reading. He'd been to work for a few hours and brought a pile of papers home with him. They were currently spread all over the coffee-table in the den. Tattie had made them afternoon tea and was sitting curled up in a chair, reading.

'Via mental telepathy?' he asked, looking amused.

Tattie wrinkled her nose at him. 'No. She rang while you were at work.'

'What else did she have to say?' He returned to the documents and sorted them into a different order.

At the same time Tattie examined her reluctance to bring up the subject of her returning to Beaufort, although she knew she had no choice.

She said, 'Doug has an exhibition opening in Perth this weekend. They want to be there for it.' But she wasn't sure, as she said it, whether the fact that she now had his undivided attention was a good thing or not.

'So. Are you all set to hotfoot it back to Beaufort, Tattie?'

Not a good thing, his undivided attention, she decided, nor the fact that she couldn't read his expression at all. She closed her book and swung her bare feet to the floor. 'Alex, of course not—unless you can come with me—'

'I'm afraid that's out of the question at the moment.'

'Because of your mother? I can fully understand—'

'That and business commitments.' His tone was clipped and curt.

She opened her hands in a helpless little gesture. 'But the thing is, I just can't leave Polly to cope with a houseful of guests.'

'The thing is,' he parodied, 'we now need to make different arrangements for Beaufort.'

She swallowed. 'Naturally, I realise some things will have to change—'

'Yes, they will, Tattie. From now on you belong here.'

She stared into his determined dark eyes and couldn't believe this was the man she now slept with so joyfully. How could he go from that to this rising sense of anger that was about to escape?

'Don't take that tone with me, Alex Constantin,' she said grimly. 'If we can't discuss this rationally then there's no point in discussing it at all. It was never my intention to run Beaufort from Darwin and...it was you yourself who suggested the whole thing in the first place and told me how I would be the one to hold it all together—I can't just walk away from it!'

'You don't agree that your place is here?' he shot back dangerously.

'Yes. No.' She shut her eyes in sheer frustration. 'I put my heart and soul into getting the tourist operation off the ground and I intend to see it through. *Of course* I'll have to make some adjustments, but why can't we both make the necessary adjustments? Why do I have to be *told* where my place is like a...a chattel? Or a partner in an arranged marriage?'

'I would have thought,' he drawled in a way that made him even more dangerous, 'it was a requirement even for marriages made in heaven to live together.'

'It is! That doesn't mean to say some exceptions can't be made for certain circumstances. That doesn't mean to say you can order me around and refuse to have a sensible discussion—'

'I have the perfect couple in mind to put in place on Beaufort. They've had previous experience—they ran a lodge adjacent to Litchfield National Park—'

'Listen to me, Alex,' she broke in, now truly incensed. 'I will make any decisions regarding that kind of thing!'

'So this isn't a marriage belatedly but nevertheless made in heaven?'

'Not if you're going to treat me like this.' She dashed at some angry tears.

'As a matter of interest, Tattie, what means more to you—me or Beaufort and Carnarvon?'

'It's not a question of that!' she protested.

He looked at her cynically. Then he shuffled his papers together and stood up. 'I think I'll go back to work.'

'Why don't you?' she whispered with her throat working and an awful sense of desolation in her heart. And some demon prompted her to add tearfully, 'Just don't stop by any pub where your father is likely to be watching rugby. That's the last thing I need, more family intervention.'

She was asleep when he came home that night, and she stayed in her bedroom until she heard him leave the next morning—but she hadn't locked her door.

She might have been emotionally exhausted and devastated at the minefield her marriage had become, but one small part of her had hoped for a miracle. That he would come to her and they would sort through it all. It was such a small issue, she reasoned. Or was it? Surely he could see that she couldn't suddenly abandon a project so close to her heart?

Nothing in the preceding five days had given her to suspect he would be a law-laying-down husband—the opposite, if anything. But the supreme irony of that was how misplaced her sense of jaunty self-confidence in relation to her powers of attracting him had been—she cringed inwardly at the thought.

Finally, she got up, and knew she needed to get out.

With not the slightest interest in how she looked, she pulled on a pair of fawn shorts, a big white linen over-blouse with patch pockets and a pair of white sand shoes. She tied her hair back severely, abjured all make-up and hid her eyes behind a large pair of sunglasses. Then she drove her Golf down to Cullen Bay for a late breakfast.

Cullen Bay was the trend-setter in recent marina development in Darwin. Because of huge tide variations, conventional marinas had not been a possibility on the Darwin Harbour foreshores until someone had come up with the idea of building locks to enclose the marinas. At Cullen Bay there was much more—apartments and town houses overlooking the marina, shops and restaurants. It was always a bustling, lively place, and Tattie chose her favourite café and her favourite spot where she could look over all the yachts moored at the jetties.

She ordered coffee and raisin toast. She wasn't feeling hungry, but there was an aching hollow within her that some food might just appease.

At the same time as her order arrived, however, so did the last person on the planet she wanted to see—Leonie Falconer.

Moreover, Alex's ex-mistress pulled out a chair and sat down. Tattie straightened. 'What—?'

'I was watching you; I've just had a late breakfast myself,' Leonie said. 'You...looked a bit pensive, so I thought I'd saunter over and ask you how it's going. Alex behaving himself?' she asked blandly.

If this wasn't bad enough, Tattie thought darkly, Leonie was looking glorious. In a skimpy cherry-red little top that revealed her midriff—and a silver navel-stud—together with a short hot-pink chiffon skirt, she was colourful, and not a lot of her full golden figure was left to the imagination. Her long hair was casually wound up, she wore some stunning rings on her slender hands and her air of confidence was not to be doubted.

Tattie couldn't help glancing down at herself—in contrast she was about as colourful and confident-looking as a mouse. She had to call on all her Beaufort spirit... She picked up her coffee-cup and said over the rim, 'He's behaving beautifully, Leonie! Thank you so much for asking.'

Her tormentor's hazel eyes narrowed. 'I thought you looked a bit down in the mouth, to be honest, Tatiana.'

'How acute of you!' Tattie marvelled. 'I am, but only because I'm going to have to leave Alex for a few days. One of my cattle stations needs me.'

Leonie sat back, and Tattie thought—Take that, Ms Falconer!

'You know,' Leonie murmured, 'over the past few months—well, the whole course of your marriage, in fact—I've wondered how well you know Alex Constantin.'

'Strange you should say that—other people have said the same to me—but I know him very well indeed. Very well.' Better than I want to know him right now, Tattie added, but to herself.

'So you were quite comfortable with him sleeping with me while you were married?' Leonie queried.

Tattie shrugged. 'Since I recommended he go out and get himself a mistress, why not?'

She saw the little flare of shock in Leonie's eyes and thought, Bingo again!—then flinched inwardly and wondered what she thought she was doing.

But Leonie had regrouped. 'And you know all about Flora Simpson?'

If she'd been angry with Alex yesterday it was nothing to what was building up inside her now, Tattie discovered, and assured herself she couldn't be responsible for what she said at this moment. 'Bless her heart, yes! A two-timing hussy, by the sound of it.'

'Perhaps,' Leonie responded, but she was pale around the mouth. 'But are you quite prepared to accept that he'll never get over her? I suppose you do know she's newly back in town and she's divorced her husband?' She leant forward and added with malice aforethought, 'Don't think that the whole of Darwin doesn't know why he married you—because he couldn't have her and it didn't matter who the hell he married, Tatiana Beaufort.'

'Constantin, actually. Do they? Ah, well, that's life.' She sipped her coffee just in case she was tempted to pour it all over Leonie Falconer. 'But, you know, if that's the case I can't help wondering why he didn't marry you.'

Leonie paled all over her face. 'Because you had one thing I didn't—cattle stations. That's all he married you for.'

Tattie stood up and grinned. 'That's two things actually. But let's not split hairs. And I have to confess he has a few...assets that appeal to me. Good day to you.'

She drove, without thinking, to the legal-aid office where she'd given her time so often during the first year of her marriage. But after she'd parked the car she decided she might as well go in and say hello. Anything to take the bitter taste of Leonie Falconer out of her mouth.

One of her favourite solicitors was on duty, and for once the office wasn't busy, so she sat down opposite Jenny Jones and had a chat. Jenny was in her thirties, and adopted a hippie style of dress—long, trailing skirts and fringed waistcoats—but she possessed a shrewd brain and boundless humanity.

'Anything interesting going on?' Tattie asked.

Jenny shrugged. 'Mostly the usual. By the way, Laura Pearson has had her baby—a boy. But it's a bit sad—her boyfriend has run out on her.'

Laura Pearson had been a legal secretary in the office, a girl Tattie had always liked, and she asked Jenny for her address so she could take her a present.

Jenny fished it out. 'How's life on the station treating you, Tattie? I must say, we miss you here.'

'Fine. Jen,' Tattie said as the thought came to her out of the blue, 'how would you go about tracking down someone?'

Jenny looked surprised. 'Why?'

'I just...would like to trace someone I've...lost track of,' Tattie improvised.

'Well, you could try the electoral rolls.'

Tattie grimaced. 'I believe she's just moved back to Darwin, so she might not yet be in the telephone book or on the rolls.'

'Hmm... You said—moved back to Darwin.' Jenny chewed her pen for a moment. 'Was she socially prominent before she left, or anything like that?'

'She might have been,' Tattie said slowly.

'You could try the local newspaper. They might have got wind of her return. I'll give you the name of a journalist I know there.'

Half an hour later Tattie left the legal-aid office with a name on a slip of paper in her pocket. But she was not at all sure of the wisdom of Tatiana Constantin going into a newspaper office and requesting any information they might have in their back files on one Flora Simpson.

All the same, thanks to Leonie and her venom, she now had an almost overwhelming desire to see clearly this shadowy figure who two people had intimated might have been the love of Alex's life—two people, above all, who should know.

She was staring, preoccupied, into a shop window when she realised it was a toy shop with a most delightful dancing teddy bear in the window. So she went in and bought it for Laura Pearson's baby, then had an amazing thought.

Accordingly she found another shop and bought herself a hat, one that she could pull down on her head and hide a lot of her face beneath its floppy brim. Then she marched into the office of the local newspaper and told the receptionist she had come from the legal-aid office on behalf of Jenny Jones, who would be very grateful if they could check their back files for anything on Flora Simpson.

It took a while, but it worked. No one appeared to recognise her, and she only dealt with the receptionist because Jenny's name worked like magic. She left eventually with an envelope she didn't attempt to open until she got home.

There was no sign of Alex as she pulled off her concealing hat. All the same, she locked herself in her bedroom to study the contents of the envelope. Then she wished she hadn't been so cunning as she studied photos of her nemesis. For Flora Simpson had all the allure of a truly beautiful woman.

There was not the earthy golden attraction of Leonie Falconer, but there was something more ethereal about her, although she was tall and fair. There was not only grace and a lovely figure, but also composure and intelligence.

She let the photos flutter to the bed, then forced herself to read the couple of cuttings that had accompanied them. One of them told her that Flora had returned to her home town of Darwin after her divorce from her wealthy financier husband about two weeks ago.

How old would she be? she wondered. And judged her to be in her late twenties or early thirties. So, not only stunning, she reflected with her eyes squeezed shut, but also much closer to Alex in age and maturity. She tidied the photos back into the envelope and hid them at the back of her wardrobe.

The phone rang. She picked up the extension on her bedside table.

It was Alex with a bad connection, a strong hum in the background. 'Tattie?'

'Yes? Where are you?'

'On a plane; something has come up and I'm flying out to one of the pearl farms, but I should be back tomorrow.'

'All right.' She cleared her throat. 'Alex, I'm glad you rang—just in case you thought I'd been kidnapped, I'm going back to Beaufort tomorrow. I'll see your mother this afternoon to explain why I have to go back—'

'Tattie, don't,' he said abruptly.

'Alex, I have to.' And she put the phone down. It rang again almost immediately but she ignored it. And half an hour later she ignored another call.

She soon discovered that Alex Constantin was not the right person to ignore, however. She got ready to visit Irina in hospital that afternoon, only to discover a huge young man outside her front door, who politely informed her that he was a security guard and he'd been instructed not to let her out of his sight.

A flicker of fear and the memory of Parap came to her and she stepped back inside smartly, saying she would just like to check it out.

She leant back against the door, trying to regulate her breathing, before she rang Alex on his satellite phone. There was no reply, so she tried his secretary, Paula Gibbs.

'Oh, Mrs Constantin,' Paula said, relieved, 'I was just coming over to visit you. I tried to call you but got no answer.'

'Oh. Paula, what on earth is going on? There's someone who claims to be a security guard outside my door.'

'He is a security guard.' Paula went on to explain how Alex had been called away unexpectedly and how he'd rung her from the plane and asked her to organise it.

'But…but has something happened I'm not aware of?' Tattie asked.

'Not at *all*,' Paula stressed. 'It's just that—I guess because it nearly happened once Alex would feel happier about leaving you alone with him in place. That's why I tried to ring you, so you'd know what was going on. He's from our own security team, incidentally.'

Tattie took a deep breath and counted to ten beneath her breath. 'OK. Thanks, Paula.' She put the phone down and once more sallied forth through her front door, where she advised her guardian angel that he'd better prepare himself for a trip to a cattle station in the Kimberley tomorrow.

He looked embarrassed, but replied that he had instructions not to let her leave Darwin until Mr Constantin returned. For her own safety, of course, he added.

She restrained herself from explaining to him that the only issue at stake here was her husband's diabolical determination to have his own way, although couched in much less formal language, and did the only thing she could—went to see her mother-in-law with the large young man squeezed uncomfortably into her Golf.

CHAPTER NINE

'WHAT'S YOUR NAME?' Tattie asked as she steered the Golf.

'Leroy, ma'am.'

'Well, Leroy, could I ask you to stop cracking your knuckles?'

'Sorry, ma'am.' He squashed his hands beneath him.

'What will you do while I'm visiting my mother-in-law?'

'Just stand outside the door, ma'am,' he said reassuringly. 'You won't even know I'm around.'

His sheer bulk made this highly unlikely, Tattie thought drily.

'And tonight?'

'Same thing, but my colleague will take over at midnight. There are two of us assigned to you, Mrs Constantin, so you have absolutely nothing to worry about.'

Tattie flicked him a glance. He had a broad, ruddy face beneath fair curly hair and small blue eyes. But he looked genuinely prepared to defend her to the nth degree while being as nice and polite about it as he could, and she couldn't help feeling a bit sorry for him. For, little though Leroy knew it, his problems were going to lie in the opposite direction...

By hook or by crook she was going to get herself to Beaufort before Alex came home!

* * *

Irina was sitting up in a beautiful pink and cream silk bed jacket.

Tattie kissed her and sat down beside the bed. 'You're looking wonderful,' she told her mother-in-law.

'I'm beginning to feel human at last,' Irina replied. 'And they say I will walk out of here—maybe on a walking frame for a time, but walk all the same.'

'I know you will!'

Irina patted her face. 'You've been so sweet to me, Tattie! And I only thank my lucky stars that Alex had you by his side through all this.'

Tattie studied the pearl-encrusted pewter vase beside the bed with a fresh spray of orchids in it. 'He loves you so much. So do I. But...' She hesitated. 'I have to go away for a few days— just to Beaufort.' And she explained the situation.

Irina beamed at her. 'I think it's just wonderful that your mother has found someone to love. So romantic. She brought him to meet me, you know. In fact, I bought one of his paintings. I do hope he has a successful exhibition. How long will you be gone, my dear?'

I would love to know how much you know, Irina, and what Alex told you when I ran away to Beaufort, Tattie thought. Because she felt as if she was walking on eggshells, and ten times more so because Irina was in hospital and had nearly died.

'I'm not sure,' she said. 'Alex knows of a couple who could take over now I've got the project off the ground.' She paused. 'I haven't met them, but from the forward bookings we have I think it is going to be a success and I'm...*really* happy about that.'

Irina studied her thoughtfully. 'You know, we all underestimated you, Tattie.'

Tattie blinked in surprise.

'And perhaps most of all Alex did,' Irina went on. 'Would I

be correct in saying you're not prepared to accept anything but true love from Alex?'

Tattie almost fell off her chair, and Irina smiled wisely. 'Everyone thinks I'm a silly old woman who imagines her only son can do no wrong. And, yes, perhaps I did have to have it pointed out to me who Leonie Falconer was—too late, as it happened.'

'Who...?' Tattie stared at her dazedly.

'A friend of mine rang me the day after the anniversary party. I don't know if you remember, but that's why I rang you the next morning in a bit of a state.'

'Yes,' Tattie breathed as her mind flew backwards. 'Oh!'

Irina patted her hand again. 'And now they tell me Flora Simpson is back in town.'

Such was her surprise, Tattie was speechless for almost a minute. 'But...you weren't supposed to know about her!'

'The only amusing aspect of that, Tattie,' Irina said a shade ruefully, 'is that both George and I knew but we tried to shield each other from the knowledge.'

Tattie gazed at her helplessly.

'Of course you must do as you see fit, Tattie; I suspect you've done that all the way through,' Irina continued. 'But only you can know what's best for you in regard to Alex. If half a loaf is not good enough for you, then stick to your guns, my dear. I did.'

'I... This... You mean with George? But I thought that yours was an arranged marriage and you approved of that kind of thing.'

'Firstly, yes—I mean George. Although it wasn't quite the same situation as you and Alex. He might have thought his mother arranged our marriage but what he didn't know was that I planted the seeds of it in his mother's mind. I wanted George, you see, but he couldn't quite make up his mind about me.' Irina gazed fondly back down the years. 'Now he's quite convinced *he* made the right choice, with a little help from his mother.'

'Bravo, Mama Constantin!' Tattie said softly, using the pet name Alex sometimes used for his mother.

Irina smiled. 'As for arranged marriages in general, all I ever wanted to do was find a girl Alex could fall in love with, or, if not that, grow to love and respect. Instead, I found a girl *I* will always love and admire, whatever happens between her and my son. Of course, I hope and pray that you and Alex will resolve your differences, but that is not my main concern now. A little brush with death,' she said humorously, 'gives you a new perspective on life, I think. Be happy for yourself, Tattie.' And she leant forward to put her arms around Tattie.

'On the other hand,' she said softly as she cupped Tattie's face, 'I predict he will not give a damn about Flora Simpson being back in town.'

Back home in the apartment, Tattie tried to sort through this surprise development as well as she could.

It was an intense relief, she realised, not to be hiding things from her mother-in-law any more. It was even more of a relief to know that she had been vindicated in a sense, or at least had had her side of the story understood by his mother and was still loved and admired just for herself. So what was the fly in the ointment? she wondered.

How could anyone predict what Alex's reaction to the beautiful Flora Simpson would be. That was one of them. As for fly two, she thought with a grim spark of humour, it was quite simple. She refused to be dictated to by her husband. If he truly loved her, as opposed to finding her desirable at the moment, surely he would have been prepared to discuss the situation at Beaufort rather than simply laying down the law?

She glanced towards the front door. Surely he wouldn't subject her to what virtually amounted to imprisonment just to get his own way?

She chewed her knuckles for a while, then came to a decision. She made her plans, which included a phone call, then got out the dancing teddy bear she'd bought earlier in the day and wrapped it up. She took a cup of tea and some shortbread out to Leroy—she had already provided him with a chair.

'Thank you very much, ma'am!' Leroy said enthusiastically.

'By the way, Leroy, I'm going out to dinner at a friend's house in about an hour. Do you have your own transport?'

Leroy hesitated.

'I only ask because it could be uncomfortable for you to be sitting in the Golf for a few hours, so perhaps you'd like to chauffeur me backwards and forwards in your car, if it's bigger?'

Leroy's face cleared. 'My Holden is bigger, if you wouldn't mind?'

'Not at all! See you soon.'

'Where are we going?' Leroy asked an hour later as he ushered Tattie into the front seat of his Holden.

She gave him an address in Fannie Bay, then enquired what he intended to do for dinner, because her visit might take a good couple of hours.

'I was going to ask you if you'd mind if I stopped to get a burger, ma'am.'

'Please do, Leroy. I'd hate to think of you sitting there for hours, starving.'

So they stopped at a drive-thru, where he ordered an inordinate amount of food, then drove to Fannie Bay.

'This is it.' Tattie pointed to a house, although she'd never seen it before.

Leroy parked in the driveway and looked around alertly. 'Don't you worry, Mrs Constantin. I'll do regular checks to make sure the house and grounds are secure, and here's my mobile number just in case you need me.' He handed her a card.

Not too regular, Tattie prayed, and felt a trickle of guilt. Then she stiffened her spine, thanked him, and went to visit Laura Pearson and her new baby.

Laura was thrilled to see her, and thrilled with the present, although the baby, at two months, was unimpressed. 'Just wait until he's a little older, Tattie, I'm sure he'll adore it. Let's have a cup of tea.'

So they had tea and a little chat, then the baby started to protest. 'He's hungry—he's always hungry,' Laura said ruefully, with a spark of exhaustion in her eyes.

'Well, don't worry about me, Laura. I can let myself out. You just sit down with him and put your feet up. What can I get you? Aren't nursing mums supposed to drink gallons of water? I'll get you a glass.'

And it was as easy as that. Tattie settled Laura and the baby in a comfortable chair, put some nice music on for her and brought her a glass of water. Then she said goodbye and took the tea things back to the kitchen on her way out.

'I'll just go out the back way,' she called softly, and did so.

But instead of heading for the drive and Leroy, after a short, pregnant reconnaissance she tiptoed across the back lawn, climbed the low fence into the house behind Laura's, prayed she wouldn't be set upon by vicious dogs or vigilant householders, and stole out onto the street behind.

Then she started to walk rapidly away, thinking that the only thing that could go wrong would be if Laura noted that she hadn't heard a car start up. She would just have to take a gamble on the girl being too involved with her baby. She pulled her mobile phone from her bag and called a taxi. Within twenty minutes she was in the garage of her apartment building, driving the Golf out of it. And ten minutes later, when she was sure she was far enough away from home not to be found easily, she called Paula Gibbs on her home phone number.

'Mrs Constantin.' Paula drew a shaky breath. 'Alex will—'

'Paula, all you have to do is tell Alex I'm going to Beaufort, come hell or high water,' Tattie said firmly. 'I'm perfectly safe, I promise you. But what you need to do *right* now is call Leroy off. I don't want my friend hassled in any way, and I mean that! Nor is it Leroy's fault in *any* way; I deliberately gave him the slip.'

'But…but…why?' Paula objected.

'It's just something between me and Alex, Paula. Incidentally, don't even think of calling the police, because that would create the kind of gossip Alex would *hate*. And please don't bother his father; he's got enough on his plate at the moment.'

'How are you getting to Beaufort?'

'I'm flying. Bye now, Paula!'

Two days later Tattie arrived at Beaufort in a light plane she'd chartered.

She'd driven to Katherine and had to spend the night there. She'd left the Golf in a garage and taken a Greyhound bus to Kununurra, from where she'd chartered the light plane after another night in a motel. She was almost reeling from physical tiredness and mental exhaustion as she stepped out of it onto the airstrip, and was immensely relieved to see no other plane on the strip. The last thing she felt like doing was confronting Alex.

But there was a surprise waiting for her. Polly drove down to the strip, as was the custom when the homestead was buzzed by incoming planes. And she flung her arms around Tattie.

'Thank heavens you've arrived! Not only is Alex in a terrible mood, but we've also got a houseful of guests!'

'But what about my mother and Doug? I didn't think they were going until Friday, and I didn't think…you had…any bookings.' Tattie's voice ran down as the other pertinent bit of information sank in. 'You mean Alex is here?' She stared at Polly disbelievingly.

'Hop in.' Polly gestured to the four-wheel-drive vehicle. 'I'll explain on the way.'

She did. Alex had arrived yesterday morning straight from the pearl farm, in a combination float and wheel plane. He'd sent her mother and Doug to Darwin in it, so they could get a flight to Perth, and told them that she, Tattie, was on her way to Beaufort. Then, out of the blue, a bus-load of tourists had arrived with confirmed bookings for two nights' accommodation.

'But…how…?'

'Somehow the dates must have got scrambled; we weren't expecting them until next week. Mind you, I had everything hunky-dory, but…' Polly raised her eyebrows expressively. 'Anyway, Alex bucked in and helped. In fact he's taken them on the billabong tour, so Mum and I can concentrate on dinner. But he's been talking to all sorts of people on the phone and, well, it sounded to me as if no one knew where you were, Tattie.'

'I… I was planning to fly from Katherine, but I couldn't get a flight so I had to take the bus to Kununurra.'

Polly drew up in front of the homestead and looked at her strangely. 'You couldn't have hopped on a Constantin plane?'

Tattie swallowed. 'It…got a bit complicated, Polly. Where's Oscar?'

Polly blinked, then shivered suddenly. 'Uh…he's gone with Alex. They should be back in a couple of hours.'

They were the longest few hours of Tattie's life.

Nothing could have been more eloquent or indicative of Alex's state of mind than Polly's involuntary shiver. And nothing gave her hope that the sight of her on the homestead veranda when the billabong tour returned was alleviating her husband's state of mind.

He surveyed her, his expression darkly inscrutable, and if it hadn't been for Oscar a pall would have been thrown over the whole party, she was sure. But Oscar suddenly realised who she was and raced up to her with utter delight palpably displayed all over his body.

She bent down and he jumped into her arms. 'Oh, you've grown, young man! How long have I been away? I don't think we can do this any longer.' She staggered and put the dog down as everyone laughed, and the tension of the moment dissipated. For most of them…

Alex began to introduce her to the party and she was regaled with all the marvels they'd seen. Then he said, 'If you'll excuse us for a moment, folks, my wife and I haven't seen each other for a couple of days. Polly?'

Polly leapt into action and told everyone that afternoon tea would be ready in half an hour.

And Alex's hand descended on Tattie's elbow and he led her off the veranda.

Not far from the homestead they'd built a gazebo on a rise like a small bluff, and the country sloped away from it in a lovely wild valley to a blue ridge.

It was pagoda-shaped, with curved empty embrasures and a wooden lattice half-wall. The floor was paved, but the timber was natural and it blended in well with the country. There were benches to sit on. It was a wonderful place to sit in peace, to watch nature and to feel the vastness of Beaufort.

But Alex said not a word as he escorted Tattie to it, and she had the absolute feeling that peace was not on the agenda. Even Oscar seemed to get the vibes and become subdued.

And, as she climbed the steps, her nerves got the better of her.

'If you've brought me here to have me shot at dawn, Alex,' she said tautly, 'think again!'

She swung round to face him.

He leant his shoulders against an upright and crossed his arms. In jeans and a black shirt he looked dusty, tired, perhaps, but all the same very tough.

In contrast, although she too wore jeans, she was neat and clean in a pink blouse and with her hair smooth and tucked behind her ears.

'Why would I do that, Tattie?'

'Because I disobeyed you, because—'

'You're getting a little emotional and unrealistic here, surely?'

'Am I? I don't think so,' she flung at him. 'You virtually had me imprisoned so you could get your own way, Alex! Look, I'm sorry if I worried you but I will not be dictated to like that!'

'Go on.'

'What more is there to say? But if you want more, you can have it! You expect me to live in a place where I keep falling over your ex-mistresses—'

He straightened. 'When did that happen?'

'It doesn't matter.'

'I think it may, Tattie. Tell me.'

She swallowed but stood her ground as he loomed over her, and refused to speak.

He said evenly, 'All right, that aside, you're rather cavalier with your apologies for what you've put a few people through, Tattie. Paula, for example. She had no way of knowing someone wasn't forcing you to ring her. The security guard—'

'It wasn't his fault,' Tattie broke in. 'It was all your fault for treating me the way you did. And I swear, if there are any repercussions for Leroy over this I will never speak to you again, Alex Constantin.'

He raised a wry eyebrow. 'Your concern for Leroy is touching, Tattie. What about my mother?'

'Your mother? She knew I was coming back to Beaufort, Alex, she just didn't know the lengths I had to go to get here. But for your information, your mother is no longer of the opinion I should stay married to you if I don't want to.'

He frowned. 'Why?'

'She thinks you all underestimated me—you in particular.'

'She told you this?'

'She did,' Tattie agreed. 'With no prompting from me,' she added. 'A brush with mortality did it. She actually told me that if you didn't fit my requirements...' She paused suddenly.

'Which are, Tattie?' he asked very quietly.

'It doesn't matter,' she mumbled as some colour came to her cheeks.

'Once again I beg to differ. Would those requirements have

anything to do with the mysterious reason you keep parading before me for not wanting to stay in this marriage?'

His gaze was so intent she felt as if it was pinning her to the gazebo upright she'd involuntarily backed into.

'I can always get those requirements from my mother,' he murmured.

She bit her lip and closed her eyes. 'Alex...' She couldn't go on.

'Tell me, Tattie. I won't let you go until you do.'

She never knew afterwards what unlocked the secret she'd tried so desperately to keep from him, for so long. The bush beyond the gazebo was hot and still, the blue ridge in the distance was swimming in a heat haze, Oscar was lying beside her with his head on his paws but every now and then he was sending her an alert look.

She was in the place she loved best with the man she loved—when she wasn't hating him—perhaps it was the sum of all this that made it impossible for her to dodge and dive any longer.

She licked her lips and everything about Alex she loved came back to her, which was incredibly unfair in the light of his recent behaviour, but none the less all the times he'd made love to her came back beneath the impact of his tall, electrifying presence...

And the words seemed to tumble out of their own accord.

'I swore I would not stay married to you, Alex—' she swallowed painfully '—unless I knew you were madly in love with me.'

'Why not?' His words seemed to echo.

But at the very last moment she couldn't do it. Her throat worked and she blinked away incipient tears. 'The thing is, I understand now.'

'Understand what, Tattie?' He asked it very quietly.

She could see the line on his forehead where his hat had rested, she could breathe in the dust on his clothes and the sweat of an energetic ride, all of it purely masculine and terribly fascinating—but not for her.

'Why you could never fall madly in love with me.' She shrugged in what she hoped was a wry little gesture. 'I've seen Flora Simpson, so—'

'When?' he asked dangerously.

Her lips parted and Oscar sat up, growled low in his throat and then looked embarrassed, and bunted them both on the legs to show that he didn't think he'd meant it but he'd be much happier if he didn't have to take sides.

Tattie laughed nervously and patted him. 'It's OK.'

All Alex did was continue to look the question at her.

She sighed. 'Not in the flesh. I saw a...some pictures of her, that's all.'

'How come?'

'I'd rather not tell you that, Alex; it's a bit embarrassing.'

'Let me get this straight. You claimed earlier you'd been falling all over my ex-mistresses but now it appears it wasn't Flora—not in the flesh at least. I don't get it,' he said flatly.

Tattie squared her shoulders. 'I ran into Leonie the day you left town. She...she told me amongst other things that Flora was back in town. So I...' She closed her eyes frustratedly. 'You have to remember your own father filled me in on how Flora had affected your life, Alex.' Her lashes lifted. 'So I decided I was sick and tired of having this...person hanging over my head.' And she told him how she'd got the pictures of Flora.

'Oh, Tattie.' He said it barely audibly.

'Which is how I came to understand why you could never be madly in love with me. She's...even in a picture she's just special.' Some of her Beaufort hauteur came back to Tattie. 'Although if the reason you wanted to keep me in Darwin was part of some tit-for-tat game you're playing with her, that I cannot admire, Alex,' she said severely.

His lips twisted. 'When did you work that out?'

Tattie looked surprised. 'It's just hit me, actually,' she said uneasily. 'I can't think of any other reason for it.'

'Can't you?' He rested a hand on the curved embrasure above her head. 'I can. All this.' He looked into the distance then his dark eyes came back to her. 'Beaufort, in other words. And Carnarvon. Let's not forget Carnarvon. It has become an abiding nightmare for me.'

'What has?' she whispered, her eyes wide.

'How much more they mean to you than I do. And I'm sorry to have to disillusion you, Tatiana Beaufort...' He paused.

If her eyes were wide before they were now stunned and incredibly confused.

'But I have actually fallen madly in love with you,' he continued. 'I apologise if it's been a slightly protracted process. If you doubt the authenticity of it, though, I even went to the extreme lengths of virtually locking you up so that you couldn't come here on your own and forget about me while you got all caught up in being here, being a Beaufort and all the rest.'

'Alex...' It was a mere breath of sound.

'Furthermore...' He took his hand away from the embrasure to touch her hair fleetingly, and a nerve flickered in his jaw. 'I had no idea Flora Simpson was back in town but, yes, thanks to her, I didn't really want to fall in love again. It took a girl with so much spirit, so much life, so much about her that brings me joy to change my mind. You, Tattie.'

'But I thought you were so cross with me!'

He shook his head. 'I was so relieved to see you I didn't quite know how I was going to handle myself. I didn't know what was in your heart.'

She gazed at him.

'When Paula rang me two nights ago it was the worst moment of my life.'

'Why?'

He smiled, but not amusedly. 'I thought you might have run away from me for good.'

'Is this...is this all true?' Tattie gasped.

'Tattie,' he said abruptly, 'it only took five days after you first slept with me for you to want to come back here. If I'm a mass of insecurities, can you blame me?'

'A mass of insecurities,' she repeated. 'Alex, if only you *knew.*'

'You could tell me,' he suggested. 'You mentioned something about requirements earlier.'

'Oh. Yes. Yes, well, one of those requirements, as I told you, was that I needed you to be madly in love with me.'

'Why?' he said simply.

'Because I've been madly in love with you for a long time, Alex, and—'

But she said no more, because he'd pulled her into his arms and she could hear the way his heart was beating, fast and furiously.

'I thought I was never going to get you to say the words,' he said unevenly into her hair. 'It was driving me crazy. Oh, Tattie, I love you, sweetheart.'

'What are we going to do?' Tattie said.

They were sitting side by side on a bench with their arms around each other. Tattie had been gloriously and repeatedly kissed, and had done not a little of her fair share of participating in it.

'About life in general or our particular circumstances of the moment?' he queried.

She moved against him and laid her cheek on his shoulder. 'You know, Alex, one of the reasons Beaufort meant so much to me was because I didn't think I could have you. So long as I can keep coming back here, I'll be happy, but now I've got you—' she glinted a mischievous little look at him '—I won't need to live all my life here.'

'Do you want to keep the tourist enterprise going?'

She thought for a moment. 'Yes. For several reasons. I rather like sharing it with the world. I think beauty in whatever form—

music, art, literature, nature—may just help people to understand and cope with life better. But I'd also like to keep it going
for Polly and my mother and Doug, and Marie and the black-
smith's wife, who all seem to have a richer life because of this
venture. I do have one ulterior motive, though.'

'Let me guess,' he drawled, 'you'd still like to drag Carnarvon out of the red by your own efforts?'

'How did you know?' She gazed at him innocently.

'You forget—one of the things I love about you is your fighting spirit.' He kissed her lightly.

She sighed with satisfaction. 'I didn't really think you were
going to be the kind of husband who laid down the law. That's
why it came as such a shock, I suppose.'

'Well, I hope this doesn't come as too much of a shock but
I'm about to lay down the law right now.'

She sat up and eyed him suspiciously.

He looked around at the lengthening shadows, and then at
his watch. 'Dinner is not that far away. I don't see how we can
get out of it, but there's nothing to prevent us from retiring early
after it. So if you have any plans to be the perfect hostess this
evening, Tattie—'

'Oh, I have plans, Alex,' she interrupted. 'To be the perfect
something. But you'll just have to wait and see what that is.'

He raised an eyebrow. 'On the other hand, I may not be able
to wait that long.' He looked at her narrowly. 'You're not about
to become a law-laying-down kind of wife?'

'Wait and see,' she teased, then sobered suddenly.

'What?' he asked.

'I still can't believe it.' Tears suddenly glistened on her lashes.

He took her face in his hands and kissed them away. 'You
will,' he promised. 'You will.'

Dinner was both a triumph and an ordeal.

They dressed up, Tattie in a long cream sheath with a Chinese collar, Alex in dark trousers and a pale grey shirt.

Polly and Marie produced a splendid meal and all their guests were more than delighted, not only with the meal and the elegance but also with Tattie and Alex.

In fact, Tattie wondered if there was some visible aura around them. Then she knew there was, from the way Alex's dark eyes rested on her from time to time, and the way everything receded and all she was conscious of was him.

If she had any doubts, Polly dispelled them completely. 'Don't worry about staying around for the coffee,' she said to Tattie in a whispered aside, and impulsively threw her arms around her. 'I've never seen you looking so beautiful.'

Alex was waiting for her in the main bedroom. He had a silver tray, two glasses and a decanter of liqueur brandy, and he poured them a tot each and toasted her. Then he put the lights out and they stood side by side, holding hands, watching the moon rise over Beaufort before he turned to her.

'You had something you wanted to show me, Mrs Constantin?'

'Yes, this,' she said simply. She put her glass down. 'Although I may need some help.'

She turned around, and after a moment he began to release all the tiny buttons down the back of her dress. His fingers were cool on the skin of her back but he made no other attempt to touch her.

When the last button was released she stepped out of the dress and turned back to face him. 'And this,' she said softly. She took off her bra and stepped out of briefs then her shoes, and shivered slightly.

He put his arms around her. 'The perfect wife,' he said huskily. 'Tattie, if only you knew how much I love you.'

And there was so much emotion in his eyes, something that was so hard held within him, at last full belief came to her.

'It's all right,' she said shakily, 'I know now.'

And he took her to bed.

* * *

It was around midnight when they stirred and Tattie sat up, disorientated, still on cloud nine over the events that had passed between them—the way Alex had made love to her so that not only their bodies but also their souls had been united.

'What is it?' she whispered.

He sat up and pushed his hair out of his eyes—and the sound came again. A scratch on the door... 'Oh,' he said, and at the same time she said.

'It's Oscar! But I thought Polly had trained him to sleep in the boot room?'

Alex grimaced and fingered his jaw. 'She had. I...liberated him last night.'

'You brought him in to sleep with you!'

'I did, I'm afraid,' Alex confessed.

'So much for your disapproval of my dog-training techniques,' Tattie said gravely. 'You realise he's probably *chewed* his way out of the boot room?'

'I was lonely and miserable.'

'I don't know why,' Tattie said severely, then fell back into his arms, laughing softly, 'but I love the sound of it!'

'You're a sadist, Tatiana.'

'No. It also makes me feel...really married to you!'

He took her chin in his hands and kissed her. 'Then it was worth it. What shall we do?'

'Let him in?' she suggested. 'Who knows what kind of havoc he could create out there.'

'But I have you now,' he pointed out, and ran his hands over her breasts.

'Alex, he's probably lonely and miserable out there. And you were the one who gave him to me.'

'For my sins,' he commented, and they both stopped as Oscar whined piteously. 'You know he's an awful fraud, don't you? He can turn his emotions on and off like a tap.'

'I won't be able to sleep if I know he's out there feeling sad.'

Tattie looked sad herself. 'Besides which, he deserves to know all is well.'

'I see. You are going to be one of those law-laying-down kind of wives.'

'Only over this!'

'Promise?' He reached over and switched on the bedside light.

'Well—'

'I thought so. So we'll need to think of a system of compensation.' His words were sober but his eyes were completely wicked.

Tattie took a breath. 'Oh, I get it. This is bribery and corruption.'

'It may be all that's left to me.'

'If you let Oscar in I'll…really rethink my stance on red-hot sex in the future.'

'Done,' he said promptly, and got out of bed to open the door.

Oscar raced into the room, leapt onto the bottom of the bed and snuggled down as if he'd come home.

And Tattie and Alex couldn't stop laughing, before they fell asleep in each other's arms.

* * * * *

MILLS & BOON
Swoon ♡ Club

Why not try a Mills & Boon subscription? Get your favourite series delivered to your door every month!

Use code *3MONTHSFREE* to get 50% off the first three months of your chosen subscription plus free delivery.

Visit **millsandboon.com.au/subscriptions**

or give customer service a call on
AUS 1300 659 500 or **NZ 0800 265 546**

No lock-in Contracts

Free Postage

Exclusive Offers

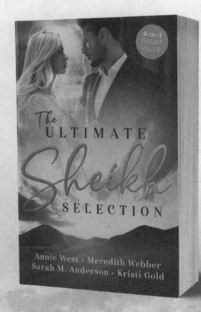

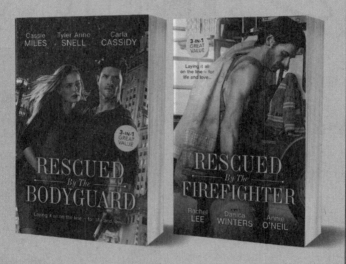

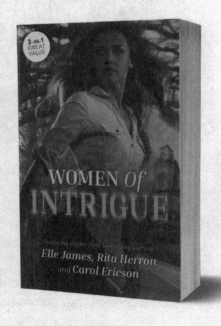

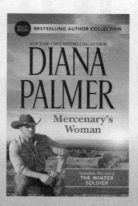